Author's Foreword

On the 18th of January, 2022, *A Requiem For Hania* (Ogham & Dabar Books) was published in Ireland. The date of the hardback publication was not incidental; on the 18th of January, 1943, in Warsaw, the Nazis began what was known as the Second Aktion: the assembling of Jews in the Warsaw Ghetto to be transported to a camp called Treblinka. A labour camp. And an extermination camp.

The paperback version of the book was subsequently published on the 19th of April, 2022, again a date not incidental. The 19th of April, 1943, was the beginning of the Warsaw Ghetto Uprising. The beginning of an ending perhaps.

A Requiem For Hania, for both author and reader, is a journey: a journey to illuminate the past of the Warsaw Ghetto and its immediate aftermath, a journey to begin to illuminate the antisemitic politics of Poland in 1968, a journey into our present. Inspired largely by true events, it is a story of identity, of meaning. It attempts to give a glimpse into a painful world gone by in order to offer a glimpse of the painful world in which we now find ourselves. It is a story of friendship. Of love. Of what was lost. What was found. A story of hope, when often there is little.

And it is a story that becomes a search for self, a search for some meaning. Some possibility.

But in a book that was already long, some stories had to be left out. And some had yet to be explored. Stories that mattered then, and continue to matter. Fragments, or as mentioned in *A Requiem For Hania,* taken from Wordsworth, 'spots of time' that tell us where we have been, and where we are going.

Fragments thus visits, and revisits, those stories. As a novel it is not exactly a follow-on from *A Requiem For Hania*. Rather, just as music was central to that previous work in both its stories and form, so it is that in a musical requiem some movements may alter, or reform, change tempo or key, move from forte to piano. Are lost, then found.

i

Some stories will be heard, and some cry out to be written. And read.

It is thus with *Fragments.* The stories explored in this novel are not simply those left out from its predecessor, or removed. Rather they are rays of light meant to illuminate the darkness, even still. They represent aspects that need to be explored, explained, followed. They take us to what came before, and what came after. Diversions. Extractions. Fragments.

For those who might have read *A Requiem For Hania,* you will find a major discrepancy of age and place in *Fragments.* In 2014, at the end of the former novel, Agnieszka (Aga), who again makes an appearance in *Fragments,* is still living in Warsaw with her husband Beniamin and small son Kuba. In this present novel, Agnieszka, Beniamin and Kuba now live in Jerusalem, where time has purposely stretched and they have lived for many years. More to the point, Aga here is older than she would have been following on from *A Requiem For Hania,* and her son Kuba is here represented as an unspecified nineteen year old. I posed the question to myself as a 'what if' scenario: what if Agnieszka was now older, rather wiser, and Kuba had been this age given the events depicted in this work, inspired by certain true events, instead of the age he would be following on from the previous novel. I acknowledge the discrepancy; for the story I wanted to tell, it is necessary to retain the character, but imagine him at this point in time as a strongly moral, principled late teenager—lessons learned from his own background. Because of the connections I wanted to make, I decided to take writer's license. Readers can hold it against me or suggest creeping senility.

Once again some of the material in this book is indeed based on true events, on real people I have known in my life and work. On experiences that left their mark, like a never forgotten tattooed number on a forearm, on our hearts and our memories, our nightmares and our dreams. And particularly at this moment in world events, at this writing, our fears.

The journeys these stories take us on--the characters, the readers and indeed this author--have no real beginning and no real end. Or as the poet TS Eliot would have it, 'In my End is my Beginning.' These fragments, these stories and memories, are but spots of time to help us understand who we are, why we are. Perhaps to give meaning to—something. Perhaps to give meaning to our very humanity.

The truth is our stories are but fragments and extractions of the time we have been, the little we have seen. *A Requiem For Hania* was not the beginning of that journey. It was simply a particular movement of the music heard along the way.

Fragments carries us further in the direction we have no choice but to follow. The music—the requiem arguably—continues to play with all the harmony, dissonance, melody, consonance that defines our lives. These fragments pose questions without an answer, with hesitations, and perhaps with a justly needed cry for hope.

Greg Dinner
December, 2024

FRAGMENTS

The frantumaglia is an unstable landscape, an infinite aerial or aquatic mass of debris that appears to the I, brutally, as its true and unique inner self. The frantumaglia is the storehouse of time without the orderliness of a history, a story. The frantumaglia is an effect of the sense of loss, when we're sure that everything that seems to us stable, lasting, an anchor for our life, will soon join that landscape of debris that we seem to see. The frantumaglia is to perceive with excruciating anguish the heterogeneous crowd from which we, living, raise our voice, and the heterogeneous crowd into which it is fated to vanish.

Elena Ferrante
"La Frantumaglia"
(translation by Ann Goldstein)

Frantumaglia: a Neapolitan word meaning a jumble of fragments.

PROLOGUE

*"They spent a long time there, mostly just the two of them
amongst the stone before any tourist buses arrived. Although
a few other visitors joined them to wander around the
monument and stone, the only sound was the sound
of the slight breeze blowing through nearby trees. These
were the ghosts that would walk beside them forever.*

*'There is no music here,' Pawel said to Aga. 'This is the
only place I have ever visited where I do not hear music.'"*
                                                    --A Requiem For Hania

The Site

Masovian Voivodeship (Northeastern Poland)
March 2019

Then there were no trees here. They came later. Then there was only emptiness, tears and fear. That was all.

Now she can hear their cries still on the breeze. Now she can see their faces too but they are not here. She cannot tell others in her team what she sees, what she hears; nevertheless those faces, those voices, those tears for her are very real. They call out to her and she knows.

Jenny sits wrapped in her heavy winter coat at the edge of the small rectangular pit the team had excavated only days earlier. It is just at the edge of the trees that were not always here. Not always. They were careful when they carved even this small memory of whispers in the dirt. Whispers from the earth. Of the earth. Only some three-quarters of a meter by one and a quarter meters. A rectangle some thirty centimeters deep. Twelve inches or so. The smallest of pits. Stepping stone, really. Still she calls it the pit.

When they were digging, scratching only the surface, they wondered if they would find anything below, far below. But they were wrong. They found evidence just beneath the surface; they did not have to dig down deeply. Evidence never touched. Barely hidden. Life and death evidence. A tiny handle probably from a teacup: porcelain. A coin. The remnants of a piece of leather. A tiny, torn bit of cloth. The heel of a shoe. So little so much. Disposed of. Hidden. Lost. Forgotten. Yet not.

And the item. That item.

Life and death remembered.

That was a few days ago.

Now Jenny has returned on this quiet Sunday, this non-working day. Most of the others came here only on weekdays: her team, her co-workers, Brian, the head of the project who was her supervisor, who was her lover only over a short time, only then, when the mistake was made and they had thought they had wanted but they had not wanted, when there was no love, only momentary desire. He like the others chose to stay in the city, two hours away, commuting to the site daily. They all said they needed relief. They needed the weekend entertainment or the airport nearby so they might fly to their homes elsewhere in Europe for a weekend visit, or the anonymity of a city where it was easier to forget.

They say they can forget. This they tell themselves. They tell one another.

Jenny, however, cannot allow herself to do so. Not for her the forgetting. So she has chosen to reside for now in the town nearby. And she chooses to leave there for the city, or for England, or for a release from the horrors, only rarely. Perhaps that is why the relationship with Brian started and stopped almost in an instant.

Or perhaps she remains nearby alone because she hears the voices still and chooses not to silence them. Not like the others, those coworkers. Those friends who are distant and kept at a distance. Not like them. Jenny needs to remember.

This is why she is here today, this weekend morning before the public arrives to stare and pray, before they enter, before they can enter, so that this moment, her moment, is the time of ghosts when all around is otherwise silent. Silent except for those past voices she can hear. And past tears she still sees fall.

And a past fear that even now she holds within. That makes her feel—what? Alive maybe? Empty maybe? In pain and in pain feeling something maybe? She asks herself these questions. She does not have the answers. Not yet.

Not love; desire.

Jenny sits with her feet in the pit. Staring at it. At the trees. At the rectangular shallow hole she and the others have created, slowly, meticulously, digging with their sharp pointed tools, their tiny rakes, their palm held brushes, searching with some discussion or little discussion. So now sitting, staring, simply knowing. Her legs hang over the edge. Her feet touch the earth. She removes her shoes, plants her toes on the cold, hard dirt, lets the whispers crawl up along her calves, her thighs, her sex, to her heart. Now her knees held tightly against her chest.

Little girl Jenny, she says. *Little girl you.* Run and play outside. But here there is no play, no laughter. Here there is only this. The knowing. The certainty of space.

Two masses moving in tandem cannot occupy the same space at the same time. Two memories moving in tandem should always occupy the same space at the same time. For the knowing. And the knowing is enough. Not enough. Or too much, she cannot be sure. Yes, probably too much.

Will you tell them why you are here? All those ghosts? Will you tell them about your memories that make you laugh? That make you cry? Will you tell them you reached out but the hand you expected to find, to pull you from the morass, the fear, was not there? No longer there? Will you ask them about their own children? Their sons? Their daughters? Did they reach out? Did they take a hand? Will you tell them? Will you tell yourself?

Jenny sits there for one hour. Perhaps almost two. She ignores the cold. And it is cold. But time has no meaning and she cannot keep track. Toes on the hard dirt. Knees at her chest. Sits, just sits. It is hard to leave what is inside. It is hard to leave this memory.

Eventually she raises her feet, settling them beneath her, sitting back on her haunches, leaning back, seeing the high green evergreen in her vision foreground, the sun then above just in her line of sight. And there sitting back on her haunches she feels the breeze on her face, the stinging slap of emptiness.

An image in her head: Native American woman. She knows to say Native American now because it is correct. But the image is from her childhood when the children on her street played cowboys and 'Indians' and she said she was Pocahantas, Indian queen warrior. So she imagined. Child imaginings. She wishes she could smile at the memory. No longer enough happy memories. She bends her legs back and places her hands at her sides, closes her eyes and wishes she was a child again dreaming and she is not and this is not a dream. Not a dream. Just a nightmare yes not a dream no.

She opens her eyes and is not sure if they are open. In that pit they dug out only a few days ago she see a young woman sitting across from her, across at the other side of the pit only thirty centimeters deep, one and a quarter meters long with her chin resting on her knees. Jenny could in fact reach out to touch her. Jenny does not reach out to touch her. Instead she stares, watches. Mirror image but not mirror. The woman looks up, looks back at her, at Jenny. Yes she is certain she sees the young woman staring, without words. Staring.

` She should tell the others what she sees when they return the next day. She should say, look there. I saw there. I heard others, there. She should explain. She should make them understand, make them care, make them know, but she cannot. No, she cannot. Not that. Never that.

Perhaps she is going mad.

You think about her as she lived, still, still think, still whispering in your head, your memory. You see her face, her crystal blue eyes staring down at you as you are born, staring at you without question. You see too those same crystal blue eyes staring in the distance at emptiness, the eyes full of emptiness, without words to give, without hope. And she, young woman old woman, Mother, ghost, looks at you in silence. And she does not reach out. She cannot reach out.

Your tears never came. You did not remember how to cry.

You struggle with that. You know she was a part of you and you cannot let go. You know you are at fault. You blame yourself. You have been sent here, have come here, to this place, work here in this place, because of her. But you will think of nothing. You do not think of her who is not. She who is not. You do not allow yourself to think of she who is not. But of course she is all you think about. All you can ever think about.

This then is why you have come. This is why.

*

Jenny opens her eyes again. Still on her knees, her haunches. Still the pit that is not a pit but simply a hole, really. Window, really, to what happened here. The coin. The leather. The cloth. A tiny broken handle of a teacup. She knew what this place was.

She found something else when digging, when dusting away the dirt. Something else that she carefully removed from the thin layer of the earth, the thin layer of the past. With her blue latex covered fingers she scratched at the topsoil with her sharp pointed chisel, thinking she might have found something. She then took the small brush and brushed away the specks of dirt. Tool, brush, tool, brush.

Rusted bit of metal. Half eaten away. Rust.

Seat for a tiny jewel not there. Here. There. Brush. Tool. Another seat, empty

4

nest of precious stone that was probably never precious but decor. Brush. Tool. Dig. Wipe.

Finally then pulling the small object from the pit. Half eaten away with time and decay and rust. Its shape still held. Still revealing. Still telling a story. Turning it over in those latex-covered hands, that small shape only a few centimeters long, narrow, tubular. She knows this shape. She knows this object. She senses this story. Turned over and over again in her fingers, blue latex fingers.

I know you, she thought.

She placed the object in the plastic bag to be recorded with the other found objects. The hollow of the cylinder examined with a microscope. Dated. Tested. Marked down. It will find its way into a museum. Where it will remain but probably speak to none.

But it spoke to Jenny. She had hesitated. Stared at it, the tubular item now in a plastic bag, oh so familiar. And she put it in the pouch at her side. She intended to return it to the other familiar objects that were found, to be catalogued and assembled and described and tested, but not then, not yet. Not yet because she needed to carry it at her side and in her memory and in her heart for a day, two, hold onto it until this weekend morning when she is alone and no one will be there to hear its song sung, its story told but to her.

And so she is here, this day, this morning, alone, her knees bent, her legs below her, her eyes opening, staring at the pit from where the story emerged. Jenny takes from her pocket a pair of blue latex gloves, thin, one of so many pairs that she always has with her, and puts them on.

Not to dig. She will not do that. But rather to feel. And she removes that half decayed, small metal tube still in its plastic bag from the pouch that she has worn over her shoulder at her side this day when she is alone, when the others of her team are not there, when there is only silence.

She opens the bag, and removes the object. She stares at it for the longest of moments, turning it over and over in her latex covered blue coloured fingers, over and over. Decayed and full of story.

Jenny looks at the pit from where it was born, this item, in her mind crying like a child emerging from a womb, welcoming life in pain and fear and hope and the blank canvas that is memory. But this is not a blank canvas. This is memory that speaks volumes.

The item in her blue coloured coated fingertips, turned over and over. The pit the womb.

Jenny stands, still staring at the item. She considers. She sees.

Jenny turns away and walks. She puts the item back into the plastic bag as she moves, but holds onto it tightly so as not to interrupt its story, its song.

She walks straight along this path that is not a path, this avenue that is not an avenue, this street that was no street but nevertheless that they called Heaven Street because it made them laugh, *Himmelstrasse* because they thought the word secretly would define the hate they felt, the pathway that is there no longer but which she and the others know is there from the theodolite and GPS mapping system and tape measures and documentation and witness recollections from so long ago now that they could see it even if it could it not be seen, that straight line from the pit as Jenny calls it towards the stones that are memorial, to the area they have marked out, a hundred meters, perhaps even one hundred twenty, to that larger rectangle marked out empty space still awaiting exploration, awaiting to dig, if permission is granted, if religious laws allow, and here she walks now in silence.

She needs to walk in silence.

*

Here then she arrives. And stands in silence.

Jenny alone.

Jenny.

And she again removes from the pouch the plastic bag holding the decomposed decaying bit of tarnished, rusted metal with its small indentation seats for jewels or fake jewels and its cylindrical interior filled once with a paste but filled no longer; from this plastic bag Jenny removes again with her still blue coated blue coloured latex-covered fingers the object that speaks to her and whispers and shouts volumes.

That small cylindrical object that Jenny recognizes as the decaying remains of a tube of almost eighty year old lipstick. A next to nothing item that weeps memory because even the smallest item from then weeps memory from this place, this hateful place dark even beneath the bright morning sunlight.

She turns it over in her fingers. Staring at it, standing here beside the string that marks another place, this other larger, deeper pit that they hope to dig if permission is granted, that they need to uncover unearth unnerve unknow but they will not unknow because in this cloud of unknowing knowledge is all and cannot be rescinded: Cassandra and her open chest of memory.

Jenny stares at this object in her palm.

And this place is suddenly silent. This place of memory and loss. No birdsong now. No insects. No wind through the tree branches. The trees that are there but that were not there not standing guard mostly not there then but there now, even they are silent. Nothing.

Jenny stares. Takes it all in. Sees all. Sees what she wishes she did not see. *Because of her. Because of her she has come with others to dig in a few locales and to mark out with coloured string and to plant short stakes in earth short wooden stakes into the heart that denote slight undulations in the earth outlines and a Site and a place and pain.* And she looks there, now, standing beside that coloured string where she and her colleagues and Brian her supervisor await the word that they will be given permission to excavate because they need to excavate to prove what they already think they know, to find the foundations of a brick and mortar building that they are sure is here thanks to measurements taken and the aerial drone footage joining the photographic imaging taken and the laser scanning and all the magical tricks at their disposal to create an image of past, that knowledge of past. This they can do. This she does with them.

Brian who is head of the project calls it non-invasive research. Jenny hears the irony in the expression. She is assaulted and invaded, at night when she closes her eyes, in the morning when she wakes. Her search deeply invasive.

And here, this place, these strings marking out place, here they wait, they attend, waiting for the time soon perhaps when they are given permission to cut into the earth with their tools. Non-invasive but sometimes, just sometimes, you need to cut carefully. And expose. With their knives. Her knife exposing and to be exposed. Knife to the heart. And so to examine the earth, the soil, the brick beneath, the entrance and exit one and the same, only one, so to feel it, to uncover. To know. Why does she want to know, she wonders? Jenny has no answer. She only has need.

7

The necessity to see what must be seen.

It is what she does with the team. Dig to imagine. Imagine then dig. Imagination becoming image so that at a later time she can create into a material world. Material life. But first she needs to draw pictures in the air. So she can say she understands. Although she does not understand. Jenny has never been able to understand.

Today is Sunday. It is morning. She does not have to understand, or pretend she does, not to the others. Not to her short term lover Brian in charge of these imaginings she can picture as if by magic. Not to her colleagues who join her. Who discuss with her. Not to herself while she draws. Models. Digs. Sees into the past now come alive. Sees what must be seen. The past.

That is History.

But History ended here.

This is the architecture she thinks. But architecture builds, not hides, not destroys. History destroys. She has learned that, hasn't she? *Haven't you, she wonders?*

This is death, Jenny thinks. *You are right she tells herself.* It is what remains. All that remains. And nothing remains, the one thing she knows. Nothing remains but memory. And the invention of memory.

She is an inventor and she hates her inventions. Their inventions. What they did. What they did. What they...did.

Site.

Cold winter's day. Breeze through trees now there not always there. Dirt. Stone. Silence. Thirst. Knowledge is thirst. Looks around. Features. Jenny always notes the features. Secret places. Like her womb. *And the womb from whence she came.* Always note the features. They matter. They speak of secrets long past. They do not forget.

In front of her, marked out space. Holding secrets. She will be one of a team that will begin to unearth secrets. They will never all be unearthed.

In that space, in front of the coloured string, she sees the young woman. The woman alone. The woman staring at her, her lips bright red. The woman who threw away the last of her treasured belongings but not before she was able to colour her lips, so that she might say this is who I am, I am woman and I am proud and I will march naked as I am told to march but you will never take away my humanity my essence my red lips because I am. Simply that. I am.

Young woman. Mother perhaps. Her belly belies a birth, Jenny thinks. Where is the child, Jenny wonders? Why does the mother not reach out for the child? Why does the child not reach out to the mother? Child without mother. Crystal blue eyes. Red lips. Child without mother.

You still dream of her but she is not. You still seek her but she is not. You would have told her, explained, painted the picture, created the image, revealed the secret place. But she is not.

And you see her, she would have been her, the mother who was not, naked now, standing, staring, looking, turning. Hanging. She is not there. Never there. Never. Mother no. Mother—no. Please.

Jenny wonders still. Then distracted when hearing as if for the first time the buzzing. Insects. And a single bird. Hymn song. Sad song. Not for the first time she looks away, realizing she is observed by immaterial spectres. How strange, she thinks.

And when she looks back at the marked rectangle of what will be a larger pit, foundations perhaps or so the instruments they use suggest, four meters by ten meters, this place of hallowed ground, pit, chamber, shower they were told, the last steps to take on that road to heaven, heaven itself, when she looks back she sees the young woman, naked, red lips not quivering but strong. Jenny sees that the woman is as her mother was, her red lips, her face, her body belying birth: the woman wanting to reach out and unable to reach out, to you. Jenny then sees the young woman nod just slightly, take a step over the string into a pit that is not, not yet, and disappears.

And yes disappears.

*

Silence again, but Jenny feels it within. Empty silence again. Except the breeze beside trees, above her and within her this breeze. And whispers heard. They are waiting, for her. Their voices. Their need.

Crystal blue eyes.

They know her. Jenny. They know her well. They have waited all these years, these decades, for her arrival. To bear witness when there are none to bear witness

9

any longer. But there is one. Jenny. She will remember just as they remember her.

She will.

And with that realization, Jenny turns, spies the Heaven Road that brought her here, that path back towards the trees, towards the train station that never was, the ticket office that never was, the train tracks that carried them all here, carried her here, sixty cattle cars loading and unloading. The tears and the fear and the knowledge.

Jenny turns. And walks towards that disappearing train. Towards the entrance to the Site a kilometer or so through the trees, and the past, and the present. Jenny returns, and can never return.

She imagines again the young woman she knows she saw at the Site, the Site beyond the string, the young woman with the red lips who threw the metal lipstick tube encrusted with a few fake jewels to the ground knowing it was needed no longer, and then marched with her red lips glistening in the sunshine. That woman who Jenny saw cross the strings of many colours. And like that woman, perhaps, Jenny too returns, and can never return.

I carry you within me. You are there still but I cannot reach you. And you no longer reach out to me. No.

So then walk away. Jenny can never walk away even in the walking. Enveloped by silences, tears and cries. Embraced by them. On this quiet Sunday, before the visitors come, Jenny walks back. And forward.

And back.

I

"*She wrote down the Babka she never knew, the relatives she never had but knew existed. She wrote down the neighbours she remembered and the childhood friends. She wrote down the names of the butchers and the bread makers and the leather tanner and the coffin maker… She wrote the Ghetto. She wrote it all…She wrote down her own name…And finally she took out a match. And she set the pages alight. And she watched the paper burn. And smoke. And the papers turn to ash and fly up from her hand and disappear. All disappeared. She stood in silence, and muttered in silence the Kaddish she had learned spoken often, too often, the prayer to remember, the prayer to forget.*

The prayer of tears. The prayer of the dead."
                                                                    --A Requiem For Hania

1. Izio

Liubar, Zhytomyr Oblast
Russian Pale of Settlement
1873-1891

I never asked to be born into this world. I was not given a choice. I did not knock on the curved edges of the soft watery cavern where I happily curled up with my left-hand first finger most precious, oh to become one day so very precious, in my fish-like mouth and say thank you very much, but no thank you, I am happy enough where I am and I choose to remain. Thank you but no thank you. Here I am and here I will stay. It did not work out that way.

It sometimes simply does not work the way you want. Even if you ask.

You do not always get to choose the path you take.

So: in my case.

They said that after the Bobe delivered Tanl from the belly of his mother, and although half asleep with tiredness, the Bobe then knocked on our door to see if I had yet been born. Because I was still making my own Mama scream, the Bobe took pity on our rather poorer circumstances and remained, although insisted that I would have to wait to see the last light from a fading day so that she could finish a bowl of kabushta that she slopped up with the final crumbs of our day's black bread baked for the occasion. Luckily Mama had made a pot of her secret recipe to be put aside, as my Tateh would never be trusted with such a responsibility. He could conduct a needle and thread like the composer of a most beautiful symphony. He could repair a wheel on a cart and in his young days cut wheat as close to the ground as any cow could feed. But when it came to preparing kabushta, such an ability was far beyond the vast experiences of his life. And so it would always prove.

Life can make artists and masters of a craft. Make the most brilliant politicians or rebbes whose prayers would be heard by God himself. But for kabushta that warmed the very soul, only Mama would do in our house.

Finally, once the Bobe had wiped her mouth on the rag my Tateh handed to her when the last bit of rich pale green cabbage had disappeared and she had loudly belched, she stood, yawned widely, retreated into the small room where Mama lay, and ordered her to push.

Push my Mama did, and so I was born. Personally I blame the kabushta for timing, place and necessity, although Mama never did.

So yes, despite entreaties and whispered protests, I was born. No choice, meshugener, you have arrived. Scream all you want until even your eyes might burst from their very sockets. Poke that left-hand finger most precious at any and all. Protest so that Czar Alexander himself might hear all the way from London where they said he was visiting with his beautiful mistress Katia (as if no one in the Pale had guessed the truth) and despair. Roar and fight.

Or don't. And I did not.

Rather I accepted my fate from the first breath, with the immediate evacuation of my tiny bowels and an acknowledged wink from a rather enlarged red member that the Moyle had yet to sanctify by slightly shortening. So it would be. That was me, ever to be. Staring wide eyed then with confusion, with only a final singular moan to greet the day, or evening as it had become, or so my Mama told me later. I was never much of one to protest nor comment for long, not then, and not even in my later days. Certainly from that very first moment I have found the world confusing. I am undoubtedly liberated by my confusion. My life has been full of such.

But at that moment I knew none of this. At that moment, being born three hours after Tanl, I looked up at my Mama's tears, my Tateh's stare, and subsequent to a slight despairing gurgle and slighter passing of gas that followed my rather sad example of evacuation, I promptly retreated into relative silence. Silence sometimes is better for confused and confusing possibility.

Tanl, my friend, did not agree on this point. He never would. He would talk with the best of them. Would recite and argue and sing as none other. But he understood that I, his closest friend in those days, could not be the same. Could not be in his image. I had to be in his shadow. It was meant to be and such was the way of our world. He accepted this fate as did I. And in the way he knew best, he comforted

13

my doubt by reminding me that he was three hours older. Three hours wiser. I generally did not comment on this fact. But I knew he was right. His might have been a lifetime wiser. Mine a lifetime of shadow. Because that is how life was for us.

*

My Tateh was not the only tailor in our shtetl in the Pale, and perhaps not the best. But he worked hard, so hard that he rarely cast a glance towards me. If I stumbled into his shop, I felt his harsh glance warning me, and more than once felt the back of his hand. I can't say he was a particularly hard man, but the needs of a young son were hardly those of a paying customer.

If my Tateh preferred to keep to himself, my Mama made certain that there would be food on our table each day, that accounts were kept, the debts and taxes paid, the clothes washed, the floor swept. Sometimes. I am not quite certain how if my Mama had not been there my Tateh would have got by. I am not quite certain how, when she was no longer there, he did still.

It was through my Mama that my family was on friendly terms with Tanl's family. His mother and my own had been friends as young girls and his own father was a good customer who ordered his coats only from my own. Tanl's father owned the wood mill in our Shtetl and his customers always paid their debts, and on time. So compared to our small lodgings Tanl's family home was in my eyes a palace, with its strong furniture his father's workmen made for him, its metal cups and plates, with food at the table carried over by a servant. A dream home to me when I was asked to stay, staring at the food with half revealed hunger. If my Tateh was silent, and my Mama distracted, Tanl's mother made certain that I had a full belly as I grew older, and would smile when my Mama rarely did. His mother could also sing, gentle songs that might wrap their harmonious arms around me and hold me tightly in the evening, Shabbos songs that I would take home to our own table on the Shabbos eve, to whisper for my Mama who would nod with approval but without smiling, complementing the inscrutable stare of my Tateh. To him I seemed a stranger, a little bird. And he had little time for little birds.

Once, when Tanl's mother asked if my own parents enjoyed the song I sang at our family table, I said that my Mama did, but that my Tateh seemed not to hear, or if heard, did not care. Tanl's mother stared at me quietly, then explained that my own Tateh heard, but that he had worries that must consume him. She tried to explain how he had been hurt a number of years before I was born, when some of the people in a town beat him and many others. She called it a pogrom but it was not a word I knew then, not like now. She said that was why he shuffled when he walked, why he might seem distant or sad. I nodded at her seriousness, but I did not understand. One day I might perhaps. Not then.

A few years after I was born, my Mama came to me one night as I nearly slept, smiling gently, telling me I would soon have a brother or sister of my own. This I found confusing, as I had always looked on Tanl as my brother. But no, she explained, Tanl might be my best friend, but soon I would have my own brother or my own sister to help in the world, and to guide with my greater knowledge and experience. And unlike Tanl to me, I would be the older this time.

I did not think I could handle such a serious responsibility, but my Mama assured me that I would be able, when the time came. She said she had faith that I would be the best of brothers. I would teach this other strange being, be it boy or girl, brother or sister, one who might have wished to hide inside Mama or who might greet the day with cries of exaltation, the songs I sang for the family. Such sibling too would hear music, she said, and one day join me in such song. I fell asleep dreaming of such a moment. And telling myself that where I would lead, my brother or sister would follow.

*

It was, however, not to be. Once again the Bobe came to our house, but this time she did not linger to slurp kabushta, did not chew black bread with grunts of approval. She did not ask for such pleasures. Rather she remained at my Mama's bedside all through the night and long into morning. She tried to urge my Mama to push, as Mama had pushed for me. But Mama was too weak to push. Could not push.

My brother, or sister, I was not to know which, decided to resist the order to appear and chose, as I had been unable to choose, to remain—within. Thus he, or maybe he was a she, would remain silent forever, longer certainly than I.

And my Mama also chose then to remain silent as well. Forever silent. Because,

15

the Bobe told me, someone had to help my unborn brother or sister, still she did not say which, in the better place, without fear.

I was told I had to be brave.

I was not brave.

I was told to be strong.

I was not strong.

I was told to be not afraid, that tears were understandable.

But I was afraid. And the tears no one saw. Not then. Not ever. I find that tears make a noise like wind brushing gently over a river. But I would remain silent from such whisperings. I would be as silent as…as Mama. So it was.

And my Tateh too said nothing. He went into his workshop. He closed the door. And said nothing.

It was many days before he would speak again. In this we were much alike, despite what differences separated us.

*

With my Mama no longer there to keep order in our house, my Tateh was not quite sure what to do with me, or if he knew, he did not know how to do it. I have no doubt that he searched the few cupboards in our house to see if he could put me within, to hang me on a hook to keep out of the rain and out of his way. Unfortunately as bare as our cupboards might be, he could not find one big enough to hide me from view. Neither could he cover me out of sight with one of the coats he spent days on end sewing for clients. Coats were too valuable to make a young boy disappear.

I suppose my Tateh was pleased when I started cheder, as such kept him free of noise, questions and boyish games for much of his day. At least that is what my Tateh thought must be the explanation for his long hours of silence and solace. And I did attend cheder beside Tanl. But whereas Tanl took to reading Torah with grace and curiosity, for me it seemed a tumble of symbols and letters of sorts that never spoke to my heart—or more importantly perhaps, to my ears. Staring out the window of the wooden schoolroom, bearing the occasional crack of the Rebbe's stick on my knuckles or the sharp barb of his odorous tongue that leaned over me and spoke loudly in my ear, I endured such embarrassments with brave indifference. Or made

16

it seem so.

If the other boys laughed at me, and perhaps called me names, Tanl alone always stood beside me and whispered to me that all would pass. All would be as God wished it to be. He alone recognized that for me there was greater joy in the music of our laughter than in any transcribed lines from Moses's good books. I might not learn to read, but I would learn to sing. I heard music, and that was well. And enough.

My Tateh of course knew little of this. For him there was only cloth, and needle, and thread. And although he never said I gave him naches in the way that Tanl's mother and father often embraced my friend with love and pride, at least I could say I worked hard not to give my Tateh cause for grief or despair. At least not much.

*

Market days were always special for us. Once a week the traders gathered in town on Grodno Street to buy foods that the peasants would bring to sell from the countryside outside the shtetl, and the traders would put out their goods for many to admire or buy if they could. Two or three times a year a Polish trader would appear with cloths from abroad. My father loaded up with those woolens he could afford to purchase, with various needles and threads he needed to replace when his stocks were low. Or he might put out his own wares for customers to admire or order for the future as was their need. Sometimes I helped by carrying coats out to the market table or a few vegetables back to our house, but often he left me to my own devices, to play amongst other cheder boys released from their studies for the day. We would meet at the edge of the square and run in and out of tables of goods and foods, or through the horse market where the farmers sold their horses and cattle, or we might wander to the backs of houses amongst the trees at the edge of town, throwing pine cones at one another in mock battles between warring Cossack armies.

The hot summer days were our favorite, of course. Tanl and I would join other boys to walk over the fields to the water mill where we were allowed to swim and splash and shout to our hearts' content. A few of the braver boys would swim around the bend of the stream where the girls had their swimming spot, to spy at their sisters' companions or sometimes throw rocks nearby to hear them scream and shout. Tanl and I oftentimes kept to ourselves, only occasionally joining in games,

17

or swinging over the stream on the rope we had tied, then letting ourselves drop with a large splash, avoiding the rocks at the water's edge.

When the weather turned cooler, and the red leaves began to drop, Tanl and I would leave the joys of the mill to explore the paths in the woods that bordered the edge of our shtetl, climbing trees or creating huge mounds of fallen branches and crackling leaves that we would hide beneath or jump into and scatter. Sometimes I could not convince Tanl to forgo his study for such adventures, so I would wander myself along the forest paths, quietly singing the songs I liked best, dreaming the dreams of the impossible. Or I might forage amongst the meadows and mossy forest floors, picking mushrooms and berries, or seeking the youngest sorrel and ramsons' leaves that I would proudly present to Tanl's mother, knowing she would turn such delights into the most delicious ice cold schav, with always a bowl for me at the table, and with a bowl to carry back to my Tateh to soup on at the end of his work day with a grunt of thanks that I might pass on.

Then as the winds from the north began to blow, turning the warmer autumn days into chill that bit through our clothes, as the snows began and the river racing through the shtetl froze, we would slip and slide on the snow covered ice, or throw snowballs, or help the ice cutters taking blocks from the river's edge that they kept in their ice houses until the spring days broke through.

So in this way we grew, and passed our days, and sometimes studied (well I sometimes, Tanl often) and saw our legs growing long and our dreams growing rich.

*

It had rained for days and the river had flooded into fields. I sat in the cheder as every day, but instead of looking down at the reading and the words scattered there like falling stars, I sat staring out the window, dreaming of fish. My stomach growled, thinking only of fish. I knew that with the floods came fish from up river, stranded on the banks for neighbors to gather, enough from the spring floods to fill many a growling belly.

I dreamed of fish.

And because I so dreamed, because I stared longingly out of the window instead of concentrating on the reading, I never heard the Rebbe sneak up behind (believe me, he did not walk; he sneaked), did not smell his fetid breath resting on the back of my neck, and only realized the fate that would follow once his stick hit the table in front of me. Snapped in front of me. Missed my nose by a nose hair, snapped, whipped, woke me from my reverie.

My reverie of fish.

I saw Tanl beside me, shaking his head in warning. Say nothing. But it was then too late in my life to say nothing and accept what punishment might be meted out. When the Rebbe asked me what was so important out of the window rather than in the sacred and profound words before me, I could but whisper a single word of answer: fish.

He stared. He moved not the slightest. He said nothing, at first. He could have lectured on Jonah. He could have remarked about Noah. He could have warned me that Lot's wife turned to salt when turning away, and it was not salt that preserved fish. Instead he did not move, did not speak, did not slam his stick on my knuckles as he often did. Instead he only sighed. Shook his head, just slightly, and told me to go. To the fish.

I looked over at Tanl. Shrugged. And left.

Towards the end of the day, as the sun was low on the horizon, I returned to my house to find Tateh in conversation with the Rebbe. I expected anger. I expected a beating. I expected—in fact I don't know what I expected. To lessen the pain I held up the three fish I had managed to collect for both to see. The Rebbe nodded, put his hand on my shoulder, and departed. In earlier days perhaps there might have been kabushta to ease the words he must have said to Tateh, to be granted some sort of reprieve or forgiveness, but those days were long gone.

Instead the Rebbe disappeared, and my Tateh stared at me, then said simply that I was no longer welcome at the cheder, that I was no student, that from now on I would have to earn my keep and earn my way.

I was not a boy any longer, I was a man. A very short man, but a man. Well, so I told myself. A man of sorts. That simply meant I would henceforth have to use the muscles in my arms and legs rather than those in my head. Easily done, as there were few if any in my head.

Thus began long days of wearisome apprenticeships as my Tateh ushered me out the door to learn a trade. Whereas some sons would learn at their father's knee, my own Tateh's knees were too busy supporting lengths of cloth and thread to put me there. Besides, he grunted, my hands were far too slow and soft to work with cloth. A tailor I would never be. Instead I was sent first to the cobbler, but here too my hands proved too slow for the demand, my eyes wandering far from soles to the street outside once too often for the cobbler's liking. I tried minding cattle, but the big cows scared me. I cut grain in the fields but wielded a scythe like a poor oaf wields a club twice his size. I spent a week at the mill helping where I could but was told not to return when I almost fell against the grinding stone, staring for slightly too long at the miller's daughter instead of sweeping away the errant remnants of pulverized wheat. Finally I found my place in the worst of all worlds amidst the blood and smell of the tanner. I had no love for leather and the work was the most menial, but for a boy who dreamed of music and laughter there was little else for which I was deemed to show possible skill and that might lead me to find my way.

The few rubles I managed to earn as a tanner's apprentice—if one called servitude the work of an apprentice--inevitably found their way into my Tateh's pocket. Without protest, I should add. We both had to find a way to live, and to live together. He did, however, allow me to keep a few rubles each week after shabbat, or sometimes barely a few kopeks, although at first I had no idea what to do with my new found wealth, or indeed where to spend such a measly sum. But even in my early teenage years I learned much from the alcohol traders about the inns and taverns further afield. In this manner I heard about the karchma, the tavern just outside of our town owned by a Jew, the shenk, with his wife, where Jews could drink, sometimes in the company of soldiers and non-Jews. So hoping that the few rubles in my pocket might go far in such a wondrous place, and of course without the knowledge of my Tateh, I found my way there. Inevitably my first night became one of many. And whilst those few rubles did not travel far, given my age and size they traveled far enough.

It was while at this karchma that two events would change my life later on. The first was the shenk's daughter. In my eyes, a wondrous beauty, a goddess, a vision. Yes, admittedly a few years older. Yes, admittedly rather womanlier than my manly attributes as yet might prepare me for adulthood. Yes, admittedly rounded whereas I, I was still perhaps within the prime years of boyhood. But she was secretly still

20

beheld by my often downcast gaze gazing upwards. And in her eyes, I...I was invisible. Unspeakable. From my lips unable to utter a remark or address, unable to find the words that might make her take notice. So she did not take notice. She may have been the daughter of Jews who owned the tavern, but to me she was Esther in my heart. And there I knew she had to remain, unknown, unknowing.

The second event was when three traveling musicians came to play, and for a few kopeks would play the most wonderful songs to any who might listen. One musician beat a rhythm on a hand drum, while another played an instrument with a reed, blowing the tune from it like a horn. But it was the musician playing the small fiddle who most enraptured me—almost as much, that is, as the shenk's daughter. I could have listened to these musicians play all night, if I had been allowed. With so few kopeks in my pocket, I wasn't. And with the tannery smells stuck to my skin like a disease, as soon as I'd had my drink for the night, I was to leave. But I left determined to be like those musicians, and particularly to learn to play as beautiful a song as emanated from that of the fiddler.

It so happened that at that time Tanl had been gifted a small violin of his own and had been offered lessons from the music master in our shtetl. Sitting in his house one day, observing him as he studied, I noticed the poor instrument on the table in his corner. Tanl watched my eyes travel, watched me, then returned to his Talmudic readings. Being bored, tired of sitting on my hands waiting for the time we might play the ball game that had become a favorite, I stood, walked over to the instrument and plucked at the strings. Tanl looked up at me again.

--I do not think it is something I will master, he said. Mama insists but I prefer the poetry of words to the harmonies of music.

He shrugged, looked away. I picked up the fiddle, simple and somewhat beaten as it was, but in my eyes made of the most magnificent hollowed spruce, dark brown; despite various imperfections, what I saw was perfection. I ran my fingers along the long neck of the instrument, picked up the bow, held it to me, and drew.

The sound I made was—terrible. Worse than the cats of the shtetl. Worse than the single moan from the cow when the schochet's knife struck and bled. At least to my ears. Tanl looked up, cocked his head to one side, and smiled.

--Better than me, he said with all seriousness. There is a musician somewhere within you.

I grunted. He smiled. I dreamed. He stared at me, long and hard, then looked away, back to his own dreams of poetry and literature. A fire was thus lit. But I knew it was a fire that would not burn, and just as quickly as lit, it extinguished.

It was perhaps inevitable, however, that Tanl would come to my rescue and give me some hope, or at least the possibility of hope. Tanl and his mother and father. That I spent too many evenings and too many rubles from one who had so little at the tavern inevitably was whispered in the shtetl. If my Tateh heard such murmurings, he did not say. But Tanl knew, and knew from me of the shenk's daughter and the magical musicians who had appeared one night, only to disappear the next. We shared our secrets. Tanl read to me the poems he had started to write, and the dream of becoming a great writer; I shared with him the song of the fiddler. And whether from his lips or another, my own infatuations, or at least the musical ones, were relayed to his mother and father.

Over a bowl of schav Tanl's mother broke the silence.

--Are you happy with your work at the tanner? Do you see a future there? There is talk of your visits to the Jewish karchma. Should a boy of your age be taking drink there? For this you gave up your Talmudic study, to become a tanner, to drink away what few kopeks are in your pocket?

Questions, so many questions. I could not reveal my dreams about the tavern owner's daughter. No one would understand how one so lowly might entertain such dreams. Tanl's mother put her hands over mine, looking back and forth between Tanl and me. Tanl smiled, shrugged. I had nowhere to hide my shame. Then it was that his mother said there was a notion. A plan. A decision. She owed it to my mother, she said. She owed it to her own son. She owed it to herself. She owed it to me: one last chance. Tanl's father nodded in agreement. And a bargain offered: Tanl's father would take me as a labourer into the sheds of his wood mill. In time I would learn to cut, to sell, to build. But for now I would have to carry and cart. A cart horse. I would have to work hard, grow muscles. I would have to pay attention, not daydream. There was, of course, a tradeoff for this offer. I would have to stop visiting the shenk's tavern. I would have to stop drinking and, without saying it, dreaming of the shenk's daughter. In exchange, with the pocket money I would keep, I would join Tanl at the music master's lesson. I would share Tanl's violin. If I worked hard at the mill perhaps one day I might learn to carve my own.

My heart beat for the girl of the karchma, but I knew she would not be mine. In the neck of Tanl's violin, however, that beautiful kley, that simple fiddle, I might find those zemer, those songs, that spoke to me, and through me might speak to the world beyond. Perhaps in this way, indeed only in this way, I might speak through those zemer to that girl who now simply remained my fantasy. And perhaps one day, through that fiddle, my kley, I might be able to seduce her nature, my kisses might yet pluck at the strings of her heart.

I could dream. And I could hardly refuse.

Except for my Tateh. Except for the tailor who took my wages, who sewed buttons for the many and sewed despair for one, me, his only son. Except for him.

I might not bring home the rubles of a king, but the tanner offered me slightly more to find their way into the pockets of my Tateh's coat, and thus the coats of his customers. He would not have his son starting from a lower position at the wood mill then spend good money after bad making bad music instead of learning Talmud as a good man should. He would not have it.

I was lost. Bereft. Hopeless. Until Tanl's father had a long word with my Tateh. And agreed to pay all my rubles directly to Tateh but for the few kopeks needed to pass into the music master's palm. The music lessons would not be gratis, but for their sake, and with Tanl's father's contribution, they would be mine, on condition that my Tateh might agree, on condition that I would honour the memory of my mother, and on condition that I would leave the karchma and the Jewish owners behind. Well behind. The kopeks these lessons would cost might burden slightly, but at least they would be not be so to my Tateh. And if the music itself might have become a burden, my promise to practice only at Tanl's served to convince my Tateh that such sonorous learnings would not overly impose upon his peaceful cuttings and sewings. That, along with Tanl's father's promise to purchase a new coat from Tateh each year, sealed the bargain.

*

The work in the timber mill was harder than I had imagined. The timber had to be brought from forests sometimes far afield, judged for value, stacked. In time it had to be cut at the mill, the giant saws carried and worked between men far taller, far stronger, far more skilled than I could ever hope to be. The planks had to be raised off the ground, seasoned, loaded and unloaded, carried, bartered, moved this way and that. The off-cuts had to put here, the center planks there, the measured planks exact, the grains evaluated. More than anything, great pieces of wood had to be carried. My back ached, my arms ached, my legs ached, but I, I was determined.

Not that I didn't still long for a quiet visit to the karchma, to cast my eyes once again on the, yes still older, shenk's daughter. I would tell myself that such disparity in age and worldly experience was a minor inconvenience. After all, wasn't Tanl older as well, by a full three months, and yet he did not despair of my existence. He was my brother. So surely the shenk's daughter might become a sister, or…well or…surely. Surely…And more than once I made the first steps in that direction when no wandering eyes cast upon me. But I always held back, in part from exhaustion, in part because of a bargain struck, in part because I was determined for once to succeed at something.

In part because of the music. And the hope that one day it would be a key to her heart, that tavern keeper's unmatchable creation.

The music master was not an easy man to satisfy. He had dreams of sending students to some sort of conservatory in Moscow. I had no idea what a conservatory was, but I strongly suspected it was not somewhere that I would ever find myself. And indeed after spending what little pocket money I had not on the shenk's strong alcoholic offering but on the lessons that followed Tanl's for over a year, with neither of us excelling in a way that pleased the master, it was clear that this conservatory would never embrace me as the master might have hoped. The master muttered he had dreamed of creating an Alexei Lvov with the finesse of Mozart. I of course had no idea who these people were, although I suspected they did not reside either in our shtetl or a neighboring town. My own dreams, however, were within my reach: simply to master the kley as best I could, that fiddle that had already mastered my heart, and to play the zemer I had heard at the karchma, or sometimes during festivals of joy where even my Tateh and our neighbors might sing and dance. My dreams were modest, no matter how many music master's shouts might ring in my ears. And there were many.

24

Slowly I improved. Slowly. And slowly my arms grew stronger in the mill. Slowly. In time one of the cutters began to take me under his watch, and one day gave me a small carving knife, with instruction not how I might cut, or rather—I was not to be trusted with the great whipsaws—how to whittle small offcuts into shapes that might amuse or please.

At first these shapes were simple: a small animal perhaps, or the shape of a house, or a simple puzzle. But over months, and finally a year having passed, my skill improved and in my spare time, left to my own devices with discarded offcuts, my imagination and ability created works that were more complex, if not always perfect.

Of course I had a dream, a secret desire. I would make my own kley. From pieces of spruce I would create an instrument that would make an audience laugh with joy or cry with tears at loss and memory. I would be as great as any traveling musician with a carved and self-assembled fiddle that would speak of my own heart, my own longings, singing the songs of our community with a bow drawing out sermons as great as any rebbe might have uttered and those neighbours of our shtetl had ever heard, becoming renowned throughout the Pale.

Yes, I knew this was nothing but a dream, but what else would a boy my age want in life? Except perhaps the kisses of the shenk's daughter. So I spent many weeks drawing, exploring proportions, weighing bits of wood, cutting and making holes, examining glues, stripping down and drying intestines from discarded cows' guts to dry as strings, pulling horses' tails to think about the ribbon of a bow. I was determined to make the most perfect fiddle one could imagine, the most beautiful instrument that sang, becoming my voice when others thought I had none. I was determined to create from the chaos something perfect. I was determined to carve out music itself.

No one knew of my plan, except of course Tanl. When I told him what I would do, he raised an eyebrow that simply said, yes, all right, why not. If he could dream of becoming Russia's greatest Jew poet, why could I not lend my meher to accompany him? A fiddler of our people. That is what he said. Why not?

Why not?

*

Some dreams are meant to be realized. But more often than not, more often, yes,

25

they are meant to be but dreams, and to disappear into the ether from which they came.

As is life. From the chaos there might be possibility, but in my world, in my shtetl, such possibility was rarely for the likes of me.

My Tateh had tried to tell me, before he gave up such lectures. Concentrate on the achievable, the stitch in cloth, the coat measured and simple. That should be enough, and is enough.

It should have been. For me it would have been. But by imagining something beyond the chaos, I was likely only to find failure, and disappointment. He warned me; I did not listen.

If I had wanted to become a fiddler of renown, I should have kept the cravings for the karchma at bay. And I did at first. But in time those cravings got the better of me. And the better of the better.

I returned. I spent my pocket change on the few drinks I could afford, staring silently but longingly at the shenk's daughter, serving me on occasion but never seeing me. Such is the inevitable way of life.

It started with the loss of a dream, when some of the cutters at the mill mistook my wondrous kley as whittled scrap, and put it on the burn pile. Or perhaps they did not mistake my fiddle as scrap, but only recognized disappointment in the imaginings, deciding such failure far more appropriate to go up in smoke, in the chaos of fire, rather than in the chaos of life. I stared at the ashes fallen to the ground for days on end, then turned away. I could have started to carve again, but knew I would never do so. Chaos cannot be controlled.

A travesty. A tragedy. But like all such tragedies in life it did not travel along the road of my days alone and in isolation.

Tavl had not noticed. He had not noticed my disappearances outside the boundaries of our shtetl. He had not noticed the small scattering of ash that littered his father's mill yard and that drew more than a single tear from my silent stare. He had long since given up on the music master's hopes at classical perfection, having withdrawn into poetry and word himself, so did not notice that I too had withdrawn with my rubles burning a hole in my trousers for only the shortest of moments before being turned over to the shenk's own version of imperfect dreams emerging out of one of his less than clean bottles.

But Tanl's mother noticed. She said nothing, but disappointment clouded her eyes. She however had other worries, other concerns. Tanl's father had grown increasingly ill and it became obvious that he could no longer carry on his business, or carry on himself.

I was not at Tanl's side, holding his hand or that of his siblings, when his father died. I was at the tavern, sitting in a quiet corner, desiring. The chaos of imperfect desires.

It was hardly a surprise when Tanl's mother then decided to sell the mill. Tanl's family was hardly poor, but the business was too much for his mother alone. Tanl also had his own dreams to pursue, his own plans. Unlike my own, his would not fall by the wayside, not then, not in the future foretold. Tanl was always right: I was not in his image. And sometimes a shadow such as I was clearly destined to disappear into the bright light and heat of the sun. So it was. With his mother's blessing, Tanl decided to go to Volozhin, to live with his grandfather and attend the Yeshiva. He had come to the conclusion that he would be a poet, a writer, a scholar. Not for him the local karchma, the tavern owner's daughter. Tanl had bigger fish to catch than those that landed on the banks of our overblown river in springtime, and he would catch them.

The day he left, as I watched him pack his small bag, he looked over at me for a long moment, then reached up to the shelf where the fiddle that neither of us had mastered rested beneath a layer of dust. He pulled it down and handed it to me. You take it, Tanl said. I want you to have it. I don't want you to stop.

I protested, honestly I did, but Tanl insisted. He had told his mother he wanted to give the fiddle to me, as a gift, as a hope for the future. She did not object. And I relented. I relented because some dreams I wanted to hold onto. I relented because no gift, no artefact so beautiful, would mean as much to me. True, it had little value, but to me it measured worth in hope. I still needed hope.

It was the one thing that Tanl wanted me to have, the one thing we might share despite the unbreachable gulf of three hours and a world of shadows.

Tanl shook my hand when he left. He promised a lifetime of a friendship that would never wane. He promised he would return.

27

It was a promise he kept. Once. He returned after a year's study in Volozhin brimming with new ideas and enthusiasm. He said he did not intend to return to the Yeshiva, that he had found no answers in Talmudic study. He spoke of a new world of enlightenment and something called Haskala that meant nothing to me. He had found a world of science and art and literature, a world where poetry mattered above all else. Religion was no longer of consequence. The future was not in wood mills, not in scripture, but in possibility, and he would be part of the possibility, in the revival of language and books and storytelling. And poems.

I listened to what my friend had to say, and realized then I would never travel that same road as he had traveled and would travel still. Despite the disapproval of mother and grandfather, he was headed to Odessa. He was headed to the future. He said he had dreams of poetry and music together, and together we must travel beyond the Pale. He promised when the time came I would join him. I would sing his songs, would play his words, would dream his dreams.

He promised, but I knew this promise, unlike his earlier ones, would not be kept.

We parted as friends. We parted as brothers. He gently hit my shoulder then turned and started down the road.

--I will send for you, he promised.

He promised. I hoped, quietly. Shadows too can hope.

He promised, but such was empty, and I knew it would likely not be thus.

I never saw Tanl again.

*

I returned to work at the tannery. I had little choice. The work in the mill had made me stronger, had made me grow. The work in the tannery diminished me, drawing me back not to boyhood, but to indifference at the world, to a loss of hope. Without the hope that I relied on Tanl to instill, I became little more than the hides I pulled: dried, empty, lifeless. The other tanners paid me little heed. The Jewish owner offered no favours. I did my work. At the end of the week he paid me my measly sum, duly passed on to Tateh. We both had to eat. But whereas Tateh found himself in the coats he measured, cut, sewed, doing so in silence but in the quiet love of cloth, I found even the shadow self that I had always been now beginning to disappear into nothing.

When I held enough rubles in my palm, I made my way back to the karchma, passing those kopeks to the fleshly palm of the Jewish shenk or his wife for the few drinks I could afford. I no longer glanced furtively but longingly at the shenk's daughter. I came to accept that a shadow would never find light in the shining star that she had been for me. Instead I sat in a corner, drank as long as the kopeks held, ignored by the travelers who appeared, disgusting some with the smell I always carried with me. The smell of the tannery. The smell, it must be said, of death.

Fortune, however, had not yet abandoned me forever. Not as yet. One evening at the karchma, after a particularly long day, I sat silently in my usual corner, noting the worry on the shenk's face as he paced up and down, and the harsh words he had with his wife. And I noted the quiet conversation that then ensued between both of them and their daughter. The tavern master listened intently. His wife shook her head, unhappy with the discussion. But the daughter spoke forcefully, nodding more than once towards my corner, towards the shadow cowering there.

Towards me.

I glanced up. I quickly glanced down, staring into the little that remained in my cup. I had rarely known fear, but now I felt fear. Had the stink of the tannery on me finally overwhelmed the karchma? Was my sorrowful countenance so off-putting that they would ask me to leave, telling me never to return? Did the shenk's daughter make up stories that my glances I had thought so unseen had offended, grown too lascivious, become far too improper for a one time cheder boy to make, and thus I should be thrust out on my ear, with a kick up my backside?

I started to stand, planning my imminent escape, planning to run, even as the shenk started in my direction. I was fast. The shenk, despite his age, was faster. I wanted to run. But he wanted me to sit. And ordered me to do so.

--My daughter knows you, he pronounced. She says she knows who you are, that her friends have told her about you. That your father is one of our most esteemed tailors in the shtetl. And she tells me you are a fiddler as well as a…as a tanner.

Words, as usual, failed me. I have never been one for words. I had always tried to leave that to Tanl, always feeling that the poetry of his heart and mine were joined as one. I said nothing.

--Here's the thing, the Shenk continued. We have a bit of a crowd coming in next week. They expect music. But our musicians are nowhere to be found. So I have a proposal. You fiddle for me. In exchange, you drink. Within reason, of course.

I stared at him. I stared at his wife, who had an expression of distaste, then turned away. And I glanced, only briefly, towards his daughter. She was watching me with curiosity, looked away, looked back. I swear she nodded at me. I swear.

I felt my heart miss a beat. I felt my loins shudder. I felt my need. I felt the slightest tremor of—hope.

--Within reason, yes?

I nodded. I agreed.

*

The free drink was an enticement. Yes. But the look on the shenk daughter's face was all I needed to give me courage. Courage in the face of adversity.

The dust had gathered on the face of the fiddle, that precious, so precious gift bequeathed by my Tanl. I so wished he could have been there to urge me forward. But Tanl had long disappeared into the bowels of Odessa, reciting his poetry and power to the enlightened Jews who would lead him forward with their voices raised to Haskala, whatever it might be. My voice, however, would only find itself the short distance from our shtetl, the voice of my own precious left hand first finger racing over my own precious kleh.

I could not tell my Tateh of the bargain struck. I could not admit to my own feelings of need and lust. Yes of unspoken lust. My Tateh would not understand. Neither would Tanl's mother, who had long given up on my need for a mothering hand in place of my own long gone mama's. So I wiped the dust from the fiddle, carried it to the woods at the edge of the town, called to the birds to crowd around and listen, and played.

I wish I could say I had aged well, improved with the mature years. I did tell myself this. I knew, however, it was a lie. Every evening I ran from the tanner's yard after completing my day's work and hurried into the hollow of the forest that I declared as my own, to practice, to remember, to seek harmony in nature and harmony with the racing movement of the kleh's bow. I convinced myself that I improved with each passing moment. I convinced myself that even the birds and forest animals listened with rapture and amazement.

Oh yes, I lied.

After the week was over, a week I should add in which not a single drop of alcohol from any alcohol trader's secret stash passed my lips, I made my way to the karchma filled with trepidation, with fear, with nerves jangling and tears just in the recesses of my eyes ready to fall when required, with a belly in knots and yes, yes, I admit it, with my loins still hot, knowing I would see her again, praying she would fall beneath the spell of composition and the notes of wonder.

A crowd had gathered in the karchma. Some drank. Some were drunk. I saw the shenk staring at me and urge me onward. I saw the shenk's wife mutter a prayer beneath a scowl. I saw the shenk's daughter, who again I swear nodded at me before turning away, feigning indifference. I had to say I was certain she feigned. Certain of it. And as for the customers in the tavern, few cared, or cared to listen, as I put the fiddle to my breast, my most precious left first finger poised above the string to race along from night to day and back again, the bow, that wondrous messenger, raised high, then lowered, then drawn, then…then the music. The song. My own poetry. My need. My art. My heart.

So. So. It could have been worse. It certainly could have been better. The music touched few, but offended none. Ears may be easily offended, but to that crowd, listening only to their own arguments, stories, negotiations, laughter, the ears were too otherwise engaged to be offended. At least not much. I played, and played, and played further. My left hand fingers all most precious now raced on the fiddle as if an extension of my life. As if it was her. Her. Thus my heart lifted, and I dared to hope. I dared to dream. And I survived the night, mostly because fiddle or no, music or no, shadows rarely offend.

When it was over, when it had passed, when the tears did not appear from the depths but remained haltered behind my eyes in silence and acceptance, when I sat with two drinks rather than a single before me, when the shenk's daughter had long since ceased to place her glance upon me but had retired to somewhere only my imagination might create in vision, I looked up to see the tavern owner standing before me, staring down.

He sighed. Shrugged. Stared at the customers, none of whom had tried to beat me, or more importantly him, for the aural intrusion, looked back at me, and said:

--You'll do. For now, you'll do. So drink and come again next week.

Bargains are so struck by necessity. I needed. Without competition to improve on my offerings, so did the shenk.

Once a week I made the journey to the tavern outside our shtetl. Once a week I pulled my most prized fiddle from the bag where I kept it. Once a week my right hand made its way plucking and bowing the songs that had been popular amongst the Jews of the shtetl, and beyond. Perhaps not well, but with my most beloved left hand first finger leading my three other most beloved fingers my hand spoke the words of music that I could not speak from my mouth. Perhaps not well. Perhaps with the same sorts of confusion that led to the chaos of my Talmudic studies. Nevertheless I played with all my soul and dreams and the occasional quiet glance in the direction of she who meant the flutters in my shadowed heart.

Once a week. And while my Tateh was not supportive, having soon learned of my wanderings and attempts at performance, when the shenk relented to adding a few rubles on a good night into my pocket even as his drink added to the pain in my forehead, if not my courage, my Tateh simply sighed, shook his head just slightly, and returned his glance and his favour to his beloved cloth and threads.

It so happened that on one such night, a night that was to prove so important and unforgettable in my life, I thought I played particularly well, indeed supported by the occasional plaudits and shouts of approval amongst the larger than normal congregation. An occasional clap on the shoulder was gratefully received. Even more so were the few glasses of the shenk's almost finest set before me as I sat back down in my corner, my cheeks red from exhaustion, drink and that feeling of hope that once again encouraged my loins. I looked around for her, the true object of my desire, but she was nowhere to be seen. So I sat back simply to savour the moment.

As I sat the shenk came over to compliment me, in his hand a bottle in which remained not a few drinks to be imbibed by those who could. All that remained within were for me. And although he had often said that he would allow me drink in exchange for music, this demonstrated generosity that I had never before experienced.

--Don't worry, he told me, it's not my gift, I assure you. You played well tonight, young man, but not that well. However, the three soldiers here—did you see them?—appreciated the effort and sent this over on their behalf.

I looked around and saw two such sitting at a table on the other side of the karchma. One glanced up, saw me and nodded, not perhaps with a smile on his face, but neither with an expression that suggested I should high-tail it back to the shtetl.

--Soldiers from the 102nd Viatka Infantry Regiment. Sometimes they protect us Jews. Sometimes they don't. But here in my karchma, they are guests. Tone deaf guests, but guests.

My heart said share it with she who might now drink with me. My thirst said simply, drink. And as she had disappeared, I drank. And drank some more. Just as shadows are not seen, so too are players of klez, however poignant, amusing or memorable their meher. I had played. I had returned to shadow. I raised a glass to my new found infantry companions who never looked my way again. And I drank.

Until I had had enough. And knew I had had enough. My head started to pound. My legs felt uncertain. And my loins spoke only of the need to pass water. My loins thus carried the day. I picked up my beloved fiddle, hidden once again by its bag, and left the karchma.

My legs did not want to move. My insides did. But my head moved most of all, as I walked outside into the warm night air. Although not a long walk back to the shtetl, it was not a walk I felt was within me, at least not at that moment. A short rest. Eyes closed. Just a short time. Piss, then sleep. Nothing more but a short sleep.

Luckily beside the tavern was a small barn where the shenk and his wife kept a cow and a plow horse, and allowed the occasional visitor or wandering musician to sleep amidst hay and rats, rats and hay. So, a bit of rest, nothing more. Just a short, small rest.

I walked into the barn. Through the darkness, through the moonlight that cut through the entrance, I saw in the back the faintest light, the faintest glow, soft sheen, evening warmth. I stumbled to the rear of the space to see, firstly, on one side the light of a single candle in glass. And on the other side of the open space, stripped of shirt, wearing only a soldier's breeches, one of the gallant soldiers of the 102nd Viatka Infantry Regiment, astride not his horse, not his saddle, but rather the prone and slightly immodestly dressed figure of the Shenk's daughter who I took to be struggling, moaning in fear, pushing at him to move away. Or so it seemed. So it seemed to me.

I stopped in my very step.

My breathing ceased.

My head burst with pain and too much drink.

My stomach heaved. And heaved again. And although my heart said no, my insides said yes, and yes again, and I vomited uncontrollably in all directions. Including in the direction of the soldier from the 102nd Viatka Infantry Regiment, who had not seen me.

But she had. She who I adored in silence, who I lusted after, who I wanted only as mine, she had heard me. Had seen me. And had screamed, none too soon.

And this is what I saw: first, the soldier from the 102nd Viatka Infantry Regiment raised his hand and slapped the love of my life and loins, thinking her protests, rightly I have no doubt, she directed at his informality.

Secondly, he felt the cold evil slop of my inner despair spew onto his bare back and neck.

Thirdly, he shouted out, standing. And he charged. And I stood, dumbfounded. Afraid. And determined to protect the honor of she who I adored by standing firm.

Thus the soldier raised himself tall, marched towards me, and as he did I in turn raised myself not nearly as tall, bent my good arm back, jerked, and drew the bag with the kleh so dear in an arc above my head onto the head of the marching soldier from the 102nd Viatka Infantry Regiment.

I may have heard the slight crack of wood on skull. Or perhaps I heard only his roar, then laughter, as he grabbed me and threw me against the side of the barn. He looked at me, shook his head. But I refused to relent. Instead I stood quickly and reached within my tunic, grabbing the small knife I kept there to strip the gut string I kept for emergency should my fiddle relent. I held the said knife up. He looked at me, grinned wildly, ran over and grabbed my shaking arm, my shaking hand, pulled the knife from me.

--Leave her, I demanded, even then feeling the pain of his grasp on my hand. Leave her alone!

--Leave her? Is that what you say, boy? Musician? Music be damned. Music for mutes, but I boy, I am no mute. And I hate the sound you make.

34

He pushed me to the ground. Kicked me once. Twice. She who I loved screamed out; I remember that. Screamed to no avail.

--You shall hurt no man's gentle ears ever again. Boy.

And laughing he took the knife. And he cut. First my most beloved first finger on my left hand, most beloved. Cut to the bone. Cut off. Then the second finger so it would serve as no replacement for the first. Then he put the knife to my tongue, even then screaming in pain in fear.

Two things I remember. Another voice, male this time, another soldier yelling for my assailant to stop.

And the sight of my finger most precious lying in a pool of blood in the dirt beside my eyes.

Which closed, as I lost all consciousness of the night. And my most beloved.

*

When I awoke I saw hay. Daylight and hay. A throbbing in my hand served as a reminder. I raised my arm and saw rags covered in blood swaddling in a great lump over the stump that had held the first finger on my left hand, most precious, most precious no longer. I thought perhaps I had died. I hoped perhaps I might die. I lowered my arm to my side. I waited for death, my shadow of a shadow.

--I know what you are thinking. But no, you are not going to die.

I looked over. She who had been the desire of my heart stood at the open door of the barn, the sun seemingly emanating from her perfect form. She walked towards me and I saw, in her expression, not love, not care, not pity, but only—nothing.

--You have slept now for a day and another night. My father did not have the heart to lay you onto a cart and send you on your way.

--My work. The tannery.

She shook her head. I looked away. With what strength remained within, I managed to sit up, my back supported by a standing post behind.

I stared at my hand.

--First finger gone. Second, half gone. Won't be playing more music, least not easily. Way you played, not sure such a loss. Or maybe you can change sides, once that hand heals. Use it to move your bow. Maybe. Maybe not. Not something I'd know.

--The soldier?

--Long gone. No thanks to you. He would have been my escape from this place. Promised to take me with him. Promised to love me. Not now. Thank you very much tanner boy.

--But…but he wasn't like us. He wasn't…

--A Jew? No. He wasn't. Exactly so.

Her expression, or empty expression, did not change. She turned to leave the barn. Hesitated, looked back.

--You'll be on your way. I saved your fingers if you want them.

I didn't.

*

I returned to the shtetl. Returned home. Tateh came in from his workshop. He'd heard. He stared for a moment at my bandaged appendage. Looked at me. Sighed.

--Not sure you'll be able to have work at the tannery any longer. Not sure if any apprenticeships left for you. I'll need more clients for my coats.

All he said. I went into my alcove. I pulled back the curtain. I removed the fiddle from the bag that had carried it home. Looked at the crack running along its back. Lightning strike, not of the creative sort; the destructive sort. I turned it over. One string snapped. The other I plucked with my undamaged hand. Music reduced to one single note. Note of despair. I threw the kleh into the corner. It would sing to others, would sing to me, no longer.

I lay down. Closed my eyes. Slept again.

I woke to see Tanl staring down at me.

--I thought you were in Odessa.

--So I am.

--But I am not.

--Are you certain? Think instead you are with me, as I with you.

I understood. He was not there. I was not here.

--My poetry needed your song.

--I can play no longer.

--No.

--Are you enlightened? You said you sought the enlightenment. So have you found it?

--I do not have an answer for you. The enlightenment is in the future. Now we have to seek it.

--I as well? I see only darkness.

--Then the future is dark for you.

--Do you think it is?

--Dark, light, who can say, really. Whatever it is I will be with you. That's a promise.

--But you promised you would take me with you.

--And so I did.

--But I am not with you.

--Of course you are. As you were. Behind all light is a shadow.

--So I am shadow.

--You always were. Shadow. But shadow is but the echo of one's soul, wouldn't you say? An echo of who we are. And were.

--I did not ask to be born.

--No. Nor did I. But the decisions are not ours to make.

--My sister or brother, he or she made such a choice.

--Maybe. Or maybe he or she simply began a different journey. Now then. Time to go. You and me. Our time. See what there is.

--Enlightenment.

--Yes. The journey. Hope. We will.

--You were always wiser, Tanl.

--No. You thought I was such. I was not. You and I, always the same. Simply, we are. A story we tell. The beginning of a story. To tell.

I nodded at him. I felt him reach out, put his hand on my shoulder. Nod, smile. Took my damaged hand in his, looked at me, at my hand not entirely whole, as indeed my life would not be entirely whole.

--We are still poetry. We are still the poem.

With that he was gone. With that, I slept still.

*

Several days later, with my few belongings I put in a sack to carry on my back, I started my journey from the shtetl where I had been born. I knew I would not return. I did not turn in the direction of Odessa. I would not find enlightenment there. I did not know where I would find it, but I knew I would look. So it had to be. There might be music, or not. Poetry or not. But there would be life, whatever that meant in the world.

As I started down the street I heard a voice call my name.

My Tateh.

I turned as he hobbled quickly in my direction. He stopped, stared at me for a long moment, and handed to me the bag holding the violin once gifted to me by Tanl who I loved, the fiddle, the kleh.

--You should take it, my Tateh said.

--I cannot play.

--You'll play. In your head and heart at least. You always need memory. This is memory.

I reached up. Took the bag holding memory within. Nodded. And walked on, with my Tateh standing in the road, watching me, he growing smaller. I continued on my way. Tateh faded from view. In time perhaps from memory.

I kept walking.

2. Lera

Babiński Clinical Psychiatric Hospital
Kobierzyn, Krakow
September 1941- June, 1942

Lera organizes the Head of the Hospital Office's shoes in his closet in exactly the same order every Monday, Wednesday and Saturday. The Head of the Hospital Office calls her Lera instead of Waleria; she does not object to this. Others are not so familiar with her. Her mother called her Lera when she was a little girl. It made her feel safe. The Head of the Hospital Office however is not her mother and does not always make her feel safe she thinks, although she does not say this. But still she does not mind when he calls her Lera. Just as her mother did. When was that? Long ago.

She likes organizing the Head of Hospital Office's many pairs of shoes and his suits in exactly the same order those same three days when she cleans in the closets of his private quarters. This is one of her many tasks when she does not spend time with the doctors herself or tends to the other chores that the nun sisters and the nurse sisters request of her. Organizing his shoes, light to dark, perfectly placed, always in exactly the same order beneath the few dark coloured suits. Lera knows this is a great responsibility. No one else could do this work as well as she does. The Head of the Hospital Office has told her this and she blushes when he does. Perhaps that is why he calls her Lera.

It is early in the month of June in 1942. Waleria Białońska knows this because she recognizes the date on the calendar sitting on the Head of the Hospital's desk. One of her tasks is to dust this desk. That is how she knows it is also a Wednesday, according to the calendar. And the shoes are in order.

There is a war on somewhere. She is certain about this fact because she sees men in grey, brown and black uniforms come and go. Sometimes they do not come in uniforms but mostly they do. They are not the same uniforms as the doctors wear, with their white coats and polished shoes. Like the shoes she polishes for the Head of the Hospital Office. Or those that Director Kroll wears, his being the most polished of all. And the uniforms, too, not like the nun sisters wear, which Lera knows of course is absurd because they are nuns these nurses, not soldiers, not doctors. The soldiers who come, those who wear unforms and some who don't, Waleria does not like these men although they largely ignore her. When they come and go. As they often do, these days.

She does not like them because when they first started to appear many months ago, after a short time they took away with them a number of the patients. They took away Mr. Sliozberg. She misses Mr. Sliozberg.

His is a different story but she thinks about him often. She thinks about his story. About the story he told her.

Mr. Sliozberg was an old man. He walked with a stick. It went tap tap tap, unless he walked on the grass. Then it went quietly, as if the stick had nothing to say to the grass. Mr. Sliozberg has disappeared now. She is sad about this because he was her friend.

And she thinks about him. And his story.

And she misses him.

And she wonders if they will bring him back to the Institute hospital, to his bed off to the side in Ward IVa, so they can chat like they used to. Mr. Sliozberg. Who disappeared one day. With the others. When they took them.

Since today is Wednesday, as the calendar tells her, she will not be sitting for her talking treatment with the old doctor and the young doctor later this particular morning. She does not have her talking treatment on Wednesdays. The old doctor, Doctor Schimansky, she does not really like. She had started her treatments only with him at first. But he became a bit too personal, or so said Sister Bronisława Bąk, the duty nurse on Women's Ward VIb when she found Waleria weeping in a corner in Waleria's own Ward Vb. When Waleria said that Doctor Schimansky had touched her in her private place and that she had not liked it much, Sister Bąk listened, nodded and said she would have a word with the young doctor, Doctor Cechnicki, studying at the Institute that had become Waleria's home.

It had been Mr. Sliozberg's home, too. And many of the others. But they were taken to another home many months ago. Another hospital, somewhere near the city of Warsaw, so said Sister Bąk. Waleria has never been to Warsaw. She wishes it was near to this hospital institute. Waleria hopes Mr. Sliozberg and the others might return.

The young doctor has always been kind to Waleria whenever he passes. She likes him. He is not like the old doctor, with his rough skin and offending smell. Following the incident that she whispered about quietly to Sister Bąk, Doctor Cechnicki now sits in on the talking treatments so that he can learn from the experience of the old doctor. Waleria suspects he joins in these talking sessions more as her friend than simply as another doctor, but at least old Doctor Schimansky no longer bothers her, or puts his hand on her secret place.

Because Waleria Białońska has no talking session with any doctor this fine summer's Wednesday morning, she quietly gets on with the tasks she is charged with doing: not only helping to clean the Head of the Hospital Office's private rooms, but once finished she walks outside and down the hospital lane, amongst the trees and carefully manicured lawns to the laundry building, where she folds the cleaned bedding that has been drying slowly in the drying rooms once the uniformed assistants have completed their washing. They are pleased to have Waleria help them because they know that Waleria folds the bedding in exactly the right manner, with each crease carefully cutting across the bedding in exactly the same place, one piece of bedding following the next, and exactly as might be suitable for an institute such as the Babinski Institute Hospital where she resides.

The assistants know that Waleria will do this task better than any other resident of the hospital because Waleria's sharp creases, like her polished Head of Hospital Office's shoes, demonstrate order that she worries might be lost in the chaos of the world. She has seen the chaos of the world and knows it threatens the peace of mind that she desires and of which she dreams. The doctors have explained as much in her talking sessions.

Once the final sheet has been folded just so, Waleria bids goodbye to the assistants and leaves the laundry building, passing the various buildings that include the trades building and the rooms where the women patients sew with the machines that make a clinking rat tat tat rat tat tat that reminds Waleria of the rhymes she sang as a little girl, rat tat tat, and finally through a manicured lawn and carefully cut hedge to the kitchens. Here Sister Jadwiga Trawniczek allows her to stir the large vats of food used to cook for the patients and staff. This had been hard work for Waleria, but it is not so hard any longer, as Director Kroll has decided that the patients like Waleria herself have long had too much food at their dinners and so has cut the rations given for each meal and for each patient. We do not want fat patients Director Kroll had stated, and, as this is a time of war we must keep the rations to a minimum for all but the staff who must do most of the work and most of the thinking.

Waleria has not always understood why Director Kroll decided that the patients are overweight and over fed, but he must have good reason, which is why he is the Director of the Hospital. Waleria also does not understand why, if the patients are overweight, their stomachs continue painfully growing ever so much larger when they are getting such little food. She has heard the cries and seen the tears of hunger, but Director Kroll must surely know what is best for those who reside here at the hospital. Surely he does.

She wonders if Mr. Sliozberg has more food at his new hospital than the patients get here at the Babinski Institute Hospital. She hopes he does, although Mr. Sliozberg was never one to say he was hungry, even in the weeks before he disappeared with some of the other patients.

Waleria knows she could possibly ask the kitchen help for a little extra of the turnip soup that she now stirs, but she won't do so. All must share as share must be. Of course she would not mind an extra small sip of the watery soup they all eat, since she is stirring it now in one of the large kitchen vats, one of the few vats still used because three or four are no longer needed. And she does think that it would today taste so much nicer than the marjoram soup or the nettle soup that they have to eat on Monday and Thursdays respectively. But Waleria is not one to ask for herself only. She would not do so.

She is very hungry, but she would not do so. And because there is so little soup that needs stirring on this Wednesday morning in June—Waleria remembers that it is Wednesday and it is June—she is able to leave her final morning's task early. As there is no talking treatment this particular morning, and as the early summer sun shines gloriously, Waleria walks out of the kitchen building and decides to find her favourite stone bench on the side of what they call the theatre building, to sit and enjoy the smells from the flowers and the grass so carefully manicured. This has always been her favourite place at the hospital, a place she keeps secret so largely for herself.

And for Mr. Sliozberg, too, before he disappeared.

So Waleria goes to her favourite stone bench now and sits, quietly, sometimes humming a remembered song for her own enjoyment, sometimes just sitting there, thinking simple thoughts, remembering.

While she sits there on this particular Wednesday, her memories float back to certain places, certain moments, certain faces. These are the secrets she prefers to keep close within her own thoughts. She remembers being a young girl. She remembers the boy she loved once. She remembers…

But those memories are interrupted by a voice beside her.

--Waleria? Are you unwell, Waleria? Lera?

She opens her eyes and sees Nurse Stanisława Pałys, the duty nurse from her own ward of Vb, standing beside her, watching. Waleria shakes her head, smiles. Nurse Stanisława watches her, then sits down beside.

Waleria likes Nurse Sister Stanisława and Nurse Sister Stanisława likes her.

--Were you dreaming?

--Maybe.

--It is all we have these days. Dreams. So little else.

Waleria does not understand what Nurse Stanisława means.

--You have no chores this morning, Waleria?

--Finished. I was in the kitchen, stirring. Sister Jadwiga tells me I do a good job there.

--Yes. Are you hungry after?

Waleria shrugs.

--What they are doing…The Director, I…I hope you had a small bit of soup, for yourself. You deserve it, Waleria.

--Oh I would not do that.

--No. I know you of all would not.

--The flowers smell nice.

--Yes. The flowers smell nice. If only you could eat the flowers.

--No.

--No…You'll come for soup soon? For your dinner with the others?

Waleria nods. Nurse Sister Stanisława stands. Waleria likes Nurse Sister Stanisława. Nurse Sister Stanisława likes Waleria and sometimes calls her Lera.

--I'll let you dream, so, Waleria. I hope you see the faces of those who are kind to you when your eyes are closed. I hope they sit beside you and hold your hand.

Waleria thinks about these words, sitting on her favorite stone bench on the side of the Theatre building. She remembers the first time she met Mr. Sliozberg, sitting here, right where she sits now.

She remembers.

She had been listening to the small men's orchestra practicing their songs in the garden there, just beyond. They had held their brass instruments with great pride, practicing one or two songs they would play in the concerts for patients in the building called the theatre. Waleria knew enough to hear the odd note out of tune, a bit of a crow's caw instead of a robin's sweet chirp, at least to her ears. But she nevertheless liked hearing them practice. It made her feel normal. It made her feel alive in the world.

She did not always feel that way.

After the men had put away their brass instruments and retired to their wards, Waleria had continued sitting on her favorite stone bench, still hearing the delightful music although the music had stopped, carrying the song in her head like she carried so much there, so much crammed within, when this old man with a stick quietly appeared and asked if he might sit for a moment on the bench with her.

Shy as she was, Waleria simply nodded, and the man sat down, sniffing at the air, watching the leaves wave ever so slightly in the breeze.

--Did you hear the music?, he asked, but didn't wait for a response. Music, our love for life I say. Do you play?

Waleria shook her head no.

--As alas I do not. Not now. Once, a long long time ago. But I hear it. Always hear it. That is enough.

He smiled. Refolded his folded hands. When he did Waleria noticed the deformity on one hand, despite it largely hidden by his other. She did not ask about this. It would not have been proper to do so, especially as she did know him, at least not yet.

The old man sighed. Stood.

--Ah well.

He looked at her, smiled again.

--Sliozberg. My name. Yitzchok Sliozberg. Or Izio, like the good sisters say. Izio remember to say your prayers. Izio remember to wash. Izio remember where you are. Izio remember us. Izio remember…Some things I remember, some I do not. Old men forget. Or choose to forget. And you, if I may ask?

She is not sure if she should answer. She considers whether to do so was proper. She considered whether it would add to chaos or add to order. She blushed, then came to a quick decision, unlike the her she knew, but under the circumstances and given this man's advanced years, even older than old Dr. Schimansky who she does not like much, she decides he seems kind to her, so answered.

--Waleria.

--Waleria. A pleasure. I will see you again no doubt…Oh, and whoever you are thinking of, I would suggest he is a lucky young man.

The man called Mr. Sliozberg winked, chuckled, hobbled away.

How did he know, Waleria wondered? Does he read minds, she wondered? Because she had been thinking of…of someone. She had been...

Aleksi.

Aleksi with the blue eyes that sparkled when the light was just so. With the tussle of blond hair and a warmth that made her laugh. They had played street games when they were children. They had grown older and he had smiled at her. Secretly held her hand. He had laughed with her. She remembers. He had laughed with her. With Waleria. Her. Before the hospital. Before the visions. When it was easier for her to laugh. When she had held his hand in secret. As children. But now she was much older. Or was she? And Aleksi had disappeared from her life. Like Mr. Sliozberg. Not there. Not. The words in her dreams talking loudly, ordering her about. Talking to her. Before the—the bad days. Where would he be now?

Aleksi.

Waleria closes her eyes. When they open she can no longer see Mr. Sliozberg and she knows that the voices have been speaking to her, that only his voice has been speaking to her, because she knows that Mr. Sliozberg disappeared from the Institute Hospital many months ago. Disappeared with others. To go to another hospital the sisters said. To be happy they said. She hopes he is happy.

She hopes Aleksi is happy. The sisters do not say where he has gone. They do not know that once so long ago he held her hand. They do not know.

She dreams of him, even still. She remembers him as she remembers Mr. Sliozberg.

She misses them both and hears them speaking to her and hears their laughter and feels their gaze upon her and feels—lost.

Waleria Białońska stands up, leans for a moment against the stone bench at the side of the building they call the theatre, and starts back to Ward Vb, to the corner of the ward she now calls home.

*

That night she says her prayers like she always does. She asks that Mr. Sliozberg, who was her friend, who disappeared, be looked after, and that Aleksi, who laughed with her and who she wants to marry someday if she can find him again, be looked after.

Before she closes her eyes she sees in the sisters office at the far end of Ward Vb, where the nurse sisters sometimes chat to one another when the patients cannot overhear, Sister Bąk speaking now quietly with Sister Stanisława, who even in the near darkness Waleria can see is weeping. Waleria sees the tears falling silently down Sister Stanisława's cheek. She sees Sister Stanisława shaking her head, back and forth, again back and forth, and sees Sister Stanisława put her hand to her mouth, as if something has suddenly surprised her.

Sister Bąk turns now and disappears from the room, disappears into the darkness.

Mr. Sliozberg disappeared from the hospital.

Sister Stanisława, her eyes glistening even in the dim light, as if they hurt, turns and stares into the ward. She stares at Waleria. Waleria closes her eyes and falls into

46

a dream.

Waleria does not remember her dream.

*

--Waleria? Waleria, wake up. Waleria?

It is Thursday morning now and she feels tired, so very tired, that she does not want to wake. But Nurse Sister Stanisława wants her to wake and so she does.

--Dress quickly, Waleria. We are going into Kobierzyn this morning. I will get you some bread there.

--I need to stir the dinner in the kitchen for Sister Jadwiga.

--Not today. Today you will take some air with me.

Most chaotic, Waleria thinks. She rarely goes into town any longer. The doctors prefer that patients remain at the hospital. Although she does not understand she likes Sister Stanisława so does as she is told.

As they walk out of the wards building they pass young Doctor Cechnicki on the walkway.

--Out for a stroll today?

--Waleria and I are going into Kobierzyn for some needed cloth and thread. Waleria can help me.

--Director Kroll will not approve.

--Director Kroll does not have to approve everything. He is a busy man. I will return with Waleria later in the morning.

--Of course, sister. I agree.

--I do not have a talking session today, young Doctor Checnicki.

--No Waleria, you do not…Sister, if any of our military friends say anything, tell them you are going at my request.

--Yes, Doctor. Thank you.

Nurse Sister Stanisława and Waleria walk down the pathways, passing patients who are working in the gardens, past the beds of orange flowers at either side of the wide metal gate that blocks the road and away from the Institute Babinksi Hospital grounds. They walk past a number of people on the road. When anyone looks at Sister Stanisława she nods, but says nothing. Waleria watches her and decides to nod as well. Some soldiers in grey uniforms pass them. Sister Stanisława does not nod but Waleria decides to nod anyway. One of the soldiers laughs quietly but says nothing.

They come to the road that leads into Kobierzyn but Nurse Sister Stanisława oddly turns left instead of right. Waleria does not understand this.

--I have changed my mind, Waleria. We could use some air. We will walk for a while.

--But young Doctor Checnicki thinks…

--Never you mind Doctor Checnicki. He has told me air is good for you as it for me. And walking. You must pay close attention to our route so we do not get lost. Can you do that?

--Yes, Sister Stanisława.

Waleria does not understand chaos but she likes Sister Stanisława and wants to please her.

They walk for what seems to Waleria a long time, although Sister Stanisława promises they will not be long. They walk past numerous houses that Waleria does not know, until the houses cease and Waleria sees only fields and occasional farms in the distance. On two occasions large motor vehicles carrying soldiers in grey uniforms pass, but they do not stop. Sister Stanisława does not nod but Waleria nods because she thinks she should. They walk often without speaking. Waleria enjoys the warm summer sunshine. They stay on the first road, then turn right where there is then a small road. Waleria takes careful note of the fence posts at this road as Sister Stanisława had told her she must. A little while later, at another crossroad, they take the left turn this time.

--Can you remember this way, even if it might be in the dark, Waleria?

Waleria nods. She can see well in the dark. She is used to darkness because she often closes her eyes. She points to a strangely shaped ash tree that reminds her of a giant bending back and laughing.

--Tree. Like a giant. It is in my head now.

Nurse Stanisława nods at her like she sometimes nods at people she sees, and smiles. Mr. Sliozberg used to smile at her when he met her in the garden. Aleksi too. The smile makes Waleria feel warm.

After some time walking Nurse Stanisława points to a farmhouse and asks if

Waleria can remember it. Waleria says she can. They stand staring at the farmhouse for a short time when a farmer comes out of it and walks towards them. When he gets near he removes the cap he is wearing and nods. Waleria notes when he removes his cap that he does not have much hair on his head and his head is red from the sun. Waleria nods back as she had seen Nurse Stanisława do.

--Waleria, this is Farmer Purchla.

--Hello, Waleria.

--Farmer Purchla is my friend, Waleria. You can trust him. He can help you if you ever need it. Do you understand?

Waleria understands.

Nurse Stanisława nods at Farmer Purchla. Waleria does as well because she has seen Nurse Stanisława do so. Farmer Purchla smiles slightly. They talk about the nice weather and the moonlit warm nights. They talk about bees for a few minutes. Waleria does not understand bees. They seem chaotic but Waleria likes the buzzing sounds they make and likes how they gently greet the flowers in the mornings when she sits on the stone bench watching them. Finally then it is time to return to the Institute Babinski Hospital. Nurse Stanisława says Director Kroll would probably be unhappy if they stayed away too long and best not even to tell him of their walk. In fact she says best to say nothing because other patients would want to walk as well and there is too little time.

--Little time, says Sister Stanisława. So little...

Sister Stanisława almost seems to forget the word she wants to say. The chaos. She looks at Waleria and her eyes are not happy. She tries to smile, but Waleria knows the smile does not laugh. As if the laughter has disappeared like Mr. Sliozberg. Like her friend Aleksi who she thinks of. Then Sister Stanisława starts to walk with Waleria, starts to walk back to the Institute Babinski Hospital. Farmer Purchla watches them disappear. After a while Waleria turns around but cannot see Farmer Purchla. He has disappeared but she thinks it is not a disappearing like Mr. Sliozberg and not like Aleksi so she is not sad. Waleria closes her eyes for a small moment and Waleria remembers the route she takes.

*

It is yesterday. Or maybe it is many yesterdays; Waleria cannot remember them all. She likes lying in her bed not moving, nighttime, tired even now from her long walk with Sister Stanisława. She has closed her eyes to see in the dark but instead she sees the yesterdays and sunshine.

So now she sees herself, sitting on the stone bench beside the building they call the theatre. And it is autumn. There are no patients working in the gardens today. The flowers have mostly disappeared. She looks at the ground and sees spotted colours scattered. Waleria knows these are leaves that have fallen from the trees in the early autumn breeze. She likes the colours of the leaves: red, yellow, some brown, some still green. There were not so many trees on her dirt road in her town when she was very young. She likes that now she can see the many colours of the leaves floating down from the trees particularly when these leaves lie on the ground after the wind blows, scattered hither and thither. Some people say it makes them sad but this is not so for Waleria.

Mr. Sliozberg comes around the corner of the building and waves his stick towards her. As he approaches Waleria hears the familiar click click click it makes. He sits then on the stone bench beside her, puts the stick leaning ever so carefully against the seat and smiles. He takes a deep breath. He says he likes this time of year. Waleria likes it as well.

They are friends now, Mr. Sliozberg and Waleria. He had said she could call him Izio but Waleria does not do so. She does not find this the proper way to address him because Mr. Sliozberg is an old man and she thinks he is a Mr. Sliozberg not an Izio. However she told him once that her mother called her Lera. She did not tell him that the Head of the Hospital Office will call her Lera because then she has not yet been asked to help the Head of the Hospital Office clean his private rooms. But she does tell Mr. Sliozberg that her mother called her this.

She does not say also that Aleksi whom she dreams of still also called her Lera.

--Would you like me to call you Lera, like your mother did?

She considers this, then nods.

--Well then, Lera it will be. A very nice name.

She likes Mr. Sliozberg now. Yes, they are friends. She had decided after many times sharing the stone bench with him, or taking a short walk amongst the flowers, that they should be such. That she did not need to be afraid of him.

--So Lera, another lovely day for we the mad people of the Babinski Institute, eh?

--Yes, the colours here are nice.

--Truly. Life moving forward.

--What does Mr. Sliozberg mean, the mad people?

--That is a very good question, my dear Lera. A good question. With all these German soldiers around, I think the world has gone mad. Or sad perhaps. In town the people, like the soldiers out there, they say we are mad. But then I look at this world. I look at you and I think how could anyone so sweet, so gentle, be mad, when you are not. And some of us are just old. Or hungry. Or alone.

--I see.

--Do you? I hope not.

They sit quietly for a long while. They look at the colours. When she was young, and Aleksi had secretly held her hand, they sometimes went for just such a quiet walk along the small river in town, walking into the countryside for a short time. He said little, Aleksi. He mostly smiled, shrugged.

--Maybe we are mad, Lera, Aleksi once said. Maybe we should be sensible.

Then he shrugged, laughed gently at her, kneeled beside the river to fill his cupped hands with water and threw this at her.

--It is much more fun to be mad.

She had laughed too, and screamed, just a little bit, to make him laugh. Because they were friends and she decided best to be mad together.

Waleria remembers. Maybe we are mad.

--It is much more fun to be mad, Mr. Sliozberg. My friend said that.

--Your friend?

--Aleksi.

Waleria had not meant to say his name. She blushes just slightly.

--Your young man? And where is your young man?

--He disappeared.

--Ah.

Mr. Sliozberg looks at her, then away.

--I have had friends who disappeared. And girls I loved, Lera. But I am old and have learned they do not disappear. Not really. They remain here.

He hits his fist against his chest, not hard.

Waleria is not sure she understands, but as Mr. Sliozberg is old she does not disagree. She looks at his hand, no longer in a fist as it opens and falls back into his lap. She looks at where the missing fingers once were but are no longer. She wonders if they too disappeared. Mr. Sliozberg sees her looking at his hand. He smiles, just slightly. Looks away.

--Like the music, Lera. It never goes away. It never really went away. Even if they take us away, they cannot take that.

--Who would take you away, Mr. Sliozberg?

He looks at her but says nothing.

--I wouldn't like that. Why would someone take you away?

--Oh, these days. These dark days.

Waleria looks around. The sun is out on the bright autumn day. Yes there are leaves scattered in colours she likes, but the sun shines on the leaves, on them. It is only dark at night. Waleria is trying to understand.

--Why would they take you away, Mr. Sliozberg?

--Because we are…

He does not finish his sentence.

--There are things, Lera, that I do not understand either. I am a simple man. I lived a simple life. For some, even some here, age, simplicity and poverty are a form of madness. I do not think so. I would like to show you my secret. My treasure. Can I do that?

Waleria nods.

--Come my young friend.

Mr. Sliozberg stands and starts to walk slowly towards their wards building. Tap tap tap. Tap tap tap. Waleria walks beside him.

There are very few patients in the building at this time. Most are out doing their tasks. Waleria did hers early in the morning and so is allowed to sit quietly on her stone bench. Or walk to the wards with Mr. Sliozberg.

He leads her into his ward room, Ward IVa, to his own corner in the back at the side. He has no other beds near his own. At the foot of his bed, pushed mostly underneath, there is an almost blue large rectangular case shoved below, dirty, worn.

--My case. They let me keep it. Respect for the old ones whose small world rests within a coloured box. Mr. Sliozberg struggles to pull it from under the bed. Waleria watches him, then leans down to help him.

--Thank you, Lera. It was not always so difficult.

Once the case is free of the underside of the bed, Mr. Sliozberg stares it, then opens the lid for Waleria to see.

--All my possessions. All that is left of a life. Not much, eh Lera? But treasures abound.

He looks at her, smiles. He begins to pull out the contents, putting them carefully on his bed. An old pair of trousers. Two shirts. Some undergarments. A pair of shoes with holes in the soles, so Waleria notices. Some old worn papers half torn. Some stones. A child's drawing. A life. But Mr. Sliozberg stares at each garment, each piece of paper, each stone, as if each had untold value.

When the few items that had been in the blue box case sit on the bed, the case is empty.

--A life, Lera. You see, it is empty. This defines who I was. Yitzchok Sliozberg. Not much I suppose. Life is sometimes like that. Fleeting. Just a few—things.

She looks at the empty blue case and nods.

--But another treasure remains. My most valuable treasure. A secret. Will I show you? I would like to do that.

She looks at him, confused, and nods. The items from his case, in a carefully ordered pile, seem complete, the order of their laying out not subject to chaos. Even the worn, torn papers do not seem chaotic to her. What could break that order, she wonders?

Mr. Sliozberg smiles, laughs quietly to himself. He reaches into the case and pull at the smallest thread on one side of the floor of the case, then the other where there is yet more thread hardly seen against the case wall. First one side, then the other. And again. After a couple of efforts, Mr. Sliozberg is able to pull up the floor of the case to reveal a thin compartment below that Waleria had not realized was there. Mr. Sliozberg rests the thin layer that had been the bottom of the case, covered with faded paper but made of thin wood, standing against the side of his case. From within, previously hidden, he pulls out a small sack and from this he withdraws a small musical instrument.

--My most precious treasure. Do you know what it is, Lera? An old violin. Here.

He hands here the dark brown musical instrument. She has never held such before. She is not quite certain what it is despite his telling. It has one string from head to toe held tight by a small broken round tightener. And another string hangs loosely from it. Waleria shakes it just slightly. The wooden instrument is silent. Waleria turns it over and sees that a crack in the wood on the back, and a quarter piece of wood missing.

--It is pretty, Mr. Sliozberg.

--No, Lera. That it is not. Rather it is tired, like I am. Old, like I am. Of value to no one. But to me, worth all the money in the world.

--What is it called? Its name?

--…Memory.

Waleria nods with great seriousness. She hands it back to Mr. Sliozberg. He holds it gently, like a newborn baby. Waleria has seen a newborn baby before. That is how he handles this memory.

--If I should die here, Waleria, you will look after my memory?

--Yes, Mr. Sliozberg. I will. Yes.

*

Waleria misses Mr. Sliozberg now. After he disappeared, late one night as autumn had turned to winter, although she was not supposed to, she quietly went into Ward IVa and saw the blue box case pushed against a back wall, with some scattered torn papers and torn clothes thrown over it or cast upon the ground. They had been left there when Mr. Sliozberg and some of the others disappeared. Waleria looked in the case and saw the box's paper covered thin floor in its proper place. She quietly knocked, then pulled it up as he had once showed her, just a little. She saw the bagged memory still there. She decided to tell no one until she might find a place to keep the memory safe. Memories must always be kept safe, especially Mr. Sliozberg's memory.

*

In the morning all of the patients are wakened and told to dress if they can. Some of the sisters try to help those who need help. They are told to move to the dining room in the front of the kitchen building as usual. Those few who are too ill, too weak to do so have been moved to beds into Ward IVa, the ward having been empty since the previous autumn.

Sister Stanisława bustles around, holding some patients' hands when they seem uncertain. Waleria does not need her hand held, although she feels confused by the sense of chaos around. She tells Sister Stanisława that she will be needed at the Head of Hospital Office's rooms, but Sister Stanisława takes her hand for a moment, tells her to go with the others to the dining room. Waleria does as the Sister asks. Waleria likes Sister Stanisława.

In the dining room all the patients are treated to a bigger plate of food than they have seen for a long time. There is not only jam to put on their black bread, there is thick porridge and an egg for those who ask. There is even a dab of real butter and a hot drink that Waleria knows is not real coffee, but it could almost be so, with milk and one spoon of sugar each for the patients. All are desperate to eat but unsure if they should do so, until the many Sisters tell them they are allowed to on this particular day, as they can look forward to a long journey.

To Waleria this seems chaotic, but she does as she is told.

Some of the patients find the food too rich. Their faces reveal their hunger, but the pain some now feel in their extended stomachs is perhaps too obvious. Many are surprised that Director Kroll has suddenly granted them, even for just a single meal, the possibility that they might not know such hunger albeit but for a short time.

Waleria is surprised to see the Head of the Hospital Office walking around the room talking quietly to some of the sisters and a few of the patients. He stops beside Waleria, smiles. She sees his eyes glisten.

--How are you today, Lera?

--I am sorry Head of the Hospital Office, I know I was supposed to clean in your private rooms today, but Sister Stanisława told me to come to the dining room in the kitchen building to eat with the others.

--And so she should have, Waleria. And so she should. It is a special day for all.

He smiles again. Waleria is confused. Behind his smile there lies something she does not understand. Chaos, perhaps. He leans down and whispers in her ear.

--Whatever Sister Stanisława tells you to do today, you must do exactly as she says. Do you understand, Lera?

Waleria nods, but she does not understand. Not really. She feels chaos.

The Head of the Hospital Office pats her shoulder and strolls away to have a short word with a few others. Some of the patients stuff food in their mouths as if they have not eaten in two years, which Waleria considers and decides is not really correct as she remembers how she stirred the large vats in the room at the other side of the building, in the kitchen, stirring the thin turnip soup, the nettle soup, the marjoram soup as best she could. True the portions were not large, but Waleria would not say patients had starved because Director Kroll said the daily rations where enough for patients who were not mentally fit and they should be happy with what they had. And who was Waleria to disagree with the hospital director?

After a short time the Head of the Hospital Office tells all the patients in the room that they must now return to their wards and to wait at their beds. Staff members will come to tell them what to expect on this special day of days. Waleria thinks he could almost be angry the way he talks, but she realizes it is not anger in his voice, but something else. Something that frightens her. The chaos, she thinks. It must be the chaos. Or perhaps, she thinks, his shoes have not been polished enough for a special day as this must be, a day they were given jam.

She hopes the Head of the Hospital Office is not angry at her. She would ask him, but he has already left the room.

Their meal is over. The patients return to their various wards in the few buildings. Some seem confused, upset. The chaos, Waleria thinks.

As she walks into her building, Sister Bąk stands off to the side of the entryway.

--Waleria, you are to come with me, she says. Sister Stanisława will wait for you in your ward until you arrive.

--In Ward Vb.

--Yes Waleria. She knows you will be coming.

Sister Bąk waits until the last of the patients have entered their building and marched off to their particular wards. She then asks Waleria to follow her down the corridor, to a large room at the back, the sewing room. Sister Bąk leads Waleria towards the alcove side of the room where materials, threads and needles are kept to make the machines do their job. The two wardrobes there are closed but pushed away from the wall a bit at odd angles. Waleria sees more chaos. She does not understand chaos.

--You must pay very close attention to me, Waleria. There is space there behind the wardrobes, not much but a little space. Do you see?

Waleria looks behind the wardrobes pushed in such a way that the back disappears into shadow and darkness. Mr. Sliozberg also disappeared into shadow and darkness but Waleria does not think she will find him behind the wardrobes. She looks back at Sister Bąk.

--Later Sister Stanisława will be told to bring the patients from the wards to the courtyard outside. You are to be the last to leave your ward. When she leads the patients past the sewing room she will stand in front of the door and nod to you. You are to quietly enter the room without the others and you are to quietly hide yourself behind the wardrobes there. Do you understand, Waleria?

Chaos. All this chaos. Waleria nods.

--You must squeeze back as far as you can into the shadow and make yourself as small as you are able. Sister Stanisława will come for you sometime in the night but it could be a long wait. You must stay there even if it is not comfortable. You must do this, Waleria. You cannot let anyone know you are there. You must do this for your own sake. Please tell me you understand?

--But the Head of the Hospital Office's shoes?

--This is his wish, Waleria. He has asked us to do this for you because he cares for you and we are doing this. You must hide here when the time comes.

--Yes Sister Bąk.

--You must live, Waleria.

Waleria does not understand chaos. But she understands the tears in Sister Bąk's eyes. She understands how they glisten. She has seen much glistening in eyes these last two days.

Waleria follows Sister Bąk to Ward Vb. Sister Stanisława is helping some of the other patients, most now sitting quietly on their beds. Waiting. She looks at Sister Bąk who nods towards Sister Stanisława, just slightly. Looks once more at Waleria then leaves to go to her own ward.

The patients sit in silence. Waleria too sits in silence on her bed. Waiting. Sister

Stanisława waits in her office. She seems to be staring into space, at nothing, at the wall. This is what chaos does, Waleria thinks.

She also thinks she should now be shining the Head of the Hospital Office's shoes and placing them in exactly the right order beneath the suits in his private office. She thinks she should be in the laundry building folding the bedding just so, because no one does it better. She thinks too she should then go help Sister Jadwiga Trawniczek in the kitchens, although Waleria knows that they have already been given their meal today and Sister Jadwiga probably needs no help just now. So Waleria sits and waits.

She waits longer. She looks out of the window near her bed when she hears a loud motor outside. She sees a large motor vehicle with quite a few men in black uniforms driving up to the hospital. They are soldiers. There is a war on. Waleria does not like the soldiers. She tells no one this. She says to no one what she now can see.

After a while, perhaps late morning, or perhaps it is just in the afternoon, a loud siren goes off. The patients look at one another, confused. This is not ordinary. Sister Stanisława comes out of her office and tells the patients to remain on their beds for now.

Waleria looks out the window again. She cannot see the soldiers. But she sees almost all the Nurse Sisters and other Sisters and the doctors and the gardener and almost all those she sees almost every day emerge from their buildings and offices and rooms to the front courtyard of the hospital. There Doctor Schimansky who she does not like very much and there young Doctor Cechnicki. There the other doctors too. There Sister Jadwiga and the other sisters from the kitchens, and those who work in the laundry rooms. There the gardener, and the administrators. There Sister Bąk. There the Head of the Hospital Office. There so many.

Waleria sees the Head of the Hospital Office read from a paper on a clipboard that he holds tightly in his hands. Some of those around him raise their hands as if to say yes, I am here. Yes…I have been here. Director Kroll, and a doctor Waleria does not know, and a soldier in a black uniform now emerge from Director Kroll's office building. The Head of the Hospital Office hands Director Kroll his clipboard. Director Kroll looks at it and nods. All those people who Waleria knows and who she does not know, those who have jobs at the Babinski Institute Hospital that are far more important than the few jobs Waleria sees now start to march down the hospital drive, and away. Waleria watches them go.

Chaos, she thinks. Chaos everywhere.

Sister Stanisława emerges from her office.

--Sister Bąk walks away with others, Waleria says.

--I know, Waleria. I am to look after both Ward Vb and VIb.

--She has disappeared, Sister Stanisława.

--Yes.

--Mr. Sliozberg disappeared. Aleksi disappeared. Perhaps they are together?

Sister Stanisława does not answer. She turns away, returns to her small office. Sits straight up, saying nothing.

They sit for a very long time. It begins to grow dark. Still they sit. Finally another siren rings. Sister Stanisława emerges from her office.

--You must all now come with me. Do you all understand? There must be no talking. Waleria it would be best for you to be the last one out.

Waleria understands. There must be no talking.

They follow Sister Stanisława into the corridor. She stops just outside Ward VIB. She goes into the room, then reappears after a few moments with the few patients from this ward who join the patients from Ward Vb. Waleria stands at the rear. They march down the ward and take the stairs in the back down to the ground floor. Sister Stanisława points to the front of the building. Far down the corridor several soldiers in black uniforms wait at the entrance. The patients march to them. Some of the patients hold hands. Some cry. They are afraid.

Sister Stanisława stands to the side at the doorway to the sewing room as the patients walk towards the front entrance where soldiers in black uniforms wait. Waleria is the last of the patients and as she reaches the sewing room Sister Stanisława quickly takes her by the shoulder and pulls her alone into the sewing room. Their eyes meet for the briefest of moments. Sister Stanisława nods quickly, slightly, and closes the door, disappearing.

Mr. Sliozberg disappeared. Aleksi disappeared.

Waleria remembers what she was told. She remembers chaos. She hurries over to the wardrobes pulled slightly away from the wall and climbs behind them. Climbs into darkness. She makes herself small.

She hears nothing at first. Then later, doors opening, closing. She hears some voices calling out but she cannot hear what they say.

She hears the door to the sewing room opening and some whimpering. Then two women patients she does not know appear just at the opening to the back of the wardrobes, crying, pushing their way into the opening.

Waleria makes herself very small. She makes herself into a ball.

She hears words in a language she does not understand. Waleria does not know what these mean. Almost as quickly as the two women patients, who she does not know, squeeze into the space where Waleria has made herself small, hiding in darkness, the black-coat arms of a soldier appear, followed by his angry face, as he reaches in and pulls the two women patients out from behind the closet.

The angry soldier has not seen Waleria.

Waleria is afraid. She makes herself as small as she can.

Sound of a body thrown against a wall. Sound of crying. Sound of a scream. Sound of uncertainty. Sound of words unknown. Sound of whimpering. Sound of pain. Sound of terror. Sound of feet dragging. Sound of fear. Sound of terror. And sound of chaos.

Then silence. Sound of silence.

Waleria hides in the shadow behind the closet. She makes herself very small. Into a small ball. And she does not move. And she barely breathes.

From beyond, she hears people shouting, doors slamming. From beyond she hears shouts and crying. From beyond she hears names being called, the voice of the Director saying names, men shouting in a language she does not understand.

Waleria remains silent. Waleria does not move. Waleria makes herself disappear.

*

Waleria Białońska remains motionless behind the wardrobes for a very long time. She barely breathes. She does not cry when she hears others cry. She hears shouting and screams, doors slamming and boots marching from room to room. She is not seen. The noises eventually recede. Later she hears boots once more, marching towards the stairs, heading above. She hears bangs. She does not understand. After a while she hears boots march back down. Then again silence.

Still she does not move.

She thinks I have disappeared.

She thinks this is what it means.

She thinks again this is what it means. This.

The room grows dark, darker still. Noises in the distance but the voices are gone. Sounds of motor vehicles come and go. No one sees the small young woman crouched low, like a ball, crouched behind two wardrobes. No one comes. She waits.

She thinks much about Aleksi. She sees him now, standing beside her, holding her hand as he once held it when they walked along the river. She sees him smiling at her, laughing with her. She remembers the games they played as children. They were not afraid when they were children. They were simply children. She loved Alexsi then. He made her feel safe. Waleria has not always felt safe, but he made her feel so, even as children.

--You need not be afraid, Lera. I know some laugh at you. I know sometimes you get confused. But you need not be afraid with me. That is why we are friends. And when I get older I can look after you. You will see. I promise. You will see.

Waleria hopes he may still keep his promise. Waleria hopes she will one day hold his hand again. That they will be friends just as they were when they were children. That she will not always be so—confused.

The world now is so confused. So chaotic.

She remembers too Mr. Sliozberg. He too is her friend. He said he trusted her. He showed her his secret.

The memory.

His secret. Will you look after my secret, Lera? Will you look after my memory?

She had promised, as Aleksi had promised. Promises are meant to be kept.

It is dark outside now, warming darkness she feels. Her legs hurt, her arms. She needs to move. She needs to keep a promise. Waleria needs to look after Mr. Sliozberg's memory.

Waleria quietly, slowly climbs from behind the wardrobes. The room is without light. The room is silent. She hears only sounds from far in the distance. She had said she would not leave the space behind the wardrobes, but she also made a promise, and promises must be kept. She knows she must be silent because she said she would. She knows she must make no sound, show no light.

Slowly Waleria walks out of the sewing room. She looks around. No one. She made a promise. She knows what she must do. She tiptoes up the stairs. No one there. No noise in the ward. She walks down the corridor, hesitates. No light. She carefully opens the door to Ward IVa. Silence within. No voices. The patients who were too tired, too ill to move, had been lying on the beds in Ward IVa. Sister Stanisława had said they would be looked after. But they have disappeared, leaving only emptiness. Disappeared like Aleksi. Disappeared like Mr. Sliozberg.

She made a promise. His memory.

She walks past the beds where the ill patients had been lying. Even in the deep shadows she sees the beds are stained, the walls behind the beds stained too. Stained brown. She puts her hand on the stain because it seems curious. The stain on her hands. Stained brown. The stain sticks on her hands. She does not know what this means.

It means perhaps chaos, she thinks. Waleria is afraid of chaos.

She walks to the side of the room where once Mr. Sliozberg had his bed, his world he had said. Off to the side of this she sees his blue box case, turned over, some of his belongings torn and scattered. But she promised.

She pushes the box over. Feels its bottom. Finds the threads just slightly sticking up from the thin surface covered with paper. Quietly she pulls until the bottom comes free and she can pull it out.

The small space remains untouched. A bag. A memory in wood. The musical memory.

Waleria keeps the memory in the bag. She knows she promised. And quietly she carries it down the stairs, to the doorway of the sewing room, into the darkness. She finds the wardrobe pushed slightly from the wall and climbs behind once again.

But she is not alone, not this time. She has memory.

She waits. She thinks perhaps she sleeps. But the darkness does not bother her because she has often closed her eyes. She feels at home in darkness. And after a short time, or a long time, or she does not know because she does not understand time, because time is chaos, she hears the sound of a door opening. She hears quiet

62

shoes walking across the floor. She hears breathing.

--Waleria? Waleria are you there?

Waleria does not hesitate. Even in the empty shadows this whispered voice she knows. She climbs from the shadow now black behind the wardrobes.

--Yes, Sister Stanisława.

Sister Stanisława hugs Waleria to her breast.

--Oh Lera, my sweet Lera. May God always protect you, my Lera.

--I do not understand Sister Stanisława. Everyone has disappeared. Like Aleksi. Like Mr. Sliozberg. Are they together?

--…I believe so. Yes.

--I have Mr. Sliozberg's memory. I promised I would look after it.

Waleria holds up the bag with the wooden memory within.

--Lera, I don't have much time. Come.

Sister Stanisława quietly leads Waleria out of the sewing room to a room down the corridor where the Sisters store bedding and bits of clothes. She does not have to unlock the room, a place patients normally cannot enter, because Waleria sees that the handle and lock are broken. Waleria follows Sister Stanisława within.

The room is small. Emerging moonlight illuminates it. Sheets and some clothes have been thrown about. Near the single window high at the top of the room is a small table and two stools. Sister Stanisława pulls the table below the high window, and puts a stool on the table. She looks around and sees a loose half brick on the ground where it had broken from the wall. She wraps this in a torn bit of cloth that Waleria can see had once been a smock. Then Sister Stanisława carefully climbs onto the table, and from that onto the stool. She bangs on the window with the brick wrapped in cloth, once, twice, as quietly but as strongly as she possibly can. On the third time the window shatters. Some of the glass falls to the ground outside. Sister Stanisława gasps, holding her breath; she does not move. She listens. She hears nothing. Waleria hears nothing. They wait another moment. Still nothing. Then Sister Stanisława climbs down.

--Listen carefully to me, Lera. You must go from here to Farmer Purchla. He will look after you. He knows you will come to him. You remember the way? The moonlight will guide you but walk only in shadow. You must go very quietly but as quickly as you can. You must do this now, Waleria. You must not stay here. You have to go right now. Do you understand?

--You will come too, Sister Stanisława?

--No, Lera. It would not be safe. Maybe one day we will see one another again. You must go. Hide. You have to live. You have to. Tell me you understand?

--Yes, Sister Stanisława.

Sister Stanisława helps Waleria onto the stool. Waleria stands, reaches up, then stops.

--The memory, Sister Stanisława. I promised Mr. Sliozberg I would keep his memory. Please...

The ward sister hesitates, then looks around, sees the bag on the ground where Waleria had left it. Sister Stanisława picks it up, hands it to Waleria.

--Now go, Lera. Go...

Waleria, holding the bag with the memory in her teeth, pulls herself up to the window with the glass broken. She grabs onto some bars on the outside of the frame, and pulls herself through, carefully dropping the bag. She starts to drop down. Her smock gets torn on the bar, just slightly, but she pulls her hips and drops, falling gently onto the ground. She stands, picks up the memory that had fallen beside her, turns and looks back up at the window.

Sister Stanisława is not there. Sister Stanisława too has disappeared.

Waleria looks at the shadows, made larger in the moonlight. Moon shadows. She hopes that Farmer Purchla will take her to Mr. Sliozberg. And to Aleksi. And to Sister Stanisława. To all who have disappeared.

And with that, holding the memory close, Waleria runs into the shadows, until she too disappears.

*

It is 19 August 1942. Yitzchok Sliozberg—Izio—a simple man, at times confused, a peddler, 71 years old, painfully climbs down from the crowded cattle wagon, one of sixty or so wagons of the train, and stares up at the blue sky. At least this is a change from the Otwock Hospital he thinks. And a change from the Kobierzyn Babinski Institute Hospital where he had lived for several years before being taken to Otwock. Here openness. Nature. A sense of finally being free.

He looks into a cloud above. In it he thinks he sees the innocent gaze of the young girl Lera, Waleria Białońska. He wonders how she is. He wonders if she is alive.

There is a young woman standing nearby. She stands tall. Her face is taught with anger. She pulls out something from her pocket. Izio sees it is the sort of rouge women sometimes put on their lips, rouge in a metal tube. The young woman stands tall, putting the rouge on her lips, bright red, beautiful. She reminds Izio of a girl from so long ago, so very long ago, a girl who refused to look at him and who stood tall and who carried glasses of drink in a karchma. What was her name? So very, very long ago. Izio does not remember now. He does know if in fact he ever knew her name. His memory was left somewhere else, somewhere in a box in a room in a place of memory. Gone.

There too another woman, old, helped by a young girl with a single leg, her second leg made of wood. They hold one another. Perhaps they are mother and daughter. Perhaps not. But Yitzchok looks at them and thinks how fortunate they are to have one another. How very fortunate to be here—together.

He thinks he hears someone call his name. Tanl? He wonders. Is it Tanl he hears? Or perhaps Tateh? But as the water clears from his eyes, he sees that it is a German guard in a grey uniform yelling at him, angrily.

--That way, the guard screams. Through the station! Move! Go that way. That way! The wash chamber that way!

Yitzchok Sliozberg, slightly confused, wonders where he is. He wonders if he is home. Call me Izio. You can call me Izio. Am I home?, he then mutters quietly. He is not certain. He wonders.

--Welcome to Treblinka, a German guard yells to him, to all, to the men and women and children as they march past the ticket office that is not a ticket office, as they emerge from the railway station that is not a railway station, where they are ordered to remove their clothes and stand naked in the heat from the summer sun. The beautiful young woman standing naked now in the summer sun, indifferent, standing tall. And her lips reddened in pride and defiance. And standing there, too, standing as upright as he can like the young woman he saw who has disappeared with so many others, men to one side, women and children to another, Izio standing tall and refusing to bow as best he can, Izio thinks he hears, quietly but with a great

65

deal of love, the meher played by his own lovely kleh. The fiddle's sound. The song.

--Now move, a guard yells at them all. Move! This way! Himmelstrasse! The road to heaven! This way! This way! This way.

Yes, Izio thinks. I am finally home.

3. Aleksi

Otwock Forest, near Warsaw, to
Nowy Wiśnicz, near Krakow
February, 1943

Aleksi has never known it to be so cold. Cold that cuts through the layers of his clothes, through his coat and hat. Father had warned him the nights would be hard and they had to travel mostly at night. He had thought he was strong enough not to feel the cold. But he had not expected this. Cold that cuts more than the knives they keep sharpened at home to slaughter the sheep. Cold that burns and screams within his chest as they march along the back roads, as they lie hiding in the fields, as they sleep in the forest. Cold and hunger. He has never known.

He sometimes feels as if he will never escape the cold. That it will always be a part of him. Or that it will kill him long before any German bullet might. But he does not want to die. He wants to live.

He loved a girl once. A childish thing perhaps, but he loved her innocence. When he too was innocent. Yet he has never made love. Not to her. Not to another. He does not want to die before he can make love, to feel a woman's warmth, her breast, her hair falling on his. To feel her life. To feel her touch.

He is afraid.

He cannot tell anyone he is afraid. He cannot show it. But he is afraid.

The first few days they travel alone, Father, his younger brother Mikołaj, himself. They had picked up some radio parts and communiques from their contact across the Slovakian border, then started north again. This is countryside they know well. Home country. They know the route they will take towards Warsaw, where they will pass on the letters and the parts to comrades.

The storm hits not long after re-entering Poland. Winter storms this time of year come as no surprise, but this storm hits harder than most. The snow falls for the first few days and the wind never lets up. They have to be careful to keep from the open where their tracks might be spotted. The few safe houses along the way give respite and usually hot soup, but they cannot remain in any one place for long. Many nights they have to sleep in forests, unable to light even the smallest fire for warmth, eating only the dried meat and bread they carry with them.

Aleksi knows this is necessary. He knows what they do is important to the effort. He knows if they are discovered and caught they will likely be killed. He knows he is afraid. He will not stop though. Any more than Mikołaj, two years younger, will stop. Or Father. They will not.

After travelling for several days they meet with two others who have been sent to walk with them. Aleksi has never seen the man and woman before. They exchange the verse they had each been given to confirm they were contacts. No one exchanges names. Names are never spoken. A rule of their resistance group. The couple who come from Warsaw then lead the way towards that city for the next two days. Aleksi knows they will not go into the city, which he has never seen. He knows it would not be safe. They speak little other than short comments about the weather, about where enemy soldiers have been seen. The man and woman seem to be together, lying tightly against each other on beds of branches at night. Aleksi wonders if they are lovers. Or are they simply trying to keep one another warm. One another alive.

He thinks of that girl, whose name he has lost somewhere in this ice and cold that wraps him it its frozen arms but does not warm him, instead makes him shiver with pain and loneliness. He cannot remember her name because he cannot remember his life as a child as a boy an innocent laughing in the heat of summer sun. He cannot remember.

Where would she be now?

On the third day of their journey the weather lets up, just slightly. They travel now only at night, listening carefully for the sound of any vehicles or foot patrols. Twice they have to lie in fields of snow and remain silent, shivering in the darkness. They reach forest again in the middle of the night, walking in silence along what is most likely an animal track for a number of hours. Aleksi can barely make out the path through the forest but the young couple never hesitate, clearly knowing the way north. The night now is overcast, which makes the going more difficult but slightly safer.

At a narrow clearing they stop, wait. Hear a bird cry that is no bird but a signal. After a short time five others appear, two women and three men. Father knows two of the men and they embrace. Aleksi guesses that they know that he and Mikołaj are Father's sons, but they do not greet them with names, rather only with nods and slight smiles. Father and the two men then walk away from the others for a quiet discussion. The rest of the group sit in the clearing, exchanging a few words, passing around bits of meat and bread from their packs. Aleksi looks over at Father talking with the two men. Even in the darkness Aleksi can sense Father is concerned, not happy. Aleksi sees him listening carefully, sees him shake his head slightly, a few quiet words exchanged. One of the other two men offers Father a cigarette, lights it for him. Father sucks on it, cupping it in his hands to hide the orange glow, listens but does not speak. Finally Aleksi sees him nod agreement; the men turn and walk back to the group.

--Give the others our gifts now, he tells his sons. We will go together for two hours.

Aleksi and his brother remove the radio parts and documents they have been carrying, as does Father, which are handed around so that no one person holds everything. Then all start to walk, single file and in silence.

They hear dogs bark in the distance. They see no one. Through a break in the forest they see farmland, a house in shadow lit only by stars and a single glowing lamp. They turn away from it, staying hidden, skirting the openness.

They approach another clearing where all stop. Two of the group continue to the far side, disappearing, then return several minutes later, gesturing that it is safe. The group skirts the clearing. On the far side waits a new man in a workman's suit. He nods but says nothing. He points; in the dawn light just beginning to break Aleksi sees a young woman in a long coat, lying on a bed of branches, asleep.

The weary group now sit down against trees and on a couple boulders jutting out against the forest incline, passing food amongst one another.

The man in the workman's suit kneels down beside the sleeping young woman, shakes her awake. Her eyes opened with a start, like a deer unsure if it will be shot or will escape. The man puts his hand on her shoulder to calm her.

--I must now return, Aleksi hears the man tell her. The Germans, they left the Ghetto alone again today. They never expected to have to fight. But they will return. You must not. Never return. Go with God.

The man stands, nods at all in the group and disappears into shadows, leaving the young woman with them. Aleksi can see that she is in fact not a woman but still a girl, yet a girl who looks exhausted and much older than her years, unsure and somewhat confused. She is very thin, probably ill. The man had mentioned the Ghetto, so Aleksi decides she must be a Jewess, just as other Jews had been moved to ghettos all over Poland. And from there he does not know. But he knows that many have died.

And he knows that if they do not help this girl, help her however they can, she too will die.

Father walks over to her.

--Come; we will go further into the forest. Safer.

They walk for about thirty minutes, then sit down amidst some rocks, seeking what warmth they can muster. The girl hesitates then walks over to the young woman who with her partner had first met Aleksi, Mikołaj and Father a couple days previous. Aleksi hears the girl ask the young woman if she is Eva.

The young woman freezes, clearly taken aback that her name has been spoken, but then nods. The ill girl removes a letter from her coat.

--…your sister…

The young woman whose name must have been Eva takes the letter, stares at it, then walks away to read. Aleksi can see in the dawn light that the letter she reads has made her cry in silence. Aleksi turns away. He understands grief, as these days everyone lies beneath cloaks of grief. He knows that grief sometimes needs silence and solitude.

Some minutes later Father walks over to the sick girl, kneels before her.

--My name is Henryk, he tells her, to Aleksi's surprise, his father breaking the resistance rule that he himself had often been told.

--You do not need to know anything further. Tonight I go south with those two, he adds, nodding at Aleksi and Mikołaj. You must not ask them their names, but

70

they are my sons. We will need to walk for ten days, perhaps two weeks. It will be difficult. We mostly have to travel at night. There are patrols. Cold. We will cross the border into Slovakia. We have business there. You will come with us. I know you have been ill. You are not strong. But for us you must be strong.

The sick girl nods. She understands.

Father turns his back on her, but then hesitates. Looks back at her for one more moment.

--You can trust my sons. You can trust me. We will do what we can to keep you safe.

--I know, she whispers.

Aleksi watches her for a long moment as she sits, staring at the ground. He can see in the girl's expression that she is afraid. And he can see her need to live is strong, that whatever she has endured, whatever she has witnessed, it has given her a strength that will fight for that life. And he knows that the journey ahead will be difficult for them all, but Father, as indeed he and his brother, will do whatever they can to help this girl survive. They will help her to live.

As in her way, she will help them feel her strength hidden somewhere within her physical weakness.

*

It is dark when they gather their belongings to depart. Father shakes hands with each member of the group. The woman named Eva embraces the girl they will take south. Aleksi knows whatever was in the letter from Eva's sister must have meant a great deal to her. He sees in Eva's embrace, in her memory, that she has wrapped her arms around her own sister even as she holds the weak Jewess as strongly as she can. He sees that Eva does not want to let go. That she would do anything not to let go.

But she lets go.

Few words are spoken. Few words need to be spoken. Aleksi, his brother and his Father, and now the Jewish girl who they will lead and support, give a final nod and turn away, beginning the long journey back to the south of the country.

They do not speak much as they walk in darkness. There is little to say and they need to retain what strength they have. Aleksi takes it upon himself to look after the girl, to reach out to her when she slips, sometimes to lift her small, weak frame over fences, to stop the march when he can see she can walk no further without a short break. They keep to shadows as best they can. When they come to open country they hurry through darkness, resting during the day, cowering low amongst weeds or grasses, or when they can lying in drainage ditches. At any sound, any dog's bark, they fall to the ground, lie low. They wait. They listen. At the sound of a motor, regardless how far away it might be, they lie flat on snow covered earth, their faces against ice, hiding their warm breath, motionless until the sound recedes and they feel safe.

In this way they pass the next few days, walking at night, hiding from the moon, sleeping a restless sleep during the day, protected by woods or in deep grasses.

After several days travel, they can see the girl struggles, fighting exhaustion and illness. Father decides they will stay in the woods without pushing on for a few hours. Although the risk is great, in the depths of the forest Father feels it is safe enough to light a small fire. He takes Mikołaj with him to see if they can catch a rabbit to roast over the muted fire. Aleksi remains with the girl, who closes her eyes, weary. He puts on some water to boil for chicory root, never taking his eyes from her. He has spoken little to her and does not want to ask what all she has witnessed in Warsaw, in the place they call the Ghetto. He can tell from the dark circles under her eyes, and now from her sleeping mumblings and near silent cries, that she must have experienced great pain, great loss. He finds her pretty if thin. Weak in body. But determined.

It makes him remember the girl he had loved as a younger boy himself. That refusal to submit to fear, that center of calm. He wonders about that girl again. He wonders about the Jewess lying here, all her fears and pain bundled within. He wants her to live. He wants them both to live.

He needs to know that they will live. One day, one long day beyond. He will want to remember always.

The chicory comes to a boil and he pours a cup for himself. He sees the girl wide awake now and pours out a cup for her.

--Drink, he tells her. This will warm you. Help you find strength.

--Strength. She looks at him, part statement, part question. I should have died. It should have been me.

--No. If you live there is reason to live. Now you have to live, for what you lost perhaps.

--Perhaps.

He sits down, sips the hot drink. She stares at him. Into his very being. Into his heart.

--Boy: I do not want to slow you down. You, your father, your brother. I don't want to…

--You don't. It does not matter.

--Why?...Why help me?

He hesitates. He looks for words.

--My mother… she died when my brother and I were young. Illness. My father says he will not bend. We must never bend, not before hate. Before evil. He says there is a very fine line between what lives, and what lives no longer. And that we have a duty to help those who can live, to live. Those who are afraid. To show them they must not be afraid. Dark times. He says in the mornings there will be light. Help always to carry the light, he told me. Those who need…need. Now there is so much need.

--Your father is a kind man.

--Kind. And strong.

They sit silent for a few minutes. She looks away, sips the hot liquid. They wait. After a few moments, she looks back at him.

--I cannot know your name, she says.

--It is safer. Those are the rules we follow.

He thinks he hears his father and brother returning. He stands to look through the trees. He turns his back on her for a moment.

--Hania Stern.

He turns, looks down at her.

--You need to know who I am. Because if I die, I want to die with my name. Because I am here. And will be here, however dark this night. And because you have helped me see the first light in morning, boy.

He looks at her. Sees within her. Sees her warm, beating heart. Her pain. He turns away as Father and Mikołaj appear. They will roast the rabbit they killed over the small fire. And find nourishment despite the dark night.

*

Moving again. Fighting against the cold. The snow. Clear days clear nights followed by a blizzard that bites at their faces and their shivering bodies, while giving them some protection from those who would alert an enemy occasionally heard, occasionally seen.

The girl Hania Stern whose name he wishes he did not know and whose name he will nevertheless carry in his heart and hold in his thoughts and one day shelter in his memory stumbles but does not stop. He can see she is as damp from the sweat of her illness as she is from her struggle through fields of snow.

She will not give up. Her determination to live speaks when her words remain mostly silent.

They come upon an abandoned barn and spend the night, then remain through the day until dusk. But they must keep moving. They must do what they can to avoid leaving noticeable tracks in the snow. It is better to make their way when the snow falls to cover their path. The evidence of their being. The evidence that they exist, and march, and refuse to die.

Several times they hear motorized vehicles, near or far they can never be certain. In the blanket silence of snow it is hard to tell where the enemy may be. Then they remain still, listening, waiting, fearing a shout, fearing the shot of a gun. Fearing death. Death sometimes would be easier.

The Jewess, Hania, grasps that they are in territory Father knows, that he now reads the back lanes and roads, the forests, the streams, as though he has been here many times. So he has, sometimes traveling alone, sometimes with one son, or both. He reads the signs and as Aleksi tells Hania, helping her stand when she has sat, the signs are like the birds warning Father when he must be warned, urging him to move on faster when they all must move quickly. Calling out to him as friend. Allies in nature.

They walk. They are still. They hide. They walk. The girl stumbles, struggling. Aleksi takes her arm with his hand. We are one, he thinks. She is afraid but she does not want to show her fear. She is afraid she holds them back. She is afraid she will

74

die here, unknown. She is afraid perhaps she will live. Life itself has become fear. Still she stands sometimes with Aleksi's help. Still she walks.

At the edge of a forest as night falls Father tells them to remain in shadows, to wait quietly. He needs to leave them all there for the moment, promising to return soon. Aleksi and Mikołaj clear a small area to sit just within the forest, careful to leave evidence of their stay largely hidden. They pull over a tree trunk to sit on, wiping the snow from the ground where it first lay. They sit. They wait.

--Your family?, Aleksi asks the Jewess.

She shakes her head.

--I am sorry, he says almost in a whisper.

She looks up at him. Stares into his eyes. The pain of memory. The memory clear.

--My father was first. They took him from my uncle's apartment in the Ghetto. The typhus took my brother. My mother, she...My mother and Alicja. Marched to Umschlagplatz, to the cattle cars. Carried away. Carried away to die.

Aleksi does not ask further. She looks away from the two boys. That pain of memory.

After an hour, Father returns with another man. The man nods, says nothing, gestures they should follow into the darkness. He leads them to his small farmhouse, mere shadow in the night. Inside, two candles and a small fire light the room. A woman who must be the farmer's wife sits waiting. She nods to each as they enter, telling them to sit. She disappears from the farmhouse, returning a few minutes later with a few eggs that she proceeds to fry over the fire in pork fat she keeps in a bowl. She places these before each with a large piece of bread. The two boys and Father eat with real hunger. The girl Hania stares at hers, as if afraid to eat, as if the food is not real. The farmer's wife kneels before her, gestures to the Jewess Hania that she must eat, so she does, slowly. Her eyes are vacant, far away, chewing each small bite slowly so that it might last forever. Or perhaps so that it tastes real, rather than of a dream, or nightmare.

They leave the farmer and his wife an hour or so later, after they have managed to warm their bodies, even a little. Father looks at the girl.

--You can walk?

--Yes, she says.

--I will help her, Father, says Aleksi. She is strong. I will help.

--I know. I know.

The four disappear back into the night. The farmer and his wife close the door behind them. The minimal light disappears. The moon is not out.

Again they walk. And again they lie in a ditch during the day. They remain still. They can hear a dog barking somewhere nearby. It does not approach. They do not move. They spend the day like this.

Father watches over them. At night they move again. In the day they stay in the forest. When there they follow animal tracks. If they come to an opening they circle, regardless of whether it takes them in a different direction, a wrong direction. They cannot be seen. They must not be seen.

The girl Hania grows weaker still. She stumbles often now. Aleksi, sometimes Mikołaj, holds her arms, helps her to walk. Father watches her, but says nothing. They can all see she is determined to continue. But sometimes she cannot continue.

They walk through much of the night and come to the edge of another farm with a barn and stables at its side. Father tells them all to wait well in the distance where the fence meets brush, then forest. They watch Father cautiously make his way towards the farmhouse, stopping after each step to listen, to make certain that no one waits, no one sees. Once at the side window he knocks quietly. Even from the distance they can just make out the quiet tap of his finger. Tap. Tap tap tap. Tap, tap. A lantern appears in a window, then the door opens. A farmer appears, holds the light up to Father. The two men embrace. Father disappears within.

The boys and the girl Hania remain at the edge of the farm. They keep their gazes towards the road, searching for any appearing lights. They see none. They remain silent, listening. They hear nothing but the slight wind. They crouch low. They shiver. The know not to leave unless they see danger. They sense it all the time, but see nothing.

Aleksi looks at the girl. He knows her strength is failing. He takes her hand. She looks at him, nods, weakly. Not yet. Death, not yet.

After a long time the door to the farm opens. Father walks quickly out, hurrying in their direction. Dawn is about to break.

--It is all right, he says.

The two boys, both helping the girl Hania, limping badly, follow Father to the farm, their eyes purveying the landscape just beginning to appear in the dawn for any approaching lights, listening carefully, keeping within shadow. Father opens the farmhouse door for them where they are greeted with warmth and the smell of soup boiling over an open fire. The farmer, an old man with thick white hair and rings around his eyes, ushers them quickly in. At the hearth, his equally stooped wife stirs a pot of soup for them. Looking up, she stares at the boys, and the girl who limps between them.

--Come, she tells the girl Hania. You need to wash.

The old woman leads Hania by the hand to a side room, where Aleksi sees a small bed. The old woman returns to the fire and places a kettle of water over it for a few minutes, takes a bowl of balm from a shelf that she smells, nods, then disappears behind the curtain. The farmer meanwhile pours homemade nalewka into cups for each of them, encouraging the boys to drink. The alcohol burns into Aleksi's chest, but warms, quietly soothing against the winter snow that has been biting for the last few days. Or is it weeks, he no longer remembers. Aleksi begins to feel his hands and feet for the first time in so very long. The flush of the alcohol brings life where he had thought it had been frozen out.

From behind the curtain Aleksi hears the girl Hania groan in pain, and hears the murmurs of the old woman, soothing and gentle. He hears this woman begin to sing, softly, and the Jewess's moan begin to subside. After some minutes the farmer's wife draws open the curtain. Hania lies on the bed, her boots and socks off, her clothes loosened where the farmer's wife has washed her. Hania's back is to them, silent now, perhaps sleeping.

The farmer's wife puts the bowl and a rag off to the side, draws the curtain. She walks over to her ancient husband, whispers in his ear. Then she pulls some small bowls off a shelf, shuffles over to the hearth and pours some soup from the pot into each one. These she hands around to the men, then sits on a small stool beside the fire, looking from one to the other, then away.

The boys sip from their bowls quickly. Father takes his time. After some minutes, the farmer's wife stands and takes the bowl from each, refilling them with the warming broth.

--You are very kind, Father tells her. We cannot thank you enough.

--It is nothing.

She then pours some into a bowl for the girl. She pulls back the curtain of the alcove, quietly. She sits on the side of the bed, gently places her hand on Hania's shoulder. Hania, dozing, turns sharply, startled. Looks up at the farmer's wife who simply nods at her, encouraging. Hania half sits in the bed, and the farmer's wife begins to feed her as if she was feeding a small child. Hania coughs with the first spoonful's of soup, then begins to settle.

Aleksi looks at Father, who stares at the girl, then away. He looks at the girl's feet, streaks of blood still staining her skin around her soles, to her ankles. The men quietly sip at the soup. The farmer reaches over, taps Father's knee, then speaks quietly.

--She is not in a good way.

--Can she stay here?

--They come every few days. They take what they want. Milk, our chickens. Bread. If they found her they would know she is not our own. They would know she is a Jew. She would not be safe here.

--Nor would you and your good wife.

--We are old, friend. We do not matter. But the girl...I do not know.

Father nods. Says nothing further. Considers. The farmer reaches for some tobacco on a near table, rolls a cigarette in some paper. Gives it to Father, who nods thanks. The farmer puts some tobacco in a pipe. The two men retreat into thought and smoke.

The girl Hania sips at her soup, helped still by the farmer's wife. Once she has finished, she leans back on the bed. The soup has brought some colour back into her face. The farmer's wife draws the hair from the girl's face, placing her hand over the girl's cheek, offering warmth, kindness.

In this gesture Aleksi feels the hand of his own mother placed against his cheek when he was a boy. He feels a pain in his chest, the pain of longing. He wishes life had not become as it has. He wishes his own mother was alive, that he could embrace her now, feel her warmth now.

But she is not alive. And he pushes the memory into a back room of his mind, and closes the door. Knowing it resides there will suffice as best it may.

Father stands, walks over to the girl Hania, stares at her. The girl's eyes, which had closed, open and stare up at him.

--They do not think you will be able to continue.

She hesitates. Stares at him. Looks away for a moment, then back at him.

--I will walk.

--Are you certain?

--I will walk.

Father stares, thinking, then nods.

--Rest. We will go again tonight.

The girl Hania nods at him. Her gaze shifts to Aleksi and she sees from him the slightest nod in her direction. She had asked for Aleksi's promise and he had given it. He will remember. She then closes her eyes, turns her back on them to sleep.

The farmer's wife closes the curtain so that she has privacy.

Father sits down beside the farmer. Neither man speaks, instead smoking quietly, waiting for the day to pass.

*

Aleksi dozes off. In his dream he is surrounded by pure white snow. In his dream he sees the girl from his childhood. They play in the road, walk along the river, sing a song. Laugh. She runs. He chases. She turns. He sees the face of the Jewess Hania. She smiles at him. A shot from somewhere and she falls. Bright red against empty white snow. Spreading red. They killed my father simply because he was a Jew, he hears the dream Hania say. They have killed me too.

He wakes with a start.

The curtain to the alcove room is drawn but not tight. He hears the quiet voice of the farmers's wife within, humming a song. From the break in the curtain he sees the farmer's wife washing the hair of girl Hania, sitting in a chair by a bucket. Aleksi sees that she is naked. Aleksi sees her small breasts.

He stands, turns, walks quietly out of the farmhouse.

Outside Mikołaj chops some logs in the yard. The day is closing into evening. The younger brother stops when Aleksi appears.

--I fell asleep for a while too. Woke and felt like chopping.

Aleksi understands that feeling well. Something mechanical. Focused. Wood. Not death. Not walking. Not snow. Wood.

--Where is Father?

--Checking the fields. Walking boundaries. Listening. Making sure we are unknown.

Aleksi nods. Mikołaj carries on.

Aleksi wanders into the small barn. Dusk winter light cuts through darkness. The farmer sits on a small stool milking a single cow. He looks up when Aleksi enters.

--They have let us keep her so far. We have to give them milk when they come here but they have not taken her. We have a bull up in the field backwards. This one gives us a calf in the spring. They will likely take the calf. They are happy enough to see us starve.

--At least you have the cow to milk, says Aleksi.

--For now. We don't need much, my wife, me. We get by.

--Yes.

--What you do, your Father...He is a good man. You are his sons. May you go with God, always.

Aleksi nods.

--A good man, yes, he says.

Aleksi looks around the barn: a bit of hay, some old tools. He runs his hand over a rusting plow in a corner.

--Had a donkey to harness to it. Ate him first year of the war. Hardest days. Neighbors was hungry too. We helped that way. Now have to plant by hand. Harder.

Aleksi sees two scythes hanging from a beam. He runs his fingers over the blade.

--Keep 'em sharp. Rub with fat, sharpen once a week. Won't let you down.

--My father says the same.

--Your father knows what he is about, boy. Like I said, a good man.

Aleksi wanders. Looks at the tools. Behind a bale of hay a piece of dark wood sticks out, catching his eye. He reaches down and withdraws an old slightly battered fiddle, of all things. He holds it in his hands. Not large, only one string, the wood of its back broken by a crack with a piece of wood missing.

The farmer walks over to him, looks at the fiddle.

--You play?

Aleksi shakes his head.

--Was a young 'un that left that by mistake. Simple girl. Another farmer I know from a ways south asked us to look after her for a week. The Germans were doing searches of his area, did not want the young 'un to be found. Simple girl, like I says. Came here with nothing but a few rags, and that thing; seemed to mean a lot to her. Can't say why.

--But she left it here?

--Hoping she might come back one day. Never know. The farmer I know came to fetch her, said he had people further west would look after her. Them people had lost a daughter apparently. Needed help. She could take over their own's identity papers. Way to keep her safe.

--Perhaps she will come back here then.

--One day, yes, maybe. Might remember. Memories what we will be left with I guess. Maybe it will be enough. Maybe it won't. Maybe it will be safe. One day. Maybe.

Aleksi places the broken fiddle back on the shelves nearly hidden by the bale of hay. A memory he thinks. Just a memory.

Maybe she will return. One day. One future day.

*

They walk again through the night. Clear night and they have to take care. They find a woods where an old makeshift hut had been abandoned some time before. They tell the girl to rest within the leaning logs that form a collapsing roof. They can tell she struggles still.

They wait through the following day, and once again, come the night, they walk. A storm has settled in once more. They work their way south, heading in the direction of the Slovakian border still some days away. They come along a path over a field; in the darkness and falling snow suddenly they hear voices just beyond a hill, German voices.

Father signals sharply: lie down in the grass, keep your bodies flat, your heads flat, do not move. Breathe quiet as you can.

The voices become louder. Aleksi feels fear in the pit of his stomach. But the voices stop. Some laughter. A match lighting. The smell of cigarette smoke, they are that close. More words.

Then walking away. Receding into snow and shadow.

Safe this time. Aleksi does not know if they will always be so safe. Aleksi is afraid to be afraid. But he is afraid.

They lie there for an hour, another. Yet another. Until Father decides they must get up, must hurry towards some woods to the east. Once there they see no boot marks, no evidence of soldiers or people or animals.

They walk despite the light of day above them.

Aleksi sees the girl struggle. He knows her fever is worse. They all know her fever is worse. She stumbles twice but refuses to fall. Refuses to stop. She will not stop. She will never stop.

Father and Mikołaj in front. Aleksi watching her. Feeling her pain as his own. Feeling for her. Feeling too his own pain. Keep moving. She stumbles again and he grabs her arm.

--I am all right, she insists.

He can only nod.

--You will remember. My name. You will remember?

--Yes.

She nods, marches slowly and with pain, on before him.

*

Mikołaj has been gone for hours.

Father had told him to go, to find the woman, to be careful of the landscape, of the place. Mikołaj had known her once, the woman. He had played with the daughter at the market, the daughter who had told him secrets when they were much younger. About her own father. About her fear. The mother had always been kind to Mikołaj despite seeming a hard woman to others.

Father told Mikołaj to go. Best he do so. Besides, Father wants Aleksi to keep a close eye on the Jewess. He knows the girl trusts the older son. If anyone will keep her alive it will be Aleksi, Father thinks. And he thinks too she may not live. Will to live, but the fever burns, and the will sometimes cannot defeat death.

To have come so far; not yet. Not yet.

So Aleksi must look after her. Trying to keep her warm against the freezing snow. Trying to keep her alive.

But now Mikołaj has been gone for several hours and Aleksi knows Father is worried. They wait at the edge of the woods, just at the edge of a farming valley with a town they can see in the distance. Mikołaj had hurried on before the sun rose, intending to skirt the town and continue on. With possibly more people about later the route would be more dangerous. Father had hoped that his young age might help render his youngest largely invisible to any who might notice him; a farming boy out for morning chores. Yet he had not returned and Father is concerned. Twice he has left the shelter of the trees to walk a road up to the top of hill, hoping to see his returning son, or to see if any locals might be out. The snows keep most people inside, but farmers have to work. And farmers have eyes.

On both occasions Father sees no one, returning to the trees to smoke, to sit, to wait. Saying nothing.

Then Mikołaj is there. He had taken a different route; there were soldiers on the road so he kept to fields. He had made it to the woman's farm.

--I spoke to her. She agreed.

--Did you see anyone on the journey?

The boy shakes his head.

--She says we will be safe, but to travel with care. She says she will expect us.

Father, clearly relieved, considers. He looks at the Jewess. He knows her fever has risen. He looks at his sons, strong despite the fears. He makes a decision: they will travel over fields for the first hour or two, but travel with the sun now low. He says they are behind schedule as it is. They need to move quickly and risk the light. They need to go.

For the next three hours they walk, travelling in silence. They keep to fields, always alert to any sound, particularly to any vehicles along back roads. They hear only crows and far away a farm dog barking. They circumvent another small village, see smoke rising from chimneys, but not a soul is seen. Luck is clearly on their side. This time.

The land begins to rise from fields into woodland. Aleksi knows it will continue to do so all the way to Slovakia. The hills, then low mountains, will protect them, as much as they could hope for protection. Eventually they come to some small open fields with woods along the edges. Father has them walk along the edge of the fields. They can see a small farmhouse below, which they ignore. Just after entering the trees above, passing the sliver of a hill stream, they come to a large, partly collapsed barn that will serve as shelter from a coming storm.

--We will stay here now.

Aleksi knows where they are. He says nothing. He points to a dry corner in the back of the structure, finds some hay and scatters it.

--Sleep here, he tells the girl Hania. We'll keep an eye out. You need to sleep.

She does not argue. She looks at him, nods. She is so tired. Her fever is up. She does not know how she has made it this far. All she can think of is sleep. She is not afraid. She longs for sleep. It finds her, without joy, without peace, only with empty silence.

Aleksi watches over her for the hours her eyes are closed.

He wants her to live.

He wants that the girl of his youth, childish love, should live. He remembers now. They said she was ill. They said she needed doctors. She went away. She will have grown, just as he had grown. Where is she? May she be alive. May she survive. May she live. May he see her again.

He thinks of his mother. He will not see her again.

But memory matters. He takes his memory with him. He holds onto memory. And remembers.

Father disappears to the farm below. He is gone for some time. When he returns he carries some warm broth, some dried food they can carry with them. They are not far from Slovakia. From the meeting.

--She agrees. It is best, he says.

Aleksi knows Father is right.

It is not easy. It is necessary. It saddens him. It is necessary.

He will take memory with him, knowing he belongs with Father, with Mikołaj. This is what they can do. What they have to do. But he will take memory with him and hope to return when this ends. It will end, some day.

When the girl awakens, the three men already have their satchels on their back.

The girl starts to put her own bag together but Father stops her.

--You are staying here.

--No. I can walk. I will not hold you back.

--We have decided. A woman owns the farm below. She knows you are here. Her barn. She has helped us before. We are not far from the Slovak border but the German patrols have increased. It is not safe for you. The woman will bring you food, another blanket. It would not be safe in the house with her but she says you should be safe here. You can trust her. We will return from Slovakia and will come for you. Yes?

She looks at Father, at his sons. She nods. She has no other choice. Father and Mikołaj turn and start out. Aleksi hesitates, staring at the girl. Her eyes meet his.

--Boy, she says. Thank you.

--I remember, he says. I will always remember. You will be safe.

And then after the shortest pause that lasts forever:

--Hania Stern, he says.

He half smiles, turns and walks out. She watches them go. Then lies down on the hay, and closes her eyes.

*

After a day and a half of climbing higher into the mountains, always keeping an eye out for German patrols, Father, Mikołaj and Aleksi cross the border into Slovakia.

The cold, and yet another storm bites. Life bites. Aleksi wonders if he will ever escape the cold. He wonders if it will always be with them. He dreams of warmth, real warmth, one day. But just now they have to do what they must.

He thinks of the Jewess. He will carry the memory with him as he promised. He thinks when they see her again she will be healthy. He thinks when they see her again they will find safety for her, real safety. And for others. And for themselves. This is what he can do.

They travel through the night, following the border fence for a while, then heading further south. The moon disappears behind clouds. They feel safer when it does. It has been clear up until then. But they have seen no one, heard nothing out of the ordinary.

Now they walk at pace, heading southeast. They have papers to collect, perhaps some radio parts, even a few guns. They will take them north again, towards Warsaw. The papers, the parts, the guns that they can carry are needed there. This is what they can do.

They walk in silence through the night. Aleksi knows that at the end of this walk there will be coffee and some hot food waiting for them. A short rest. They have been on this route before. Soon this journey will be at its end. Soon there will be another. But first each of them looks forward to a day or two of warmth, just as if they are home. It is a long time since they are home. It will be a long time before they can return there, Aleksi knows. But one day. A journey has a beginning and an end. This journey. All the journeys. And they can go home.

First they will return to the girl they left in the barn. They promised.

The memory.

And help the girl from the Ghetto to be safe. The girl from the Ghetto. Her name, Hania Stern. The memory. And funny but the name of the girl from his boyhood finally comes to him. Lera. He had not forgotten. Not really. Locked away. The memory. The name. He carries them both within.

He will not forget. No. He will not.

A long journey. A very long journey ahead.

No. He will not forget.

What Aleksi does not know, however, what Father and Mikołaj also do not know, because they could not know, they would never know, is that beyond, whilst on this journey, they have in fact been betrayed

And that soon they too, like so many countless others before and after will lie without life, fallen into the snow.

They will not again feel that warmth that now they seek as they walk through the woods, and over fields.

Very soon, they will no longer feel anything.

But even so, somehow the memory will remain. And the memory will be carried in a heart in those who came before.

And those who would come after.

II

*"They wandered into a couple buildings. Nothing but mildew,
a few broken chairs. An old wooden chest of some sort that
had once been papered over with blue or green flowered paper.
A few people had written their initials on it, memories of tourist
visits without memory. If there were ghosts, the ghosts were
silent."*

--A Requiem For Hania

1. Jenny

Ostrów Mazowiecka / Masovian Voivodeship (Northeastern Poland) June 2019

Jenny knows she is looking for something here. She simply does not know what it might be. Ghosts perhaps? Plenty of ghosts. Her mother? A lover? Something. Someone. Some…thing.

She lies on the bed, staring at the blank ceiling. She has come to know every inch of it. All faded white, slight markings of a bad paint job. A hint of a brush stroke. A scratch. A speck of dust. A small insect, indistinct. A void, infinite. A screen running a never ending movie. She stares nightly, looking for something, the film running over and over and never finding its third act completion. Her life.

It is June, 2019. Her mother dead almost five years to the day. Suicide. You do not put suicide into this film. So instead empty frame signifying: loss.

Run the reel backwards. A story in requisite acts. A story needs structure. These images, this moving picture, running through her head tonight, every night, needs structure. So begin again.

I am Jenny Unger. I reside in the town of Ostrów Mazowiecka. Well I do for the moment. It is not my home. I have made it such but I have nothing here but these walls, this ceiling, this film.

Okay, so I reside in Greater Manchester, England. No, I don't. No longer. I did once. While my mother lived. My father: I did not know him. But my mother lived. And then my mother died. And I discovered it was no longer my home. It had not been so for a long time. Greater Manchester. I did not know it. When she was hanging her body swayed, just slightly, ever so slightly as I found her, and I could not find a knife to cut her down. Could not bring myself to cut her down.

Not Greater Manchester. Not…

No, no, no. The wrong image to begin a film, surely. You need a beginning. That seems a beginning, but it isn't.

Nathalie is the beginning. Professor Natalie Spencer-Wright. She was the opening gambit. Professor and to your surprise, both your surprises, a once upon a time lover. Nathalie.

So then, this is how it begins.

I am a student. I have been for a number of years. I have two loves. No, three. I love history. I love archaeology. But not archaeology of far off places, temples rising above the Mediterranean set against magnificent sunsets. Not something...distant. Rather something I need to touch. To feel. Knife to flesh; the knowledge of blood. Need it, perhaps. So something that still talks to me. Needs me, perhaps, somehow. Archaeology like an invited stranger, toying, placing its stone imagined historical fingers on my breast, my thigh, making me laugh, making me moan.

And the third love, which is the love of form, made. My hands, made. Something I can touch and by touch I can feel. The body. The place. The sheer eroticism of form become art. I am not an artist but I need to create in the present something that is the past. How is that possible? How can I describe what it is I am trying to touch?

I do not know how. And then I meet Nathalie. Professor Nathalie Spencer-Wright, who stares at me with a sidelong glance taking everything in and whispers one night over a talk where I do the talking and she does the listening, over a glass of decent whiskey (Irish I say almost as an apology, and young as I am, I mutter it has to be Irish. I need the burn, not the inhalation of smokey scotch, but something that burns the senses and speaks of pain and a past not mine but somehow always mine) I say this is who I am.

She puts her hand on top of mine and says I know you, I will know you, and I will allow you the freedom to find what it is, this that you seek.

And she does.

Thus that is the beginning. The opening moral imperative. It needs to be. I need to be. It is erotic. It is shocking. It is a moment, then past.

Like history, archaeology speaks of the past. Or perhaps speaks of the present. Volumes about who we are now by understanding who we were. And what we did. We all did. Uncover the past from the present. Dig, just slightly, dig to seek knowledge. To understand: something. Dig. Nathalie taught me to dig—deeper. I could have stayed. But I was not meant to stay. Not because she is a woman, but because I needed to find something else. Myself. We were lovers. I had had other lovers, only men. But that was not the reason. Nathalie knew that. She knew she needed to give me space, to breathe, to seek. She knew.

Perhaps it is the way with my professors. My mentors. My need is apparent, but my need to move forward also grows. Nathalie. Now Brian. I inhale as much wisdom, as much knowledge, as I can from them, but it is not enough. It is never enough.

Nathalie said: you need to find a way.

Nathalie said: you need a path that makes demands yet remains forgiving.

Nathalie said: you are torn between your interest in history, in archaeology and your love of art. You think they are not compatible. They are compatible.

Nathalie said: follow me, my work, my lectures. You will discover you can take many lovers at once, man and woman, art and archaeology, history, the past discovering voices for the future, the future discovering voices from the past.

So I followed. I listened. I learned. I searched for a way forward, a statement of self, a direction. And I thought perhaps I might have found what I wanted. Just might have found who I needed to be. No longer lovers but bonded together by my need and her desire to open doors. I thought. I took exams. I listened to lectures. I explored theories. I had ideas and dreams and plans and an intended calling. I created images. I created myself.

And then I disappeared. I was, no longer. I needed. I needed to disappear.

I came home one night. I thought it was time to return. I had been keeping a distance but I felt a need to talk. To explain. This is me, Mother. This is who I am. So I came home. One night. I came home. I took the train from Manchester Victoria towards Wigan. I got off at Hindley and jumped on the bus. I sat for the requisite eight minutes, thinking of Nathalie, thinking of what lay below the earth, what sat above in the heavens. I casually descended the bus at the stop I knew so well, knew as a child, as a shy, gawky teenager, as a young woman with dreams but unsure where they might lead, as myself, I descended the steps, walked down a back road, past one rural house, another, to a house I knew well, a house that spoke to me past and present, I opened the gate, up the path, up the way, pulled out my key, set it firmly in the lock, not locked but latched, turned it just slightly, opened the door in front of me, closed the door behind me, put down my knapsack, picked up the post by habit, dropped the post again by habit, walked into the kitchen, opened the refrigerator and took out a bottle of already uncorked white wine, poured myself a glass, left the bottle on the counter, carried the glass to the back, no one around, opened the back door to go out to the old barn I had once used as a studio when I had dreams of creating, of painting and sculpture, dreams of imagination, three dimensional, imaginings you could touch, no one around still, opened that barn cum studio door still holding the glass of chilled white wine, walked in, left the door ajar, walked out of the night into the silence of light and shadow dominating closed-in space, chiaroscuro, past the interior door hiding the small toilet, down the short corridor of the studio once upon a time barn, into the large room, into the room, the room, into the…

And dropped the glass of chilled white wine onto the hard concrete floor.

And heard the glass shatter on the hard concrete floor.

And felt spilled wine drip at my ankles, the thin shards of glass at me feet, my toes, my world, on the hard concrete floor. Spots of blood. Cut.

Cut.

And stared. And maybe screamed, just a little. Or no, maybe just said no, no, no, no. Then fell silent. Looking for words that might emerge from the wordless. No words came.

I could not move, standing there, wine and fragments of glass on my shoes, could not move, staring at the straight motionless back, or maybe hunched slightly, lower vertebrae, shoulders, head hanging head taut, hanging body, silent hanging, hanged, mother, swaying ever so slightly with the movement of air, and the fallen chair, and the rope, and the hair hanging down her long back, and the wet stain along her trouser leg, and the slightest motion caused by so little weight these days weight hanging from rope from ceiling hook from white ceiling from movement of air and I do not know where I am I do not know what to do I do not know who I am I do not know—anything. More.

*

I find that sometimes the perception of the world that is your own, your sight, your words, your tears, knows nothing of the Other. Knows nothing at all. Sees nothing at all but is blind behind your own gaze.

*

I did not finish the degree. I walked away. I became a ghost. I simply was not. I went north. I went east. I went south. I went west. I did not know where I went. I simply moved. Perpetual motion.

I drank. I fucked. I snorted coke and fucked some more. I no longer cared. Mindless. Feeling nothing. I did not remember. Memory did not matter. I disappeared from everyone. But I could not disappear from myself, much as I might try.

And then one day I was back where I started, sitting at the bar of an anonymous pub in Hindley near the b&b because I could not return there, not to that house, not there. Sitting with empty thoughts. Seeing nothing. Seeing no one behind me, beside me. Hardly noticing, hardly hearing or seeing, just sitting, when a hand beside reached over and rested on top of mine. And I looked. And Nathalie said nothing to me, just stared. Then said to the young man behind the bar two Irish please. No ice. Two please.

Let it burn.

After a while she said I looked for you. I put up pictures. Someone rang. I looked for you.

I said nothing.

And she said: I know. I'm sorry. Sorry that it's you. I know.

And that was enough.

I started to cry. We drank, left, walked, said nothing. She let me cry in silence.

In that way I slowly began to reenter the world. I slowly began to reappear. I told her I could not return to the course. I did not want the degree. I could not go back. I needed to go forward. I needed to escape.

She said she understood completely. She said she could not help the inside. That it was a journey I would have to make alone. But she had a suggestion, a possibility. You are very good at what you do, she said. You need to find what you seek, she said. I want you to meet someone. I will talk to him. I think this might work for you, for what you are good at, for what you need. I will talk to Brian.

I did not want a shrink, I said. I did not want grief counselling.

No, she said. Not grief. And not lying on a sofa making up words and thoughts as you go along. He is an historian, an architectural historian. He has a project. I think he can use you. I think you might need him.

And that is how I met Brian.

*

He was a bit mad, perhaps. A bit of a genius, perhaps. He became a lover for the shortest of times. That was an accident. It happened and it was over.

Brian was in charge of a project in northeastern Poland. He was exploring the archaeology of a satellite work and execution camp that had disappeared after 1943. He and various teams under him had done so for the previous six years. A work camp at one side. A death camp nearby. Now it had reappeared. He had been utilizing methods of archaeology and architecture that allowed for non-invasive exploration, unless religious authorities agreed that digging was allowed. Was necessary. Not exhuming the dead. Allow the dead to lie in peace. But the stones. The architecture that archaeology would uncover. The space. The remains that last forever. Brick. Mortar. The secret truths the earth holds at her breast, feeding, nourishing, mothering, protecting. Mother. Birth. For the living still. To see. To know. To remember. His non-invasive technological approach was preferable to authorities, both religious and political. It was preferable in his academic work. It was preferable to the ghosts. Some digging, yes, but little. Rather mapping, explaining, imagining. The nightmare of dreaming and creating the past from the air, to the air.

He found stories.

For this he also needed assistants. Workers. His teams rotated yearly, joining him by need, availability, desire. He had mostly assembled a new team for the coming season. After years of research, surveys, GPS investigation, working with Ground Penetrating Radar, he had mapped out areas of likely foundations of buildings. The Site. The deceptive facades that lied to populations. The chamber called shower house, where no water ever entered. Where no cries ever escaped. The hopeless echoes of a dark world.

He could use one more. Perhaps I would be interested; given Nathalie's words about me, he thought there might be a fit. He would train me with others to use the equipment he used. Laser scanning. LIDAR data from light detection and ranging instruments. Creating digital interfaces. Witness statements and historical documentation to research and understand. To listen to their words, to feel their tears. Total stations and GPS units. Basic trowels and brushes. Kneepads. Kneepads always help. Some of these I knew. Others I did not. He said the work was not physically difficult, or not too much so. Mental anguish was another matter. He said he knew some of what I had recently seen, experienced. He said the digging would either destroy me, or give me meaning. Or both.

I said I was not an architect. Not an archaeologist. Not an historian.

I know, he said. But Nathalie told me you feel the processes within, through your fingertips, in your heart. She said you were right for this. And she said you have art in your blood, lying just next to architecture and archaeological curiosity. That you have a need to imagine. So therefore I can perhaps use you. To imagine. And in the imagining, the seeing.

He asked me to think about it.

I said I did not need to think about it.

I said yes.

*

It was not the beginning.

It was not the ending. The direction of travel from then to now. From within, to without.

It was but another step. I, Jenny chose to take it, one step at a time, hoping the direction was right, hoping that it moved me forward, moved her forward. But Jenny, now Jenny, was not sure she was ready to move forward. She knew only she was ready to move.

Then.

And now.

*

And so Jenny lies on the bed in her small rented apartment in Ostrów Mazowiecka. The town is near enough to the Site. She can drive there daily in the small Fiat she had driven to Poland from Manchester, arriving after one engine breakdown and a struggle to find decent vegetarian food in rural Germany. She spent a month in Warsaw, now almost ten months ago, commuting daily with Brian or others. She learned some Polish. She learned some German. She slept with Brian, Brian who almost accidently became her lover. Then was not. Brian who was sometimes a genius and sometimes a monster. Who knew his way around her body. His way around her need. And then did not. Brian: always a mentor.

She soon realized that she could not stay in Warsaw. After she started spending time at the Site, spending time talking to ghosts, she knew she needed to be close to it. To them. After a month in Warsaw, she rented the apartment in the small town of Ostrów Mazowiecka, to be near to it, to them, near to where they waited for her. This apartment, womb like, nurturing her real needs. She needed. And at night, if she did not read, if she did not research artefacts and background information she might access online, if she did not study languages and words that were not her own, she lay in silence on the bed, staring at that blank ceiling and the bad paint job, even as they sat beside her. Staring at that void, infinite as it was, asking questions of her as she asked questions of it. Seeking the infinite that she discovered there. Seeing them from so long ago. The men. The women. The children. The child. Seeing too Mother hanging. She had hoped she might escape once away, but she did not. Could not.

Over weeks she worked with the small team that Brian had gathered. He had not asked her to return with him at night, and she did not do so. But on weekdays she listened to his direction, his instruction, his musings. She carried out his wishes. Contributed somewhat to his suggestions and hypotheses. Spent further hours reading documents and witness statements that she would research at the library or online, at his request, or sometimes because of her own curious search.

She spoke to Brian, to the six others of the team, only once about the ghosts. They neither dismissed her words, nor embraced them. Rather one or another often looked away, nodded, said 'I know' or 'that will pass' or 'may they be at peace' or 'I can feel it too but not hear it, Jenny, not hear them. It will get easier.'

It did not get easier. But she no longer told them.

The permission to dig was finally granted. The strategies for the work examined, evaluated, reevaluated. As much research as they could do had been done. Years of planning by Brian and various teams over so many seasons.

The initial ground breaking for three small dig locales felt to Jenny like an assault. Like rape. She had to walk away to vomit. No one saw her.

Slowly methodically, they worked away the earth. The earth that bore witness. At first Brian insisted that they be minimally invasive to confirm what the previous non-invasive work had bequeathed them. Three small pits, a meter wide, a meter long. It soon became apparent that they had indeed reached foundations of what clearly had been a chamber of death. A confirmation of place. There was no joy in the confirmation; simply an acknowledgement.

So then a decision to commence the larger dig. A chamber for gas execution of the thousands. Tens and tens of thousands. The strategy triggered their secondary approach for a larger excavation. Five meters by four meters. Layers of the earth stripped away, carefully, painfully, slowly. Brick appeared below. Foundations as expected appeared below. Tiles from a wash room, a room that gave no wash, stamped with the imprint of a star, a six pointed star, there perhaps to welcome those whose light would soon be extinguished. Bits of metal. Bits of mortar fallen away.

Bits of death.

A timeline in layers. A timeline leading to the beginning where once, built up, brick by brick, tile by tile, led to an ending.

The Germans thought they had dismantled and burned everything back in 1943. They were wrong. Look closely, look close enough, the earth kept its secrets. And whispers. And memories.

It took several weeks for the foundations to reveal themselves. After each day the whispering grew louder to Jenny. Cacophony of anguish. Sometimes she would stay later than the others, to sit, to listen, to hear. Sometimes she left early to go lie on her bed in her room in her small apartment in the town of Ostrów Mazowiecka in the east of Poland in a world of madness, staring at the white ceiling, forgetting to eat, not wanting to eat, just lying there perhaps watching the ceiling fan go around and around and around, or watching nothing at all.

She started a letter to her mother.

Dear Mother…

She did not know what else to say. She did not find any other words.

Dear Mother, she thought; I saw you hanging. That still hurts.

She wanted to write this but could not. She stared only at the two words she was able to write: Dear Mother…Then nothing further.

She took out a lighter from her bag and burned the piece of paper. She recognized the irony, watching it become smoke, become ash, become nothing. Emptiness. Existence extinguished in flame. Like for like. Gift for gift. Burnt offering.

Over more weeks, carefully removing earth, brush away time and dust with small brushes, every spec inspected, then the outline of a building. Brick on brick. Scorched remnants of a building the occupiers had wanted to disappear. Fire burns much but cannot burn all. Dig deep enough you find. Supporting wall here. Semblance of steps here. Chamber foundations here. Changing space likely here. Outlines. Ghosts. Imaginings. Pictures in the air.

One thing intrigued Jenny; she could not say why. Buried in the internal edge after the foundations of the first chamber, a cut length of wood, scarred and charred, blackened with time and age and a fire that had hoped to obfuscate memory, to obliterate history. Petrified by its age and significance. After spending days brushing away soil and the dust of time, Brian decided it should be block lifted from the bottom of the site as the wood had become too fragile to lift, particularly as it was embedded in sediment. Jenny helped the team cut into the earth in a border around the two meter or so length of wood, somewhat worm eaten, relatively hard still despite the age. Preserved despite the attempt to hide any preservation. They worked their way beneath the length and eventually cut it from the borders and from below, finally lifting it from the dig floor.

Jenny stared at it as Brian confirmed measurements. She looked at its rough surface on top, its smooth surface underneath as the soil was brushed away. She ran her gloved fingertips over the wood, taking in its texture, its edges, its slight defects on one side, its worn edges at the end.

--Interesting. I think it may have been the sill of an entry way. That side edge might have faced upwards. See how worn it is in the middle but rougher at the sides. The traces of mortar there, and there at the end. Perhaps this was the sill at the entryway to the changing room. Or given its location, the shower room itself. We'll take measurements. The shower room would have needed to be sealed, of course. But they may have laid concrete on either side of it with this wood a threshold piece at the center of a doorway. See there, mortar in the grains of the wood. We'll carbon date it, chemical test it, see what story it has to tell. Research anything we can find on the door seals. It will be a nice piece for display perhaps if we keep it like this.

Brian walked away to look at some of the tiles they had found in the pit. But for reasons she could not understand Jenny could not take her eyes from this simple piece of wood that perhaps spoke volumes, yet remained silent. Again she ran her latex covered fingers over its worn grain, its smooth, worn underside. She needed to feel it, its textures, its life, its death. She needed to know it. Over and over. She stared at it from all angles, carefully enveloping each centimeter, each tear of hardened wood and caked earth and defect and tiny knot that stood out with her fingertips, her eyes, her breath. This simple piece of wood spoke to her, as if carefully running her hand over a lover's body, gently, feeling the pores, feeling the beating heart, feeling the life.

The last moments of a life. Of many lives lived, lost. Gone.

--Jenny? Jenny? Earth to Jenny.

She returned to the time and place. Looked up. Avi, one of the team, stared at her.

--You all right?

--Yes, I...Sorry, yes.

--Something for your mantel piece.

--What? Yes. No.

--Joking. If the earth could speak. A meaningless piece of wood that holds much meaning, I'll bet. A lot of memory.

--Yes.

--Don't get too lost in your head. Not good for you. We're taking a break. Want a coffee?

--No. I'm fine. Thanks.

He looked at her, smiled, and nodded. Left her alone. She sat there still, staring at the wood length, the threshold of so much disappeared. She looked away, towards the trees, hearing the whispers of ghosts. She felt her own body, diminished

98

somehow. She felt the breeze against her cheek. She felt nothing and everything at once. She felt confusion. She felt her mother's hand taking hers as when she was a little girl. She felt immense loneliness. And immense need. And at once both warm and cold.

Jenny stood up from the edge of the dig. She turned away from the edge of the excavation after a final glance at this silent piece of deadwood livewood. She looked over to the far side of the Site, where the others had gathered at the tented work station to drink coffee and eat sandwiches. She saw Brian staring back towards her, expressionless, watching. She did not feel she could join them, not now, not at this moment. Instead she walked away, towards the tree line and the coolness of the woods surrounding the Site.

She walked amongst the trees. She looked at a ravine, at some undulations in the forest floor. She could see what had happened here, once. They would inspect this area in coming days. Survey it. Use imaging. But she already knew, just as they all supposed. They would not dig here. They would never dig here. Too many whispers. She kept moving, deeper amongst the trees, until she found a fallen tree surrounded in a grove. Here she sat. Here, alone, she listened to the breeze speaking to her. Here she acknowledged those voices that said, simply, remember, remember me, know that I was here, that I lived and died, know me.

And Jenny acknowledged them. And Jenny nodded and thought, I hear you, I do, I know. And Jenny turned her gaze away, taking in all in her glance, and nothing in her glance, with the ravine now behind her sheltered by trees. And Jenny sat with her forearms wrapped around her knees, sitting on this fallen tree. And her body shook, just slightly, shivers of the living.

And Jenny wept.

*

That night as she lay in bed, staring at the white ceiling, watching the film of her past and her present and perhaps her future, as she lay there sweating not from heat but from life itself, her life, as she lay there motionless, in silence, seeing the images before her eyes, she saw another. And she knew. And she felt it; and she knew.

*

Ten days later. A Saturday night. Late. Jenny still nibbling on some takeaway pizza, staring at the computer screen. Her eyes weary, heavy. Her body as well. This is her life. She no longer chooses to stare at the past tense; instead she breathes in the present. This moment. The computer screen, here. She closes her eyes, opens them. Only here.

Her phone rings and she checks the caller i.d.

--Hi, Brian. It's late.

--I know.

--It's Saturday night.

--I know that too.

--What's up?

--I want you to come to Warsaw tomorrow. Meet me at the lab. The doors will be open. Two.

--Brian, it's...

He hangs up. Brian.

The laboratory is a space set up at the University of Warsaw, arranged by the Polish Center for Holocaust Studies that in part supports his project. The doors are open as promised. Brian sits on a stool at a workstation staring at a computer when she comes in. He does not look up when she approaches.

--Uh...nice to see you too, she says finally.

--Just a minute...I need to finish reading this.

She finds a stool of her own. She sees he is reading text. She does not read over his shoulder. She looks around the room. Textbooks, some artefacts from the Site, tagged, bagged. Three dimensional Site models. Photographs. Various architectural plans from different parts of the examinations and some excavations. Electrical imaging survey results both in black and white and colour taped to the walls. Various graphs and penetrating radar survey imaging. After so many months all these are ingrained in Jenny's memory and imagination and experience. More than simply the layout, she knows the place. The Site. It has taken over her life. It has taken over all their lives.

In the middle of the room is a long table with various boxes of removed artefacts, all bagged. On some coloured cards a few items wait to be photographed: an old key, the sole of shoe, a cooking pot, a bent frame of a pair of glasses, a hair clip. A number of brick and roof tiles, broken, meaningless and full of meaning. Jenny walks over to the table, staring at the items sitting in their plastic bags or on the photograph cards. In a box she notices a familiar partly decayed lipstick holder, bagged and tagged. Jenny puts on a pair of white cotton protective gloves resting on the table. She picks up the bag, removes the decayed tube, stares at it. Her glance travels backwards by months, by decades.

--You found that.

Brian is staring at her now from his stool.

--Yes.

--Months ago.

--I know.

He simply nods as she puts it down.

--It's Sunday, Brian.

--Yes, I remember.

--Why did you want me to come to Warsaw?

--Maybe I wanted to sleep with you.

--Did you?

--Come to think of it, yes.

--And if I say no?

--Then you say no. But that's not why I wanted you to come down here. Come.

He walks around some shelving units to another small table covered in lights. Jenny puts the tube back, follows. On the table are six or seven of the chipped or broken ceramic tiles, browned yellow, orange, each with the faint imprint of a six pointed start. A Mogen David—star of Jews. They had found a number over the last weeks as they excavated to the foundations of the building. The one time chamber.

--Now these: these are interesting.

--I saw them. Mogen David tiles.

--No. I thought that too, but that's not exactly what they are. See, we assumed they were tiles in the gas room, the dressing room too. Six pointed Stars of David. I wondered: why there? What does it really mean? Make your thousands of guests think they were indeed coming for a shower? Checking in but not checking out. Put them at their ease. Then…then.

101

--There was always deception. Everything was meant to deceive the victims.

--Yes. Largely true. But I've been looking into these. In fact that's not what these are about. Or not exactly. These aren't intended as Stars of David. Believe it or not, it was a logo used by a tile ceramics factory in Opoczno. You can almost make out their name there on that one, although it's pretty worn down. Dziewulski and Lange. This just happened to be their insignia.

--Ironic.

--Yes. Ironic. But: read between the lines.

--Go on.

--Some of the few witnesses who survived have said the gas chambers were modelled on bath houses to give the impression that it was the true purpose. That they really were entering a shower room. There is testimony about red clay, orange or yellow tiles and these match perfectly.

--The illusion of a bath house.

--The illusion of it. But what's also interesting about them is to try to discover whether they were manufactured as new and sent to the Site of all places, or whether they were taken from somewhere else.

--Meaning?

--Warsaw, mainly. There were a lot of Jewish ritual bath houses here in Warsaw, in Lublin too, here in the north. Destroyed, but we know there were many in the Ghetto.

--So they may have been removed and used in the construction of a gas chamber.

--A death chamber with all its illusions. The ultimate deception. Taken from the Jews for the Jews. Yes. I want to research it a lot more, but…well, we'll see.

--A footnote of history.

--Not a footnote. A statement. A warning. Even…a truth. Proof of life but here, proof of life extinguished.

Jenny picks up one of the tiles, holds it carefully with her white gloved hands, runs her fingers over it, touching the imprint. Star of David that became a star of death.

Brian walks to another side of the laboratory. She puts the tile down, goes to join him. On a table at the far side, covered, Brian having removed some plastic sheeting that had protected it, is the decaying, worn wood length, the likely sill they had extracted from the floor of the excavation site.

--You were drawn to this. I watched you.

--A piece of wood.

--No. It isn't. We both know that. You could barely drag yourself away from it. Why is that?

She hesitates, trying to find the words that might explain. She does not think she can find them; his curiosity may be little more than that. And it is not something she feels she can share.

--I don't know, it just... I don't know.

--Don't you?...

Brian turns away, leaves her standing at the table. Still with her white cotton gloved hands, she runs her finger tips over the wooden sill, if indeed that is what it was. And that is what it is.

In her mind something born. An idea. Nurturing. Awaiting birth. Awaiting air and voice. A need. It has been created within her many days ago. Almost erotic. Almost human, the need. Now it is taking form. Even as it had done so probably to Brian.

She finds him back at his computer, staring at a screen of images, objects, artefacts. He says nothing for a long moment. Finally, nodding at the computer images:

--These were gathered at Auschwitz. Held now at the museum there. Some of them: beautiful is not a word I would use. Memories maybe. Memorials. Sometimes I've seen people tear up when they see them. Weep. Sometimes they walk by in silence. And sometimes, they shrug. Artefacts without history. History with artefacts. But history is the past. What we do in archaeology sometimes. Try to ignite the past into the present. I'm not sure one can.

--But we try.

--But we try. Each to our own journey. You've been looking for something since you came here to work with the team.

--Have I?

--Yes. We both know it. The team knows it. Looking for something and have not found it.

--That's not true.

--Yes it is, Jenny. You can try to lie to me, but you can't lie to yourself.

--I thought I was helping. You think I should go?

--No. Not at all. That's not the point of asking you to meet me here.

She waits. Still he does not look at her, but she can see his eyes narrow, just slightly, his mind moving forward in space and time. Finally, he exits from the computer screen image. Sits for another moment. Turns to her.

--Nathalie said your career was torn between the past and the present, to build in architecture or dig on a site, or create. She said you are an artist without art. Did you know that?

--No.

--Do you have a way to speak? A voice to speak to others? How would you do that?

Jenny stares at him for a long moment. She turns away, thinking, her mind working in quick motion. The images of her mind's eye, seen on the white ceiling in the small apartment in the town near the Site called Ostrów Mazowiecka, seen by a life put on hold a life in a film never shown flowing in her imagination, rush back. Voices of the past. Whispers. Tears. And her mother.

She sees and knows. The birth. The idea. The need.

She walks away, back to the table in a far corner where an anonymous piece of wood rests, waiting for her. Waiting.

Brian behind her.

--I still want to be a part of the team.

--I know. You will.

She hesitates. Does not look at him.

--It's not simple. I don't simply want to create images. Photographs do that. I don't want to recreate. I need to create. Do you understand?

--Yes. And?

--I'll want to make a cast of the sill. To start. I can protect the artefact but I want to make a three dimensional cast of it.

--I'll need to approve your methodology first. It will need thought, care. But in theory it can be done I think.

--I'll find a studio here. Space. Some others to help me. But I remain a part of your team.

--That's fine. I just said.

--Without the art of our lives to speak, there are no lives. No humanity left.

--No.

--Thank you.

He does not respond. After a moment he puts his hand against her cheek, gently. And looks at her. But says nothing.

*

She knows it will likely never repeat, not again, not after this time, this last time, but she needs to feel him enter her, needs to feel him inside of her. She needs his flesh on hers. She needs the urgency she feels inside. She needs the release to last forever. And if not forever, then for a night.

Flesh on flesh. Life.

For a night, a night only, a moment only, she desperately seeks the release that he provides. She needs to forget, and remember, neither and both, one moment and many. Still life.

And for a night even as she cries out, her Mother sleeps soundly.

She leaves before dawn. Brian does not wake when the door quietly shuts behind her.

*

The following weekend Jenny flies back to Manchester. She had always thought this journey would be difficult, raising feelings of fear, confused memories, but once she is in the air she feels only release and a purpose she has not felt in some time. Even when she arrives at the house in Hindley the fear that had for so long defined her life seems lessened, no longer dominating.

The next morning she ventures to the converted barn building behind the house. She takes a deep breath as she enters, the first time in many years. She had asked the post-doctoral tenant who had been living at the house until recently to leave everything in the studio alone; four years previous she had locked its door at the time, thinking she would never be back.

105

Now she is back.

The room where her Mother had taken her life is silent. The memory is not, not entirely. Jenny thinks back to her Mother, to the many mistakes she, Jenny, had made. To the mistakes too her Mother had made.

And for the first time Jenny recognizes that, although not reconciled to the past, perhaps never reconciled, neither can she any longer define her own future simply by those events. For the first time she understands the need to move forward.

She spends the day collecting supplies she wants to ship back to Poland: sketch pads, charcoal and coloured pens, her camera equipment that she had locked away so long ago, boxes of plaster and wire, textbooks, epoxy mold release tape, tools, rulers, tubes of paint and brushes. Anything she can think of that might be useful she carefully places in boxes, wrapping, protecting. The studio becomes a package, a gift to herself, a gift to define a need and a direction.

The following morning a shipping company services van arrives to take the numerous boxes of supplies away to be forwarded to Warsaw: they might once again create image and possibility with her hands, with her imagination. A side road taken along the journey.

Later she goes into a local estate agent. She leaves without the keys to the house. Her own direction will now take her elsewhere. As she emerges, she hesitates only slightly. Looks up. A small murmuration of starlings flies on the horizon, a sign to her of coordinated possibility. She thinks inside: it is right. It is what I have needed to do. Hope is an incorrect word. Hopeless an incorrect emotion. Now.

That night she has dinner with Nathalie. They have not seen one another in over a year. Nathalie listens quietly as Jenny tries to explain, not always succinctly, the feelings generated within over these months. The sense of loss welled up, breaking out. The lack of meaning. And now the possibility of meaning. She listens as Jenny speaks of voices and ghosts, of bricks and tiles, of whispering foundations, of archaeology that lives within her, of architecture that took lives, and has given back one life. Of images. Of creating. Of meaning. Nathalie understands and supports.

Then they talk of little things. Insignificances. Signifiers and signified, the semiotics of signs and language The signs are there.

Finally, as it grows late, after quiet smiles of memory over a final shot of Irish, no ice, for old times' sake, as they must each move in separate directions, at separate velocities, Nathalie puts her hand on Jenny's, just as she had in the past, as she had as lover. As mentor. Finally as one who saved and forced back life that had appeared extinguished.

--It's a journey, she tells Jenny. You'll find a way. It won't be easy but it's good. What you'll create, ultimately, it matters, it will give some light, but it's only part of it. Remember that. You'll find something but the finality of what you'll manage to create with your hands, your heart, that won't be it. Remember that always.

Jenny nods. Nathalie smiles, removes her hand. They take the last swallow of Irish. Let it burn. The burning needed.

--It's time.

--I'll get the bill, answers Jenny.

--No. That's not what I meant.

Jenny looks at her, smiles slightly, understanding then, a bit of pain there, a bit of knowing. A bit of moving.

It is time.

*

Jenny stores her art supplies in a closet room at the university laboratory. She spends weekends there, weekdays at the Site. The constant trips into Warsaw after the week's work tires her, a tiredness she embraces. Often she works alone at the laboratory, photographing the length of wood from every angle she can, running her gloved fingers over its surface, burning into memory and thought every tiny knot, every millimeter of grain and texture, the ends, the surfaces. She draws when she can. She researches to understand, to find what it is she seeks to do.

And yet she is not comfortable. Not yet at a place within where the work without can settle and truly begin. In this Nathalie again comes to her rescue, with a short text message: a name, a number of a Polish student once at the university but back in Warsaw for some time now. Nathalie tells her to contact him; he might be helpful.

Janusz is short and sharp on the phone, suggesting they meet at an address in Kolo on the north side of Warsaw. At the appointed time Jenny finds the door of a small two story industrial building where Janusz waits for her—in person not short, and serious rather than sharp. He had been an art student in Manchester. Nathalie had contacted him through a colleague at the university and told him about Jenny's work and her project. Nathalie thought he might be able to help.

Janusz leads Jenny into the back of the warehouse, a large space filled with boxes, timber, tools, junk.

--It needs a good clean but Nathalie told me you could use a studio.

Jenny is taken aback. She had said nothing to Nathalie, yet her friend sensed, and knew. Once again to the rescue, answering need.

--Yes, I…but…

--Don't worry. It's mine. I keep it for my junk right now. One day maybe I will have a use. You only have to pay for electricity. There is only one other cost: one day you may need an assistant. When you do, I assist. Otherwise for now I give you the key. No one bothers you here. Not even me.

Jenny looked at the space, looked at the serious Janusz.

--You know where I work during the week? You know about the Site?

--Yes. Of course.

--I can't take you there. Not at the moment.

--No. But somehow, here, I think you will take me.

--…Will you want to go?

Janusz hesitates. His thoughts turn inward, then outward.

--I am Polish. I have no choice. Necessary. I know what is inside you. I know from Nathalie. I also have friends, artists, fabricators. They are good. I can help. Them too. When you need. When you are ready. Meaning: when you wish.

She nods and the deal is done.

Jenny spends two weekends scrubbing the space clean of dust and dirt. She brings over all her supplies from the university lab and sets them in an order that helps make this new studio space take shape in the image she needs, space for her to call it her own, to call it her studio. She finds herself growing ever more at ease. It becomes familiar and in doing so it becomes her.

Near a back wall but centered in the room, Janusz helps build a low platform and then angle spotlights; she will need it later in her work. He arrives one day with a large, smooth table top and builds a work station for her as well. Jenny buys herself a large light panel that she hangs on a wall beside the work station, hanging up both photographs of the Site and many images of the wooden sill that she had taken, as well as some of the digital terrain models from the Site and excavation, and a few magnetometry images and LIDAR images of the entire site area that Brian had told her to keep and use as she needed. In front of the platform she puts up a large image of ground penetrating radar that they had used in first detecting the structural remains for the excavation. The studio begins to take on a look of part archaeological investigation laboratory, but as more and more drawings she makes find their way onto the walls as well, part artist's studio.

Between archaeology and art, construction and deconstruction, a sense of controlled chaos. A sense of someone trying to define meaning.

At the Site, the excavation continues, day after day, week after week.

And in the studio, the work progresses, slowly, in her mind and mind's eye.

*

Jenny spends much time researching. She needs to find the image. She needs to understand why this piece of wood. Why this length. What happened there? What is happening now? She needs to reach deeply inside herself, while reaching out to the places and the people who have given explanations to dark history. To form. To architecture. What is it she can create that will mean life and death, one and the same: hers, her Mother's, the thousands, the Others? The Ghosts?

She begins to spend more and more time at her Warsaw studio. It envelops her like a womb that nurtures. She moves in a camp bed to sleep there on weekends. She finds herself sitting at her drawing table in the middle of the long nights growing longer, staring at blank paper, then drawing images from her imaginings: buildings, rooms, people. Hollow faces. Munch-like terror. Her face. Her Mother's eyes.

She needs to understand. She needs to find it.

Then one night, lying in bed in her small apartment in Ostrów Mazowiecka, she realizes what it is she will create. She sees it. She knows it was always there, a door to be opened. And a door to close.

She invites Brian to come to the studio one Sunday afternoon. She shows him all her drawings, some in charcoal, some in watercolour, some in anger, some in fear, some in hate. Some. She shows him too the photographs, the files of research, the stories read, the concepts, the intent. The project.

He listens carefully.

--You wanted to show this all to me. Why? For approval?

--No. Maybe. Not entirely.

--No. Approval I gave a long time ago, Jenny. And not companionship I take it.

--No.

--No. My loss.

--I have an assistant when I need. Janusz. You'll meet him.

--A lover?

--No. In fact he's gay. He told me. He has a partner.

--So then…What do you need?

--I want to continue with the team. You know that. But I want to cut it down to three days a week. Would that be all right?

--Under the circumstances, yes. Besides which we will break next month to return to England. Collate and write up the research there. Lectures. Then Christmas holidays. Will you return to England?

--No. No…One other thing. I want to bring the wooden sill artefact from the dig here. For a while. I'll keep it safe. I want to make some small maquettes of it at first, but then use it to create a mold.

--A mold will require priming its surface, Jenny.

--Not what I have in mind. I've discussed it with Janusz. He's done work with 3-D mobile scanners. We can scan the artefact from all available angles, or what's exposed of it, then go to a metal fabricator to recreate it. I can use the fabricated metal artefact to then create the mold. The original wood will never be touched, except by my gloved hands. Easy.

--Easy. Right. And you couldn't do that in the lab with the LIDAR equipment? You could, you know.

--No. I need to keep the original near me.

--Why?

--Because…It's hard to explain, Brian. Its song, its tears, I…I need it near. I'll be careful. You can trust me.

--Yes. I know…Do you want to say what you're doing?

--Not right now.

Brian stares at her. He smiles. The request is not simple. All of the artefacts are owned by the institutions funding the work. All are valuable in many ways. And fragile. All are history. History does not come without cost. Like memory.

--…All right. You can do that. One condition: as you work, you photograph. You update me periodically on progress. You show me the path you take in pictures, in words. And in the spring we take up where we left off at the Site.

Jenny nods. Smiles.

--Yes.

--Good…good.

And he looks around, one more time. Looks around, nodding his approval.

--Jenny's studio; hm…yes, it's good.

And he leaves.

After the few days up at the Site, Jenny returns to Warsaw, asking Janusz to meet her at the university lab so together they can move the wooden artefact. Together they carefully wrap the wooden length in special packing materials and place it in a metal box, Jenny shows Janusz around the lab. She gives him a pair of white cotton gloves so that he can pick up some of the collected artefacts from the dig, as well as showing and explaining some of the archaeological equipment that they use to collect data. Janusz says little as he picks up some of the smaller items they have brought back from the various surveys or surface exploration of the Site early on in their investigations.

--What will happen to these items?

--We catalogue them, both in terms of their identification and the exact location they were found. It helps to build a picture. Some will remain in archives. Many will find their way into museums, one at the Site in time, when it's built, or elsewhere.

--Build a picture. And is that what you are doing?

She thinks a moment.

--No.

--Then?

--Looking.

--And what will you do when you find?

Jenny shrugs.

--I don't know. I really don't.

Janusz nods, puts down the identified broach he had been holding. He looks at a small woman's hair comb. Runs a finger over it. Looks away. Shakes his head, quietly, wordlessly. Jenny watches him.

--Janusz? What about you? What will you do?

He hesitates, then he too shrugs, purposely echoing Jenny. She smiles.

--Come on; we should put this in the van.

After they have carefully placed the container within it, they get into the van to return to the studio. But Janusz considers something first.

--Detour.

--…Okay.

He starts across the city, and north, slowed by traffic. After half an hour Janusz turns to a side street, parks.

--Come. The van and its cargo will be safe here.

Jenny nods, follows him out of the van. He points at the large building beside them.

--Psychology Department of the University. They like to be separated from other departments. Typical.

They start up a main street, across from another large building.

--A technical college. It wasn't always like this. These buildings weren't always here. Like much of Warsaw. Flattened like a pancake during the war. This way.

Jenny follows him across the road, down the block, where the buildings end and a small monument stands: a wall in grey granite some three meters high, closed in except in its middle, and along the corners which are open. They stand within it.

--Do you know this place?, he asks her.

--Yes.

--Yes. Umschlagplatz. Or it was once. All around here. Before the buildings. There was a railway siding once here, you know? In 1942 the Nazis brought the Jews here, here in their Ghetto, loaded them into cattle cars, took them to the camp. Hundreds of thousands from here, from around here. This is what remains.

--I know.

--These walls are supposed to represent such a cattle car. But they don't. Not

112

really. Your project. What you are trying to find. Is it such a representation?

--No.

--No. It goes deeper I think. It goes into you. Like I tell you, I understand.

He nods, smiles, just slightly. He walks over and runs fingers over the stone.

--From here, my great grandfather, my great grandmother on my father's family side, they too are forced up into the cattle car. From this place, Umschlagplatz, from here, they too find they are on a journey. Like you. But they do not return from their journey. Here, they disappear. They cease to be. Right here. A journey. Like me too. My grandfather, he is their only child. Years before they send him to a sister in Switzerland, to my mother's family. He comes back here as an older man, with a wife. And my father is born here in Warsaw. And am I. But you see, Jenny, their journey it is my journey too. Perhaps something like yours. So yes, I understand. In your piece of wood, in your artefacts as you call them…perhaps maybe one is my great grandfather's, my great grandmother's. A hair comb. A broach. A lipstick container. Maybe.

--I see.

--Yes. You do.

Jenny places her fingers on the granite, closes her eyes. And sees.

*

13 September 2019

To: Nathalie@gmail.com

From: Jenny@InstituteHistoricalArchaeology.manc.ac.uk

Hey, it's me.

Have I sent my thanks for bringing Janusz into my work, my life? He has proven to be a life saver. You were right: he has contacts in the art world, amongst crafts people and university folk that can be called upon when I need. I'll need. I'm lucky to have him here when I ask and his help is always forthcoming. So thank you for that, Nathalie. Or for him.

The work continues slowly, as I explore, trying to find the image that I have needed to define not just this place, or the Site, but to define me I suppose. Self-examination, true self-examination, is not always easy.

I have been drawing as I can, ideas but also impressions. At first I thought I needed to exorcise the ghosts within, but I see now that is not what I am doing. Rather I think I am learning to accept them, to walk with them, to hear their whispers without fear. Especially, but not only, Mother. Does that make sense?

I'm now at the Site only three days a week, with Brian's approval. He has been supportive. I don't know why that surprises me, but it does slightly. As it is he will close down work at the Site in the next few weeks. Everyone is anxious to return home—everyone but me I suppose. Not sure where home is any longer. In any event Brian wants to get back so he can begin logging the findings and working on his book I suppose. He has a series of lectures arranged at several universities and one at the Royal Academy over the next few months. So it suits that I'm not spending as much time with the team at the moment: suits me, probably them as well. I can be a bit obsessive. I know, I know.

I continue nevertheless to commute up to Ostrów Mazowiecka, spending many of my nights in my small space there. Many rather than most. I've put a portable camp bed into the studio and often spend the night there. I've rather made it into my space. My image. Womb-like. But I am surrounded there by the drawings I'm making— sometimes, not always, for the project. Sometimes images that appear in dreams. Or nightmares. Sometimes doodles that hold interest. They make me happy, pasted up beside the various topographical and imaging graphs we have from the Site itself. All artwork in their way, I suppose.

A few days ago Janusz helped me to bring over the wooden sill artefact found at the site. At least that is the theory, that it's a sill at the entrance. It remains my starting point. Over the next couple of weeks we'll use a high-spec mobile 3-D scanner to build up its image, with all its deformities. My suggestion in order to protect it from elements that don't belong. Janusz knows a place we can hire equipment. I want to build up a picture of every detail, every knot or scratch or smoothed out surface before I begin. Then from that we can have it fabricated for a mold plug to create and work on fiberglass molds of it. I need to build up two or three to experiment with the project. It won't be easy but it is the way I want to proceed. Proceed as in moving forward. If I only knew where it might take me.

So that is the plan. I hope you approve. Your approval is important to me.

Needless to say I will not be back in the UK at Christmas. In fact I have no idea when I'll be back. If? I will of course, one day. But right now, I think I belong here. Breathing it in. Living in it. Life.

I'll write again soon.

Jenny.

*

28 September 2019

To: Nathalie@gmail.com

From: Jenny@ InstituteHistoricalArchaeology.manc.ac.uk

Hi N

Thanks so much for your emails of support. Means the world.

So I received the first polyisocyanurate foam mold back from the workshop a few days ago. The 3-D imaging was tricky to handle at first as you know, but ultimately the image we built up seems complete. I was rather nervous working with the engineering guys who built the model, but ultimately it seemed to pick up every detail, every imperfection of the original. Perfection in its imperfection. It's a class 'B' mold finish. They seemed a bit confused when I explained that the scratches and imperfect details needed to be retained, rather than a perfect class 'A', but they acceded to need. My need. I had them seal and harden the entire surface as well. They will make two further secondary molds for me in the next two weeks, once I've started to fabricate the fiberglass mold composite from the plug. They want to ensure I'm satisfied before proceeding with secondaries.

In fact we poured the first composite yesterday. It's still setting but so far it looks right to me. All a beginning—beginning to take shape in many ways. And even as I write, shape is beginning to form from imagination. It is a process.

In the meantime, we had a goodbye party for all the team a few days ago. Between the multitude of bottles of vodka and slivovitz I'm not sure how anyone was left standing. Quite a few weren't. Unlike me, I should add. I drank my share I suppose, but made a quiet exit early on without attracting too much attention. Those who saw me sneak away wished me well, hoping we'd meet up in late February at the start of the next team on Site. That is the intention, anyway. Brian was aloof, but wished me luck. Avi, who I am probably closest to, has been the most curious as to my work here in the studio but I've let on little. It may yet all fall apart. May be disastrous.

Or may simply be…empty. That is what I fear the most. But hope not.

The first composite mold is still a bit rough—and I don't mean in texture. But still, holding it in my hands, thinking what it might become, provoke, it gives me hope. Janusz too seemed pleased enough with the result. He has offered to deal directly with the engineer chaps on the secondaries, and to pour the fiberglass with me on the next attempt, to steady an unsteady hand. I think we're both getting the hang of it, however. And I think as an artist himself, albeit more a photographer (so much of the 3-D work was due to his careful eye). He's fascinated by the process. It makes it that more enjoyable.

Just realized I jumped back to the studio work, away from the team, when I was writing about that. I suppose this place, this project, is an obsession. It always was going to be that. But the goodbyes with the team were fine. I'll see most of them again in four or five months anyway. At least I think I will, if I don't wrap myself in fiberglass and disappear forever in this cocoon. Now there's a thought. To be honest, the team going separate ways is a relief right now. It's been both a blessing but often hard for me. I think right now the freedom of isolation, or relative isolation, is what I've needed. Just my thoughts in silence. The discoveries at the Site were sometimes amazing, sometimes heartbreaking. Remember I told you about the lipstick holder? But I think here, in my way, in my hands, there is still a discovery to be made. Wonder what I'll find?

Will try to let you know.

Sending love

Jenny

*

17 October 201

To: Brian@ InstituteHistoricalArchaeology.manc.ac.uk

From: Jenny@InstituteHistoricalArchaeology.manc.ac.uk

Morning, Brian

Pleased to get your email and that you all made it back safely, instruments and data in one piece.

Sorry I did not see you and the others in the team after the 'wrap party'…funny expression that, as the work is hardly wrapped. I wonder if it will ever be so.

And pleased to learn of the interest from all in the 'Project' as I've come to call it. At this point I need space on it, but in time hope the others in the team will still be curious, will want to know more. And will not think it the whims of a foolish woman. Or that you will.

As promised, I'm attaching a couple of photographs. As you can see, the fiberglass molds from the plug have turned out well. We made five in total—that allows me to experiment a bit as I build, particularly with colour. The texture was what I sought in the first place, and although the material is of course different than the wooden original, the defects and marks and feel from the original have been retained in the 3-D plug we made (with two extra in case of damage.)

The wooden artefact original we've carefully put back into the protective container. I'll hold onto it for the moment. It's safe here, but, whilst difficult to explain, having it nearby offers a sense of comfort. No, wrong word. Offers a sense of possibility. And memory too. Funny that such an object should become a memory. When I say that, oddly I hear sound, I don't know: the sound of a violin quietly weeping. Does that make sense?

I know, I know: it doesn't. It is simply Jenny. But so be it.

I also have a theory. I know, I'm not supposed to have theories. But perhaps you might mull over this. I think the wooden plank was not the center sill of the frame. I think it sat in front. An illusion of warmth. That would explain how it became so worn, and was not used as a seal but as a pre-threshold. The normality of its substance, its form. They were so eager to give the illusion of safety, in a way, of confidence. To lie. I cannot help but wonder if it was a part of that lie. What do you think?

So the photographs, courtesy of Janusz: these are the 'base' molds of the artefacts. And now I know that this will work, or think it will, I will begin to consider how to build up. What to build up. And what to make of it all... as well as why. It remains important to continue to use molds, I think, rather than originals. In part because what I have in mind will have weight. The weight of...what? The weight of the imagination, I guess. I don't want the original, I want that which can come from thought, from my dreams, my imagination. That explains a lot.

Forgive me: I ruminate as I write. And you won't have the time for it.

117

I will continue to send you photographs as things progress, and explanations. Will try not to waffle on.

I do hope the lectures go well, and the book of course. I so look forward to seeing where it takes you—and by you, through you, takes all of us.

I am comfortable here; you need not worry. And I will be back to you soon, further on I hope.

One last thing: I do want to thank you, Brian. From within. You've helped me. You've helped make this possible. And you haven't made demands—well not really. For all that I'm grateful. So I send my thanks, and my love.

As always

Jen

*

3 November 2019

To: Nathalie@gmail.com

From: Jenny@ InstituteHistoricalArchaeology.manc.ac.uk

Oh Nathalie!...

I know, I know. Too silent too long. Remember remember the 5th of November and it is approaching; with it a remember remember to write. I am truly sorry.

I've been busy. That won't surprise you.

I've been working on the mold made from the wooden artefact. Happy with it now, and the industrial paints using for it. You wouldn't know the fiberglass isn't wood. It took a couple of attempts but I found what I was looking for in colour and texture. The worn brown colour effect took a while to figure out, but we've mixed it with deep blacks and the results seem to work. But I still need to think on it. Still not certain it's the right direction.

We've also started working with the plastic engineering people on a box frame for the Project. All the research done has paid off, as I largely know exactly the look I want having spent so many hours researching. I decided that this too should be created from a mold plug, albeit it will result in a large fiberglass composite rectangular sheet. It could have been argued that it would be easier to use original materials rather than working on a mold, but I chose not to do this. One of the reasons was because of weight: to use metal sheeting, or even a metal and wood

composite, would create a work that is simply too heavy to manipulate and design.
That is a big part of it. The other reason, however, is that I need all of this to be
imaginings, all created from air, like air, from what I see when I sleep, when I wake.
It's imaginary: made to look real, in some ways, to take weight, but to be weightless.
Dream weightless. The weight of water and the weight of dreams.

So we have started to buy the materials we've needed to make the mold itself,
once I have the plug made. And to think of design from fiberglass; that will be the
most difficult part, probably more difficult than the mold of the wooden plank.

Did I also tell you what I've come to the conclusion as to what is, or was, its
purpose? I think that Brian was right: it is a sill, of sorts. But I think it sat in front,
not within, or covered, on the flooring. I think it too was part of the illusion: the
illusion of warmth (wood), of going into a welcoming environment, rather than a
sill to the frame. That would explain its worn surface—worn from feet crossing a
threshold, exposed rather than hiding: yet hiding realities of the shower room, the
purpose, and I could almost say warn rather than worn. 'Beware all ye who enter
here...' Do you think Dante would have had more to say? Or said less, as there was
no escape perhaps. No escaping the circles of Hell; no Virgil to bring you to
Purgatory. No Purgatory: only a very dark emptiness and the ashes of the
crematorium, when it was later built.

Sorry; I digress and grow into a dark mood. Too much on my own? Perhaps. In
this place.

I've been buying, lots. Most people I know, with Christmas coming next month,
buy dresses, or champagne, or frilly underwear, or a dream holiday. I on the other
hand buy in hardware shops and metal bric-a-brac at Saturday markets. But it all
pleases me and I've found some materials I can use for the molds: large hinges, old
bar locks that would have made their way from some dungeon or another—
appropriately; heavy bolts, a wire egg basket (explanation for another time I think).
All sorts of hardware toys I'll experiment with, design, colour, love and grow to hate
at the same time. What this is I hate. Yet need. And in the need, love. I wonder if that
makes sense?

All for the Project. The Project I desperately need to find my way to. And through.
Do drop me a note when you get a chance. Tell me about the autumn colours.

About your classes this year. About your plans and dreams.

I'd say think about visiting me, but not right now. Next year maybe. For now…I need the isolation and the space. I need the imaginings. I need to make them real, and only I can do that.

In a way I need you. And I realize I needed Mother too. Funny that. The need keeps me going; I just cannot fulfill it right now.

I do miss you. I will buy a bottle of the best Irish whiskey I can find, and raise a glass in your direction.

It is not the same. For now however it must suffice, must satisfy need. I hope you understand that.

I send warmth and love, as always.

J.

*

21 November 2019

To: Brian@InstituteHistoricalArchaeology.manc.ac.uk

From: Jenny@InstituteHistoricalArchaeology.manc.ac.uk

Brian dear Brian:

I know, I know. I promised I'd keep you well informed. I'm so sorry. I've been so up against it. I promise I'll write very soon, with pictures. Forgive me. I haven't run away. Not yet.

Love, Jenny

*

4 December 2019

To: Brian@InstituteHistoricalArchaeology.manc.ac.uk

From: Jenny@InstituteHistoricalArchaeology.manc.ac.uk

Dear Brian

So better late than never and I'm finally sending you various photos and drawings—with apologies for taking so long to update you.

The photos of the mold from the wooden artefact you'll recognize, although you can now see what I'm trying to achieve in painting them. I'm particularly pleased with the second composite; I think the colouration is more natural. I'm also attaching a photograph taken of the original wooden length from the lab for comparison. You can see they are almost identical; I'm pleased about that. You could say one is simply a copy of the other, but that is not quite so. The molded fiberglass comes from within me, I'd argue. It's part of the imaginative exploration explicitly because it is not the real artefact. Therefore an imaginative journey. Call that artistic license, if you like. I like. It's what the Project is about.

The remaining photos are a collection of sheeting, hardware and wooden backs I've used in order to create a new—quite large—plug, from which we can then begin to build the fiberglass molds. Because of cost, I could only afford to do this once, and had to separate certain elements of the project, which we will then reattach with molded hardware elements and using specially created molded screws. Nothing will be 'real', therefore all will be real.

The Project is coming along, albeit the processes are not fast.

We, that is Janusz and I, spent some time discussing a supporting frame: not something a part of the project, but effectively a hanging frame that is static, yet does not 'intrude'. I came up with a minimally invasive steel support. Janusz felt that inwardly protruding static support cables were too numerous to be necessary, becoming too apparent against the Project itself. He found an engineering firm in Warsaw that has agreed to help us, however. Working through the design with them, they have suggested simply four stainless steel static supports to hold the Project in its place, in turn welded on a three sided cylindrical frame. The two sides will sit in a three sided concrete base that will be strong enough to hold the Project, but low enough to the ground to make it barely noticeable. I think it will work. The entire supporting structure will be of stainless steel, which will mesh with some ideas I have for the Project further down the line a bit. Anyway, that is the plan.

I hope you find the plans, drawings and few photographs stimulating and interesting. The Project has been both a challenge and a journey so far. You were right; it is something I needed to do, less for others than for myself.

I have heard from a few of the team that the lecture you gave in London went terribly well. I'm pleased that there is interest. How is the book work going? When you have data analysis sheets and conclusions from some of last year's dig, do forward them if you can; I would love to see the work. I understand too you've had letters of support sent to both the press and the Institutions on the works done at the

121

excavation from the chief Rabbi here, as well as in England. I was surprised to see letters of concern in the press, at first anyway; I'm pleased they've come out so to argue that what we are trying to accomplish, and the primary methodologies, are not contrary to Halacha law.

I suspect you'll be slowing down for the holidays now. I hope you have a good break. Raise a glass to me. Raise a glass to the Project. And to the memory of all. I will keep mine quiet. Preferable. But I will be thinking of you all.

Sending fond regards

Jen

*

4 December 2019

To: Brian@InstituteHistoricalArchaeology.manc.ac.uk

From: Jenny@InstituteHistoricalArchaeology.manc.ac.uk

Dear Brian

Thank you for your good wishes and cheer. But more to the point, thank you so much for approaching the Institute about funding! That's brilliant. Costs have risen and if they could help out that would be fantastic. I'll keep my fingers crossed. And if it's not possible I hope to have the sale of my mother's house done in the coming weeks, so will cover costs this way. The Project is my responsibility, and my journey. I always expected it to be my problem.

But thank you. I want to stay that. I owe you regardless of the outcome.

Happy Christmas, Brian. I'm sending warmth.

Jenny.

*

8 January 2020

To: Nathalie@gmail.com

From: Jenny@ InstituteHistoricalArchaeology.manc.ac.uk

And to you, sweet Nathalie.

Celebrate? With the noisy boiler wishing each other cheer. It's what I wanted. Not sure what it wanted.

Chose to sit quietly. Read. Consider.

I've given up the apartment in Ostrów Mazowiecka. I had stopped going up there *some weeks ago anyway. I might move back in the spring when the team returns, but I'm not sure about that. Not sure about a lot of things.*

So now the camp bed and studio are home. Warmth. Well usually. The boiler and I are only sporadically on speaking terms.

Have been testing paints. Found what I like for the Project. Janusz is away in Hungary with family, then skiing somewhere. But I like the isolation. Not lonely. You?

Not sending photos right now. Will in time. At moment simply want to think, read, research a bit more, think still some more, the occasional glass of wine and a bit Thelonious Monk streamed through my computer. Calms me. That's enough.

Will write again soon. Not much want to say right now. Miss you.

Jenny

*

28 January 2020

To: Brian@InstituteHistoricalArchaeology.manc.ac.uk

From: Jenny@InstituteHistoricalArchaeology.manc.ac.uk

Brian that's brilliant. Can't thank you enough. My mother's house sale completed so have funds but this will help. Let the board know how grateful I am. I'll write to them too.

Found the paint I want, finally. Attached is a photo. Stuff is used on the Polish naval fleet. Very strong. Very grey. Very dull and perfect. I use heavy duty sandpaper for textures before it dries. Messy but seems to do the job.

Yes I've moved into the studio. No you needn't be concerned. I'm happy with my own space.

Can't say more at the moment. Will soon. Working. Looking forward to reading some of those papers of yours too.

Jx

*

12 February 2020

To: Nathalie@gmail.com

From: Jenny@ InstituteHistoricalArchaeology.manc.ac.uk

Dearest N

Yes I've heard about this thing. Just what is this virus? Certainly isn't the flu. I do hope it doesn't get out of control. Not a lot being said here about things but have heard of deaths and lung issues in other places, mostly in the Far East.

I keep mostly to myself so not too worried, but look primarily after yourself. Sounds quite contagious and you're at risk in those classrooms.

Everything else continues, my pace. No Janusz. Attaching photo of my seafaring paint efforts. What do you think? Happy with it myself. At least I think I am. The metal support frame seems right, but not sure about a number of things. Have had an idea want to explore for partial silvering on it. Can't explain right now but have spoken to one of Janusz's mates. He didn't know but has arranged for me to meet a chemistry professor from the university to discuss. Am intrigued.

More on this anon.

Your Jx

*

23 February 2020

To: Brian@InstituteHistoricalArchaeology.manc.ac.uk

From: Jenny@InstituteHistoricalArchaeology.manc.ac.uk

Shit, Brian! Shit! It killed him? What is this virus? I knew Italy was bad but this is terrible. His poor family. I'm sure you must be devastated. Be careful where you are; it seems to be moving fast. Keep me informed too on the team. Damn.

I'm okay. A lucky one perhaps as I'm largely isolated here, only going out for groceries. Otherwise working. Sleeping. Janusz checks up on me ever few days with a phone call; we've thought it best to keep a distance while we can. So I work. I've started to listen to Bach a lot—his violin concertos transport me somewhere gentle. All this is enough. Am also experimenting with a process called silvering. More on that soon. Silvering to the sound of a weeping violin. That's me.

Please please be careful. This virus sounds awful. You don't want it.

Jen

*

14 March 2020

To: Nathalie@gmail.com

From: Jenny@ InstituteHistoricalArchaeology.manc.ac.uk

Sorry, meant to respond more quickly.

Heard the rumours of a stay at home there. Sounds like UK has been hit very badly. And I just heard from one of our team who is Glasgow. Brian has come down with it. He's in hospital but thank goodness not on a ventilator. I so feared this.

You need to keep isolated too, Nathalie. You can't get this. You just can't. Please! Be smart.

I've got almost everything I need. Have managed to arrange grocery delivery so don't ever really need to go out.

I met with the chemistry 'professor' a few weeks ago. In fact she's a she, about five feet tall, hilarious. She walked me through silvering processes, of which I understood perhaps 10%. Then she looked me in the eye and asked what I'm trying to achieve. After listening she suggested another solution. She'd heard of a relatively new process to "create a solution from cheaper crystalline materials and (get this—the words I've learned) sequestering the silver with appropriate chelating agents to maintain the silver solution. Thus once a reducing agent is used it cases the precipitation of the silver in a smooth, non-crystalline form on an adjacent surface."

Right, you guessed it: might as well be ancient Abyssinian articulations; she wrote this to me in an email. But the long and short of it she bought the chemical solutions I'd need and directed me on processes. I've been experimenting and whilst the silvering isn't exactly what I'd thought, I continue to work and see how it will progress. With a little bit of luck it might just be the answer I needed. And given that I have enough time—as does the rest of the world it seems—I can experiment until I find what I'm looking for. Easy. Well, no, but wish me luck; it might just work. It might.

Listen, do please be careful. This bloody virus—you don't want it. No one does. The world may or may not survive it, it seems. But in the meantime, I'm trying to finish the Project. Not far to go and not willing to succumb beforehand. I hear the sounds of the violin carrying me back so I'll say little more. Please, please be careful. Think of me and write.

JennyX

*

2 April 2020

To: Brian@InstituteHistoricalArchaeology.manc.ac.uk

From: Jenny@ InstituteHistoricalArchaeology.manc.ac.uk

Dearest Brian

I know you've been very ill. I've heard you are on the mend. I have heard nothing from you, understandably. I have no idea when you'll be able to read this. I hope you will get well very very soon.

I realize the surveying and excavation work will have to wait and the team won't be able to return for some time. May it be soon.

But I am safe and well. Being isolated is easy for me. I suppose I'm a bit afraid but the work keeps my mind from anything else. I've successfully found a way forward with the silvering. I think now it will work, and I can see the light at the end of that tunnel at least. Or perhaps I can't. I'm still not quite happy with it. Something... isn't quite working. But I have come too far to give up. I just have to find the solution. For that I need to understand the problem. Hope for me, will you? As I hope for you.

I won't send photos now, but will soon. May you be well enough to look through them when I forward.

Almost done.

Please get well. I think of you.

I hear the sad tears from a Bach violin playing through my computer. My company. It reminds me of the work at the Site. Funny that. Music as memory. I guess my memory.

I still hear the whispers; if anything they've grown louder. But the music soothes them as well. The music and the Project. A way through. A way forward.

I hope you are able to read this.

I send you warmth and strength, and love, my friend.

Jenny x

*

7 April 2020

To: Nathalie@gmail.com

From: Jenny@ InstituteHistoricalArchaeology.manc.ac.uk

The silvering worked. But something is not right. I don't know. I don't…know. I'm sorry but lost in it all.

My head is spinning with it. Maybe too much. Maybe it's this virus. Maybe it's memory. Just feeling lost in it the Project and the Project is me and the door is not ajar but I need it to open I don't know Nathalie. Space to breathe. Breathing has become so hard hasn't it.

Something missing. The last step through the open door.

Perhaps I am going mad. Perhaps I have been headed that way for so many days since Mother died. No, since she took her life. She took part of mine as well. But I don't think so, Nat…I think I've never been saner, and it's the world that has gone mad. What do you think?

I will be growing silent. Like I have done before. Disappearing just a bit. No posters looking for me this time please. I'll come back.

And I love you in my own way.

Jenny

*

Jenny stares at the Project, lying on its back on the podium she had built. Raised up but not upright. She sits on her camp bed in silence, simply staring at it, lifeless on the ground. Dead body. Dead space. She feels tired, so very tired.

Something is not right. She is not certain what it is. Something not quite—finished. Complete.

She has missed something, after all these months. Missed the finishing. The final act.

What has she missed?

She has no answer.

What is left to do? What final word?

She hears only silence. Deafening silence.

Forgive me Mother, I know not what I do. Forgive them. Forgive me.

The voices too are silent, but she can nevertheless feel them, even here, whispering confusions to her, watching her, waiting for her to act. What do they want, she thinks? What do they want of me? I have done this for them. I have done all I could. I have listened to them, their words in my head, what remains to be done?

Jenny looks for answers, for an answer, but finds none. She stands, walks over to the work table, looks down. Nothing. Walks over to the side of the studio, packed with supplies, discards, tools. Has she missed something? Nothing.

She picks up a long piece of rope they had used when they first started. Rope to make the artefact container even more secure. She stares at it in her hand. Stares at it over long minutes.

She sees her Mother, hanging, just the slightest sway.

She looks up at the studio ceiling joists, exposed.

Just the slightest sway.

She carries the rope back to the design table, covered with tools, chemicals, plans, ideas, imagination, fear, hope, greater fear, need. She stands there, motionless, trying to understand, trying to see.

Until finally, the glimmer of a thought. The whisper of a voice. The tear along her cheek. Mother. She looks back up at the Project, staring, and yes, finally she understands. She drops the rope onto the floor, throws many of the tools onto the floor. She picks up a small mallet amongst the dropped tools, stares at it. She drops a silvered maquette she had experimented with onto the now bare table, a maquette shaped into a large rectangular bit of silvered fiberglass that she'd work with trying to find the right visual, the right feel earlier in the process. She stares at it, at the nearly finished Project, back at the maquette. She raises her right arm with the small mallet held in her hand, raises it just slightly, then without anger, without too much force but with intent, strikes the maquette. Strikes it once. Again. Again. Again,

She stares at the unbroken but now defective silvered maquette lying on the table. And she feels the tears falling down her face, unstoppable. And she knows she has found the final act, the final motion.

After so many months, Jenny knows she can complete the Project. Can discover its final act. Its conclusion. So it is time. Now.

Days later she asks Janusz to come, to help her in a final movement of her composition. He arrives wearing a mask. He removes it when he walks in. He says he needs to breathe here, and here he can breathe.

He walks into the studio, into the space where the project lies on one side. He stares at it.

--Will you help me to raise it back up?

He looks at her and takes one side. Together they set it vertical, then take the thin stainless steel supports and lock them into the project's framing metal with the nearly invisible small clamps. Two on each side. Firm. Unbreakable. Unmovable. The Project thus stands, static, imposing,

Janusz walks around it. Three hundred sixty degrees. He returns to where he started. Takes a step back. Stares with no emotion in his expression, a lack of emotion that speaks loudly of emotion.

Finally he turns to look at Jenny, in turn looking at him.

He simply, slightly, nods at her. An acknowledgement, and an understanding of what he too had sought.

*

14 April 2020

To: Brian@InstituteHistoricalArchaeology.manc.ac.uk

From: Jenny@InstituteHistoricalArchaeology.manc.ac.uk

Dearest Brian

I hope this finds you getting stronger now. I know it has been awful.

I am very tired myself. Not the virus. Just…tired.

I am not sending photographs. Forgive me for that. I cannot just now. I am not despondent, just expended.

I will leave something for you at the lab when you return. You can see for yourself. And the repacked wooden artefact will be returned there stored in the case. It is safe. There is more to say perhaps; when the time comes.

I cannot write further. Not just now. Cannot speak more. Hope you understand. Everything else is a gift. A gift from me, for me. Somehow I think you will understand. I have lost things, found things and I will continue now moving forward. I know that. I say that. Last words.

Very tired. When ready to speak, will speak. When ready to be, will be. There.

Love you, Brian. And thank you. I will always be grateful for your trust.

Be well.

J

*

Brian returns to Warsaw late in May. Some of the team he has handpicked will follow perhaps in a month, if the virus has waned enough, if all have their vaccination certificates in order. The Polish government is rightly being careful, just like all the world. The virus is everywhere.

Brian still feels slightly weak. His sense of taste has not returned. His breathing is slightly shallow. But he needs to be moving on. The research matters. The Site matters. It has been his life for too long not to carry his investigations forward as soon as possible.

He drops his bags off at the flat he has retained for all these years. It is not home, but could be. He'll arrange to have it cleaned.

He tries to telephone Jenny one more time but just as it has been for many weeks now she does not answer. He is not surprised. He no longer expects her to answer. He thinks perhaps he should not be concerned but of course he is concerned. He will try to make sense of it. He will find out.

He also misses the touch of her but that is long past. There will be others. Or there won't.

Brian walks to the lab. He prefers to walk. The weather in Warsaw has turned warm. Walking allows him air to breathe. A bit of space to think.

Avi is waiting, having opened the lab as Brian has asked him to. They will not shake hands. For the most part they will keep a distance. The world has changed. At the edges of their humanity fear sits quietly watching.

--All well?

--Yes. Unsurprising. They told us to stay at home. Most did. It could use a dusting but nothing out of whack. How about you, boss? Must have been hell.

--It's better. Covid: Christ. I hope I never see it again. You heard nothing further from Jenny?

--No. Not in weeks. I tried her again a few days ago but no answer.

--No.

--The packing case is over there. That assistant of hers probably helped her carry it in, but no one saw them. Most people are still staying home.

--Yes.

--I found this on it.

Avi hands Brian an envelope. Jenny had written his name on it. Brian opens it and removes the key. A note is within. He stares at the key, looks at the note. Thinks. Looks up at Avi who is watching him. Hands him the note.

Please close the door when you leave.

--What does she mean? The lab door?

Brian hesitates. Looks around.

--You have your car?

It takes only fifteen minutes to get to the studio, with so little traffic on the streets due to the virus. Avi parks. They try the building door, but find it locked, unsurprisingly. Brian takes out the key and tries it. A click and the door opens.

They walk down the corridor to the inner room door, the studio door. Brian pulls it open. Inside it is completely dark, the only light coming from the sharp but minimal shard of light from the corridor where they stand. Unsure where to find a light Brian takes out his mobile phone and turns on its flashlight app. He sees a row of switches off to the left, but finds the bank all taped over with gaffer tape, save for two. These he flicks on.

Four beams of spotlight, directly and specifically angled, illuminate the room towards the back, their angles crisscrossing over the low pedestal where the Project stands upright, completed, like an actor on a stage standing silently before an audience that does not know how to respond, that does not applaud, that simply stares in confusion, or in awe.

Brian and Avi walk up to it.

The Project is a large door of sorts, a door that is monument, and memory.

Neither man says a word.

Door that is art, art that is door. And always memory. The Project stands slightly ajar, illuminated by the beams of light. On the side he stands the door is of a deep, heavy grey paint giving no reflection, no sense of possible space, flat rather than dimensional. Its outer frame, also grey, is supported by two tall cylindrical thin stainless steel poles, each bolted at the base into a steel plate to keep them upright, it too stainless steel. From each pole two short, static, thin angled supports hold the door's frame in clamps barely seen, clearly tight enough to hold the project upright.

The door itself is made of several panels that look like vertical wooden slats, although Brian knows that they are a single piece of fiberglass made to look like vertical tongue-in-groove wood, a perfect replica illusion that is the product of research and imagination rather than the true materials that would have been used. Some ten or twelve centimeters from the top of the door, and ten or twelve from the bottom, the heads of a line of bolts, or the illusion of such, spaced equally apart, emerge and run parallel both near the door's top and the door's bottom, their unseen and unreal thread covered by fake large square washers to tighten, and hold in place. Or the appearance of such. None of this is real. All of this is real.

He understands what Jenny saw. What he too has seen. And sees still.

Below the row of top bolts, face height, in the middle, like the painted false wooden vertical slats and the painted false bolt heads and washers, is a bird's nest-like convex metal grill with no visible means of attachment, covering a spy hole, rendering it untouchable.

No handle. No lock. No surface to pull. Nothing to hold onto. Nothing to grasp. No means of escape. No possible hope.

A door that cannot be opened from this side, whatever the materials that make it.

A door entirely in a dead grey colour.

A door that says 'no exit'. No exit ever.

Brian looks closely and sees that in various places on the painted finish, Jenny has etched in a few scratches, a few barely emerging fingerprints. These he knows are meant to be scratches from fingernails, hands clawing to find a way out, any way out. There is no way out.

He looks along the foot of the door and sees the only colour set against the dead grey paint: there a fire-scorched brown wooden replica threshold, painted so closely as to represent slightly charred wood, such that one would not know that it is fiberglass. Worn even from its mold to resemble the thousands of feet that would have walked over it into the space beyond. Brian thinks now that here she was right. This is how it was. And this is how it is. But not artefact. Art. Art that whispers. And weeps. And is found in an excavation at a site where some search so that it will not be forgotten. Buried, burned, remembered.

Brian takes a deep breath. Avi standing just behind him stares in silence.

Brian now walks around to the other side of the door rather than through it, to what would have been the exterior of its meaning. Looking towards the far wall he notes the camp bed resting where she had rested, where she had slept but never slept, staring for months at her Project that had been born within, that needed to emerge, that had emerged, that had taken all her will and talent and need and imagination. That had taken her.

He turns to look at the Project from its front side and stops short, staring at what Jenny has created. The door here is silvered, luminous with what looks almost like silver jeweled sheeting, perfect silver plate, shining in the light. The silvering technique she mentioned in an email, but he could never had imagined. Here however she had taken a decision, a bold decision that he would never have expected. With hundreds of small depressions and knocks created from a hammer or a mallet, the door's front is deformed with hundreds of different slight angles, picking up broken reflections of his form, Avi's form, hundreds of different Brians and Avis, undefined, out of focus, but human, moving in silence as they appear and disappear with his own movement right, left, forward, back. Right, left, forward, back. The silver reflects the shadow images in all angles, depending how one stands before them, beside them; they become not one, but hundreds, thousands, tens of thousands, hundreds of thousands. Souls marching into a grey hopeless shower room beyond. Crossing over a false wooden sill threshold that they will wear down in time. Closed in by dead grey from which they will see—nothing. Shortly, nothing.

Impaled into the silvering door front are two silvered large heavy bar locks, also likely made of fiberglass but with the exact appearance of two large, unrelenting metal bars, one above, one below, that in reality would have locked such a door tightly, completely, inescapably into place. On this side the door may have been metal; the silvering suggests it might. The peep hole has a fiberglass as metal cover over it to be drawn aside so that one might know, one might stare, at death. The meaning of death, when it arrives, strangling, choking, diminishing, ending. Stretching from the bottom of the door perpendicular to its silvered vertical base are thin slats leading way from it, a dozen in a row, like the slats of a bathhouse keeping feet from the floor, so that unseen is the metal frame seal jutting up against the faux wooden sill, ensuring that when the door, the real door, would have been closed, no air could possibly have escaped. Death would not breathe. All the slats have been silvered but the vision is clear: air would not have got out; air would not have got in. The air inside could then become toxic, drawing its poison from the opened cans of Zyklon B pellets becoming gas dropped down through ceiling towers to the ground. To the room. To greet thousands waiting for the shower water that would never fall.

And greet their screams when they understood. When they knew. Life would have walked in, but would never have come out. Never escaped.

Brian knows the images. He has seen them from other places. Jenny would have known and in her imagination would have lived. And died. There.

Brian stares at the hundreds of Brians, the hundreds of Avis, the thousands of souls. He hears their whispers too. He hears what Jenny heard.

He knows she did hear.

And knows why she had to stretch the limits of her skills, her imagination, the pictures in her head, to create this Project. This door that is not a door. This entry that is not an exit. This memory. That one might know, and remember.

Brian steps back from the door, ajar, gazing within. Gazing and unable to turn away, he knows Jenny too had gone through.

And once through, Jenny had disappeared.

Jenny disappeared.

He reaches up, and as she had requested, he slowly closes the door, pushing the fiberglass silvered bar locks carefully into the hold on the fiberglass frame, supported in turn by a stainless steel frame of poles so that the Door will stand. Always stand.

Avi looks at him and understands as well. Her request was more than a request; it was a need. Close the door but do not forget. Remember always what happened beyond there.

The note had said please close, and it had been closed as she wished. As she knew it had to be.

Brian does not know if he will see Jenny again. He thinks he will somewhere, sometime, but knows also that she will not be able to return to the team on the Site when they reopen it for their work, their ever necessary work, reopening after a virus that had appeared, and killed indiscriminately, and caused them to weep. Weeping still.

This door, this threshold that is wood and not wood, this memory, is Jenny. She had lived it, in a way, imaginatively, died by it, and would now continue her journey that will take her elsewhere. What she had to do. Needed.

Need is a funny thing.

Brian stares one last time at the reflected out of focus silver Brians, images of souls without definition, staring back at him, the multitudes who might have passed through one final time only, and he realizes that for the first time on his own journey, his own need, professionally, he is seeing himself in the silvered mirror of his experiences and seeing how that journey has also affected him. Drawn him forward. Made him perhaps. He stares at the door before him and he understands he is not simply seeing a replica of the past, what happened, what it was, he is seeing a mirror of himself here, now, the present, perhaps the future.

That realization pains within him in a way he would never have expected, had never sought. But perhaps with a need unspoken but always there. A necessity.

Brian and Avi turn and start out of the studio space. They leave in silence. Brian closes the lights and the door disappears. They walk down the corridor without words and out the front door. Brian reaches towards the lock to seal the front door, but immediately realizes this is one door he cannot lock. Perhaps a door he could never lock, just as he can hardly bear to close his own door, lock his own way, past, and forward.

He hands the key to Avi to do as he must, then turns and walks silently away, passing the car that brought him here. He needs to walk now, walk through the city, through the Ghetto that was once here, the places and streets and buildings long ago destroyed, past the Umschlagplatz that he still recognizes for what it was, where it was, feeling the fear that was there, the cries and screams that were there, hearing the cattle car doors slam shut, locks drawn, hearing them still, then along the markings in the street where a ghetto wall once stood but stands no more, so that he can hear the cries and the whispers from ghosts and can feel their tears and their loss, loss that has become his own.

And as he walks he somehow thinks he hears the sound of a violin weeping out the notes of a sad song. Jenny had said in an email that she heard it. Now he understands. The notes speak quietly to him as well. The notes of something that came before, a long time ago, before the door closed and was locked and the notes were removed forever from those listening. So Brian hears it too, now, just slightly, as he walks, he is sure he does, and he knows that that quiet song from a violin is the song of memory. The memories of others. The memories of Jenny. The memories that are his own.

Brian understands what it meant, and what it means.

It is not enough, but it will suffice. This memory. This self.

Brian disappears down the streets of this city. Into the evening settling in. Disappears along his own way, his own journey.

Brian disappears.

2. Tom

Jerusalem
January 2019

Tom finds him entrancing from practically the first moment he sees him. There is something about this young man, more boy than man and yet not boy, who somehow connects the enthusiasm of youth to the quiet seriousness of experience, a sense of something that Tom cannot quite put his finger on. A combination of intensity, a semblance of irony, the slightest turn of a smile, a deep inward-looking glance in his dark eyes. Something attractive about him that makes Tom wants to know more. Wants to know him. A mystery. A warmth.

Maybe Tom sees in the young man an image of himself. Maybe that is it. Or the desire to see himself as he too once might have been. Or maybe it is simply Tom's need to find life again, in all its complexities, and for some reason he recognizes it now. The first time around is so long. So very long…

No. Wait. Start back at the beginning. Or at least at the beginning of place. This place. This time. Here to hide away from all that has gone before. And in the hiding, finally found.

So: click. Still shot, close up, tight angle. Click again. See at a slight angle, gaze away, to his right, to his left, to his past. There is no gazing forward. Not just now.

He is Tom …

*

The aperture of a camera lens, simply put, is the hole within the lens through which light passes, determining the exposure of the final image. The larger the aperture, the more light reaches the unexposed image awaiting definition, or with technology now the camera's sensor, resulting consequently in the exposure of that light against the image. Think then of the human eye, its pupil growing larger or growing smaller depending on how much light enters into the eye, into the brain itself, determining how one sees an image. And depending on the conditions, the brain like the camera sees an image as darker or lighter, in full light or in near black. The image as it is, or as the camera like the brain wants it to be. Distorted. Exposed. Revealed and remembered.

Light exposes the final image to a semblance of reality. But by playing with exposure through aperture, just as in the development process, the image is manipulated by shadow and light, defined in time and in space by the brain, by the camera, until it becomes apparent that what is real is not. Indeed that perhaps nothing is real except as the photographer chooses to see the image in his mind. To record it thus. To remember it thus. To frame it: thus.

At that point, all reality comes into question.

*

It begins for him on a rough small weed covered playground in front of a low apartment building.

Or perhaps not there.

Perhaps instead it begins when he is eleven. His parents are out for the evening and he pulls down a movie cassette to load into the VHS player. He loves movies, any movie; he will watch anything and everything. So he pulls out a film sitting on the back of a high shelf, poorly hidden from his eleven years old grasp, directed by a famous director he has never heard of, neither knowing nor caring what a director does. This dust covered VHS cassette tape contains a film about a war that is not his war, a time that is not his time, a film in which to watch madness unfold. And the film is just that: loud, angry, chaotic, a driving narrative, a driving soundtrack. At the end of the movie, just before all hell in narration breaks loose, an apocalypse breaks loose on that television screen attached to a VHS player by an umbilical cord that now gives him nourishment, the story introduces the character of a half-insane photojournalist, a man like an oily snake seeing the world and all its madness through the character's own reddened, mad eyes. The voice singing the song on the soundtrack says 'this is the end', but Tom, wide eyed, recognizes that for him it is not the end. It is but the beginning. The photojournalist character, not the actor, not the event, but for this boy of eleven, the role embodied by the here and now, on a screen but alive, is his beginning. And despite the insanity, despite the chaos around him in a moving picture on a screen, he too is there. Simply: he is there. With a camera to record all, a camera to protect from the madness, to bear witness, to define. Time, and place, and moment, and truth, and laughter, and fear and humanity in all its inverted glory. Necessary to be there from that moment forward.

So even at the young age of eleven Tom knows that this will be him. It has to be him. It has to be his life as it is the mad character in a movie playing on the television screen thanks to a dusty VHS cassette tape not carefully hidden on a high shelf in a cupboard. It is the dream. The vision. The possibility and even the necessity of his dream.

From that moment Tom begins to learn cameras so that he might one day follow this dream, making it into the real. That it indeed might be him, the eye behind the camera. Thus the ins, the outs, the functionality, the speeds, the focus, the lenses, the distortions, the light. Always the light. And the image.

The camera will become his eyes, like the character in the movie who molds him, defines him, urges him to reach out, reach forward. He will hide behind a camera, and through a lens he might see all. The chaos and the fear and the humanity. All.

The beginning of his journey.

He tries formal education. He tries university. But it is not for him. He has to be there, the place, the zone, the moment. He spends all his savings on this camera and that camera, learns developing processes and exposure, and takes himself off to make a name for himself. This he thinks will be simple.

It is not simple.

Even when it is time. Even when he drops out of college almost as soon as he begins, pays his own way to a country he does not know, a war he does not understand, a time and place, photojournalist, war journalist, even then it is not simple. He is one of many and others are more professional, more experienced, under contract, more of a time and place and at the right time and right place than he is at his young age. Yes he eventually sells some photographs to publications, but not many. Few give him time. Few care.

He knows cameras. He does not know life. Not yet.

Not until the rough weed covered playground in front of a low apartment building. On a clear, sunny day. In a place some know, some do not. A city called Sarajevo. And a dream he has had from the age of eleven, from a story on a VHS tape cassette running before his astounded eyes finds voice. And a voice finds the song to sing through a photograph, like the weeping of a sad violin.

So this is how it truly begins. He keeps at his side his beloved Leica M4, a camera he calls Annabel; he does not know why. She is always with him, this Annabel, who lives not by the sea. Lover. Sometimes too he takes one of his heavier Nikon F2 bodies, a short lens, a long lens, the camera companion of a hero, that hero a half-insane chaotic photojournalist he once saw in a movie as a boy, now replicated. But not this day.

Not this day.

This day he has not expected assignment. He has not planned locale. Motion. Instead he wanders down some back streets in the city being strangled, siege city, with time for some thought, to wonder where this will all take him. And there in that rough, weed covered playground in front of a small apartment building, sheltered there, safe there, he sees four young boys and a young girl playing football, shouts and joy and laughter in a language he barely understands. One in goal, two in offense, two in defense.

He watches them as the minutes drag by, minutes of laughter and shouts and arms waving and play. Only play. And he himself almost boy, dreamer of images, dreamer of the photographic moment.

Finally Tom, for it is Tom, takes off his jacket, puts his camera beneath, and strolls over to these children on this weed covered small stretch of playground, gesturing me too, me too. And it is then three boys and a girl against one, with one more boy moving side to side in a goal defined by sticks and shirts, thus five children against Tom who imagines he is one of them, when it does not matter, when it does not matter at all. Five against him, he against five. And the laughter. And the shouting. And a goal here, a block there, a foul that is not a foul, a fall that is not a fall, a pass to the right, to the left, around him, through him, through them. He and they are one, laughing and charging and playing. Until youth wins out, and he falls on the field of play, weed covered field of play. Laughing and panting and drenched in sweat and acceding defeat to warriors half his size but full of righteous bravura.

Tom laughs, waves, shakes hands with each of the four boys and the one girl. Pats them on their backs. You win, he proclaims. You win. You win.

He walks back over to his jacket, allowing their own game to continue: two on two, a fifth in goal. He laughs. Shakes his head. Kids. For a moment, he too a kid. He puts on his jacket. He picks up his Leica that he calls Annabel, beloved Annabel, he does not know why. And even as he turns indeed a wind blows out of the sky, chilling, just at it had done in the poem by that poet whose words and thoughts these are. That poet, Tom tries to think: who was it? Who was it who said this? A wind blows out of the sky.

But it is not wind and is not chilling as that poet said, he remembers, as that poet wrote, but is hot. So incredibly hot. So incredibly loud. Deafening. That summer's day on a playground covered with weeds, a small playground in front of a small supposedly sheltered apartment building, heat that burns and chills at the same time.

He does not hear the shell from above before it hits the earth. He does not see it.

But he feels the blast, pushing against him, tornado of wind that is not wind.

And in one motion, even as his body twists and falls and turns, he stands in a single motion, one single motion, his hands holding tightly his beloved Annabel, his Leica M4 lover, his finger pressing the shutter to release, to shoot. To shoot—back.

So freeze frame and press the shutter. Click. Click again. Faster. Click. Focus. Focus. Not thinking his fingers simply doing. *Doing.* And images freezing in time and in motion. Images of a weed covered playground blackened now. And the arm of a child. And the foot of another child. And the head of another child. And death around.

And the blast around.

And the images that would define him hereafter. The images of death. The death of a child. The death of one child. The deaths of three.

And one boy child still alive, covered in blood and tears lying on the ground screaming, lying where a once defined goal of sticks and shirts is now but a crater of muted fire.

And one little girl standing somehow, stock still. No scratches. No blood. No understanding. Motionless. Her face unable to express anything but emptiness as life was there, but is now taken away, the shock of what it means for her now to be alive, will always henceforth mean for her to be alive.

He, photographer, he who is Tom, in his heart he knows he should run to her, embrace her, cover her eyes, carry her away, run too to the one covered in blood, screaming still, in his heart he knows he should run. Embrace. Human to human. Be.

But he does not run towards them. He does not embrace. It will henceforth become his trademark. Capture the instant in an image but do not become a part of the landscape. Hide behind the camera. He invisible. The camera the eye. The camera the brain. The camera only, the heart. So instead over and over he presses the shutter release of his beloved Annabel, his beloved Leica M4, over and over, angle here angle there high shot low shot the expressions of pain the expressions of emptiness the expressions of death the expressions of shock the faces. Blood. Close up, and the faces of those who have died and those who live and those who live with death forevermore. To shut them up in a sepulcher. In a kingdom that is not by the sea. A kingdom that is fated now to become the conscience of the world for a short time only. That appears as image through the aperture of his beloved Annabel. And not from his heart. Not from his heartache. But from what Tom has become.

Photojournalist who is there, but never really there. Not really. Instead exists only the exposed image. The photograph. The lives that were, that are, that may be or not. The captured expressions. The red eyes, red with tiredness and fear and too much, too much. Instead there is war.

*

The calls hence come. The photographs make him famous. The messages do not stop this time. They call with staff offers but he values his independence. They ring with assignments; some he accepts, some he rejects. They telephone with questions, with possible headlines, with titles and subtitles. Print journalists ask to join him. Television anchors raise their glasses to him from the safety of their far away news desks and beg him to be a part of their teams. Wire services seek to sign him up.

All from a few photographs of a small playground in hell itself.

From that moment Tom finds his place, his vision. And from that moment Tom learns that he needs to disappear, for the camera to disappear, for the image and place to become paramount to his own existence, his own being now no more than the end of an index finger pushing on a shutter release: no matter how painful, or dangerous, or broken, or lost, the subject will have its own voice, its own singular

142

reality, on this day, this time, this instant, this history. Its own place. Sometimes its final resting place.

Tom finds ways to embed with one group of soldiers or another, day or night, front line or on leave. He finds the enemy who seek the limelight: the murderers, the politicians, the mercenaries, the diplomats. Moments of thoughtfulness or bravura, moments of hate or kindness, moments of life. Moments of exhaustion. Moments of homecoming. Moments when there will no longer be a homecoming. Moments of death. He finds them all.

And he finds in the faces and expressions and tears and blood of others his subjects. Children. The disturbed. The lost. Elderly. Ordinary people. The Others. His voice is only the voice of the subject. His eye a singular eye. The eye in the camera. It becomes him, is only him. In this way Tom ceases to be. And in this way his fame increases, fame as photojournalist, as photographer, as one who records through the lens of his Anabel, that Leica M4 and his Nikon F2s, the story. He will never be the story itself. He will be the storyteller who speaks without words. Nebulous cipher.

The calling.

He spends another year in Sarajevo, occasionally, smuggled out through enemy lines, dangerous enough, but they allow him passage because they want his eye to show them for what they see of themselves. What he sees of them is not always the same. But for some reason it does not antagonize. For some reason it gives those who hate him and what he stands for a semblance of power and pride.

He travels to their killing fields. He stands staring up at the woods of Srebrenica: clicking at ghosts. Aperture closing and opening at the disappeared. He sees what they do. What happens. He becomes invisible so that the camera might speak for him. It does. It does not lie. But neither does it weep. The camera is not an enabler. But it helps shape and mold history. Selected history that will remain forever, whispering into the ears of readers of magazines and newspapers, witnessing on television screens and searching in books, so that his audience too might know, might say I too was there, even while Tom himself is not. Aperture closing, opening, always closing, opening.

Tom is not there. Behind the camera he is not there. To be there he will have had to reach out. And he never reaches out.

At the end of that year, that year filled with blood when he witnesses but does not bear witness, when he records without recording, weariness sets in finally and the enemies in that place stop killing. But they do not stop hating. Tom decides to remain in this country, tired and tired of, to journalize the hate, to show the lines of exhaustion and confusion that remain on the faces of those who survive as well as the poorly hidden remains uncovered of those who do not. These photographs, quieter, etched with the remnants of violence, win him further plaudits. Further recognitions. An award or two. He understands, however, that such recognitions are not the achievements he seeks. What he seeks is anonymity, a medium to tell someone else's story, someone else's experience of exhausted pain in image. When all is said and done, there is only the image. The scars of the moments will never be his.

Other conflicts quickly draw him into their spheres, their worlds. He lives on the border between Turkey and Iraqi Kurdistan for a year. He flies to the Congo and lives in a small village recording massacres he could never have imagined in his nightmares; he does not imagine, allowing only his cameras to be the soothsayers. He returns to the Balkans and Kosovo, rejoining many he has worked with before. He sees some local fixers he knows killed. He sees nothing. The price paid. Then the event that comes to so dominate, so define all that will come after that 11 September and he immediately flies to Afghanistan. He knows what will happen. He knows he belongs *here,* embedded with the firestorm that soon erupts. For years to come he will follow the so-called war on terror. It becomes his battleground, but for Tom the battleground only of the mind, the eye, not the battleground of the heart.

His heart is empty. His heart is silent.

In every conflict he seeks out the ordinary, the everyday, those who do not desire to suffer but who inevitably do suffer. He allows them to tell their stories not in words, but in glances towards the middle ground. They never see Tom. They see only themselves and one another, and the hopelessness of events over which they have no control. And sometimes a flash of hope.

This too Tom captures. But more often than not this too remains elusive.

He plays hard too. Drugs keep him going harder, further. He shoves coke up his

144

nose and rubs it on his gums so that he can run faster, be there first, hidden by a camera to get a shot, any shot, to see, to be. He drops acid at night so he can be somewhere else, imagine the unimaginable, be not himself, be everyone and no one, be the camera. He parties. He makes love. He has no lovers. He dreams. He has no dreams. He keeps special mushrooms in his camera bag so that the witnessed explosions become fires of joy and fires of hell. He simply is, and is not, racing a course that will give him a reputation sometimes for daring, sometimes for carelessness, but always for possibility. He gets the photo by not getting himself in the way, because he is not. He is the camera and the camera is him. His calling card. Leica and Nikon and somewhere there might have been a human consciousness focusing, touching that shutter button, controlling. But he controls no longer. The camera is all. The picture is all.

The picture is all.

For a decade, pushing two, this is Tom's life. Tom's world. A world in which he does not allow himself to exist. A world in which he will never allow himself to feel.

Later in the second decade of the millennium, after working in so many areas of conflict, so many wars passed or passing that one begins to flow into the next, that death no longer shocks, when at times he does not know if he is East or West, North or South, when the hotel rooms all look familiar because they are in their way one and the same, when the reddened eyes of so many, fatigued, have become his own reddened eyes that see everything and nothing, Tom is offered a retrospective of his two decades of journalistic record at a gallery in lower Manhattan, New York. The opening night reception proves a great success, with tears and applause, loud congratulations from the glitterati and literati, from critics glowing and guaranteeing brilliant reviews not only in the New York papers, but in national and international reviews as well. Tom is referred to as artist, as necessary witness, as humanitarian, as brave soul.

But none of it is true. Not to Tom. Not who he is.

At two in the morning, when the familiar crowd has gone home, when the warm wishes have grown quiet, when the door has closed, Tom asks the gallery owner, a friend, if he might stay alone in the space for a while, promising to set the alarm when he leaves. Last man standing.

Left thus by himself, dimming half the lights, Tom's soles echo off the wooden floor as he moves from photograph to photograph, some blown up to the size of the wall, some on a wall as a line of photographs no larger than four inches by six inches. He picks up a half empty bottle of wine on a table, sipping as he stands before each picture that represents almost twenty years of work, trying to remember each face he sees in each photograph. Each place. Each gunshot or bomb or tear or expression of joy or fear, hope or loss. Each moment. Each human being. Each human life.

And as he moves from photograph to photograph, between rooms, between wars, between each and every experience, then around again, Tom begins to realize that he cannot name one individual from memory, one moment, one place name. He cannot tell himself when he might have once reached out. Once cared enough to put down the camera. Once shed a tear himself.

Mostly, he cannot remember himself.

Tom spends the next two hours standing in front of every photograph, staring, trying to understand what he felt at the time, what he feels now. After two hours he realizes that the accolades and the congratulations and the warm words mean nothing. Absolutely nothing. He realizes that so much has been simply a lie. And he begins to sense that the photographs of so many in that room, from so many countries, experiences, fears, hopes, so much of what Annabel had seen through her mechanical aperture, the Nikons had captured in a single moment, so much of life is not his own. Because arguably his own has never been. Because in the process of the finger pressing over and over, as quickly as possible, the echoing click of shutter's mechanism, his own humanity may well have disappeared from himself.

Tom leaves the now empty bottle of wine on the table.

He closes the lights in the gallery. He sets the alarm. He locks the doors. He slowly strolls down the steps into the still dark night air, with a few stragglers yet walking the streets, a few cars passing. A taxi. A radio playing somewhere.

He walks down another street, turns and walks a few blocks further into deepest Manhattan. He finds a small weed covered playground not far from the Hudson River, opens its gate in its surrounding fence, goes within to sit on a bench. He looks around the space, overlooked by a small apartment building. He imagines he sees four young boys and a young girl playing football even there in the dark, one boy standing in a makeshift goal, the other four playing at offense and defense. He imagines he is there with them. Only this time, in this kingdom so near the sea, as an early March breeze comes out of a cloud by night, Tom realizes that the love that should have been stronger than the simple aperture opening onto an unexposed image and that should have brought in light, revealed the light only in others but not in himself.

For the first time that he can remember, with the recollection of a weed covered playground lot that was protected and that was not protected, in a country few now think about, in the memory of the sheer joy at joining five children who he realizes now he had loved, truly loved, and lost, Tom feels the tears on his face, allowing himself to silently weep.

*

Later in the morning, still early, Tom returns to the apartment he has borrowed for the past months. He packs a small bag with all he still owns: not much. He leaves a note for the friend who had loaned the apartment to him with a simple message of thanks. He puts Annabel, that Leica M4, as well as two Nikon F2 cameras with four associated lenses into his camera shoulder bag. Then he leaves the apartment, locking the door behind him. He puts the apartment key into the apartment's post box.

He leaves the city, telling no one where he is going, no friend, no agent, no stranger. He is not sure himself where he is going. For the next three or so years, Tom is silent.

*

Cameras today have the ability to focus automatically on a subject. But a good camera, and a good photographer, in many circumstances will utilize manual focus of a lens. A camera focusing automatically can occasionally miss the sharpest image of the subject that a photographer can define with the manual parameters for opening and closing the aperture. Focusing manually a good photographer ensures the sharpest image, or, for some reason, may choose to pull focus so that a subject or background may present out of focus to varying degrees. Tripods make manual focus easiest for most photographers, but tripods are often not appropriate, particularly for a photojournalist on the move.

Manual focus is often preferred when shooting a subject in closeup, or extreme closeup. In such a situation the photographer takes control of the image sought and then revealed. This is particularly important and valuable when trying to define the etched lines on a face, or a tear, or when focusing on a subject needs decision to reveal a glancing emotion, time passing in a moment, confusion, loss, fear. Automatic focus might catch the emotion, but the photographer behind the lens focusing with one hand, pressing the shutter button with another, defines the emotion. Definition humanizes a subject as it does a photographer.

Manual focusing on a subject also allows the photographer to play, and define, depth of field. In doing so, the primary subject dominates, becomes more important, unless the photographer decides that events surrounding the subject, or behind the subject need the kind of clarity that impacts the subject, causing him or her to react in an unexpected way.

Should the photographer prefer the bomb to the bombed, the gunshot to the wound, the implement to the torture, manual depth of field control is essential.

Manual focus puts the photographer in complete control. Or at least the illusion of complete control. In fact it is only the illusion of such because, when all is said and done, only God creates, and God destroys. But together God and the camera give life to the subject.

Or death.

*

He has rented a small cabin in upper Maine. He tells very few where he is. He has no guests. He has few needs. He spends much of his time fishing, thinking, reading. He desires only a quiet life. Tom does not seek to belong. He seeks to forget. He cannot forget.

When the call comes from one of those friends who knows where he is, who sends a Christmas card once a year but does not seek to intervene, in fact who understands well, Tom is not surprised.

He hesitates when the offer is set before him. He is not certain he needs to reenter the world, anyone's world. But the friend assures Tom this is not an assignment to photograph but simply to teach eager students ingredients of composition, of chiaroscuro, of images defined, of aesthetics and professional practice. Tom will be free to do his own work, to forge a new path if he wishes: nature or still lives if he wishes. And although there is conflict enough in this place of history, he will not be in demand as a conflict photojournalist. Tom is simply wanted as a practitioner, as a professional, as a mentor to younger voices, as an expert in camera art.

The residency is in Jerusalem. A flat is included in the offer, as is a studio of his own to work in, to create as he might wish. Interested students. A salary. A curator's role of student work at an end of year exhibition. And no questions asked.

Tom can be who he wishes to be. He can be simply the present, not the past. He can teach, and he can observe. After an initial hesitation it seems a safe move, away from trauma, away from what came before. He does not have to engage with the ills of the region. He can look at the world around him but he does not have to immerse himself in it if he does not wish to do so. He might find a way to touch a heart. He might find a way to touch his own.

The apartment is near the Old City in the Musrara neighborhood, around the corner from Jaffa Street, with its multitude of shops and restaurants. Despite that, the apartment is quiet, its front door through a small courtyard half hidden behind flowers and shrubs. It is only a few minutes' walk to the Bezalel Academy of Art and Design, where Tom teaches a group of twenty-five young, curious students. Here too he is given a large studio with printing and darkroom facilities both to work with his students if he wishes, and to work on his own.

He is rarely asked about that work, past or present. No one seems to care about the ghosts that haunt him. The students themselves are far too engrossed in their own hopes and dreams, in the statements they want to make. He finds these young people largely apolitical despite living in a political world of extremes, in some ways extensions of the cameras they bring to his workshops but not so far behind the cameras that they disappear from the images they wish to create. Those images are effectively reflections of themselves, their intellect and curiosity on show, so different to Tom's experiences. He does not try to lead them down a different path. Instead he concentrates on technique, on the manipulation of images with the camera, on fundamentals. He helps them discover and define the images they wish to explore, where images are art and art does not document. The images they wish to tell are photographs that do not tell a story but that are a story. The students simply want to create art as they see it, as they understand it; they do not really seek to tell stories with that art.

And in this way, without quite knowing it, the students themselves are the story. Without quite recognizing it, while they rarely put themselves in front of the camera, they are nevertheless there, in every photograph, in every idea. The art and the artist merge into one.

How different to Tom's past life, in which he had managed to disappear, insisted on it, defined himself in this way: he had thus ceased to exist while the shutter opened and closed, sublimated and destroyed by the images before him. War does that. It destroys him even as it destroys the world through the view finder. The loss of the human.

In this place, this new city filled with history, some of it violent, Tom tells himself he can be human by simply disengaging from the world around him, the events that define a generation, the flare ups of violence and distrust existing but ignored. And if his world here lacks intensity, it does manage to calm with soothing indifference to this world. He spends his own time photographing people, but no longer trying to reveal them. He photographs places somewhat like a tourist might, except that the images he seeks are there to define texture rather than the object itself: the threads of a carpet; the cracks in an old wall; the warming terracotta curves of a tagine; the colour of a prayer shawl, blue against black. In the glint of sunlight, or the long distance photograph of a surreal moon with focus pulled so that it rests upon shoulders. There are no statements and there are no tears. Here Tom feels safe.

This is what he wants. His statement of self. This is the religion of place. Not the religion of those around him, so much in evidence here in what so many refer to as the Holy City without a trace of truthful irony. Here where prayers are uttered with belief that requires an out of focus view of the world, where background pushes into a close-up depth of field and clarity thus blurs what is in the foreground. Here too where one's God exists simply so that the responsibilities of what might happen, what does happen, all sit on God's shoulders, not man's. Perhaps it is a derogation of responsibility, this human not in human image, but it allows Tom to be someone else, be somewhere else. To forget the playground. To stop remembering only to realize when trying to remember that he never has. Memory has no place for him here.

Tom is to the students an expert in the art of photography.

He becomes so too to himself.

And in doing so he manages to cease being an expert in humanity, replacing it with the art of, ultimately, artistic mediocrity. The art of perfection, where perfection does not tell a story, it simply exists in and of itself. For itself. It simply hides humanity that has long since disappeared behind the camera lens, and here, now, disappears before the lens as well.

Still, stories need to be told. One cannot ignore the world beyond forever. And the world beyond cannot ignore Tom.

It never could, really.

*

Most non-professional photographers today prefer to use digital cameras. With a digital camera the photographer needs to think a great deal less. The camera becomes the photographer, at times subject to little more than the click of the shutter button. Modern cameras also have the capability to automatically adjust the settings needed for exposure, so that images are defined with a clarity one might seek in order to make the perfect photograph. And the perfect holiday snap, in which image is neither too exposed—too bright—nor underexposed, thus too dark. In either of these negatively considered scenarios, the image might become undefined, the aperture having remained opened for the slightest second too long or closed too quickly to bring in the light of day.

A person might go blind, but not so a digital camera.

However not all digital cameras, intelligent as they may be with their digital metering systems controlling the flow of light, react to images in a manner that some photographers, particularly professional photographers, find true, or pleasing, or satisfying in terms of the image they wish to create. Or manipulate.

Digital cameras effectively evaluate available light by that which is reflected off the subject. These interior meters are standardized on a middle gray. This is referred to technically as eighteen percent gray. Middle gray has become the default position. Thus when the camera eye points at darkness, the meter brightens the exposure; when the light from the subject reflects strongly, the meter works to darken the image. It does so without thought. Without asking.

Sometimes, however, one has to ask.

Sometimes, one has to command the camera's glance to approach middle gray as closely as possible. Or to demand that the camera embraces more light, or less, because the world is sometimes not as dark as we fear, or not as bright as we need. Sometimes either overexposure or underexposure produces a desired effect. An image needed so like life.

The solution to this issue is generally referred to as exposure compensation. Through compensation of the digital meter buried in the depths of the camera body, driven by simple algorithms of 0 and 1 to define the very meaning of light, in fact by overriding those chosen algorithms the photographer compensates for more light, or less light, thus brightening or darkening the exposed image to the desired effect the photographer seeks.

Photographers, like most of us, realize that light is not only important for survival, it is paramount. Unlike a digital camera, indifferent to the effects of light to life, the photographer knows that in order to live, one must reach towards light in such a way that it gives a viewer of an image as well as the photographer himself not simply the ability to see, but the ability to breathe, to reach, to be human.

And yet too much light itself is a danger. Too much light, too much of the wrong kind of light, can be lethal. And in such case, some professionals might in fact pursue varying depths of shadow, growing deeper, richer, complete. The oncoming death. The inevitable mist that is end of life.

Therefore the photographer must carefully compensate exposure of the subject. Too little and the subject disappears into darkness, disappears into nothing. Too much and the subject burns Icarus-like, flying too close to the sun and burning into a bright flame of heat and destruction.

The lines between that which lives, that which grows, and that which either disappears or burns in heat is a fine line, and one that a good photographer wrestles with constantly, by necessity and by desire.

To do this, Exposure Compensation, the manual reach for more light or less light by the photographer is necessary. In order to affect this compensation the photographer needs to identify one of the digital camera modes that will use the interior, automatic and life-indifferent commands forwarded to the camera meter. It may be access to aperture priority. Or a selected program mode. Or another scene mode that relays a command to the camera for shutter priority or a preferred exposure adjustment. Once a proper mode can be identified and selected, the photographer then has the ability to adjust brightness manually by utilizing Exposure Compensation.

However this is a constant battle of wills between man and machine, between photographer and camera, between artistic endeavor and the need for mass produced marketing content. This is not simply the push and pull of desire over commercial need, of a world where all are artists therefore none is such. Rather it is reflected in the human need, the human ethic, the humanizing touch demonstrating that the brain and the heart and the soul are in fact within us and not dictated to us.

To regain humanity one must overcome fear, to become the center of the universe, to become God in a godless world. To remember why, and who, and what we are.

It is easy to forget such.

It is easy to keep a digital camera on automatic exposure rather than compensate, allowing the photographer to define through manual means. Forgotten Manual Compensation.

It is arguably, however, sometimes also too easy to overcompensate and over define and thus in the process lose definition. And yet one must never forget that those flaws in vision, that the processes of erring for too much or too little, are the very things that make us human.

In order to be human, we need to take that risk. To seek more light in darkness, more shadow when the light becomes too bright. We need to compensate so that we might see. And by seeing, breathe. In so compensating, we find who and what we are. The resulting exposure, perhaps imperfect, thus reveals an image that is wholly, singularly, our own. And ourselves.

*

The lecture on environmentalism and photography in nature has gone well enough. It is a subject that seems to interest his students more than it interests Tom.

The relationship between ecosystems and environmental change in the modern age reflects a lexicon that young people need and want, far more so than in Tom's work. He can understand and develop the argument in his mind, if not his heart, and in this way engage with his students. It is enough.

As he collects his notes and puts away his slides, Ilana, a young woman whose work he admires, walks over.

--Thank you.

--For what?

--It is interesting. This lecture.

--Good. I'm glad you found it so.

She smiles. He has always found her confident. Her photographic work is somewhat unusual. She focuses on houses in black and white, but she both overlays varying exposures and overlays the silent exteriors with images of rooms, as if the exterior becomes interior, the interior exterior. While what at first might seem mundane takes on a solitude that is somehow startling. Always one room in the image seen from without and within has a single person, naked, but largely out of focus. Somehow the photographs capture both isolation and need, emptiness with a question of the human. She calls her work identities. Her photographic explorations demonstrate both an artistic journey and an artistic curiosity simultaneously mature and conceptual. Tom likes her work, even if its artistic bent is self-conscious. It asks questions, something he feels is important. Although a different path than he has ever chosen, it always catches his attention.

--I wonder if I might do some printing work in your studio. Use the darkroom if it is all right?

--Of course. Whenever you wish.

--Thanks, Tom.

Tom has always insisted the students call him by his first name. He does not like formalities. It reflects the way he works. And he is always open to students sharing the studio space with him. If he needs the space himself he might occasionally refuse, but this is rare. He is always interested to see the students' processes as he is to comment on their progress. He likes their company. He likes them.

--I have another favour?

--Go on.

--I'd like to show a friend of mine around there as well.

--A student?

--No. Does it matter? He's interested.

--No. It does not matter.

--He wants to meet you.

--Why?

--He's interested.

--I'll look forward to it.

Ilana smiles. Nods. Disappears.

He puts the conversation out of his mind. Two days later Tom is working in his studio when Ilana appears with a young man in tow. Tom barely looks up as they enter, Ilana smiling.

--This is my friend Kuba. I mentioned him to you.

Tom glances up at them, Ilana's hand tightly grasps the young man's arm as if protecting. Tom nods, smiles slightly, then turns back to his own work spread out on a long table.

--He's going to help me in the darkroom. That okay?

--Of course.

Tom neither minds, nor gives it much thought. He smiles to himself, just slightly, wondering how much work might get done once the darkroom door closes and the red light within turns on to protect the light sensitive paper. They are young; he shrugs, focusing on the prints he has spread out before him. The young need space; the young have gifts.

He loses time. He can be like that. He does not know if they come or go. He notices later the light just outside the darkroom door is still on. Still working, or not. No matter. He remains absorbed in his own project.

Sometime later, as he puts away the notes he has been working on, the photographs of the last weeks that absorbs him so, he notices that the darkroom light is off. He turns and sees Ilana's young friend Kuba wandering around the studio, staring at photographs carefully, intently. Tom watches him for a moment. The way the young man moves. The way his hand raises to trace one image, then another, as if drawing it. Seen from behind, the young man gestures with his fingers, like a conductor before an orchestra, someone drawing both sound and definition from silence. The gesture strikes Tom as somehow strange, as if this Kuba reaches for something hidden within the image that he stares at so closely. Photographed secrets.

He must realize he is being watched. His hand drops and he turns.

--I'm sorry. I did not want to disturb you.

--Is Ilana in the darkroom?

--No. She left.

His intonation has an accent Tom does not recognize. His dark eyes pierce, staring at Tom without flinching. It reminds Tom of some of the wounded he had so often photographed: staring at him for answers, for hope. Staring through pain. The intensity of such a stare always had unnerved him even as his camera shutter did not turn away.

Tom looks back at his work table, retreating from that stare.

--I thought I'd wait while you were working. I hope you don't mind.

--Not at all. Kuba—is that right?

Kuba nods, slowly.

--You're a student?

--Not here. I'll study in Haifa when I can.

--Photography?

--Philosophy. That's the plan. After I'm called up.

--Of course.

--I like Ilana's photographs. I wanted to see them. And the studio.

--Ilana is good. She's growing into her work. She will do well.

--It frightens me.

Tom now looks back at this young man, still staring intently. There is something about him; Tom cannot quite grasp what it is. An intensity, a seriousness with a hint of irony, even as his words are not ironic.

--Really? Why?

Kuba shrugs.

--It has truth, maybe.

Tom stares. Nods. Weighs those words that hold weight.

--I understand. But it's good. Maybe the fact that it is unnerving is a good thing. I think that is a response she seeks from her audience.

--Perhaps. It's one of the things I love about her.

--She's a talented young woman.

--Yes. She's special.

Tom smiles. He senses the young man's feelings. He is almost jealous: not of the girl, but of the innocence of it all. And the need. He turns away.

--Ilana said I should talk to you.

Tom looks back at him.

--I know your work. A lot of it anyway.

--Should I be flattered?

--Sometimes it frightens me too.

--Like Ilana's?

--No. In a different way.

--The subject.

--No. The photographer...I was at an exhibition of your work. A retrospective. In New York. I was there with my mother for a family event. I wanted to see your photographs when I read about the exhibition, so we went. It was a few years ago.

--Yes.

--I already knew some of your photographs. It was my idea to go. My mother too was moved by them. Maybe for different reasons, I do not know. But both of us felt something.

--You were pretty young to have followed my career.

--Maybe. But I chose to. And then you disappeared.

--No. Just withdrew a bit.

--Why is that?

Tom finds this young man, the intensity of his eyes, his questions, disarming. It is hard to move his glance away from Kuba's stare.

--I needed a break.

--And now you're not doing this sort of work. Conflict photographs. War.

--You get burned out as a photojournalist in conflict zones. Burnout happens

157

often. I did the work for a long time.

--Stress.

--Maybe.

--Trauma. Or fear.

--Both I suppose.

--And questions I guess.

--I guess.

Kuba, this young man, gazes around the room. A number of Tom's photographs hang on the walls, photographic images occasionally of people Tom has seen in the old town, but mostly of the extreme close up details that have become his subject of late: the lines in a face, the misshapen faults in objects, cracks in walls, stains on a table cloth. Images that have no life in them.

--I think your photographs still speak in the same way.

--Really? I wouldn't think so. Still lives in extreme close up.

--Lives that are still.

He looks back at Tom.

--Isn't that right? They haven't changed. Your photographs. Not really.

Tom does not respond. Just watches the young man.

--I want you to teach me.

--Teach you what?

--Cameras. Photographs. What you do. Who you are.

--I don't take outside students, Kuba. I teach here, or teach what I can. The students have their own voices; I just try to guide a bit, help a bit. You should get Ilana to help you. She's very good.

--I know.

An opportune moment, as Ilana indeed then reappears holding a couple of coffees in one hand and two books under her arm.

--Hey.

Kuba smiles at her.

--I didn't get you one, Tom. You were so absorbed with your work. I can go back.

--No matter. I'm about to head out anyway. Did you get some printing done?

--Some.

Ilana smiles at him, irony in her eyes.

--Good. I'll catch you later. Kuba: she'll teach you. She has a lot to say.

--She does.

Kuba smiles again. They watch Tom as he leaves.

An interesting young man, he thinks. And the first person to comment on the life he had before. The life Tom strives to leave behind.

*

Some days later Tom wanders through the back alleys of the Arab Souq market, carefully seeking images that he wishes to photograph. Although lost amidst a sea of tourists taking tourist pictures, Tom seeks something different. In the religious icons he photographs he sees not the icon, but the stroke of a brush or the cut of wooden frame against wooden carving. Amongst the carpets he sees the weave of colour and tries in a photographic image to define the hand of the weaver in the grain of thread. In a rich array of spices he finds a concentration of intense hues in powders and seeds and through these he looks for the defined fingertips and stained hands of those who pick from the flowers, the tastes and aromas hinted within a close-up photograph.

To the traders he is simply another tourist, unlikely to buy. Still they try, bargaining even as he shakes his head no. When they look away to tend to another, he raises his camera to shoot dark rings below an eyelid, a scar on a neck, stained fingers in a bag of flowers, a woman trader's mouth as she sits back and pulls smoke from a cigarette.

Rather than people, rather than things, Tom seeks essence. In essence he seeks a reality of existence. He does not expect that he will find such, but neither will he stop until he discovers either a fundamental truth, or the realization that there can be none.

Exiting through Damascus Gate, Tom wanders for a few more minutes before stepping into Bassem's Café and Bookstore/Gallery for a coffee. He has always liked it here, thumbing through books and staring at the junk pieces that line the walls, each piece telling its own story that he will never learn. Tom sits sipping his coffee, looking at some pages in a book he pulls from a shelf of worn books, when he hears a mumbling voice behind.

--May I sit down?

Tom looks up to see Kuba, smiling slightly. That piercing glance again. Tom hesitates only momentarily.

--Sure.

Kuba sits.

--The souk is crowded today. Like always.

--You were following me, Kuba?

--No. Watching. There's a difference.

--In what way?

--Not following. Rather, learning. Or trying to.

Tom leans back in his chair. Kuba asks for a coffee. After it comes:

--What are you hoping to learn, Kuba? Photography?

--Ilana could teach me that. What I don't know. So no, not simply photography.

--And what do you know? About photography.

--Not much. I have a camera. I'm not particularly good. Not like Ilana, the others you also teach I should think.

--Yet you want me to teach you?

--Yes.

--What do you think I can teach? How to hold a camera? How to capture and manipulate an image? How to focus?

It is Kuba's turn to look away. His slight smile, that slight irony, disappears. He thinks for a long moment before answering. His glance drops: not away, but within.

--All that, but not just that. I want to understand how a photograph tells the past.

--You mean reveals?

--No. I mean tells. Like a story without words. But talking.

--A photograph captures a moment in time. All of my work captures a moment in time. An instance. Happenstance.

--I don't think so. I looked at some of your photographs in the studio at the Academy. The breaks in the wall. The bits of a rug or pottery. The far away stare of a woman on the street. You feel it.

--That's what I do now. It's what I want to do.

--Maybe. But it is no different to the images I remember from your exhibition in

160

New York. From the newspapers and magazines that I looked through. From wars. Soldiers. People in need. They tell a story. They speak of history. Photographs speaking in words without words. They talk.

--What I do now: no. Just a single moment captured through a lens. Hardly the same genre.

--Maybe. But your photographs now also speak of the past. That is what I want to understand. What you can teach me. A detailed weave of a pattern on a prayer shawl or the tears of a mother who finds her child in a mass grave. No different. They speak to me in the same language. History. His story her story in time, past time, speaking. I'd like to find it I guess.

--You're looking for an answer in the past?

--Maybe in the present. But in the wordless story of the past. What do you think, maestro?

Tom is silent for a long while. It is his turn to look away. His turn to think about this boy turning man, young man more boy, who has somehow now touched a nerve. And who speaks something that Tom has for the last few years hoped to deny.

--Your accent...

--I was born and lived in Warsaw. My mother is from there. All her people. Mine too I guess. There were many. Then there were none. My father is from here. It is our home now.

--Warsaw. A city with history. A place of stories.

--Many.

--...You said you will likely study philosophy.

--After the army.

Tom shakes his head; a note of impatience if not disapproval.

--Of course, yes. The army. I've known too many armies. I grew weary of them.

--I have no choice.

--...What are you really searching for, Kuba?

--...Myself.

--In the past or in a present moment frozen in time by the printed image on sensitive paper?

--Like I said: a photograph speaks the past as it reveals the present. And maybe the future, I don't know.

--Philosophy and photography.

Kuba shrugs, and Tom has to smile, just slightly.

--Do you have a camera?

--An old Zenit. Soviet. From my great grandmother.

--You're kidding.

--And…sometimes I use my father's digital Canon. Usually on automatic. I tend to be stuck there. In automatic without control.

--…Bring it. And six of your photographs. Six will do. In six if I find any eye, any vision, maybe. We'll see.

Kuba nods. Says nothing. They sit longer in silence, sipping their coffees.

*

How a camera analyzes the light of a scene in order to determine the correct shutter speed, or the aperture, or the ISO—the all-important number that determines the camera's sensitivity to light, allowing more or less light to enter the aperture—is through its meter setting. Digital cameras contain an automatic digital meter with different modes in order to manually decide how and how much light enters the camera and becomes etched into an image. Older cameras do not have such an interior digital meter. With these older cameras the photographer has to use a light meter to determine optimal exposure, and of course the photographer cannot preview an image or see immediate results, leading both to chance mistakes and occasional chaos of image.

Sometimes, however, chaos and confused judgement is necessary for the moment. It is chaos that some of the best photographers harness. The unexpected. The theory that is chaos suggests there is always an unknown factor at the edges, waiting: this inevitable element of uncertainty also leads to possibility. It is chaos that makes us human, with all its many facets of hope and despair.

Of the numerous modes for evaluating light in a modern digital camera, center-weighted measuring is often desirable. This mode evaluates light in the very centre of the image the photographer is about to shoot as well as to a degree the subject's surroundings, but ignores the corners. This mode is strongest for close-ups and relatively large subjects when such sit in the middle of the frame.

The risk, however, is that the light at edges loses its texture, its exposure time. Becomes chaotic. A good photographer remembers that the edges of an image can be as important as the centre. Sometimes, when ignoring or even forgetting those edges, the subject might be exposed, but the story might dim, or even become lost.

*

Whether or not Tom finds something in Kuba's work, he never says. A unique voice. A unique eye. A yearning. Potential. What it is, Tom also never says. Perhaps never understands. But for whatever reason, Tom finds Kuba both engaging and challenging. He likes the challenge.

Over the coming weeks, irregularly at first but soon more habitual, Tom sits with Kuba in studio, looking in detail at the IPOs on the boy's camera, the different modes and how these relate to light and shutter speed, the possibilities of different lenses for capturing or manipulating images. Sometimes Ilana joins them, discussing and arguing about her work, her point of view. Sometimes Kuba disappears into the darkroom with her, emerging with a slight grin but both showing evidence that prints have been made. Or at least a few. Tom enjoys seeing them together, finding their way; he also enjoys the time he has alone with Kuba. He appreciates the boy's curiosity. The questions. Indeed the search.

Kuba never presses Tom on his work as a photojournalist. He never asks in detail about life in war zones. About victims. He never asks about pain. Once in a while he might remark about a particular photograph of Tom's from those years ago that he might have looked at, indeed might have studied. He might query the angle and how Tom achieved it, or the shutter speed, the relationship between shadow and light. He might argue about depth of field with Tom, or the focal length or the ISO setting. But he rarely comments on content, on image, on the photographer himself. He never asks Tom how he felt. He asks the how. He does not query the why. He asks about the making, but not necessarily the maker or the moment.

As Tom grows more comfortable with Kuba, and Kuba with Tom, the two of them, sometimes with Ilana or another student or perhaps two, wander the streets and alleys of the Old City, the markets, the landmarks. Kuba has an interest in faces, particularly the elderly, shooting subject after subject, sometimes with permission, sometimes surreptitiously. Tom watches how people warm to him, or frown, or eye this boy up and down, or turn away. He watches how Kuba seeks the shot he wants, retrieves it, at times successfully, at times not. He also sees how the boy engages with children, laughing, instructing curious young faces in the workings of his camera, accepting a young child's attempt to become his older self; they eye Kuba with interest and wonder. Maybe they are all Kuba.

--You are looking to capture them, the old, the ancient?

Kuba smiles and repeats an oft uttered phrase.

--I know who they are. I am trying to find who they were.

--And the children?

--Who they will be.

For some reason, Kuba makes Tom smile. They boy has that effect on him, disarming, the same way he disarms his subjects, even those who turn away. And yet all the while, even as this boy becoming man tries to define his Voice both technically and thematically in his own work, he retains a close, learning eye on Tom's photographs as well: a mentor's photographs that explore form as well as content, that open textures and physicality, not asking of the present or past, that simply are a statement of a material presence. This is Tom's work in Jerusalem. He seeks these textures. He seeks the central presence, the essence, rather than the temporal. In trying to define the existence of an object, perhaps he seeks the meaning of identity, of light defining being. Yet all the while, despite its distance to Tom's former life as a photojournalist of conflict zones, Kuba insists that he sees in this work a natural thread in all that Tom has done. He insists that one does not disguise the other. Or hide the other. It is all part of the same ellipse, the boy says, then leaves the comment hanging.

Tom does not push Kuba further.

Kuba does not push Tom further.

In the process, a real friendship develops. Mentoring, yes, but more than that. A cooperative need at a certain time, a certain place, without a clear definition why. The central image is in focus yet out of focus at the same time, so much a part of both their visions, where the edges of the photographs remain unnecessary at the time. The center will hold. So they think. They put the edges out of the frame of their minds.

At the end of one particular week Tom is in the darkroom printing some of the images he had made during the previous few days. He has not seen Kuba during the week. It is not unusual for Kuba to be away for days; theirs is never a particularly defined schedule. Tom has never pushed Kuba about his family or life beyond the body of a camera. That is an aspect of his own work that Tom always retains: the photographer disappears behind the camera entirely and there is no life beyond that moment, that image, that photograph. This is something he and Kuba disagree on, something he can see frustrates the boy. But about this Tom engages only slightly, and only occasionally. As Kuba is not a student at the academy his time is his own: he appears when he appears, or when arranges, as simple as that.

When Tom emerges from the darkroom into the studio he finds instead Ilana, gathering some of her own work she needs for an exam presentation.

--Working?

--Not today. I said I'd help my mother at home. Will we see you tomorrow night?

--Why? What's tomorrow night?

Tom is confused; he has made no plans to meet her or Kuba or any of the other students over the weekend.

--Kuba didn't mention it to you?

Tom shakes his head.

--He was going to. There's a concert tomorrow night. Classical. Partly in honor of his family. You didn't know?

--About a concert? No.

--Or his family history?

--No. Sorry.

--Ah, well: his story to tell, not mine. But he said to me that he hoped you might come.

--I haven't seen him in a week or so.

--He's wrapped up with a couple things that are important to him. I'm sure he meant to tell you about tomorrow. Jerusalem Theatre Hall. It's not far. There should be tickets available. You should come.

--I'm not much of one for classical music. Or socializing.

--You should come anyway. See the real world through your own eyes, not always a camera.

She winks at him.

--Later alligator.

And she is gone.

He has not planned to join them. He has never been at ease at such cultural events. He has never found it easy in crowds when he does not have to be, especially these days. But despite himself Tom is curious about Kuba, about his family. Ilana said the concert was partly in honour of them. Kuba has always been circumspect about his background. It is neither open nor closed for discussion; it is simply a subject that he keeps at bay. So although last minute Tom decides to put on a jacket and tie, a most unusual costume for him, and to make his way to the theatre.

His seat is in the balcony. A concert for young musicians. He notes the program: the 'Warsaw Suite' by a composer Pawel Weisz and a work by another composer Tom also has not hear of, Marek Kopelent, make up the first half of the concert; the second half after the intermission is Bach's 'Concerto For Two Violins', followed by another Weisz, 'Yeshua: the Journey of Loss and Light (From Requiem For Hania)'. Unsurprisingly, none of these works Tom recognizes. Not that this matters.

Tom sits back in his balcony seat and joins the applause as the conductor marches onto the stage, acknowledging the young orchestra. He then points to a box of seats at the edge of the balcony, not far from where Tom sits, and applauds. Tom leans over and sees Kuba sitting with Ilana and two older people, presumably his parents. Tom looks back down at the program and sees that the concert is gratefully attended and supported by Janiec-Zuckerman family of Pawel Weisz.

Quietly Tom removes his beloved Leica 'Anabel' that he has hidden in a bag at his side, quickly focuses on his proteges, and clicks the shutter, nearly silent. Just as he does, Kuba turns his head and seems to look directly at him. In the viewfinder Tom sees a slight smile, ironic, appear, just as the lights dim further.

Tom lowers the camera. He sits back, listens.

And as he listens to some of the music, evocative in its way, his mind wanders to images from the past. Images that have been dormant for some months if not years, but never removed from his unconscious. It makes him think, even as the music flows over him, how music performed in the present inevitably speaks of the past.

He cannot help but wonder about the relationship between music and the photographic image, and cannot help but wonder if this is at the heart of Kuba's argument over all these weeks. To capture the past in art. In the frame of a photographic image like the notes of an orchestra.

When the concert finishes the applause is long, the audience clearly appreciating both the works performed and the young musicians. Tom almost surprises himself at having enjoyed the music, in part for itself, but in part because it causes him to think in images. It is something he not often feels in listening to classical repertoire, perhaps because he does not understand its methodologies or language, never having had a musical education. But he admits to himself this music sets his mind working in pictures. Images of the past; images of the present.

As the crowd thins Tom pushes his way into the foyer. He starts towards the exit, when someone takes his arm. He turns to see Ilana grinning at him.

--You came.

--I couldn't miss it.

--I hoped you would. Come with me.

--Ilana, perhaps…

He does not finish the sentence. Ilana is the type of young woman who gives orders and sticks by them. She leads him over to a far side of the room where Kuba stands with his parents, smiling, nodding, engaging with the warm words of concert goers. Kuba sees his mentor and girlfriend approach.

--She yelled at me because I forgot to tell you. I apologize. I'm happy you came.

--I didn't have much choice. Not with Ilana on the case. But I'm glad I did.

--This is my father, Beniamin Zuckerman. Tom Clark, the photographer.

Kuba's father has turned to look at Tom. He is younger than Tom would have thought, grey just beginning at his temples. He shakes Tom's hand warmly.

--Mr. Clark. A pleasure. We know you've been kind to Kuba.

--Tom, please. I think he's the one who has been kind to me.

--And my mother, Agnieszka Janiec.

Another woman she had been speaking to is turning away. Agnieszka Janiec nods at her, then turns her glance to Tom. Her gaze is warm but intense. Kuba's eyes are hers. Tom understands now where the boy gets the intensity of his stare. And his accent, Tom realizes, when Kuba's mother speaks.

--Tom. And it's Aga. It pleases me to meet you at last. Jakub has said many kind things of his days with you. He said he hoped you might be here tonight.

--Mother…

--He does not like the formality of Jakub. I like to needle him, just a bit. I think a bit of needling does him good. I offer that as a suggestion.

Tom takes her in, takes her all in. She is likely older than her husband, but not by much. Although her hair has more grey, perhaps as much grey as black, youth retains its hold on her face. It speaks of a confident intelligence, as does her gaze which, like Kuba, she holds when others would have turned away. Her expression also speaks of curiosity, again as Tom has seen in her son. Her face immediately strikes him as forthright and honest. Everything about her is beautiful and strong.

--Did you enjoy the concert?

--Yes. I did. I guess there is a family connection.

--To Pawel Weisz. Yes. He was quite special to us. But that's a long story for another time. What did you think about the music?

--The second piece lost me a bit.

She laughs, a laugh that Tom finds endearing and warm, rather than sarcastic.

--I think Kopelent confuses everyone. He certainly does me. But Pawel liked his work, so…

--I did like that last piece.

--Yes. Part of that story, Tom. A long story as I said. The word Yeshua from the title of this piece: you speak Hebrew?

Tom shakes his head no.

--The name Yeshua in Hebrew is Joshua. But through the Latin it became the English spelling for Jesus. Pawel knew this. But he also knew that the word in Hebrew is derivative of the verb to rescue or to deliver. From Pawel I learned that this meaning was important to him. The ending of a long story and a long search. Delivered after so long. Pawel's story, my family's, is perhaps about deliverance, or rescue. So it touches me too.

--I hope to hear it sometime.

--I'll let Jakub tell you then.

Kuba rolls his eyes.

--Okay, Kuba. If it's Kuba, Tom, it means you are truly a friend. Perhaps I should have called my son Yeshua. Or in Polish: what do you think Beniamin: does your son seem a Jezusa?

--I think my mother who is also Polish might have approved. Or maybe not. You see Tom, a Polish wife, a Polish mother, how I survive is beyond me.

--I'd say you have lived to tell the tale.

--I have. Indeed.

Tom smiles at Kuba, holding Ilana's hand. Ilana grins back at Tom. Kuba again rolls his eyes.

--Kuba: will I see you this week?

--Yes. Not Monday, but…Tuesday I'll have a break.

Tom nods his goodbyes and makes his way out of the building.

Later, in the studio alone, he prints the photo he took on the balcony. He stares at the family image, particularly at mother and son. How alike they are, he realizes, and not just physically. A beautiful woman; a beautiful son, he mutters to himself, intrigued.

He stares at the faces, caught in the moment.

And he smiles to himself because he senses he stares too at the past. A distant past in a glance. In that, there, that moment, he surmises that Kuba has been right. It speaks a story. It does not reveal. It speaks.

*

For long-focus on a subject a photographer removes the usual lens attached to the camera body and adds a telephoto lens, also called a telens. A telephoto lens increases focal length, used commonly to show faraway objects within an accurate perspective. It defines detail that was not always possible to see except in close-range photography. Utilizing a wide angle telens also expands the horizontal of the image. But most telephoto lenses produce a narrower field of vision to a standard lens. They are often used by sports or wildlife photographers although are useful for anything the photographer wants to zoom in on. When a digital camera is placed into burst mode, which is a mode of continuous shooting, images can be taken in quick succession, so that the photographer captures movement in time as well as a particular space. With a telephoto lens that which is faraway and moving is captured in burst mode into a series of photographs so that the photographer can define an action in motion, continuous, even when not close to the scene or the image itself.

When continuous shooting and utilizing a telephoto, even from a great distance, the photographer tells himself that he can understand a scene happening before him. But a good photographer also recognizes that this is not really true, even if motion is captured. A particular angle, a specific point of view, remains an inevitable part of the noise and chaos constrained by the photographer's depth of vision and angle of vision. Sometimes such 'noise' is because of choice; sometimes it is by accident or circumstance. Sometimes it is because of necessity: to shoot from afar, at a particular angle, so that the photographer does not have to engage directly or can increase his own invisibility.

Even a telephoto lens, shooting in continuous succession on burst mode, trying to reflect every minute moment of motion and activity, does not really tell the truth. A good photographer knows this.

And admits that truth does not really exist as a finite concept. Or a moral one.

*

As Tom in fact quietly hopes, Kuba appears at the studio on Tuesday before Tom is to head over to the classroom for a meeting with several students.

--You're early. I've got to meet some students, then I'm planning to walk to Temple Mount. There's an archaeological dig I want to get some shots of in close. I met one of their people who said that would not be a problem. We could have a coffee, walk up together. I'll be an hour or so first.

--I can't, Tom. I'm sorry. I can't today. I'm working with some friends in Al-Bireh. You know it?

--No.

--West Bank. In the Ramallah district. An interesting city. Some people I work with we try to do some humanitarian type work there. Bring people to hospital in Jerusalem, talk to locales, foster relations.

--Is it safe for you?

--Usually. We get grief from both sides, especially recently. You stand in the middle you hear the noise at the edges. Like some photographs. There have been some incidents. We try to help calm.

--Standing in the middle is not always wise. I know.

--Yes, I think you do. But survival is a lesson I've learned from my family. Speaking of which, I brought you a present.

Kuba reaches into his backpack and pulls out a book that he hands to Tom. '*Pawel Weisz's Hania: A Requiem* by Arthur Schamus'.

--My mother suggested I give this to you. Arthur Schamus was Pawel Weisz's partner. Also a family friend. He too is now dead but before he died he wrote this about some of the music you heard last night. It is also about Pawel's life; and about us, about my family.

Tom reads the words on the back of the book: '...A story not just about the creation of a moving piece of music, a piece of art, but the story of Pawel Weisz, of the family he finally came to know. This is a story of what was lost, and what was found.' Tom looks up at Kuba.

--Thank you. Interesting. Something was lost, and something was found. Your family?

--The past and the present maybe.

--What you seek in a photograph.

--What you give in your photographs too. All of them.

Tom smiles.

--Will you take your camera with you today?

--No. Cameras are not a good idea. And I'm not as brave as you are.

--Were. That's why I go to archaeological digs instead. Nice and safe.

--No. I don't think that is so.

--Be careful where you're going today, Kuba. I know places like this. Always expect the unexpected.

--The chaos. It's safe. I'll see you at the end of week.

Tom nods. Kuba smiles, then is gone. Tom looks at the book still in his hand. He puts it in his camera bag to read later; he's late to meet his students so grabs his coat and closes the door behind him.

*

Taysir P.'s father always says about his son that he has the sharp eyes of an eagle. Beautiful eyes. His father says if he should ever find himself lost in the desert, lost in the deepest Sinai, he would only need to call out his son who with those eyes would see a lost farmer wherever he might be. Taysir P's father is deeply proud of his son; and why wouldn't he be? Even at the age of twenty he has shown himself to be a trustworthy talent. Others have taken note.

Taysir P. grew up in Jerusalem. He was a fair student, not standing out. But he has his talents and he is obedient; he is never one to question authority or to take initiative. He pays close attention to explained information. There are of course times when he reacts somewhat beyond the expectations of those in charge, but this is largely because of an incomplete understanding of his responsibilities or the instructions handed to him for any particular course of action.

Basically, Taysir P. is a safe pair of hands, someone you can usually rely upon to be steady in the middle, good at editing out extraneous noise. That perhaps goes some way in explaining why powers that be choose him to develop the skills of a scout and protective marksman. His eyes are good, but so too is his patience under fire, his calm. Taysir P. is known to react only by necessity, not by desire.

Trustworthy.

On that particular Tuesday morning Taysir P. and his unit are easily briefed on the job at hand. Nothing particularly unusual or out of the ordinary. Routine patrol. Everything calm. No outlying orders or expectations.

Expect the unexpected.

A briefing and business as usual. Photographs are shown: satellite, street level. The unit will commence its patrol here, depart there. A ninety minute stroll at most. No reports of belligerents. Simple reconnaissance. Group A in the front. Group C take rear. Eyes open. Group B chat respectfully with locals. Two high observation posts: at the entry corridor, in a four story office building, top floor office, empty, one hundred eighty degree view along the main patrol and traffic route; a second at the end of the patrol corridor, from the roof of a six story office building with a possible three-hundred sixty degree angle view of the patrol route. Taysir P. will be located here, with ability to see almost all of the patrol's entire route forward as it approaches from street to street, along the back, cutting again towards the primary corridor passage.

Expect the unexpected.

Before dawn Taysir P. and a two person local support group, civilians, pass in front of the office building for which they have a key. The two civilians continue walking up the street, arguing loudly, pushing one another right and left, creating a visual distraction while Taysir P., pretending at first to stop and urinate in a doorway, quickly lets himself into the building and disappears up the stairs. The civilian support members turn down a side street, then walk quickly, disappearing into the dawn, no longer seen. No longer noticed, if in fact they ever were.

Taysir P. signals to his unit that he is in position and all is quiet. He would like a cigarette but knows he cannot smoke. His rooftop location is the highest in the vicinity; he would not be seen from above. But cigarette smoke travels. He has been trained to remain invisible from start to finish. Even the water bottle he carries in his pocket must be completely full or completely empty when moving, so that even the slightest sound of water within will not be heard. Nothing is left to chance. He remains invisible.

Taysir P. removes the short rifle he has hidden beneath his long shirt and lays it on the ground beside him. He takes out the scope he has in his small shoulder bag and places it beside the rifle. Then he sits and waits. His role is observation and backup protection. He expects to be on the rooftop for half a day, no more. He closes his eyes and rests. He will not sleep. He never sleeps when on duty. He does not close his ears to any sound, however distant or unthreatening: a dog barking, cars starting their morning journey on the streets below, people talking, laughing, a baby crying, pots and pans, shops opening: everything is ordinary. Nothing is ordinary. He keeps his eyes closed, his ears listening for even the slightest aberration. Or silence. Silence is always a warning.

There are no warnings. Everything is ordinary. Nothing is ordinary.

In this position Taysir P. now remains for the subsequent two hours. He admits to himself he is tired. The effects on him of a family celebration two days prior have not quite ceased to make themselves felt. But he would never admit to such to any in his unit. He has a job. He does the job.

As it grows brighter, as the head of this day begins to take hold, as the morning's noise grows louder, Taysir P. sits unseen and quietly on the rooftop, his back against a low wall, resting silently. After a time he opens his eyes. He looks down at the rifle at his side. It is a piece of protection, of support, that he knows well. Indeed that he has come to love.

The rifle is an M89SR, his pride and joy. His best friend. It weighs only four and half kilograms and its length, only eight hundred fifty millimeters, makes it an ideal companion for Taysir P., with his specific skills. He knows this companion inside and out: a muzzle velocity of two thousand eight hundred ten feet per second, range one thousand meters, magazine feed of twenty rounds, constructed of light-weight carbon fiber. Perfect. And the attached scope is his preferred Schmidt and Bender 5-25x56PMIILP, as good as he could ever wish for observation. That is his role: to observe. To protect as necessary. Mind their backs. Mind their fronts.

Taysir P. knows how to shoot. He knows how to aim. He has been required to shoot warning shots only twice in his year's military career, aiming high towards a brick wall once, high into the air in open ground once.

Taysir P. has never killed anyone.

He is good at what he does.

And now he sits. And waits. And sips from his bottle of water that he will need to empty if any water remains when he will eventually leave, ensuring that he makes no sound, leaves no trace.

Twenty minutes before the agreed commencement time of the patrol Taysir P. rolls onto his knees, hidden from view behind a large air conditioning unit. He picks up the scope from beside his rifle and slowly, methodically, stares through the scope at everything he can see below, three hundred sixty degrees, taking in the streets, the buildings, the alleys and the primary thoroughfare. He looks for anything that does not seem right, anything out of place. The day promises to be very hot. There is no wind. That suits because if he sees a blind moving awkwardly he knows that something might be amiss. If doors are not opening or close en masse it tells him that, as the day is beginning, something might be wrong.

But nothing seems amiss. Nothing seems in any way wrong. The day is beginning as days before and likely days after. Everything seems normal.

Expect the unexpected.

The theory of chaos: no matter how perfectly planned an action, a motion, an intention, there is an element that has the ability to always result in chaos. To malfunction. To reveal the unexpected.

Below a car drives along the route. Taysir P. stares at it through his scope. Lettering on its side suggests it is part of an NGO out of Jerusalem known to assist those who live here in this district, ferrying those in need to hospitals in Jerusalem or further afield. They are a group dedicated to support and peace in all communities. Taysir P. knows of this group but has no political opinions about them, indeed about any such NGO. He has no interest in politics. He does the work he is asked to do. He trusts his ability to see but he does not see beyond the vision of his eyes. He has no other opinions. With his scope he watches the car stop at a building. Two young men, three young women emerge, wearing T-shirts emblazoned with their NGO's logo. They knock at an apartment building door. An elderly man appears, limping heavily on a cane. The two young men help the elderly man slowly into the car, then stand back. At this point Taysir checks his calibrated watch and sees that the patrol is to begin its movement in three minutes. He lowers the scope that has been angled towards the NGO's car and attaches it to the rifle still lying on the ground where he has been sitting. Quickly, efficiently, Taysir P. makes some corrections on the scope and commences a final check on the rifle itself. All is in order.

He crawls over to the edge of the building, lying in position, able to angle the scope and weapon towards the far streets beyond, starting at where the team will slowly make their way after the first ten minutes or so of their patrol.

Nothing amiss. Nothing out of the ordinary.

He knows of course: prepare for the unexpected. Taysir P. does not expect the unexpected.

After the long wait, through the scope he begins to see members of his team cautiously make their way down an alley, emerging then onto the main street. He watches as they slowly, methodically, walk along the edges of each side of the road, Group A in front, Group C protecting their rear. He can see their faces. He knows their faces. His team. His friends. They carry their automatic weapons with shoulder straps hanging down for the appearance of nonchalance, indifference even. They can react in an instant. They have been taught to do so. But it is always imperative that they do not instigate anger or reaction or instill particular fear. Control, yes, but they are not here to fight. They are not looking to hurt or take anyone prisoner. Or kill. That is not their assignment.

They patrol. They eye. They nod and do not antagonize. No more unless something not expected in fact transpires.

Taysir P. watches them, the minutes dragging on. Watches them and keeps watch and protects as best he can from on high.

Expect the unexpected but react, do not act.

Taysir P. watches them still. And after a long period, the patrol gets somewhat close to his position. Through his scope he can see their faces, this team he knows well. Their expressions are easy. Smiling almost. Some of his team stop to chat with a shop owner, local traders with faces that if not particularly friendly are neither particularly hostile. All is as it should be.

All is as expected. Nothing untoward.

Nothing unknown.

Taysir P. breathes easily, sighs almost. And just as he does, from far behind, behind C group taking the rear, from back in an alley a good distance away, sounds of shouts, sounds of bangs. Not gunshots. Those he would recognize. Rather stone on metal, stone on stone. A car backfires. Not gunshots. Doors slam. Not gunshots. Shouting louder.

A group of young men appears in the distance. Teenagers really. Taysir P. can see them through his scope. Running towards his unit. Stones thrown. Shouts. Sticks raised. Is that a knife? Another? More stones. Running towards the unit. Shouts and stones and more stones slamming at metal doors and gates and pavement and anger and shouts and more stones.

He sees it through the scope. He hears it from afar growing near. He sees his unit taking defensive positions. Guns raised. Warning shots aimed high. Birds at risk. The shouting does not diminish. The stones become a hailstorm of stone and concrete. From an upper window items are thrown down. More stones. More hail. More anger. More.

Taysir P. goes into automatic reaction mode. He swings his rifle and scope to the left, scouting, scouring for sources, for weapons. He swings his rifle back towards his unit who have taken cover and have their own weapons at the ready. He sees two of his team at the rear, C group, firing shots into the air. He sees their Negev7 weapons pointing up in the air, discharging. Negev7: four hundred twenty millimeter long barrel, six point six kilograms, seven point sixty-two millimeter ammunition, he knows it, has it written in his mind so that he knows but does not need to think does not need to remember because his M89SR marksman's rifle is his weapon of choice, his companion, with its Schmidt and Bender 5-25x56PMIILP scope through which he stares now without thought yet automatically, knowing. Now from somewhere, he cannot be certain, he thinks he hears a single shot. He thinks he hears a burst not from the automatic arms of his unit but a single shot small calibre from somewhere, somewhere, as the rocks still fall still bang on doors shouts growing louder.

A rare moment of uncertainty. A rare shadow across his face. He thinks he hears. Does he hear? The rocks slamming right and left. He thinks he hears but does he hear? His finger twitches. Does he hear? The rocks pound against walls, doors, pavement. Stones thrown. Anger and shouts. Does he hear a small calibre single shot? Does he? His head twitches, just slightly. Not sure. Not sure.

His unit C group crouching in doorways, pointing this way and that, not firing, defensive positions. He looks to where they aim but sees no one. He swings his own rifle to the right to see if there are any perpetrators in the front of the unit. Nothing. It does not seem to be a pincer ambush. Back to the rear. A few more shots he thinks. Likely two perpetrators, perhaps three without warning but not currently hitting near to anyone. Are there belligerent shots? Does he hear? Does he…hear? He is not certain. He cannot be certain. Chaos. His unit moves between sheltered doorways, scouting. Taysir P. again swings his rifle and scope quickly to the right, beyond his unit, in front of them keeping his angle of vision ahead to protect, to warn, to aim. To fire if necessary. But to remain calm unless his acknowledged talents are needed.

What he sees: suddenly a group of very small children in school uniforms walking towards the melee.

What he sees: the small children, in their uniforms, starting to run away.

What he sees: in the middle of the street, near his unit, almost on top of them, three other small children emerge unaware from an alley and freeze. Two children quickly now turn and run, disappearing back up the alleyway.

In his scope he sees the third child, standing in fear, stock still. He can see a face, a little girl. Blue uniform. Her eyes are wide. A shot nearby. Does he hear a shot? Blue uniform. Is that a shot? He hears it. What does he hear? He cannot be certain. Cannot. Alert. He hears much. He hears a little girl cry. Blue uniform.

Blue uniform.

What he sees: in his peripheral vision, from up the street to the right, he sees two figures with orange shirts. Or maybe orange vests. He sees one, a man, in a t-shirt with an orange vest or perhaps orange combat shirt he cannot be certain, Taysir P. sees in his peripheral vision this figure running towards the unit. Running towards the little girl in a blue uniform still standing, as he can see again in his scope, still motionless, paralyzed with fear, screaming. He can see the man with the orange shirt or vest running towards her which means he is also running towards his unit. He can see the man's face: young face, he could be anyone. One of them, one of us. One of them. Does he hear? Does he…hear?

Chaos. The unexpected.

He can see the flash of orange running towards the little girl, towards his unit.

Everything in a flash.

Expect the unexpected.

Taysir P., on automatic reaction in his mind, no thought, in a flash, as needed without question, needed, stares through the scope at the little girl in the blue uniform. And a young man with an orange shirt or maybe orange vest that may in fact cover combat gear or may not and the girl screaming and the girl crying and the fear and what does he hear? What does he hear? And he feels his finger tighten on a rifle trigger.

And he tells himself nothing but if he told himself anything he would say shoot high but he is not thinking not talking not listening simply on automatic doing what he does and what he does he does well and what he does is to look through the scope and sense particular danger and think nothing other than his responsive instinct telling himself he must do what he is trained to do what he is so very good at with his eyes that his father always said were as sharp as any eagle as he looks through the Bender 5-25x56PMIILP scope with one eye shut and one eye perfectly placed to see an orange shirt or vest running in front of a little girl in a blue uniform an orange shirt or vest protecting the girl hiding her covering her and is that a weapon in the hand a weapon just raised in front of combat gear beneath the orange vest and is he a threat are they all threats remember the threat is always there always belligerent remember that trust only your team and his own role is to protect that team and to eradicate threats and he feels the trigger of the M89SR the rifle he has always loved for its perfection and he puts just the slightest necessary stress on that trigger, the slightest touch, the slightest pressure, he feels it and he sees it and he hears it and he does not think and he does what he is good at doing. His work.

Taysir P. pulls the trigger.

And shoots.

*

The theory of chaos: expect the unexpected. And even then, with that knowledge, you never expect what is unexpected. There is simply, and only, chaos.

***

All photographers need to be cognizant of lens distortion, whatever kind of lens is utilized. Put simply, distortion causes a lens to put curved lines where straight lines should be. There are two common types of lens distortion: barrel distortion and pincushion distortion. With barrel distortion, straight lines as normally seen bow outward from the center of the image. This might occur when the photographer stands too close to the subject with a wide angle or zoom lens at the wide end. Body parts are made to look abnormally large. Pincushion distortion, on the other hand, is a common enough occurrence with a telephoto lens. This kind of event makes people look thinner than they are, or is often the result when looking at images in straight lines. The further the lines are away from the center of the image, the more distorted they will be.

Photographers sometimes use lens distortion with intent, manipulating the image they photograph. Others might be able to rectify unintended distortion in the light room when printing. Distortion can usually be avoided when shooting by changing the plane of the camera in relation to the subject. While it is probably best to avoid distortion unless the effect is sought, it can however be addressed at a later time. But sometimes too distortion, when unintended, can be seen as a cheat of a subject, the resulting image taking on more character, a greater warmth or sensitivity than the reality of the image might suggest.

If distortion cannot be avoided, there are ways to address it, if not accept it. For professionals the cheats in the lightroom are at times considered falsehood, not a true understanding of a real situation. For those photographers it can seem a fabrication when trying to address a mistake, so that the image is never reproduced as an actuality, but rather becomes what was imagined. Or for the professional photographer who does not seek a truth in reality, a desired effect. A creation.

The imperfection of an image reveals instead the almost perfect desired creation. And a lie thus becomes truth.

*

He spends many hours in the quiet of darkness, lying beneath the angled light of his bedside lamp, reading. He reaches the point where it becomes hard to focus. Smiles to himself: wrong lens he mutters; you will need contacts next.

He thinks about this book he is reading, the story of a composer who did not know his past, a young woman who did not think of a future. Kuba has a lot to take on, he thinks. A lot both to live up to, but also to release from. The past taints a future no one ever expected. Had it not been for that young man's mother, Agnieszka, connections might never have been made. And a requiem never composed. A beautiful piece of music, he thinks; that last movement he had heard performed. A work of wonder.

He will finish the book in a day or so. Then much to consider. Mull over. And to discuss with Kuba, this young man who has become not just a simple student, but perhaps a part of his life. A family story has touched him. This young man searching in the face of all that has gone before too has touched him. This boy. This man. Tom shakes his head, just slightly. Closes his eyes. Long day over. Long day ahead.

Even before he wanders blindly and gently into sleep his phone rings. Unexpected, unwanted. He opens his eyes, looks at the screen at a caller name. Ilana. He is to meet her early the morning to discuss her project submission. But she should not call at this hour even if cancelling.

He clicks the answer button, puts the phone to his ear.

--It's late Ilana. Can it wait?

He hears her words as she speaks. He hears and hears too much and does not wish to hear, not wish to know not now not ever not…

His eyes close. He listens.

*

He is told he can remain in the waiting room with others. Many stand in the corridor, most in uniform, some talking on phones even at this early pre-dawn hour. As he approaches the waiting area a uniformed officer stops him.

--These are not visiting hours.

The officer speaks first in Hebrew, then in English when Tom does not respond.

A voice behind him:

--He's with us.

The officer looks at the man standing behind Tom. Hesitates. Shrugs. Walks away.

The man takes Tom by the arm.

--I'm Ilana's father. She said you would want to come.

Ilana's father leads Tom to a large waiting reception area. A number of people sit mostly in silence, including some young people, probably fellow students from Kuba's school. Two of Tom's own photography students are there as well. Some people talk quietly in groups of two or three. Against a far wall Tom sees Ilana sitting with an older woman, her face turned away. The woman, likely Ilana's mother, holds her hand. Ilana looks up, sees Tom following her father. She stands, hurries over, gently pressing her father's arm with thanks.

She looks at Tom, then puts her arms around him and buries the side of her face against his chest. He too holds her, tightly. After a long moment, she pulls away. Searches in his face, hoping for an answer perhaps. Something. There are no answers.

--He is still in surgery. They have put in him a coma. All they would tell us is that it is a head wound. They say it is serious but they do not say how much so.

--I'm sorry, Ilana.

--They are investigating. They always say they are investigating. They first said they thought he was wearing combat gear, that he had a gun. Tom would never carry a gun. He does not wear combat gear. He does not fight.

--I know.

--They say none of their people would deliberately shoot anyone, that he moved. That he ran.

Tom looks at her. Nods slightly. Puts his hand around her arm.

--He was with two others of his group. They were drinking tea with a family when they heard noises in the street. They said he ran to protect a child when he saw her. A little girl. They said he saved her life, this child.

Tom looks away. Kuba should not have been there. This should not have happened. Tom has been here too often; other wars, other hate on two sides of an argument, two side of a divide, Tom thinks. Seen this too often. His camera has always protected him. Now he has no protection.

Her voice almost a whisper:

--Kuba said once to me that you do not break, that you never once break, not in your work. You have seen this, this…But not break. How does one not break? Teach me that.

He looks at her. Reaches up and dries a tear slowly falling down her cheek.

He gently considers. Gently responds.

--It is better to break. Your strength will be there. It is better to feel.

For most of the early dawn hours nearly all sit in the waiting room. Waiting room waiting. Occasionally someone stands to pace. Another closes his eyes. A woman leans against her partner. An older man sits with his head in his hands.

Tom does not know. Tom knows them. Has seen them too often. He sits isolated in his silence. He feels emptied. He closes his eyes to rest. To remember.

--I didn't think I'd see you here.

Tom opens his eyes. A journalist he knows, or he knew in old places, hard places, stands looking down at him.

--I thought you'd left the game.

--…Do you ever leave?

--I suppose not.

--Family friend.

The journalist nods.

--Word is this kid may have been involved. You want to give a comment?

182

--Off the record? Bullshit. On the record? Bullshit.

--Yeah. That's my reading too. There'll be an enquiry then an enquiry of an enquiry. Way things work here. Like always. Like everywhere…Nice to see you Tom. You're lucky you left, although you're probably right: you never leave.

The journalist strolls from the room, greeting another colleague in the corridor. They both disappear.

Tom looks over at Ilana. She rests her head on her father's shoulder, her head turned away. Her father holds her tightly to him. Tom closes his eyes so that he too might disappear.

After more hours have passed, time ticking slowly indifferent to pain and worry and fear, a woman comes into the waiting area to address them all.

--Um, I'm Mira, I'm Jakub—Kuba's--aunt. Kuba's parents know you are here and want you to know how much it means to them. Kuba is out of surgery. He is in a coma. The doctors cannot say right now what his condition is other than very serious. It may be hours, even days, before they have a better idea of what is going to happen. As you can imagine this is very hard on all of us, particularly Aga and Beniamin. Your prayers are greatly appreciated and greatly needed. His parents have asked me to tell all of you that it is best not to speculate about what has happened or to suggest anything to the press or others while everything remains unclear. In the meantime we hope for the best. We…

Here Kuba's aunt struggles. Seeks words. She takes a moment to catch her breath, looking away, closing her eyes.

--It is not easy. Kuba is a young man full of life, a life to live. It has been a very long night. Go home now. Get some sleep. We have authorized the hospital to give updates as appropriate. For now go home. Pray.

*

Tom sleeps.

He finishes the book about a composer named Pawel, a young girl named Hania.

He cancels student evaluations for the day. And the next.

He needs time. He needs silence.

He is never supposed to enter into the frame. To put himself inside the camera. The camera has eyes. He does not. How often has he told himself that?

But this time Tom sees. This time Tom hears. He cannot shut his eyes. He cannot close his ears. The aperture is wide open. The moment in motion caught in an image.

He sees this boy, Kuba, this young man, this mind looking for answers.

Tom has no answers.

He telephones the hospital. They have nothing further to report. He visits again. Sits alone. Leaves.

He does not telephone Ilana. He knows that she will be waiting just as he, Tom, waits. Trying to figure things out.

He has always expected the unexpected.

He has always known there is chaos in the wings. He has always known it is so. Now he understands he had forgotten this first lesson of all. There are no expectations. There are only five children playing on a weed covered playground, playing with soundless laughter.

Tom thinks he does not know. But he does know. He probably always has known. The endless passages of possibility are finite after all.

As he expects. As he knows.

Three days after surgery, his brain having ceased to function, an enquiring mind no longer with any questions to ask, his search having ended, the monitors are turned off and Jakub Zuckerman dies of a massive trauma to his head without having regained consciousness.

*

Tom attends the funeral for Kuba at the Beit Shemesh Cemetery, about half way between Jerusalem and Tel Aviv. A large crowd of family and friends gathers. He keeps well away behind the crowd. He feels this is not his place, not his time. Ilana and her parents stand close to Kuba's parents; Tom notices how somehow this strong young woman keeps herself together, her face set, her pain in evidence although she refuses to let it take control. In this she is like Kuba's mother Agnieszka; Tom senses that woman's strength revealed even through the emotions expressed in her face. When she turns to leave Tom just notices her glance in his direction before turning away. As he starts to walk back towards his waiting taxi, Ilana's father, who has separated himself from his daughter and wife, catches up with him.

--Professor...

--Tom. Please.

--Of course. Ilana asks me to tell you that you will be welcome at the Zuckerman house. They will sit shiva, the period of mourning, for the next week except on the Sabbath. Tomorrow it will be family, but come the following day. They will like it if you do, I'm sure. As would Ilana. You've meant something to her, to Kuba. Here: I wrote the address on my card. Please.

Tom takes the card, nods, and Ilana's father returns to his family.

Tom wants the aperture to close tightly. He wants the exposure complete, the image set. He wants the image to remain but he the photographer to disappear. But he cannot disappear; not yet.

Two days later, in the afternoon, Tom finds the address in the Ein Karem District on the outskirts of Jerusalem, a small, airy two bedroom single story house with a quiet courtyard filled with flowers. A crowd of family and friends stands in the entrance; as much as Tom struggles with crowds, he makes himself ease his way inside. A woman hands him a glass of water, which he gratefully accepts, struggling with the heat, the people, the reason for his presence. He keeps to a far wall, watching, taking all in as if the eye behind a camera. He does not think he belongs but neither can he escape. Kuba would not have allowed him to escape. After a few minutes he wanders into another room, a study library filled with books. Kuba's father Beniamin stands talking to some others, quietly. Whispering almost. Seeing Tom, he makes introductions.

--This is Tom Clark, our photographer friend who was kind enough to take Jakub under his wing. Thank you for coming to us.

--I do not know how to say in words; I...I'm so very sorry.

Beniamin grasps his hand, tightly.

--You touched my son with your work.

--As his work touched me. Truly.

--I am aware you came to the hospital. Waited. Thank you for that. We are grateful. I don't know...exactly what my son was looking for. But I know you were helping him understand this journey.

A woman reaches for Beniamin's arm. He nods at Tom, is then pulled away.

Tom slides into another room. More books. Some art he finds interesting. But one display shelf unit particularly catches his eye. On it, in a large perspex case, he sees a violin displayed as if artwork. Walking over to it, he sees that it is an instrument in some disrepair. There are some chips in the wood along one of the holes shaped like an 'f', a crack in the other. One on the strings hangs off but has not been replaced. One of the key pegs is half broken away. Tom does not know if the instrument is an antique or not, of value or not, but it catches his eye. It does not seem as if it is something particularly unique or beautiful, but somehow it must have value to the family. He finds its display odd, as if it belongs to another time, another place. This rather basic, rather broken violin somehow demands his attention; Tom finds it hard to turn his eyes away from it .

From the front of the room Tom hears the rabbi of this family speak in Hebrew, then English, inviting all to join in prayers and say Kaddish for Jakub. Tom turns but loiters at the back. Although the words Tom does not know, he remains in the crowded large room whilst the Rabbi chants the first prayers in Hebrew, with most joining in the subsequent readings. At the end of the service all recite the Kaddish, lines that Tom has heard before in his many travels, from so much loss he has witnessed over many years. Too many years. Heard too many times. These are the prayers recited in mourning. Prayers over the dead. Prayers of loss and remembrance. And whilst he does not understand the words, nor could he recite them, he knows, as he has been told, they suggest that loss, painful as it might be, will not be forgotten, that memories remain. Once the words are said, once Tom realizes that he too will remember, that the image is ingrained within even if not printed on paper, he quietly leaves the house.

He has a sense that Kuba would have walked with him. Is walking with him. His father Beniamin had said that Tom had tried to help this boy on his journey. What the father could not know, that even Tom could not know, not then, not later perhaps, but it is there, within, is the realization that this boy, this young man, this Kuba has helped Tom on his journey as well. And that he continues to do so.

*

All photographers respect that the outcome of any photograph is not guaranteed to be the perfect image. Too many factors come into play to distort the intent, whether mechanically, digitally or because of a choice decision made by the photographer him or herself. Chance always plays its part. Sometimes these distortions, unintended, unwanted, can be rectified in the development and subsequent printing processes. One such example is when chromatic aberration appears on the photograph.

Also known as 'colour fringing', this can be a common optical problem on a print caused by a particular lens distorting colour wavelengths, unable to bring a specific colour wavelength to the particular focal plane, or sometimes when specific wavelengths are focused at different positions on that plane. The resulting photograph may look blurred or demonstrate an intense colour range around edges of an image, particularly so when high contrast exists between image and background noise. Consequently, an intense colour range may appear around the edge of a central image, with ranges themselves differing at different points of the image edge.

And while black and white photography utilizes limited and specific colour channels, chromatic aberration can also result in image blurring in these photographic prints as well. These distortions, whether in black and white or in multi-chromatic wavelengths, can be countered and addressed by utilizing certain colour filters, or in the case of a monochrome photograph in black and white by converting that colour plane into singular black and white without any chromatic intensity.

The issue of chromatic aberration can also be addressed through the development process by understanding the mathematical and physical properties of colour wavelengths.

That said some photographers choose to use chromatic aberration to their advantage, often in the case of art based photography rather than photojournalism.

All photographers see images in colour but some seek to define image through a hyper-realistic black and white. All realize too that colour, like image, like imagination is physically finite but ultimately has no finite boundaries when subject to the photographer's perceptions. A rose is red if the photographer says it needs be red. If in black and white it may be grey. With aberration it may have purple or blue at the edge. Sometimes the photographer defines for him or herself what is red and what is not, even if in the final photograph the viewer sees an entirely different colour saturation due to the reaction to colour wavelength within the viewer's own eye. And should that viewer be blind in one eye or both, that which is red takes on entirely different meaning.

What is clear is that the photographer reaches for some kind of truth, only to discover that truth is mutable and ultimately an empty concept. But this does not stop the photographer from seeking elemental truths. And this is where story itself comes into play. The photographer, particularly the photojournalist, seeks truth from every angle and ultimately finds a way to tell a story that finds many truths, many moments, and acknowledging such. Truth and the image are relative. Relative to the photographer. Relative to the viewer.

But without such stories, there is no truth or even the approximation of such. Without reaching for a truthful reality, there remains only emptiness, a world of darkness where even shadow dissipates into nothing.

A photograph continues to reach. It is a process that is necessary. It is also a process that is absolutely, and ultimately, completely human.

*

It is three months since Kuba's death. At first Tom follows the media information about the events, the press notices about the enquiry, but then stops doing so. He cannot bring himself to want to know what had actually happened that day, what truths and falsehoods are written or said. He needs to find his own way to move forward.

Late in spring a heavy rainfall hits Jerusalem, a rare enough event but a gift for all; the water is desperately needed. Some of Tom's students refer to the torrential rain as 'rains of blessing', so dry has it been. Tom works at his computer in his apartment late in an evening on such a night when he receives an unexpected email from Agnieszka Janiec asking if he might like to drop in at some point; she has something she wishes to give to him. He thinks about the mother, the father. He knows their loss will have been unbearable, perhaps as was his in ways he struggles to understand. But he also recognizes in her note the need. Theirs. His. He goes to the house the following afternoon.

Tom watches her as she pours the tea she has made. Her face is drawn, her hair showing more grey. He can see the last three months have taken their toll.

--It has not been easy. I'm sure you understand.

--Yes. I know.

--Beniamin, my husband, he especially struggles. He spends hours at his work. He teaches at Hebrew University. History. He loses himself in it. He comes home. We talk. We don't. Sometimes he cries. Sometimes I cry. We say we will move on. I do not think we will ever truly move on. Kuba was our beating heart.

--Yes.

--I remember seeing images of your work at a gallery in New York. I was there with Kuba.

--I know. He told me.

--I remember him pointing to some of the photographs. He smiled and said this photographer— you—thinks he is not in the photograph. But he is there. I said I do not see a photographer. He laughed, that quiet laugh of his, and said you probably would think you are not, but he could see you. Yet he had never met you then. Funny. I did not understand what he meant. And then you appear here and agree to teach him. Maybe it is something he willed; I don't know. But it is as if he always knew.

--Yes.

--Do you think he knew? Do you think he was he right, what he said, seeing you in a photograph when I did not see?

--He said much the same to me. I did not think he was right then. Now, I don't know.

She smiles, just slightly.

--Do you know why he approached you?

--To see what he alone could see. Or what I did not.

--Yes, perhaps that is correct, Tom.

--And he was looking for something. He told me once. The past speaks in a photograph through an image. A photograph tells the past is what he said. I argued somewhat, saying it reveals, it does not tell, but Kuba insisted this was not right. He insisted there was this difference between revealing and telling. As if a photograph might speak. As if the photographer does not stop it speaking. He felt that an image captures a moment in time and that moment might help reveal what had occurred to reach the point of an instant. That of course is what photojournalism does. It tells a story. But he argued that a photograph would further speak the past, not reveal it, and he was trying to understand that. I suppose that was the journey he was on. He may well have been right. I don't know.

--He so reminds me of my grandmother.

--Of Hania.

--Yes. My grandmother Hannah, who became Hania, who was always Hania inside, then out.

Tom looks away from her deep gaze. He thinks about Kuba. He thinks how the boy's mother who sits before him and the boy himself are echoes of one another as well.

--I read the book that Kuba gave to me. The story of the composer Pawel Weisz. Of your grandmother.

--Yes.

--It is a remarkable story in many ways.

--Hania, the woman whose requiem music Pawel composed and you partly heard, yes she was my grandmother. And Pawel Weisz was—like an uncle, although not. A cousin. A friend. A part of me. He was born Jakub, and for that our Kuba was Jakub. They both were two lost people who somehow were found. Their names. Their place on this earth. Their selves. Bearing witness in the process of seeking meaning. And finding who they were. And are.

--Speaking, not revealing.

Agnieszka is silent for a long moment, staring at him.

--When you came here, during shiva for my son, I saw you staring at the violin in the case there. You went to stare at it again just now while I made tea.

--Yes.

--I watched you.

--Do you play?

Agnieszka smiled.

--No. None of us, not my husband nor me nor…We do not play. But it speaks. You know Pawel's story, a bit. Not all of it; what his partner, his manager and friend and our friend too, Arthur Schamus knew and wrote, but not all of it. Arthur felt the

190

need to speak, just as I spoke of what I learned from my grandmother Hania, from her notes and diaries and records. I spoke, and Arthur spoke. Those are the words you read.

--Spoken, those words, not revealed.

--Spoken those words, not revealed. So: the violin, cracked slightly, a string broken, chips in the wood…A few years ago I was invited to speak about my Grandmother Hania's story. At Yad Vashem. It is something I am asked to do every so often, largely because of Arthur's book. It is a story that is known, even as Hania was not known once. Her words not heard. Even as she did not know.

Tom sits back slightly in his chair. He knows this is a story she wants to tell. A story Agnieszka Janiec needs to tell. And needs to remember.

--Not long after I gave that talk, I received a letter in the post from a woman I did not know. But I have learned to look at letters carefully. Like a photograph, they sometimes speak and you need to listen. The woman's name was Daria Wojewoda. A Polish name, like mine. And she wrote in Polish. So yes I was intrigued. The note simply said she would like to meet me. That she had something she felt belonged to me.

Agnieszka stares at Tom intensely, then looks away, running a story through her memory, and a memory into words.

--A driver brought her here. She was in a wheelchair. He pushed it where you are now. He put a large bag on her lap then waited in his car for her. 'You do not know me', she said. 'You do not know who I am. You would not. And I did not know you until I heard you speak about Pawel, about your grandmother. So: a long time ago, so long, I grew up with a boy named Robert Mandeltort.'

Tom nods; he knows the name.

--Arthur Schamus mentions the name in the book.

--Yes. But Arthur did not know him. Nor did I. Daria Wodjewoda explained that her father, like Mandeltort's, had fought with the Russians in World War II, then the two men returned together to rebuild Poland. Her father became a doctor; Mandeltort's was in the government. So Robert and Daria, they had been young teenagers together. Very close, like brother and sister she said. She sat there, Daria Wodjewoda, and I saw in those tired, old eyes of hers tears swell. She must have loved Robert Mandeltort. She looked away, then back at me.

For a moment, that moment, Tom sees Agnieszka become this old woman, Daria Wodjewoda, speaking for her, and as her.

--I wrote down her words after, so I would not forget. This is what she said to me, sitting there, just there, remembering as she spoke.

This woman in grief, grown tired, resembling her lost son in such a way that almost unnerves Tom, picks up some papers sitting on the table before her and places them on her lap, looks down and reads:

--'Robert was the most wonderful violinist. Remarkable. Everyone knew this. Pawel too when he first heard him. I think Pawel was attracted by Robert's playing, but also by the boy. Robert was rebellious. Funny. Beautiful... Robert and Pawel Weisz: I never asked questions, but I knew they were in love. Those days in Poland—this could not be. People watched. The government agents watched. These were hard times. Hating times. Robert, I, others, we marched on behalf of students. The police fought us. People were hurt. Attacked. We sought a more open society. Yes different times. And on top of this, Robert--Robert was a Jew. Unlike your relation Pawel Weisz before he met you, Robert knew where he came from. You see, there were factions in the Polish government that used the Jews as an excuse to condemn and to hate and to push their agenda. We went to Krakow after some marches in Warsaw. There had been violence in Warsaw and we knew it was a possibility again. We went to Krakow for a students' meeting before we were to go to Poznan. But I could not go. I had to return to Warsaw. I was not there in Poznan. I could not look after my Robert. I was not there. I... In Poznan they took Robert. They beat him. They purposely broke his fingers so that he would never play the violin again. They broke his spirit. They broke so much and it could not be repaired. Never. Some weeks later Robert took his own life. Pawel Weisz—I saw him only once more. He had not known what had happened to Robert. He had not known that Robert could not go on. He had not heard that Robert had died. Pawel was distraught I was told later. And I heard he ran—not from Robert but from himself.'

Tom looks at Agnieszka Janiec carefully. Her eyes stare inward. She is more than remembering a story and relating it to him now. She is living it: living the life of a young violinist she would never have known, living through the eyes of her relative, the composer Pawel Weisz, who was in love with that young man. And living too through the eyes of an old woman who then, who now, sat and sits before her telling a story. A story that Agnieszka Janiec now in turn needs to tell Tom, because of her son Kuba, that namesake Jakub who she had so loved, and who perhaps in a different way Tom too had loved.

--Those are the words she said to me. Daria Wodjewoda said that she and Robert Mandeltort went to Krakow before Poznan, as she told me, as I told you. While they were there, one day they went to a flea market. At Hala Targowa. The market is still there. I know it. They were wandering around, acting silly, laughing, being young, when Robert noticed an old broken violin in a box that a farmer wanted to sell along with his other tools and things of so little value, the poor man. Daria told me this. How I remember. Robert Mandeltort looked at the violin. He, a wonderful classical violinist, brilliant even, but this old broken violin, with a crack in its back, a broken string, worth nothing, this he fell in love with. So he offered the farmer twice its value or what the farmer wanted for it. Daria asked him was he going to repair it, play it? Mandeltort told her it must never be repaired. That is was perfect as it was. A memory of other days, he said. And before he went to Poznan, he asked his childhood friend who was like a sister for a favour: give this violin to Professor Pawel Weisz. Pawel Weisz who he so loved. And who loved him back.

Agnieszka looks at Tom with great sadness. Sadness for the loss of Pawel. The loss of Kuba. The loss of her grandmother Hania. In doing so she almost becomes an old Polish woman who needs to tell her story. And a younger Polish woman who tells it now, as she is: somewhat broken, hurting.

--'Tell Weisz that the violin is me, Robert said to me,' Daria had continued. 'Tell him he will always remember me when he looks at it because it too is the sad treasure of a sad musician.' I did not realize at the time that within a few days Robert would never be able to play the violin again, and within a few weeks he would be dead. I had made the promise, but I only saw Pawel Weisz again briefly, late one night, in Warsaw. At that moment I could hardly talk to him. I did not know if I hated him, blamed him, I did not know anything really. And although as a well-known conductor years and years later he conducted orchestras here in Israel, I could not approach him. I could not. And then he died. And one day I heard you speak at Yad

Vashem, a story as rich as any music he might conduct or compose.'

Agnieszka looks up from the pages, stares at Tom. Takes a breath. Remembers. Smiles sadly to herself.

--This is as she said it to me, an old woman who I learned only later was dying herself. That violin is the violin in the case we had made. Daria Wodjewoda had it on her lap while speaking. She had come here to give it to me. After she took it from the bag she held and handed it to me, she asked me to call her driver. I never saw her again.

--A story.

--A memory. Kuba—my own Jakub--always loved that instrument, that broken piece of wood and string. He would take it out for hours. Stare at it. I never quite understood what drew him to it. If it had been cloth it would have been filled with moth holes. But despite the cracks, the broken string, the chipped wood, for him it was a treasure. Perhaps for all of us, as it was once a gift for our Pawel from one young boy who must have loved him deeply. A gift for us. For Kuba...

Agnieszka stares at him, then stands.

--There is something I need to show you now.

Tom follows her to a room at the back, its door closed.

--This is Kuba's room. He called it his sanctuary. We have not had the heart to change anything. We both, Beniamin and I, we do not want to create a shrine. One day, it will be the right time, the right moment to change things perhaps. But not yet.

She opens the door and leads him inside. Tom adjusts his eyes to the light. Pinned over all of the walls are photographs. Some are the purposely blurred figures that Kuba had photographed with Tom, then printed in Tom's studio. Some are moments and images from the Old City, mostly of people who looked at the camera or looked away. But what immediately strikes Tom are the dozens of photographs of the violin, from every angle, from every part of its structure, its faults, its existence. He begins to walk around the room, to look carefully at each and every image. He does not notice that Agnieszka has left him alone, disappearing back down the corridor to another space. He stares particularly at photograph after photograph of the violin, taken on a table placed most likely here in the room but lit so that only the instrument is seen against blackness. Some of the photographs are shot from a mid-distance. Some are extreme close up. Every angle, every fracture or change in the grain of the wood is captured. There the split in the back, wide like a canyon, and another small mark like the slightest imperfection. There the broken string hanging against darkness, lit to shine against black. There the f shaped holes in the violin's body, in close up, then from further away. Dozens of shots over, and over, and over. Although the photographs of blurred faces interspersed are interesting, the photographs of the violin are the most striking. Urgent. Not art, but earth. Kuba had been looking for something, all along looking in details almost unfathomable. That much Tom knows. And that much Tom understands.

He does not know how long he stands in the room, examining every photograph. Five minutes? Ten? An hour? It could have been. He does not think the photographs represent an obsession. Rather they are taking the photographer on a journey. Urgent for Kuba. And in a way, haunting now for Tom.

When he finally returns to the sitting room he finds Agnieszka Zuckerman again sitting in her chair, staring off into the distance. She sits quietly; Tom can feel the sadness emanating from her.

--They're remarkable. The photographs, they...

He is uncertain exactly what word or words he reaches for.

--They are Kuba. And Jakub. Both of them... Do you think he found it? What my son was so desperate to find?

Tom is quiet for a long moment. He glances behind him at the violin so photographed, now in its Perspex case.

--He was looking. And he was right: those photographs of the violin, his work, none of them reveal. They all--talk. They all speak of a story that had meaning for your son. He sought not just the past. He sought memory itself. I think he knew that was what he was looking for.

--Memory then was life.

--No. Memory is life.

She looks at him, nods, just slightly.

--Beniamin and I, we looked through some of his things. We found this. It is why I asked you here. It is for you. Not from us, from him. Please, take this, but open it later, in the quiet of your space. Think about what you saw in there. Perhaps this will have special meaning.

She takes a large manila envelope from the table, hands it to Tom. She does not stand as she does so and Tom has a vision of an old woman from years ago, sitting in a wheel chair, passing over a package holding a broken violin within. It is memory, Tom thinks. Then. Now. This is what memory means.

That night, after working in the studio, looking at photos the students had been working on, looking at some that Kuba had also left behind, when the dark hours are creeping into the studio space and the night surrounds him in silence, Tom finally takes out the manila envelope that he had put aside on purpose, opening it. A single large photograph is within. On the back Kuba has written Tom's name. That's all: Tom. The photograph itself Kuba had taken on the outside of a storefront. On one side of the photograph, looking in the window of the shopfront, reflected in it, is Tom, unaware of Kuba the photographer off to his side. Kuba, standing where he is, catches both the back of Tom in the photograph and the front of Tom reflected in the storefront window. But he also catches himself; on another side in the window is a mirror that reflects Kuba the photographer, holding the camera to his eye. Thus the photograph captures both Tom unaware, and Kuba unaware, one beside the other, one almost reflected with the other. Within the other. One instead of the other in a strange way.

Thus Tom becomes Kuba.

And thus Kuba becomes Tom.

Tom stares at this remarkable photograph. And he knows that this lost young man, Jakub, Kuba, he who Tom realizes has so touched him, has done so for a reason: it is so that Tom does not see this simply as a photograph he now holds, sees not a single moment revealed, but rather that Tom sees this photograph and hears it talking to him. Memory talking to him. The past telling a story.

Tom is Kuba, just as Kuba is Tom. For both it was a journey, and it is a journey. Kuba was right: whether Tom is in the photograph, as he is here, or he is behind a camera lens pressing the exposure button, hiding from an aperture opening, closing, opening, closing, opening, closing…he is not hidden from view. He is there. He is always there.

Tom is Kuba. Kuba is Tom.

Both there. Both always there.

*

Spring passes towards early summer. Time does not heal. He knows they say it does. Maybe it will. Tom does not think so.

He has taken the images of a lifetime inside, put them in a closed closet in his memory. But they have not gone away. Every so often the closet door opens and he looks at them again. And again. And yet again. So it will be.

His time with the students is over. The Academy asks him to remain another year, but he refuses. He needs to move forward. He needs to be again in motion. Motion is perpetual. There are yet decisions he must make. Tom cannot yet know what they will be.

He does not photograph now. But he holds Annabel at his side; companions may be quiet, but they are not lost.

Very early on a Saturday morning with so many off the streets, making them almost empty now, he catches a number 22 bus out of Jerusalem; thirty minutes later he changes to a number 216 bus to Jericho at Giv'at Hatachmoshet station. He flags a taxi that takes him the remainder of the distance to Wadi Qelt gorge entrance. Here he finds a hikers path through the wadi, moving at the edges and along the walls of the gorge. He hikes deeper and deeper within, seeing no one as the area is quiet on the early Saturday morning. The trail he takes leads him sometimes along the riverbed where small pools of water rest quietly, thoughtfully. Sometimes the trail narrows over ledges on one side or the other of the wadi itself. Eventually he finds a trail that rises towards the heights of the high walls, until it reaches the top, from where Tom hikes over open ground, deeper into barren desert landscape. He passes a herd of goats along the way, bells hanging from their collars clanging quietly. It is the only sound.

He knows he is on the route back towards Jericho that he can see in the distance, but he is in no hurry to return there. Instead he finds a large rock to sit on, staring at emptiness, sipping from his thermos.

Tom wants to scream. To scream to the heavens. To scream in anger. In pain perhaps. In loss.

Tom does not scream.

He wants to pound his fists into the barren ground. He wants to curse the ground. To curse the place.

He neither pounds his fists nor curses.

He sits in silence, staring beyond in silence, desert earth in silence. He has no words to shout in anger. The earth around him does not reveal.

Instead it speaks to him. In silence, without words. He hears such unseen voice without words but with understood words, hears them without sound.

The image is all around.

He does not photograph.

He stands and continues walking away from the walls of Wadi Qelt, over open ground, the city of Jericho waiting for him again just beyond.

*

There is, finally, only the photograph.

There is, for the photographer, only that. The subject. The image. The perception of a certain chosen reality, subjective, created by thought or by chance, by chaos or hope. The need to understand a single something.

A photograph captures a moment. A moment drawn from time, of time. It may be simply a record for a family album or a site visited on a holiday, smiling faces or a family brought together to record their presence. But a photograph too is made of many technical elements to tell the story that the photographer wishes to capture.

For the photojournalist, recording time, recording a story, the process of doing so is not simply made of the many mechanical and digital choices needed, not simply the processes of understanding every function of a camera body and lens in order to create image, and through image a tale told. For the photojournalist, the photograph, the final image, the moment, is just that: an attempt to capture a story, the story, from beginning to end. Without words. Without commentary. With truth and ethical standards inherent within the need and ability to tell that story. A moment when life reveals itself, in all its glory, all its pain, all its soul of past, of present, even in many ways of future.

For the photojournalist, truth, a lack of opinion or bias, honesty, these are qualities that are the foundation of his or her work. The professional photographer too tries to show the multi-dimensional sides of a story, at times accepting the need to show violence or hurt or graphic horror without shying away from it. Not an easy task by any means.

A photojournalist also needs to remain vigilant to context. Context matters. The photographer is there to illuminate and elucidate context, to attempt through an image to take a viewer of the photograph down the path of understanding, to make the circumstances of a particular moment clear, and through the moment capturing the arc of a story without the need for words. The photojournalist needs to make the viewer know—something. Whatever that something may be.

The role is to touch the viewer intellectually and emotionally, to help the viewer engage. To present an image that informs, that explains to some degree, that captures a moment a viewer wants to understand, to reach, to know. To that end the photojournalist tries to open the viewer's mind and heart to the possibility of the story's present, to give meaning and memory.

In this way, memory becomes all.

Images are remembered. And photographs affect memory and moment past. Sometimes moment future. An American president bleeding and dying in the back of an open-topped sedan moments after a bullet tears into his head. A hotel waiter leaning over the prone body of a candidate for election in shadowed black and white, trying to save, trying to protect the unprotectable. A naked girl child running along a road at the edge of jungle, her arms spread wide, terrified, afraid of the onslaught. Two tall tower buildings, smoking, collapsing, define the world as it has become and will henceforth be. An emaciated prisoner, one amongst many, standing at a barbed wire fence trying to say I am alive, but alive and dead at the same time. Trying to say save me. Save us. A half burned corpse lying on a dirt road in the violent suburb of a large city as people walk past, ignoring what is around them, or indifferent. A man taking a first step onto the moon. A woman praying to god. A man dying. A woman pregnant. Smoke from a crematorium rising above a death camp. A child playing. A child dreaming. The moment. The image.

The photograph.

But it remains paramount to remember that the photograph, telling a story present, revealing what has become at a moment or in moments of history, is simply a perception, a point of view, a determined point of view. The photojournalist makes himself disappear, although perhaps he or she never disappears. Not really. Perception remains. A choice. The choice of how to operate a camera. The choice of aperture, of image manipulation, the choice of shutter speed, the choice of colour or its lack.

The choice, simply, to be there. Or no choice. The chaos. The accident. The unexpected. The luck and the loss. To be there.

What remains is the photograph. The story without words, where words are not needed.

What remains is that point of time, the spot of time past, present, and in many ways future.

What remains is memory. Memory of what we are, of our humanity, of our failings, of our weaknesses, of our hopes, of our dreams, of our frailty, of us.

We are remembered, us. We are the photograph.

The photojournalist takes us along that journey. He or she also takes himself or herself on that same journey, to say he exists, she exists. The journey that is a simple moment of time, passing, passed. And the present caught, frozen. And the future, the possibility of future, with questions asked, seeking answers. That is the journey. And in that, we are all photojournalists. We are all the photograph.

The image of ourselves.

*

Tom has no idea how many people will come to the opening of the gallery show. He has not gone out of his way to advertise it other than to put up notices at the academy. But word spreads in a small country: word about his own work, word about the others.

Although he has decided it is time to leave Jerusalem, he chooses to remain a couple months longer for this one reason, this one exhibition of photographs that he wants, no, needs to exhibit. The Bezel Academy is more than happy to allow him to remain in the apartment when he explains his intention even though his teaching contract has ended. He has also contacted the gallery owner of the Jerusalem City Gallery of Art who has several times approached Tom about putting on an exhibition, and who is happy enough when Tom responds to the idea, with a stipulation: that it will not be a small exhibit solely of his work, past and present, but that he will be showing only a few pieces of three others as well.

Tom calls the show 'Fragments'. It seems appropriate, in fact essential, that the photographic images on display are moments of time, spots of time, not simply of the stories told in the photographs displayed, but in the development and stories of the photographers themselves. Fragments of an image. Of stories. Only fragments.

The gallery consists of two rooms and Tom breaks up the work accordingly. The first room contains two photographers whose work Tom finds very different, yet echoing one another in important ways. Some are works by a Palestinian landscape photographer, Abu Said, older than Tom who had seen and been intrigued by these photographs in Abu Said's small shop in Jericho. His images on display at the exhibit that Tom curates are all of barren landscapes but in extreme close-up. Strong, large images from deserts, canyons, forests but where the close-ups make the landscape unfamiliar, indistinguishable from habitat, alive in an almost foreign, unrecognizable way. "The relation of the viewer to the image here is all important: it speaks…" Tom wrote in an introduction about the photographer's particular relationship with the land, "…with place. Where place itself is life blood, and alive.'

Tom purposely intermixes these images with some of the images and photographs that Ilana had produced during her time with him at the Bezel Academy.

Following Kuba's death, Ilana had not been able to return to his class. He knew she needed space and did not press her. After several weeks, however, he sent her a message that he wanted to meet. They did so at Bassem's Café near the Damascus Gate, the café he so liked and to where Kuba had once followed him, and where a friendship began. Tom knew Ilana struggled still and was unsurprised when she told him that she would be going away from Jerusalem, from her home. She had to break. She had to re-form, re-be. He agreed, but it saddened him. Yet he knew one day the breaking would lead to something new.

She had gone to New York and Tom had arranged with a colleague who had been leading the photography course at Parsons' Design School to meet with her. That colleague had offered her a place on the course for the autumn and Ilana had agreed to start over. It was indeed time for her to start over. Tom knew she had talent, so was pleased when his friend informed him that she would continue her work there.

Ilana was unsurprised when Tom telephoned her in New York. She listened to him discuss his proposed exhibition in Jerusalem and despite her hesitancy agreed to let him show what photographs he might choose, although she would not return herself for the show; it was something she could not bring herself to do.

Her numerous pieces, interspersed with those photographs of Abu Said, produce a remarkable juxtaposition of the interior and the exterior, with questions about land and home that somehow created an emotional vortex between the different works.

The final photograph when exiting the first space in the gallery is a photographic image that Ilana sent to Tom after he had asked her to participate. She wrote in a note to him that it will be the last of the particular series she has spent over a year working on, the images of exterior buildings overlayed with interior spaces. She told him that the series had reached its end, that she would now try to develop other ideas, other dreams, in New York.

This final photograph is essential as a statement not only of Ilana's work, but as a statement of her work juxtaposed with the older photographer from Jericho's images, indeed a statement too about the exhibition in its entirety. It is similar to Ilana's other photographs in the room, Tom notes in his introductory comments, but with one essential difference: every photographic image of Ilana's shows an exterior building overlayed with interior rooms, but always with a single naked figure, out of focus, standing in one of those rooms. In that final photographic image, however, there is no figure standing. There is only emptiness. And the title of a final work: 'We Are Here We Go On'. It is the story she tells, Tom explains. It is her journey.

Ilana's parents are there for the opening. Tom watches as they look carefully at each photograph and stop for a long time before the final image, which they had not seen. Ilana's mother tears at seeing this last work produced. Before they leave she tells Tom that they are grateful for him having included their daughter, as difficult as it has been for them, as lonely they feel with Ilana remaining in New York.

It is the second room, however, that is the most difficult, and the primary reason that Tom had wished to remain that much longer in Jerusalem. It is, he writes simply, his own beating heart.

The room displays six photographs of his on a wall to the left, six of Kuba's photographs on a wall to the right.

Tom's work consists of three pieces from his time of photojournalism and three from his time in Jerusalem. The three from his earlier days show only empty spaces and the name of the place below: a weed covered playground empty, silent, titled Sarajevo; a burned out wooden house, its door hanging off its hinges, titled simply Darfur; a torn, broken doll lying in a street of rubble, titled Aleppo. After these three photographs Tom places three others from his time in Jerusalem: an extreme close up of a woven carpet in a marketplace, a close up of a trader's aged hands in a shop, the textures of an earthenware water container, its lines and textures almost alive and moving. These have no titles; only current dates. Tom writes simply in his notes that all the images are taken with the photographer in the shot, although you cannot see him. All are related, he writes, by the journey.

On the wall containing Kuba's six photographs Tom has enlarged four images that he had asked Kuba's parents if he might borrow. These are the close-ups, from different angles, of the weathered, somewhat broken violin: its crack, its string hanging down, a portion of an f hole in its body, a side view of its four tuning pegs, one half missing. The four photographs are framed by two images Kuba shot quickly, in passing: a pair of hands caught in motion, legs rushing by, both out of focus.

In his short note of Kuba's work, Tom states simply that stories are told, and speak; that is how they relate. These are the only comments Tom writes.

One final image remains in the room, the photograph on the wall between Tom's six photographs to the left, Kuba's six photographs to the right. It is the photograph that Agnieszka had given him, the image of Kuba shooting Tom from the side, with both Kuba and Tom reflected front and back.

Tom gives this a title, but says nothing about it in his notes. The title simply says 'We Are Only Our Fragments'.

At the end of the evening, when the crowd has largely thinned out, Agnieszka and Beniamin enter the gallery. Tom does not see them at first; he is talking with the gallery owner in the second gallery room when they appear. When he turns and realizes they did come after all—he so wanted them to but was afraid they would find it too difficult—he stands completely still, watching them stare at one photograph, then another. After some minutes they make their way into the room where he is, glancing at him but saying nothing, instead again making their way from one photograph, to the next, to the next. They first stand quietly before Tom's photographs, then cross the room to look at their lost son's: one, the next, the next. Finally they both stand in front of the gifted image of Tom and Kuba together, both reflected, one and two. And one. They stand for the longest time, saying nothing. Tom moves to Agnieszka's side, looking at the photograph as well. And saying nothing, as well.

After several minutes, Beniamin turns to Tom, nods, takes the photographer's hand.

--It is hard for us, Tom. It is hard but we are deeply grateful. You find him in yourself.

Tom nods, looks at Agnieszka, staring deeply into him with eyes that speak of her son, speak the words, not revealing, but speaking. She puts her arms around him, kisses him on each cheek.

--Thank you, photographer.

She pulls away, nods both with assurance and deep emotions only partly in evidence. She then links Beniamin's arm with her own, smiles sadly at her husband, and they quietly walk from the gallery.

Tom watches them go. He had said nothing. He did not need to. He turns again to look at the image of himself, of his young protégé friend Jakub, he who is Kuba. Tom does not turn away. He hears the words in the photograph. He sees.

*

The day before he leaves Jerusalem Tom receives a small package. He opens it and finds a very small box and a note. Inside the box is a small charm pendant of a violin, with a scratch on its small back.

The note, from Agnieszka Janiec, says simply 'This is Memory. It speaks of all things.'

***

The taxi driver looks at the note Tom hands to him with the address in his language, then drives to the far side of the city and up the narrow, cold street that sits on a hill to the north side of the valley. He stops by a high wall to let Tom out.

He uses hand signals and broken English to ask Tom if he should wait. Tom smiles and shakes his head.

--No. I will walk.

--Cold. Snow.

--I know. I will be all right. Thank you.

Tom hands over the fare and a large tip, gets out, watches the driver reverse then slowly disappear back the way he had come. Tom's breath cuts through the air, cold in the early winter grey. Snow lines the paths. He listens to his feet crackle along broken ice. The world here sulks with only greys and dirty whites. Nothing distinguishes. Nothing speaks.

Tom follows the wall to the entrance of the cemetery. He has been here before, but that was long ago. Many years, and things have changed. Or they have not changed. Waiting for him is an older woman whose language he does not speak, but who knows him. Who remembers and does not remember him from a long time ago. And who, assisted by the translation from her neighbour two days earlier, has agreed to meet him, despite the passage of time, the dimming of memories.

Some memories do not dim.

They wander through the large cemetery. Their footsteps crunch over broken stone and well-trodden snow. Others have come here in silence. Left here in silence. Still silence. Dead silence. Still. Their footprints in snow speak for them. Tom glances at the many white marble stones, all shaped like obelisks, each the mirror of the next, hundreds of such stones distinguished only by the names engraved and the slightest alterations to a date: a day here, another day following the first there; perhaps the number of the month changing, just slightly. Many of the numbers are the same. This is how it was. This...

The two bundled figures, he and the woman, do not try to hurry. They do not speak. Tom stares at names in a language he cannot read. He does not remember where to turn, although he was here once before, so very long ago.

Things have changed.

And not changed.

After wandering quietly, Tom follows the woman who points to the far side of the cemetery. She too is looking. He follows in the direction she points, trying to remember, unable to remember. At the far section she hesitates, thinking right or left. The dull grey landscape of the dead perhaps confuses. Or perhaps reminds. After a considered moment she nods, takes her bearings and leads Tom to the middle of the section.

She points to a marker, then another, a third, and Tom knows he has found what he sought.

--Thank you, he tells her.

She nods. He tries to give her some money, but she puts her hands up, refusing. Instead she gently takes his arm, rubs her hand over his elbow. An acknowledgement. She smiles, sadly, turns and walks away.

Tom looks down at the marker. There are in fact three such stones together in a line, three graves. He reads the names and while not in his language he knows the names regardless. Although it is more than twenty years since he came here, he knows that this is a part of the journey he needed to make, always needed to make if but one last time.

Tom opens his backpack and removes the three small roses that he had carried since the early morning, buying them from a small shop that somehow still had colour to combat the daily empty winter landscape in the city. He places one at the foot of each obelisk. He notes the names, the dates of birth, the dates of death. Children when they died. One child was seven. Two nine.

Small red roses on white snow, lying there without words, without voice, before three small obelisks, three that in this foreign language speaks to him like hieroglyphic drawings of a day long ago, the beginnings of a story not forgotten; his story too from what seems both a lifetime passed yet only days gone by. The picture in his head offers more than a moment captured; it speaks. Kuba was right. The photograph speaks a story and the story is memory. The photograph in his head. Memory.

Tom stands back, stands quietly, looking at the three stones, side by side. He closes his eyes and hears laughter. He closes his eyes and sees a makeshift football pitch on a weed strewn playground sheltered by an apartment building, but not sheltered enough. He closes his eyes and sees five children, a ball being kicked, himself falling on the earth and laughing. He closes his eyes and begins to hear the high shrill note of a shell falling towards them, feels the heat of a shell exploding around them; he sees one small girl standing, spellbound, shocked, but somehow, he is not sure how, somehow he takes all the images rushing now towards him, somehow he removes the painful images from his thoughts and puts them in a darkroom cupboard for another day. He closes that cupboard door of his memory for now, hearing instead the laughter. And the play. And the childish joy. These are the sounds he embraces at this moment and wishes to hear speak to him in the language of children, the laughter of children. Yes: it speaks. It does not reveal. It speaks.

Tom opens his eyes and pulls from his bag his Annabel, his beloved Leica 24, constant companion, and raises it to his eye. He focuses the camera taking in three obelisk gravestones at once. He feels his finger begin to put pressure on the shutter button.

But he stops himself.

He moves the camera away from his face and stares.

He stands there, that way, for a long moment. Then without taking the photograph, the photograph that he had told himself he would come here on this cold winter's day to shoot, the image to remember, he realizes he does not need to take the photograph after all. And he puts the camera, his beloved Anabel, back in his bag.

He carries memory.

That is enough.

He carries memory.

He puts his hand on the chain around his neck, hanging against his chest, where his finger touches the small shape of a violin. And he smiles, sadly, just slightly. That is enough.

He carries memory.

III

"Aga watched them for a while, running, laughing, father and son. Their simple happiness brought her joy. She thought about her own life and knew she had always been blessed. ...Life had been rich, even if difficult. She thought too of the story, of all that it meant. Ultimately it meant everything and nothing. Everything because it told her who she was, who she perhaps had to be, but also because the story told her of the underlying belief that was the true fabric of her life. It told her of the faith in one another that was instilled deep within her, the hope and the fear, hand in hand. It had taught her about life and all that was human. About need and about survival."

--A Requiem For Hania

1. She and He

Krakow
July, 2021

They are easy lovers.

He is somewhat older. She somewhat younger. They are drawn together by separate confusions becoming one.

She has not expected this. She has come to expect nothing. Neither has he sought a release from the isolation. Neither has he wanted to forget. Needed to forget. He cannot in fact forget. Neither can she. But this is how it happens. This is how it begins. Beginnings are only the beginnings of endings.

*

He.

He had not chosen to remain here. He had desired simply to breathe, hoping to forget much, to move forward. So he descended the steps of the train that landed him here and found a nearby hotel room for a few days. Breathe, move forward. Hear other voices. See other faces. But still he found he was troubled, found he could not move. Seeing a note about an apartment for a short term let, he had decided to stay.

He had not realized that a virus would soon explode here, everywhere, making movement impossible. Therefore for the moment Krakow became his home. Perhaps that was best. Here he was anonymous. Here even closed in a remote space, unable to interact with anyone, he could read and rest. As could his cameras, his beloved Anabel, his two Nikon F2s. Let them rest, like tired lovers who have seen too much, known too much. Felt too much, the bodies within and without. Who desire silence.

He could, for a time, simply disappear. Lost, unseen, unfound.

Krakow was a city of the lost, the unseen.

For so many, the four walls of their surrounds became a prison of sorts, without interaction. The world changed and felt empty. Blank walls that did not speak. But it did not seem this way to him. In silence he could reflect, consider, await the lockdown's end; the borders then might reopen. They would surely reopen. He would wait.

Sometimes, too, he listened to music. He particularly listened to the works of Weisz, that Polish composer who had removed himself from Warsaw in 1968, escaping to Paris, eventually to New York. He felt he needed to listen to all, to understand, because in the music was story and he now needed story, this story that had kindled a small flame within. That he carried in a small charm on a thin chain around his neck.

A requiem. A requiem mass. A requiem for the dying and the dead. The music spoke to him. Requiem. He needed this music, this sound, the words that emanated from the notes because they touched him now. As the boy not boy older yet younger too young had touched him. As had the Mother.

A boy not boy not man killed.

A Mother left empty.

The notes of a broken violin in a perspex case that meant simultaneously nothing and everything.

The days melded from one into another into another. The weeks becoming some months. He bought what food he needed from a small shop around the corner opened to three customers at any one moment. An essential service. Survival and essential services. Otherwise he remained inside during the day, as did most everyone. Days would pass when he might see no one staring through the two large windows that looked down upon the once busy thoroughfare below. He, like others, rarely ventured out.

Finally, however, the need to touch the sky overwhelmed the emptiness of place and he began to walk occasionally at night, in the late hours, keeping to shadows should a police car or ambulance pass. His need to seek out images again began to beg at his desires, his urge to see, to know. He started taking a camera with him on these late night wanderings, photographing the angles of street corners, streetlights giving orders to empty alleyways, graffiti, walls, shadows.

He photographed the emptiness of the moment. The emptiness of a virus. The isolation he felt, others felt. He often walked the underground passage that led into the train station. There were no passenger trains just then. A few security guards watched empty tracks. Shops normally bustling at all hours had shutters fronting their doors and windows. Birds surviving flew occasionally down through the tunnel. The extent of life on hold. No one looked at him. There was no one to look at him.

He walked in the small hours along the back streets of Stare Miasto. His footsteps echoed on the paving stones of Rynek Główny. An occasional shadow across the square, hurrying to shelter. Cats. Many cats. The tourist shops otherwise closed. Forbidden entry. If roadway stones might cry. Empty doorways too.

He walked further along into the district of Jews, into Kazimierz. He heard voices here of what had once passed over these streets. Only to become silent. In these empty hours he often sat on a chair in the square in front of the Old Synagogue. He read on the wind words of weeping from a time not so long ago. Not so distant. Weeping for a virus of hate. He had photographed such hate in other places. It had never left him. It did not leave still. He was not one of them. But he was one of them. Shadows. Ghosts. Shadow. Ghost. He and they: he sought them and now had become them.

Sometimes he walked down to the River Vistula, staring at the flowing waters. At night their late winter reflection spoke of darkness, of death perhaps. On the far bank he occasionally saw a figure emerge. They stared at one another, then turned away. Even in this hour one did not want to meet another.

Or he stole into the grounds of the New Jewish Cemetery, new but generations old, lifetimes old, to stare into the dead cold light at the gravestones, some standing, some destroyed. He recognized them for what they were, obelisks if not in material fact than in recent mirrored memories from a distant city speaking a common language of loss. It was there that he decided he needed to bring forth the images once again. There that he decided that if he could not speak the words he felt, his cameras might. His work was not photographer. His existence was. His profession did not define him. He defined it. He defined himself.

He returned to his rented flat before dawn after one particular night's wanderings.

211

His flat that was around the corner from the park they called Strzlecki, a word he could not pronounce, with its strange holy monuments that never spoke, his flat in the shadow of the train station Głowny remaining even still almost empty of passengers, quiet but for the arrival of freight trains on the tracks. He walked up the stairs to his room, closed the door behind him. He stared at his beloved Anabel sitting then quietly on the table in his room. He unwrapped too the Nikon F2s. He saw the late winter sun just beginning to peep over trees, early morning renewal. And he said to himself it is time. It is time to speak of isolation, and loneliness. It is the time for memory. And words spoken in their unspeaking. There could be no choice in this.

He continued photographing the texture of place. Only textures. Empty images. Empty of life itself. Place reached out to him just as did the composer's work, music that he would return to the flat to listen to, that spoke softly in stories of the past brought to life. In words of memory. In the secret desires to survive. This too he saw, and photographed, and heard speak: in the damp walls of a train station tunnel, in the angled street corner greyed by shadow, in the rough, tarnished guard rails that protected him as he walked over a silent roadway, needing no protection but nonetheless stating a purpose.

He created a darkroom in the bathroom at the back of his apartment. He printed images. Destroyed them. Printed them again. Felt them. Became a part of them. He never photographed himself. He was in every photograph.

In time life itself began to whisper back into being. Slowly perhaps, but noted. An old man on a side road urinating in the shadow of a wall. A young couple desperate for human touch making love beneath a tree in a park closed by nighttime and instructions to remain at home, forbidding them when they refused the bidding. A dog eating from a fallen trash can filled with boxes of delivered cooked takeaway foods that were still delivered, called an essential service by those who defined such things. Faces walking over to the other side of the streets, shell shocked faces. Blank. Expressions he knew from war zones. This was not a war zone. Or perhaps the war was the living itself. Yes, perhaps it was.

His cameras whispered to him as they had once before.

They whispered words that spoke of a different kind of conflict, a different kind of war called life.

They spoke of humanity, and its loss.

They spoke first of desperation, but slowly then of hope.

They spoke to him. You are here. Remember that: you are here too, one of them. One of all.

Here I am Lord. He remembered the phrase. *Hineni.* A word whispered at a funeral for a boy not boy not man just…him. The word now spoke to him, and he whispered it to himself. For himself. Here I am. When are the trials of life no longer the trials but the living?

In this way, slowly, he began to reemerge into the world. Perhaps not understanding but accepting that he had yet to complete the journey he and he alone had placed upon himself. Moving forward. And in this way he found that which was within him was still need. And admitted loneliness. In this way the photographs in the locked cupboard of his mind slowly began to find their way back into the light of day. And in this way he began, once again, to live. Slowly. Uncertainly.

Until one evening he photographed her.

*

She.

She had walked through the door, and she felt it then close behind her. A rush of air; stifling in airless imagination. Yet she knew that a single door in a building was but one of many doors. A door within a building may lock. The door within your mind, the door of memory never locked. Not really. It awaited the opening, awaited the hint of light, that images might escape. Behind the door are the untetherable moments like a cupboard of photographs. Never tethered. And like the fingernail scratch marks on wood or wood that is not wood but of synthetic fabrications, a door within may not open yet but reminds always of the other side. She had seen that the stains of blood on hinges struggle to force such a door to open, even to crack slightly ajar; the scratching fingernails, try as they might, cannot push door from frame even slightly, so they take the memory of breath and air and the beating heart with them into eternity, unable to live, but unable to rest. Always there. Always. The ghosts do not rest. Memory does not die. Memory does not disappear.

This she had learned.

At the time she thought: where do I go? At the time she was not free because she could not allow herself to be free; she was a prisoner of herself. But she wanted to push the past away. The relationships. The reminders of a mother. Hanging. Tears. She knew she could only go forward, not back. But she could not go forward either, this prisoner of the locked door, the room. The Project. There were more voices that needed to be heard. Whispers in darkness refusing to be silenced.

She went south. A choice. A need. She went to Krakow. She told herself she did not know why she went there. A lie. She knew. It was not home to her but the voices said she still had to find her way, and to find a way for them. Push the door open once more, slightly, letting the hint of light in, the hint of light out.

She thought she might be able to walk away from the artefactual and architectural diggings, the scratching at the earth because from there voices whispered to her both memory and fear. But she was unable to escape, unable to forget. There were simply too many voices whispering remembrance, asking her to embrace. She embraced in silence.

She contacted colleagues who worked at other sites, those based in offices in Oświęcim, living nearby. So near to their own sites. So near too to the horror. It frightened her. It made her sweat with memory. She trembled. She could not do that. Not again. But even despite silent despair she contacted them. She suggested she might be of assistance. She suggested she had experience elsewhere, other sites. The sites were endless. And like broken glass, these cut, and cut, and cut. Self-harm in the cutting but she had no choice. Not really. They listened and said they could use her assistance, her ideas. They could find housing nearby if she wished. They could develop an endeavour if she wished. She could be one of them with their own varying directions of research. But she knew she would never know peace, not with them, not so near to their sites, not with their explorations, their own diggings in earth, in history, in memory, in what happened. Peace was out of reach just then. An accepted if unacceptable reality of her life, just then. Still, she needed to join them, without real choice, so she might define and redefine and reunderstand a vision of the world. She told them, however, she also needed space, anonymity. Krakow meant anonymity. She recognized this. She was not alone in recognizing this.

Many were aware of the Project. Word had spread. A door opening, closing, an image, a representation. Faux metal and faux wooden step threshold into darkness. A small peephole into what was, into the memories and ghosts. For her it had meant much more. Not simply a representation of the past but a representation of her private present. Her mother. Her need. Her search. And her search had not ended. She had slipped into a kind of madness and although the madness had now passed, or so she believed, still it waved back to her in the mirrors and windows of the moments that she needed while looking in, those moments trying to move forward.

Moving south. Krakow. There. The place she finally found herself in silence. The place drawing her in. She knew this was not something she could escape, not entirely, so she took those moments of uncertainty by the hand and whispered I will follow where it might take me, you, us, both: one afraid, one fighting fear. We will take it to Krakow, to another site, so many other sites, to listen there, to hear what others, so many others have to say. We will wait. We will listen. We will be.

They in turn listened to her need and pain: the curators, the guardians of memory, the historians in situ, the researchers, the local keepers of a particular flame, the museum professors, the PhDs residing nearby who saw and heard yet somehow managed to feel only peripherally, if at all. Not in the way she did. Hearing not in the echoes that she heard; seeing not through the light as she saw. They asked her if she wanted to create another Project, another architectural awareness, fill their own museum with image and creation and representation, but this she could not do. So they asked her to assist in the development of an archive that took images they already had in storage, and images they had yet to discover: with these to create three dimensional representations from two, utilizing similar photogrammetry computer programs she had used a year earlier at the Site, her Site, her ghosts, thus recreating with this specialized computer's algorithm artefacts so that others might know, might almost touch, might practically reach out and feel, or smell, or hear. The voices. So that a fascinated, almost obsessed public might remember. In three dimensions they might feel the stone of stolen, defiled gravestones discovered or yet to discover, stolen from the dead, placed as building blocks on pathways or farmyard building repairs. In the near reality of computer generation and Artificial Intelligence joining imagination and reality like conjoined twins, a curious public might almost feel the cloth of deteriorating shirts, or shoes, or woven toys, or prayer shawls. They might hear the broken watches no longer allowed to tick the minutes the hours the seconds becoming the years and the centuries, yet ticking still, discarded on pathways that led to the ashes of crematoria. They might see what another might have once seen through the cracked glass of a pair of crushed spectacles, might hear the music again from a crushed, broken hand organ or dented, half formed harmonica or cracked, stringless, broken small violin that once cried with tears of emotion, tears of loss, tears of strangled hope. These historians and museum curators and doctors of anthropology and doctors of archaeology and doctors of stories now used a computer program with its own defined intelligence for the creating. For the remembering. Blessed, restorative algorithms recreating truth, the semblance of human reality. She could work from her rented apartment in this new city, this Krakow, remaining hidden away, emerging only when she wished, only for periodic meetings in Oświęcim, or at one of its nearby sites if required, only if required. She could trample unseen forest paths finding overgrown cemeteries and memories to photograph, or walk on uncovered paths with occasional inlaid stones, their carved names worn away but somehow remaining, voices of the dead walked upon, stones that carried the almost unreadable names of a lost people, lives forgotten, faces disappeared, memories retreating into obscurity. But with her work and help they might not fade into dust. If she wished. Whatever she wished.

She wished.

She was one a team of others doing the work. She was one who was not there. She could hide away, and remain in her own domain, her rented flat, her silence, virtually unknown.

Space was still sacred. They were not in her private sacristy. She needed the prayer.

Voices still whispered. She did not have to tell others she heard their words.

And still she walked on glass. Cutting into her skin. Into her veins. Constant cutting.

Those trained, understood and revealing moments of GPR, of LIDAR, of magnetometry, of probes used for high-resolution data, those moments staring at square foundation blocks, at ditches and rectangular resting holes, those moments when watching DNA samples taken or defining areas of deception or concealment, the hours tracing, then walking back and forth, back and forth along the Himmelstrasse or feeling the hair that was no longer brushed by the thin metal teeth of a discarded comb or the feel of the cold, hard, dented metal of a lipstick container that no longer held paste but that had touched the lips once of one who loved, lover, mother, whore, daughter, those moments of staring at decayed dentures and feeling the bite, of trying to read faded words on a faded letter, those countless, obsessing moments staring at the hairs the fibres the soil the chemicals the paint the food residue the graffiti the tears, all of this she could push aside. The human reality she could push aside, concentrating solely and uniquely on the algorithmic demands of a computer program, replacing the two dimensional photographed discovery with the three dimensional created artefact simply to say: it is here now, but it was there once, and it lived.

And they lived.

I am mad still, she said to herself. I am mad still but I am mad in silence. And I did not close the door after all, she thought. And then carried on. I am here, Lord. I am here.

She took the work they offered at the central research offices located in Oświęcim. They accepted that she would work independently, based in Krakow, a part of the team who remained aloof, isolated, doing the job requested of her mostly in the silence of her rented rooms. It was easy, even desirable, to remain isolated with the virus still threatening, commanding attention. It was what she wished for.

There were times when she walked along the near empty streets of the city that was hers and never hers. Times to clear her head, to think of what she was doing, to picture in three dimensions the artefacts in her mind. To touch them herself. Feel them herself.

There were times when she sat in cafes, the odd restaurant, one of only a few, at first masked against the invisible enemy, her eyes alone able to express uncertainty, hiding, so that she could pretend to socialize. She could pretend she was like anyone else out on the town. She would tell herself this is what it means to be human. She did not, however, believe her own lie.

She passed countless hours, often in silence, keeping the virus that had swept so

217

much of human touch away from herself. She did not reach out to others. She did not contact previous lovers. She did not say where she was because in truth she did not know where she was beyond the long stare at a computer screen and her fingertips on a keyboard articulating an artefact of pain, every one of its angles, its threads, its history, its memory, its voice, what it was then and what it was now. In this way she spoke to the ghosts, and in this way the ghosts spoke to her. She became them. And they became her, in this era of a virus that no one really understood. This new reality. This new here and now.

This Krakow.

Winter months in 2020 crawled into spring in 2021. More people on the streets, avoiding one another. Avoiding interaction. Human touch kept at a distance.

She ventured out, while rarely at first, in time somewhat more often. A trip to the local shop before the computer sprang to life became a walk in a park, or a secluded seat in a café, or a quiet stroll in sunshine down along the Vistula. Not often, just enough.

One night, late, she heard sad music seeping from an underground cavern of a jazz club. She had never been interested in music, especially sorrowful jazz, but she felt the notes draw her inside and down the narrow stone staircase. She needed to empty herself of the thoughts and the three dimensional images that swirled in her brain, too sharp to cut through the fog she needed, too real to allow her eyes to close against the thousands of fragrant dpi colours that made up the image on a computer screen, the revolving, turning image once spread out in two dimensions now taking over in three. She needed something she did not understand. The music she did not understand, but it offered release.

The rooms in the cellar were largely empty. It was late. People kept away. Those who ventured mostly still wore masks, hiding their selves, the world hiding from them. She bought herself a large whiskey—Irish, no ice—at the bar from a woman with many tattoos, hair cut short and coloured blue. She quietly walked into a small underground concert room and sat down at a table off to the side. On a raised stage of sorts sat a pianist, a trumpeter weeping in brass, a double bass player, ignoring the few customers there to listen. They played pain: the pain they felt, the pain they saw. There was no real joy in the music, only thoughtful reflection emanating with

218

a sense of loss and perhaps a lack of hope. But it was the kind of music that she, not understanding its language, could sit back against, allow to envelop her, close her eyes, sip from her glass.

After some time she returned to the bar to get herself another drink. She needed the warmth. She needed the burn. She wanted the confusion of alcohol to settle. She wanted to disappear.

As she was sitting down again she noticed on the opposite side of the room a figure in shadow, one of the few there also listening. She only glimpsed his face. It meant nothing to her. What she noticed, however, was the camera lying face down on the table. It was of no consequence, should have been of no consequence. But she was surprised to see him pick it up after a time and angle it not towards the room, or the few listening, or the musicians, or the music floating, air bound, but instead he angled the camera between the wooden curved back of the bentwood chair and the stone wall beside him. She saw his finger move. Not his head. Not his eye. Just the constant clicking of a camera shutter as his finger touched the shutter release, again, again. Shooting over and over simply a bit of deformed wood on the back of the bentwood chair towards a plastered wall without meaning, without context. Or perhaps this had a context she could not see, or could not understand. Strange, she thought. Or perhaps like the music that filtered through her ears into her brain, there was something the man saw that she could not understand, or see, or hear. Something of meaning without meaning.

He put down his camera and sat back, his expression regressing once more into shadow.

She turned away, having glanced at his face. He meant nothing. Neither did the image that spoke into the lens of his camera. Not any more than the music that spoke softly from the keys of a piano and the strings of a double bass and the long held single notes from a trumpet that tried to speak yet the words could not reach. Her.

This is Krakow, she thought. I have disappeared. I cannot be found. I am…not.

Except that perhaps she was. Because if had she turned, just slightly, and reopened her eyes after another sip from a large glass of whiskey, Irish, without water or ice, just the fire on her lips and down her throat, had she turned towards the shadow opposite her, she might have seen the man she had noticed raise his camera once again, point it towards her with her eyes open instead of closed, and shoot. And again. And again.

A zone of conflict during a time of a virus. Because of a virus. Victims in a zone of conflict.

With his camera, he shot.

She did not see.

When in fact she finally opened her eyes again, looking into the empty notes that surrounded her, that held her tightly, she glanced once more over to the table on the opposite side of the room.

There was no longer anyone sitting there. She saw only the lateral wooden supports along the back of a chair, framing shadows before a wall of plastered stone blocks. Nothing else.

*

He.

He is in a present tense. He is in Krakow.

Today the sky, empty of clouds, haemorrhages deep blue. Warm. He feels the warmth. He needs it. Prays to it.

He has walked from his apartment rooms, from the darkroom that has served as his womb and kept him nourished, not far from Krakow Glówny Train Station, to the Hala Targowa outdoor flea market. He has come here a few times over the past weeks. He needs to come here because the past has spoken to him and this is a place of which it speaks. He likes to wander amidst the book sellers and stalls in the middle of the market, staring at titles, at covers with their defining photographs, at names named. He likes to rummage too through the old weathered photographs from times past, images that mean nothing yet entrance, now stored in long wooden boxes. No dates. No places. No names. Aging paper wrinkled and burnished brown. He does not buy. He has no desire to buy. He can only witness and store images in his memory as he stores images on his contact sheets and his files and his published experiences and his presence. He feels oddly at home in this marketplace. One does not buy home. One resides.

He particularly likes it on Sundays. Not yet crowded because the virus remains too prevalent, too worryingly uncomfortable. But more traders appear. More books.

More old photographs and magazines and postcards. More things. More stories and faces.

He picks up something old, a trinket of no value. Turns it over in his hands. The stall holder stares at him hopefully.

--Something good for you, maybe? You are tourist? Something to take home?

He smiles, shrugs.

--You should buy. Good things. Some maybe not so good but you should buy.

He glances at the man desperate for a sale. Middle aged and pock-marked face. He glances at the man and does not see him.

--Thank you. I am only looking. Just curious.

He puts it back on the table. The trader shrugs. Turns away, no longer interested. The trader will not find a sale here.

He notices for the first time behind the trader a violin case amidst the boxes scattered under a table on the ground.

--Can I see that? That?

The trader follows the finger pointing to the small violin cardboard case. He pulls it out, puts it on the table. Opens it and removes a rather battered small violin.

--This violin it is fitting for child. I can give good price for you. Very good price.

He takes the small violin from the trader, stares at it. Turns it over from front to back, back to front. The instrument speaks to him of another, and another speaks to him of a story, of photographs at a particular angle, then of a photograph at another angle. And others. Countless photographs of something necessary, but this is not it.

He puts the instrument back into its case, nods at the trader.

--Thank you.

The trader shrugs again. Still no luck. No hope from this customer who does not spend money, who is only curious and needs to touch things but not buy. He does not buy.

--Do you play?

He turns. He sees her standing at the side of the next table, watching him. He sees her. He knows who she is. He remembers. He remembers her.

--No.

--You held the violin like a baby. Something precious.

--I held it like a memory. But not my memory.

--Are you certain?...We've met.

--Have we?

--Almost. Over music in a cellar. No violin. Trumpet. Bass. Piano.

--Yes.

--Sad notes.

--Sad notes.

--And photographs. You were photographing but in a way that made no sense. Not the musicians. Not the place or the customers. I watched you. You photographed—I don't know.

--Textures. Angles. Life.

--Life? Is that what you photograph?

--Life. Now...As it is now. As I see it.

She stares at him. She does not turn her gaze away. She does not smile. She is perhaps curious, cautious. He does not know what she is looking for. Is she looking? He does not know. Does she see? He does not know.

--Do you photograph doors?

--Doors?

--Doors that can no longer be opened.

He considers, turns away. Looks at nothing. Looks at a child's violin, hidden away by a cardboard case, lying on the ground amongst boxes sitting below a table. He looks away, so far away. Then. Now. Photographs. Places. Perhaps not as far away as he had thought. Turning back:

--Most of the doors I see close. I thought they closed behind me. I thought they remained closed. But then I find they sometimes open. Even a little. They open like music from a small violin. You cease to hear the notes, but they remain inside of you. Like surfaces. Textures. Like being.

--Yes.

--...I took a photo. Of you. Your eyes were closed. You were there and not there. I saw you. Annabel needed you within.

--Annabel?

--My camera.

She looks at him, tilts her head, smiles just slightly.

--I'd like to see it. The photograph.

--Why?

--So I remember who I am. That I am.

--Do you not know? Are you lost?

--Are you?

He does not answer her question. Again looks away. Again looks back.

--I will show you who you are. Tomorrow over coffee. A place called U Stasi. We can sit in a courtyard. Breathe. Good pierogi, too. Noon?

She hesitates. She looks at him carefully, deeply, taking him all in. Perhaps she is attracted to him. Perhaps she is attracted by his need. By her need. Perhaps she is him, as he is her.

--I'll find you there.

--And find yourself?

--We'll see, she says.

--We'll see.

The young woman nods. Turns and walks out of the market. He watches her. She does not turn around. She does not look behind her. She does feel the need. He does not know her name. He does not know who she is. But too: he has always known who she is.

And now.

She is sitting quietly, waiting for him to arrive. He is not late. She is early. She sits at a table in the courtyard of U Stasi. She has a coffee in front of her. Milky. Froth on top. The shape of a heart on top, a heart of coffee brown against the steam-filled white milk. She has put a line across the heart. Coffee brown cutting the white froth in half. He walks through the arch into the entrance. He nods. Sits. Puts his bag beside him. Points at the coffee.

--Your heart is broken. Is it?

--No. It's not a heart. It's a shape in coffee. That's all. A representation.

--Representations speak a story.

--Speak? Do they speak, not reveal?

He laughs.

--So I'm well informed and have been corrected.

She nods. He orders a coffee for himself.

--They do sweet pierogi. Yes?

--Sure. Why not.

He points at the menu for the waitress. Speaks to her in English. The waitress nods. He clearly does not speak Polish, she realizes. She could but will not. They say nothing. Sitting quietly, sipping coffee. The waitress brings their small plate. She takes one, nods.

--Good.

--Yes. Yes…they are. So.

--So. You found me.

He smiles slightly, nods. He puts his bag on his lap, pulls out a folder. Hands it to her. She hesitates, looking at the folder, then opens it and pulls out a number of photographs. There, the textured image of wall and dark bentwood measuring the back support of a deep brown chair. There, the angle of one wall perpendicular to another. She can feel the surface, even in two dimensional relief.

Funny, she thinks: he almost accomplishes with his camera what she is asked to do in her work with an algorithm and a computer.

She looks at another photo. This time the slightly raised angle of a stage in a stone lined cellar club. No musicians, no musical instruments or crowd; simply the edge of the raised platform in detail, juxtaposed to the stone wall off to the side, behind.

She hears music without the musicians, feels atmosphere without place. In two dimensions he somehow manages to convey three.

The final photograph is a woman in profile, her eyes closed. It is not the woman she knows. It is not the likeness captured. It is not someone sitting in a cellar jazz club listening to music that she does not particularly care about. It is not the present. It is the story of the past within her. The profile of a woman, almost silhouette, that speaks of a door ajar, closing, closed. A profile with painted lips painted from an empty, slightly crushed lipstick holder. With two elbows resting not on a table but on a wooden threshold, worn away by thousands of shuffling feet crossing over, crossed. Never returning. All there in a photograph of this woman in profile.

She stares at it for a very long time. A very long time. Then she puts it down.

Does not look at him. Sips from her coffee with not a heart but in froth once a heart cut in two by a sharp stain and now simply coffee, and froth, and a moment. And a moment that is true.

Finally she looks at him.

--I think you are right. These tell a story. They speak it. They don't represent.

--Do they speak to you?

--Stories speak.

--And did you find yourself in the photograph?

--I found something else.

--And what was that?

--...In my work, which is very different, I too have to define images. I take that which is two dimensional and with a computer program redefine it as three. The purpose is to make the viewer feel as if they are holding an object, smelling it, living it. I think you accomplish that without a computer program and AI algorithms. I think you do. I think you gave me life.

--There was always life.

--No. No, I'm not sure any longer.

--So perhaps then I did find you.

--Perhaps. Is this your work? What you do?

--Yes.

--Photography.

--Of a sort.

--Art?

He laughs.

--No.

--Then what?

He does not answer. Not at first. He looks into his coffee. He looks into himself. He does not know if he likes what he sees. He sees.

--People. Places. Hate. Life and death. Heat. Loud...heat. A child. Five children. A game of football on a rough ground then...heat. The old and the young. Those who cannot get away. Those who cannot—escape. Those who do and have to live with themselves. A young man with life slipping away.

She looks at him. In not understanding, she has a feeling she understands.

--And the door closes and you can't get out. But you're always there, scratching at the hinges with fingernails bloodied.

He stares at her. Deeply.

--Something like that, I suppose, he says.

--Yes. I'm sorry. I think I understand.

He finishes his coffee. Signals for another.

--You too?, he asks.

--Yes.

--I'd like to see your computer work.

--I don't think… Not yet.

--When you're ready.

--You'd probably understand.

--When you're ready.

--When I'm ready.

The waitress brings over two more coffees. She stares at hers, picks up the spoon and with its handle draws a line across the coffee brown heart set in the white foam. A line appears, unyoking one half from the other. Two fragments. And she drinks.

He watches her.

--I don't know you, he says.

She puts down her cup. Takes him in with a long glance.

--You know me. I think perhaps you have always known me. I think so. Yes, I think so.

*

She.

She chooses when she will see him. She mindfully is careful. But there are times she desires to see him. So they meet for coffee every so often, or a quiet meal. They do not say much to one another; words are not always necessary. Neither talks of the past. Of history. They talk only of the moment. Of a world seen in two dimensions and trying hard to make it into three. They speak not of loss. Neither do they speak of hope. These are simply a moments when one might be with the other, the other with one.

They approach one another's work separately, sometimes with fear. He does not push her on her own necessary creation. He had asked her once to see what her work entails but he does not ask again beyond having said he is curious, engaged, but will not push the issue. She can speak if she wishes. She has not wished.

She however has searched for information about him. His name and his own work are easy to trace. She sees images. She sees his reputation, his fame. Some of the photographs she discovers she remembers having seen. Some touch her. Some repulse. She reads in a review that he had somewhat disappeared, taken a step back. She sees he was in Jerusalem. She reads of a photography exhibition there at a gallery: four artists, carefully curated photographs. On her computer she clicks on images of one photographer, learns that another, just a young man, had been recently killed; she reads of an investigation; she reads of government obfuscation. She chooses not to explore further. She could ask him. She does not ask.

She understands.

She does not enquire.

She sits now in her own apartment in front of her computer, working on one image collected by colleagues only recently. A single child's shoe, found covered in earth on farmland near a boundary of the Site. The leather material primarily blue, with white saddles crawling up its side. Blue, deteriorated cotton lace still within the blue lace holes. Evidence of fire and ash. She stares at it for a long while, works on it with the computer's program developing it from a two dimensional photograph into a three dimensional image almost touchable, almost real, this worn item. Child's shoe.

Child's shoe like an empty lipstick holder.

She touches them both, so it seems. Holds both in her hands. In turn she holds the child's hand. Just as she acts as mirror to the young woman putting on her lipstick then dropping it into the earth, to be found buried almost eighty years later, its red lip paste long since swallowed by time and soil and painful sand dirt mud. She closes her eyes. Memory, she thinks.

She turns off the program. Considers. Chooses to look at another unrelated website of photographs, more recent times. Or recent enough. Two in particular. The oldest, the first: five children playing football. Five children disappearing. The second, tied to the first: a single little girl, her face empty, staring in shock and emptiness. The aftermath. Her shoes are dirty. The laces dirty. Blood on knees, streaked blood. The dirt makes all into a colourized violet. She wonders if the shoes were blue. Blue laces.

They meet for coffee. He drinks quietly. She watches him. Considers then speaks:

--I will show you my work if you wish.

--Are you sure?

--I will show you.

She takes him to the apartment her colleagues helped her find, in Bronowice, a district on the western side of the city. He does not look around the unadorned rooms. He does not comment on the emptiness. The apartment echoes his own small rooms.

She carries from the kitchen a chair to sit beside her own at her computer. The chair is one of four, the only chairs in the apartment. She uses one as her seat where she works. He sits beside her as she shows him images that she has been translating for many months now. Pairs of spectacles. Cloth. Shoes. Suitcases. Some silver. Artificial legs. A doll. A child's shoe. Broken bits of metal. A few worn wooden toys, half rotted away with time. Some worn gravestones, broken, without names. Some leather ties. Torn coats. A tiny metal ring. Some empty makeup containers. Some beads. A myriad of lives dissipated into ash and air. Scattered.

She moves slowly between images. Slowly so that he sees. Understands. Sometimes he traces with his index finger the image on the screen. Sometimes he holds the image in his mind, two dimensional becoming three, thus as if holding the item in his hand.

She finally shows him the image in two dimensions of a door on a platform. From without. From within. Large hinges. A spyhole covered with wire mesh. Behind it on the ground a wooden threshold, shining, worn with thousands and thousands of people shuffling over.

--Is that real? he asks.

She does not respond at first. Then:

--Is anything real?

--Did you translate it into three dimensionality as well?

--Only inside. Here.

She points to her heart.

--Only here. When it closed on me. A different project…A similar need.

He looks at her but doesn't enquire further. She turns off the computer.

--These objects. Where are they?

--…Some, not all, are in a facility in Oświęcim. Archives. Storage. Some on display in a museum. Some for research.

--Can I see them? Can I take a camera?

She hesitates. She wonders if she has allowed him to enter too deeply into her life. She does not tell him of her past. He does not ask. But she knows that he can hear her story even without its words. He has seen much. She wonders if it is perhaps too much.

--I can ask.

She tells her colleagues who he is. The researchers and curators and specialists. She shows them his work. They recognize some of his own images. They perceive that he has seen much over the years. That he must understand. They agree she can bring him. They agree he can bring his beloved Annabel as long as he does not publish. He will not.

They take the train on a Sunday morning when no one will be around. They sit together staring out the window. The journey takes only forty-five minutes. The train car is almost empty. They stare at sunshine reflecting off newly built houses. Green fields. Tractors cutting in fields of rye and barley.

He has asked for no audience. He prefers not to explain, not to chat. She understands well. Walking through the town, she shows him the museum, now closed, a onetime synagogue where some of the team's artefacts are on display. Most however are held in their offices and research centre for archiving. She takes him to the offices, to the rooms used for archive and examination. She walks him along the storage shelves: stacks of protected boxes holding metal fragments, eyeglasses, shoes, some toys. Larger stacks for artificial limbs that in certain cases provide DNA samples and commentary on lives lived and lost. Climatized shelves of carefully preserved fabrics and prayer shawls. A room of suitcases and small traveling baggage trunks.

She gives him a pair of disposable surgical gloves so he can handle some of the remnants of forgotten lives if he wishes. He touches few, but some he asks to photograph. She knows he does not photograph the items themselves, but finds angles of texture and place to redefine meaning. He spends several hours on only a few of the pieces she shows to him. Whereas she creates three dimensions from a flat photograph in the work she is hired to do, he seeks a different definition, a different meaning: in angles, in foreground cutting across background, in a corner, a line, a particular material.

She shows him an item they have been examining in the collection that only recently was sent to her computer as a flat image: a small baggage trunk partially covered with mostly torn away blue cloth. Inside is a removable base used to hide something of value, long since disappeared.

--They still find things all over this area. All over Poland, Ukraine, Czech, Slovakia. Sometimes buried, or sold in markets, in attics or cellars. Most things probably have a story to tell but the stories are usually forgotten or lost. The carved prosthesis once worn. A suitcase with secrets. A pair of bent eyeglasses that once read religious texts or examined paintings of forgotten artists. A child's laughter in a torn rag doll. We don't know.

--You know.

--In some ways, perhaps. As a friend put it to me recently: these don't capture a moment of time; rather they talk a story still.

He smiles, just slightly, with a pain she cannot see and cannot know.

--Yes. They talk a story. Still.

His Annabel shoots the angle of the half removed chest's base and the darkness it hides, angled so that he creates two surfaces, the same but weathered in different ways. Darkness meeting light. One story meeting another. Talking to him with the possibility of memory.

--What will you do with them? The photographs you are shooting here, elsewhere?, she asks him.

--I don't know. None of these are defined or recognizable for what they are. That's important. Rather I want them to speak of what is not seen: the feel of a wire frame against the side of an eye, the pain of someone's treasure carried in a tight, secret place in a personal piece of luggage, the whispered words of a child to the secret friend that was a woven toy. The stories that define lives, perhaps they'll help define mine. I don't know what I'm after, really. I just find I need to…to search.

--When I dig in the earth, when I tried to imagine the foundations of buildings where the unspeakable—here she hesitates—I sometimes hear them. I call them the ghosts. Do you believe in ghosts?

He looks at her for a beat, at the pair of eyeglasses she is returning to the labelled shelf. She closes the cabinet door in front of the shelves, turns around to look at him to see if he has an answer.

--Perhaps the right question is do they believe in us?

It is evening by the time they are back in Krakow, having stopped on the way for borscht and pierogi. She asks him to come up to her flat for a cup of tea. He follows her. They sit at her small kitchen table with its remaining three chairs, the fourth in another room at a table where a large computer screen rests, blank now.

--You were right; our work is not so dissimilar, he tells her.

--Our work now. I looked at some of your photographs that I could find. Some I knew from newspapers, magazines. It must have been hard.

--It took its toll. I carry it.

--Yes. But perhaps what you're doing now--is not really any different.

--A young friend told me that not too long ago. He was certain of it. The friend who talked of stories spoken not captured by the moment.

--He was right.

--He was right.

He finishes his tea.

--I will show you whatever I print, if you're interested. I won't publish them as you requested. These are for me. My own search.

She nods. Walks over to the door with him. He turns to her, nods. Opens the door.

--I'm interested.

He turns again, looks at her. She reaches her hand up to his face, runs the back of her hand against his cheek. He watches her eyes. He feels her hand.

She will not turn her gaze away. It will be. He closes the door in front of him.

And it is to be. He walks beside her to the bedroom, she taking his hand.

231

He enters her gently and she feels him deep within. She closes her eyes so that she can really see him. She holds him tightly to her, feeling his shoulder blades, the small of his back. She can feel many scars that are not there, two dimensions becoming three. He moves slowly, rhythmically, resting his head in the crux of her neck, against her shoulder, moving with her as they sit with legs wrapping one against the other.

Her eyes remain closed and she sees memory. She sees her mother not swaying in the cold of an empty studio but laughing with her when she was a child, playing games, hide and seek. Hide and seek. She sees digging in the dirt not for empty lipstick tubes rusted and crushed but by the small dog she once had when she was young, the animal trouncing in water and mud and shaking and she now grown-up laughing as the dog even still shakes water in all directions. She sees a door opening, a door to her brightly lit warm studio in Hindley, north of Manchester, where she sculpts clay between her fingers into a small human form, simple in its beauty. She sees the glasses she wears to makes sense of the romantic novel she reads as a teenager, the child's ballet shoes she puts on to dance like the ballerina she dreams of being when a young girl, plie at the bar counted by a teacher she cannot see, up down, one two, up down, one two. She sees the suitcase she carries when she goes away to university for the first time, holding her treasures she knows and needs: a rag doll, a teddy bear. She feels the material of a new dress, the soft wool of a scarf, the burning of whiskey, always Irish, swallowed and warming. She feels him, inside of her, life, knowing it will pass because it has to pass but not now, his firm body pressing on hers, embracing and needing.

She sees that it has eased her pain. And she absorbs him inside of her, deeply inside of her. His sex. Her sex. His need. Her need. His warmth. Her warmth. His breath. Her breath. His pain. Her pain. His urge. Her urge. His strength. Her womanhood.

She feels him. She feels herself. And as she is seized by the rush of heat, the race of adrenalin and endorphins through her body forcibly making their way into her brain, as she weeps and cries out for what has gone before, as he shudders and holds her tighter, so much tighter becoming one from two, painfully one, as she feels him so deep inside of her telling a story being a story needing a story, as she feels his

232

texture and his skin and the touch of him the smell of him the one of him, she opens her eyes and sees that although she knows the moment will pass as it must, for this moment, this now, she is here, she lives, she is whole. She leans back, she breaks, she shudders, she cries out, and the door opens.

The door opens.

*

He.

He weighs the thought for a day, a second, a third. He decides this is what he wishes to do. What he needs to do.

He writes to the Mother in Jerusalem. He says where he is. What he is seeking. He asks a favour. He had read the book the young man hardly more than a boy had left for him, the book about the composer Weisz, written by the composer's manager, companion, lover. He had recognized that, had the young man's Mother, then a young woman, not sought out the composer, an entire history would have been lost. A life.

A story. Many stories.

The book had said that she, young woman then, now Mother in grief, had left notes and files for the composer and that when he finally read the story it had turned a heart. And spoken to him. So after considering carefully, he writes to her, this Mother in grief, grieving still:

I hope you do not mind this message to you. I hope it will neither distress nor seem inappropriate.

I read the book that I was given. A story of questions, and a search, and history. It too spoke to me as it spoke to your son, he too searching. Perhaps ours was a journey we should have undertaken together.

The book talks of notes that you once left for Weisz, notes and pages and a story that changed a life. And in a way saved a life. Hania's life becoming his.

I am now in Krakow. I do not know how long I will stay here. But I too am searching for something. With that in mind, with the hope of understanding, I want to enquire if you have put these notes, or story, or the words of a life hidden and then found into a form I might read—copies, a summation in a computer file, the life of your grandmother Hania as you knew her and might feel able to share.

233

It is a lot to ask. Perhaps inappropriate. But I too am on that similar journey and am trying to understand—your grandmother, your son, myself. I am trying to make sense of things that do not always make sense. I wonder if in the story of Hania there might be even a single answer.

Forgive me if I have overstepped the boundary of my respect for you.

Late one night, in a quiet house in the Ein Karem district of Jerusalem, a Mother now aged far beyond her years, grieving for all lost, so much lost, reads again the printout of an email received from Krakow. She places it in her lap, looks over at a perspex case where a cracked, worn, old violin of no real value but priceless lies encased. The instrument has only one string hanging loosely beside its body. Its neck is weathered and broken. It plays it tonal melodies for no one.

She thinks of the words of the old woman who gave it to her, the words that the woman in turn related of a young man who had wanted the composer to have the broken instrument: '*Tell Weisz the violin is me*'. The nature of a gift from one to another. More than a thing, it is a life. So the Mother looks over at her husband, watching her while she sits with an email from Krakow on her lap.

--I think I will send him the manuscript. I think we should.

The husband looks at her with love and huge sadness. A life that has taken its toll of sadness. And he nods his acquiescence. His son would have wanted this. He in Krakow is correct: theirs is a search together.

The following morning in Krakow a photographer finds an email and attachment in his computer in-box:

--*You may read this,* the Mother has written; *we think our journey and yours are one.*

He downloads the copy of a manuscript that one day may be published, or not, the story of the Mother's own Grandmother. Hania. And he begins to read.

*

She.

She will see him when he wishes. If he wishes. His arms around her feel comfortable. Also needy. Together they are gentle lovers. He inside of her is his need as well as her own. They rest. They sleep. They move apart. They lie together.

This is not urgent. But neither is it timeless. She knows time beginning is also time ending. This is the way of things.

He disappears for a few days but she does not wait for him to ring. He will, he will not. Instead she concentrates on the images. Two dimensions into three. A colleague asks if She would like to join with one other to seek out a hidden Jewish graveyard that locals had recently discovered. The three drive to the town of Strzegomek, northeast of Krakow, leave the car and with a guide walk for half an hour to local woods. Deep within, at an unmarked glen amongst the trees they find the graveyard they had sought, overgrown and abandoned. Forgotten. They take photographs and mark the locale on a map and a record of its location on a printed form they keep for later investigation. Finding an old forestry road they follow it to a dilapidated farm. A farmer's wife emerges, suspicious, saying she knows nothing of any graveyard in the trees. As they leave, She notices a foundation stone at the corner of a barn that has faded lettering carved on its side; it had once been a gravestone. They call it matzevot. It is not the first time she had seen such. She quickly takes a photograph with her phone to add to their archives, before they continue walking.

Two nights later he telephones her. It is a week since she spoke to him. She does not ask where he might have been. She asks no questions whatsoever, but he volunteers that he has needed to read some files received, and that he then went hiking for a few days along the Slovenian border. There was something he had hoped to find, but he found no answers to his questions. He found only more questions.

He tells her there is a park open to the public and an institute there he is eager to explore at the weekend. He asks if she will join him.

They meet at the tram entrance under the railway station, only realizing too late their tram has taken them in the wrong direction. They get off at its final stop, walk across a small intersection, wait a half hour for the same tram to pick them up again, then sit quietly for the forty-five minute return it takes to reach the other end of the line. Here they wait for a bus, ask directions, are eventually dropped off, a five minute walk from the Babinski Mental Hospital in the Krakow suburb Kobierzyn.

The paved drive up the parkland with numerous small chalet buildings nearby is long and lined with trees. They say little as they stroll quietly up the tree-lined gentle lane, staring at a few of the worn buildings slightly set back in a wide, green park. He takes a few photographs. At the end of the drive up the hill is a large, handsome building, empty, with a sign outside that says simply 'theatre'. At its side, overlooking flower beds, a stone bench of calm. She smiles: she could be happy in this place.

In the distance they can see a couple larger block-like buildings that have cars parked in front of them, still used, still working, but as they stroll they see that most of the many institute buildings are empty. It is as if a former summer camp is closed for the summer. Along the crest of the hill that defines the boundaries of the hospital the main drive circles yet other abandoned residences and offices. Behind these several empty buildings, and a few where only one or two people are seen inside, ignoring the two figures walking, the hill slopes down again in a large farm's pasture filled with sun-bleached grain, blowing just slightly in the breeze. All has an idyllic feeling.

--Why did you want to come here?, she asks him after long moments of wandering and silence.

--Curious. There was a woman I read about who came here as one person, left as another. Lost herself. Found herself. Or perhaps just the beginning of finding herself.

--You can relate to her?

--In some ways. Perhaps both of us might, in some ways.

--Was this during the War?

--After. A few years after. But war scarred her. War leaves permanent scars.

They walk further in amongst the chalet buildings. One they find unlocked and enter. Scattered glass. Some graffiti. A couple former bathrooms, shower rooms with their toilets and baths ripped out leaving only a few pipes sticking out of the walls. A rusted frame of a hospital bed. Hospital staircase with no voices. Garbage scattered around. More glass.

He takes many photographs. Glass, graffiti. The worn staircase against the faded blue stairwell wall. A broken pipe emerging from a wall where a shower once existed. Broken tiles. Garbage strewn. Bars on windows. A door half ajar.

A door she stares at but does not close.

He stands in a large empty room, with a small room off to the side. Gazes around. Puts his camera aside. He finds the living in the empty space, the silent textures.

--Do you hear ghosts here?, he asks her.

--No. No, not here.

--I think I do. Or rather, stories told. She was a patient here for a time. She found her voice. Married her doctor eventually.

--And lived happily ever after?

--No. No, he died quite young. She became a teacher, lived for many years near Warsaw. She saw her own daughters grow. Saw them become mothers. Came to know her granddaughter. Loved her. Grew old. Waited for others who did not come back. Waited for…herself maybe. Never saw her great grandson, which was a pity. But he saw her I think. Listened to her story. Went to find her. Searched in his heart.

He grows quiet as they leave the building. She does not query him further. They stroll. Behind another of the chalets in the back they find a monument to those patients killed here during the War. On one side, in Hebrew, is a wall of weathered bronze for the Jewish patients; across from it is a list of all the other patients who had perished.

--I researched it. The Jewish patients who were here were sent north to Otwock, near Warsaw, to a hospital there, then transported to Treblinka. The other patients suffering from various mental disorders were taken a year later from here to Auschwitz, or euthanized here. These beautiful quiet grounds became so dark. Like too many places.

--But that is not why you wanted to see this place?

--No. A woman named Hania was brought here. After the War, as I said. She found her voice, literally. She came here to die, to live, hard to say. I needed to come here. To see for myself. To try to understand her.

--And will that help you to understand yourself?

--I don't know. A young friend wanted me to hear her story because it formed his own. Perhaps mine now, I can't be sure.

--Then important. Worth the journey here. Worth the journey.

They come to a chapel, empty and locked. They climb its few concrete steps, stand in a portico entrance looking in through the small window of the wooden door.

She notices a plaque on a wall just inside the portico, and one across. She points.

--It seems the patients did not all die here. This is for the one who survived, the only one. It says she escaped. And the plaque on that side is for the nurse who saved her. I suppose she too found life again when everyone else did not.

--The woman I mentioned, Hania: she lived and yet you wonder. Lived with memory. Lived but died perhaps, in some ways.

--What about you?, she asks. Does memory kill some of you as well?

He does not answer at first. He considers the question. Slowly walks down the stairs away from the chapel. Stops, turns in all directions to look at the simple property on the hill, the hospital, the memories, some his, others not.

--You were right, he says. When you finally allow yourself to remember, yes, a part of you is taken and becomes a ghost. Not haunting, just beside you.

--Yes.

She says no more.

It is late when they return to Krakow. They find a quiet restaurant near his flat. They eat. After they go up to his flat for the night. They make love. This is not urgent. This is quiet. They separately and together listen to one another's memory without words. Separately and together they close their eyes and hear. Their movement one against the other ties them as one. The stories once separated are no longer.

In the morning they again make love, this time gazing deeply into one another as their bodies hold tightly. There is urgency. There is warmth. There is the pain that is life itself.

After he brings her a coffee. They sip in silence.

--I have to go away.

--For good?

--No...No. I'm back in ten days or so. To the States. Someone I worked for wants to meet. It's not time to work, but we'll talk. And with some others I know. Research. I'll come back here after I see them.

--I understand.

He gets up, disappears into his dark room, emerges with a plug and play zip file.

--You might be interested to read the file on this. The woman Hania. Her story.

238

Yesterday's. Tomorrow's, I don't know.

She takes the small computer file. Nods.

Later, when she plugs the disc into her computer, she finds three copied files. The first is a photograph, faded, of an older woman sitting in a garden in the back of a wooden, brown house, looking away into the distance, her face barely in profile. The second file in fact clicks on to a long piece of classical music, without any commentary. The third is a manuscript, again with neither introduction nor commentary of any sort.

Before she reads she plays the music, quietly in her empty flat.

When the music stops she sits for a long time. The composition lasts for well over an hour. She decides she will play it all the way through again. Without knowing why, she thinks she needs to hear it once more. She closes her eyes, sits down on the floor in her work study that has only one chair pushed slightly beneath a desk. As the music starts again she reaches up for a small throw blanket resting on the back of the chair, places it over her, lies where she is and closes her eyes.

She listens again.

She hears the words of the music. Music that has no words.

When it ends, she sits back at her computer. Although it is late, well past midnight, she brings up the file with a manuscript onto the screen.

And she begins to read.

*

He.

He listens to the offer in New York. He reads the reports, the briefing materials. He looks at wire services information. He talks to some political contacts. He builds a picture. He does not shoot one with his camera. Instead he listens. And he closes his eyes knowing what might happen. He says he will consider it.

He returns to Krakow. Autumn arrives. He sees her often but does not overstep bounds. He needs her just now. She needs him just now. Both know it will end by necessity. Who they are by necessity. So he remains careful with his time. With her time. What they want is similar, but where they inevitably have to go may not be. He knows the future. So does she. They do not speak of this.

He researches. He seeks out a town mentioned east of Krakow. Explores in the local museum. Meets the small museum's English speaking curator who has history, knowledge of the past. Finds a local priest he can talk to about the past, about those who left, those who remained. The land. The people. He travels to another town that is the centre of voivodeship administration offices and spends several hours looking through old documents to create a picture of what once was. He hires a translator to help him wade through archives. They meet with a few local officials. He needs to understand how the land has altered. Memories he finds are short. Time has moved forward. He has not.

He chooses to seek out a lost farm, lost to time, the encroaching edge of a forested national park creeping into its once existence, changing boundaries brought on by changing politics over decades. He finds what he seeks on a map and asks her if she would like to see whatever can be found there still with him. She has read the manuscript. She knows what he seeks, if not why. She will seek with him.

She too has need.

The day they rent the car the weather is crisp with autumn sunshine. Trees shed blankets of red and yellow leaves on back farmland roads. They carefully drive over a trickling stream, water splashing slightly on either side of the vehicle. In some fields a few Polish red cows watch them drive slowly by, indifferent to the human presence. They find a crossroads shown on the map, a large farm below them, beyond, forest pushing higher on the other side. The leave the car in a layby, start up the road towards the trees. The road quickly disappears but a hikers' trail leads them higher.

He stares at his map, considers, then continues. She follows a few steps behind. They say little, other than commenting on the path's route, or warning of sharp brambles, or that there is evidence of a road here once. Once a long time ago.

They find their way through wooded areas, hearing birds along the way but seeing no animals, no people. The sounds are the sounds of a crisp autumn day. In the distance, the far distance, a tractor hums a chorus of miscued bass notes. Somewhere, again in the distance, a dog barks.

They emerge into a large clearing with trees sheltering on the high side. Evidence of a track of sorts that came here. Ended here. The sun emerges from a cloud screen. It brings light to the clearing, but not warmth. He stops to consult the map. Some notes he had written. He looks around: right and left, above him, below him.

--This is it. This is where they left her. This was her home.

She looks at him, nods. She thinks so too, without the consultation to the oracle map he holds in his hand. She does not need prophecy. The pragmatic scientist side to her character asks for fact. Here it is not difficult to find such.

They walk around the expanse of the clearing. They find quantities of broken, rotting wood, fragments of rusted metal and then, eaten by undergrowth and vegetation, the half disappeared markings of foundations.

--There was a house here once. That's what these foundations means. Not much else to see. Some rotting wood there: a lintel maybe. Most of everything eaten by time. Hard to see what was here. Really here.

--We have the story of her notes. That's all really, he replies.

She nods. That's all really. Nothing else to see but the spreading layer of weeds, rushes, brambles, poor vegetation and then the growing expanse of trees. Anything that was here once, that might have whispered secrets, has long since disappeared beneath the earth or been taken away. She knows the instruments she could use to tell more of the story that was here. She does not see the point of doing such, not now. Perhaps it is best to leave the story buried.

--I'd hoped there would be more.

--Like what?, she asks.

--I don't know. I don't...something. Song. Story.

--Maybe it's here; you can't see it. Or maybe it remains in her telling.

--Probably. Let's go up that way.

He points towards the trees above them. At the edge when they reach the boundary of the clearing there they find a path, possibly an animal trail, and follow it. Perhaps two hundred meters further on they find another clearing, much smaller, overgrown. Decayed wood. No foundations here except for six crumbling short brick pillars at edges of the space where pillars once stood, barely emerging from the ground, worm housings mostly that possibly supported a barn structure.

--She spoke of living in a barn, he says.

--Yes. This was likely where it was. It's a long time ago. Nothing remains. The earth and vegetation take over. I've seen such often. Too often. Another life. Or the same life, I don't know.

--There are ways to see what was here, aren't there?

She hesitates. She remembers her own Site, her own pains at that Site. She knows her training and had wanted never to return to it. She always knew she would have to.

--There are ways to see, yes. Foundations. Place. Techniques and machines used make the invisible into material. But what matters is what it tells us. Here, maybe grains were kept. Some animals once. And a secret life lived. The machine ways you're referring to: they tell more of death than life. A story, the breath, the tears: these are not so easily revealed.

--I thought I would find more.

--You found a lot. You found the need to search. And you found the need to hear the whispers. To find her.

--Maybe. Maybe—ultimately maybe searching for her great grandson, who needed her. Needed to find her.

--Perhaps you have. In ways you can't see right now.

He looks at her, nods. Understands where she is leading him. He takes out his camera from his backpack, and a second as well. His belove Annabel. A Nikon F2. He looks around, begins to shoot: rotten wood, a few scattered brick, foundations that aren't there, a life that was, was not. He looks at this vegetation encroaching world, takes it within himself, finds it in his cameras, shoots. The photographs he needs to survive. To be.

He looks at her, watching him. She nods, just slightly. She sees, too. He returns his singular stare to his view finder. And shoots once more. Click.

Then click. Then click. Then click.

*

She.

She wanders away from him as he looks at the world through a camera body. She follows a path a bit higher. Driven. Curious.

She discovers a small brook of water seeping down. She stands at the edge, washing water over her face. Autumn day. Looks up. Sun speckling brightly off trees. Finds stepping stones and crosses. Climbs a bit higher. The land flattens, just a bit. Slight grove of woods. Trees surrounding. Peaceful spot.

She sits on a stone. Rubs her hand through her hair. Breathes. Forgets. Remembers.

Closes her eyes. Listens to the wind. Listens to memory. Listens.

It is only then that she hears the wind talking to her. Hears that which she has heard before, somewhat, calling. Voices calling. As it was once before. As she had tried to forget. As it was once before, yes. She hears cries on the breeze. Asking for her. Asking remembrance.

Asking forgiveness.

She stands. She looks at the earth. She paces forward, just a bit. Looks at the earth. Kneels and pulls some vegetation away. Looks at the earth, the greater earth. The soil and growth. Undulations on the forest floor. Altering vegetative ground cover. The slightest shifting of topography. Hints of settling topsoil, slightly apparent. Just ever so slightly, but her eyes see. Slightly more vegetation with a minimal but noticeable greater facilitated growth due to just a bit more moisture content in the earth. Disturbance. Ancient. Long ago. But there.

Disturbance.

All the training she had done, the work, the science of archaeology and forensic archaeological examination. The degrees she had been granted. The belief in her experience. The techniques she had been shown and had utilized once not so long ago at a different Site for a different reason but perhaps, just perhaps, not so different after all. She knows what it means. She fears what it means.

What she had run away from, but never escaped from.

Assessment of possibility, becoming assessment of probability. All interacting here, now.

And most of all, simply most of all, the voices. The whispers of ghosts. The whispers she knows. Remember me. Remember me.

And forgive.

She looks behind her. He has emerged from the trees, from the open earth and hints of foundations that he has sought and tried to define in his own image making his own way. He has come to find her.

He has found her.

And now he stands straight and still, staring at her. At her wide eyes. At her knowledge. At her fear drawing lines in her face, tightening her expression. He stares at her as she looks at him. Stares at her as she turns and looks there, just beyond. Waits for her to speak.

She does not speak.

He waits for her to explain in whispers.

She does not whisper. She does not move. All she now does is to stand quietly, looking at the earth that surrounds. Because she knows. They are here.

Here.

She says nothing. She hears. In hearing their silent weeping, she sees.

2. Jenny and Tom

<u>Jerusalem and Krakow</u>
<u>December 2021</u>

--So, you found it? The farm? Whatever remains?...

Jenny and Tom flew here together. They both knew it was important to do so. Necessary even. Jenny had never been to Jerusalem. Tom had not returned since shortly after the photographic exhibition. That was before the virus that became a pandemic changed the world. Or perhaps did not change it.

That was before.

--Yes. Six weeks ago. We were there. And subsequently.

Tom answers Agnieszka's question quietly. Mother in grief. Centered in grief. Agnieszka takes in his response, whispered not like a bold child's repost but rather by one who has made decisions in pain, necessary but reluctantly.

--What did you see?

Tom shakes his head.

--Everything is gone. Some slight foundations. Small bits of wood that could have been...Well. Nothing to define what was there. What she had been through. What Hania lived, saw, when she became Hannah.

Silence hangs heavily in the room. Now it is Beniamin's turn to speak.

--We were there also. A long time ago.

--Yes. I read. We read. It's in your manuscript.

Agnieszka looks at them, but does not say anything.

--When we were there, Aga and I...the outlines of the farm still existed. The house. The barn above, fallen in, little to see.

--But you did see.

--We did. Aga found her Grandmother's initials, carved into a beam where the barn would have been. I suppose this is all gone now, so many years.

--Yes. As you wrote in the manuscript, already disappearing then. Now, the forest has taken over. Just rotting wood, a few metal bits of no description. There is nothing left.

--Why did you go there, Tom?, Agnieszka asks. What were you looking for? Why were you looking for?

--I know, I… I would not hurt you. Either of you. Since I left here…

Tom shakes his head. Looks away. Stares at a broken musical instrument that continues to sing its song.

--I think Kuba was in so many ways far older than his years. My talks with him, the photographs: he was trying to understand. Now I'm trying to understand. He searched for a reason. In the notes and music from the violin you keep right there, never played. In the experience handed down within us, those we know, those we do not. I don't know why I felt the need to go there.

He stops. Eyes seeking. Eyes saddened. Gaze afar. Then he continues.

--You spent a long time trying to find your Grandmother, the Grandmother you did not know secreted away in silence by the one you did. Then you went searching for her. Her story led you to Pawel Weisz. And Weisz found you even as he found himself. That experience gave—definition. The reason. Being. It told memory. That is what Kuba said to me about his photographs, my photographs: an image may speak a story. Loss. Gain. Pain. Love. Hope perhaps. Kuba was looking for it and tried to find it through the stories of things, through memory. I think I'm trying to do the same. Your Grandmother's story, it is yours. But it is also mine: I the reader, the audience, the one who gazes at the image to see the almost hidden reflection of oneself. Perhaps I was hoping to find that as well. The humanity within us, I don't know. I felt I needed to understand somehow. To see the picture. To see—her. To see Kuba one more time.

The slightest sad smile crosses Agnieszka's face, just slightly, then disappears again.

--I understand, Tom. I always understood. It is why we thought we agreed to send the manuscript to you. My Grandmother, Pawel Weisz, yes their story. And yes mine. But Kuba's as well. Perhaps somewhere yours too.

She turns her gaze to Jenny.

--And you, Jenny? Did Tom simply say come with me, hold my hand? Curiosity?

--No. No, something else. He suggested I read your manuscript. You will think perhaps I should not have, that it is nothing to do with me. But it is everything to do with me.

--As falling in love with Agnieszka had to do with me, all those many many years ago?, Beniamin asks.

--No. Something else. Something…

--You told us you were trained as a forensic archaeologist. That you work at sites, the camps. You are not Jewish. Why?

Jenny looks quietly at Agnieszka, weighs her answer.

--Perhaps like Tom, I'm looking for something. I'm not a tourist, professionally or… It's something I needed to do.

Agnieszka and Beniamin sit quietly, considering. Agnieszka angles her gaze towards the perspex case, the weathered, broken violin within. She shakes her head, just slightly, not with disapproval, but with a hint of understanding. And great loss. She sighs. She closes her eyes. Hears the notes played in the air. Then looks back at her guests.

--So, you've come back here, Tom. You found where Hania was lost, then my Hannah Kielar was born, became. The beginning of my Grandmother's journey that found its voice only after her death. So now, what…?

--There's more.

Tom looks at her. Then at Jenny, urging. Jenny closes her eyes. Struggles with words. Finds them.

--My work, it…What I do, or did, involved being able to read landscapes. Look for that which lies beneath the surface. History. Architectural evidence. Forensic evidence. Jewish law prevents the disturbing of gravesites. You'll know that. But I am involved with looking at lost architectural remains. Artefacts. The material things that give historical evidence. Meaning. The story. They become part of the archives of what we understand. What we need to understand. Things we cannot always see but with scientific tools of the trade we can picture and describe. Things we choose not to forget, long after they are assumed forgotten. Were intended to be forgotten. Intended to be lost.

--Go on. Please, Beniamin tells her.

Jenny reaches into the briefcase she has brought to this house. It speaks, even as she speaks; she withdraws a folder.

--When Tom and I first went, we wandered up to the farm, or where it once was, as he told you. But something happened, something…Sometimes I get a sense, I…It's as if you hear voices talking to you. Calling to you. I can't explain well. I can't… I…We walked from where the farmhouse was, its clearing, barely anything remaining. We went up and found a smaller area cleared. The only things there were the remains of brick pillars, mostly gone. I'd seen this sort of structural foundation before. I knew it was likely the barn, as you described in the manuscript file. Verbal evidence supports physical evidence, and Hania's words, your words, provide images. The landscape. The architecture. As you saw, when there was still more to see. But then I went alone further up into the forest above. Wandering. Considering. There was a tiny stream coming down. I crossed over. Beyond was a very small grove. Really nothing. But…I knew it was not 'nothing.' I heard the…I heard the wind. And the wind was like…

--Like voices, Agnieszka says when Jenny grows silent.

--Yes. I know, mad perhaps, but—

--No. Not mad. I understand. I think both my husband and I understand. Perhaps we heard such on our visit. Perhaps it whispered the initials of Hania Stern. Her voice calling.

Jenny opens the file that now sits on her lap.

--Over the next few weeks, I returned to the former farm. I borrowed some instruments that we have used in our work. A colleague who lives in Warsaw joined me a couple times for a weekend. Tom joined me, but not always. Sometimes I went there alone, worked alone. Sometimes it was easier.

She puts some photographs on the table in front of the older couple.

--This…I asked Tom to photograph this. It is where the farmhouse would have been. There is not much to see but these stones are basic foundation stones. Mortar. This photograph here—

Jenny points to the next set of photographs.

--These are remaining pillars that suggested a barn. Six in all.

--Not much there, Beniamin says. As you suggested.

--No.

She now pull various pages from her file.

--This is a topographical map of what remains of the house. This, the barn. Topographical surveys are the first thing we do. I then did a GPR survey—ground penetrating radar—on both locales. These are what the surveys look like. I put in twin resistance probes; they help us to define the relationships between features, to create the varying planes of the surface and just below, you see here. These help to define the foundations. I also used a device called a fluxgate gradiometer. This helps detect the magnetism of objects below the surface. These geophysical surveys ultimately helped create a picture. Using software we have, and some that I now use, we can build an image of what was once in situ, what it once looked like.

Jenny pulls out the computer images from each of the two locales: one is a created rendition of what the farmhouse would have looked like; the other, the barn where Agnieszka and Beniamin found the carved initials of Hania Stern, Hania who hid, who disappeared, who reemerged as Hannah Kielar; so she became, and remained, until her final days, bequeathing the notes and story for her granddaughter.

Agnieszka and Beniamin say nothing, staring at the computer graphic renditions. Agnieszka runs her fingers along the outline of a barn, the foundations still existing shown clearly and giving rise to a shadow image of what had been. Then she looks up at Tom, at Jenny, who watch her and Beniamin, silently.

--It—these—touch me, Agnieszka finally says. They move me in many ways. But—these images might be the result of your interest, but they are not what you came to show us.

--No, Tom answers. He looks at Jenny. He nods, just slightly.

--As I said, Jenny explains, I went above where we found the foundations of the barn. Wandering. At a small clearing there was...Well. There was. I saw undulations, changes in undergrowth. Things I understand. Things I'm trained to understand.

She pulls out some other pages.

--This is the GPR from that clearing. And the magnetometry surveys. This mapping here, it is from what we call Lidar technology. Lidar simply means light detection and ranging. It uses lasers to map below a limited forest canopy. The lasers are mounted on drones. My colleague from Warsaw helped me with this. And here in this photograph that Tom took, these are called taphonomic markers. These are not easily seen but when combined with the other surveys, the walkover, the total station survey, here, with Lidar and Magnetometry, it reveals here the disturbance of ground, of vegetation. Also you can see here in Tom's photograph, the slight changes to the fauna just around suggest some bioturbation that...

Jenny looks up from the laid out mapping sheets. She sees their confusion. She stops speaking. Looks at Beniamin and Agnieszka, smiles just slightly.

--I'm sorry. Sometimes I forget to speak in plain English. Too often perhaps.

--What is it you wish to tell us, Jenny?, Agnieszka asks gently.

--This small grove here, above the barn. In the manuscript you compiled, telling Hania—Hannah—telling her story. What happened there as much as you knew. Imagining perhaps the things you did not know. This grove of trees I think is a grave. Unmarked. Forgotten. I think it is the grave of Helena Kielar. Perhaps someone else. Perhaps her true daughter, born Hannah, whose name she would give to Hania to help her survive. It's not a large grave but I think...I think this is where your grandmother buried Helena when she died.

Beniamin looks at Agnieszka. Agnieszka lowers her eyes to look again at the various surveys and photographs laid out before her, then looks at her husband.

--Perhaps it is. Perhaps you are right. But why are you telling us this?

--In Polish law, and...I...We would need to tell the authorities. They would want to exhume what is there for forensic examination if the truth suggests this. Even a gravesite as old as this. This is what they have to do.

--Unless they were Jews.

--Unless the victims were Jewish, because Halacha Law takes precedence. And religious leaders have the right to say no.

--Helena Kielar, Hannah Kielar's mother, and the girl born Hannah Kielar whose name became the gift to my Grandmother Hania, they were not Jewish.

--No.

--And if you are right, why do you tell us all this?

--Because...because it is the right the thing to do. This story. You. Because sometimes history must be left buried. Because Hania is perhaps one of the ghosts here. Her story here.

Tom now speaks quietly to Agnieszka and Beniamin:

--We, both of us, we felt that we should come to you, to see if you said it is right that the dead should be left in peace now, after so long. This story is yours too as it is your Grandmother's. And if you feel that we must leave the forest alone, that should this be her final resting place, or others', the forest may look after the farmer woman Helena who gave the name Hannah Kielar to your Grandmother, to that part of your story, and that is enough. We have done what we felt was necessary for us to do. It is not simply a choice of right or wrong. It is not simply a moral choice. It is about the final part of this story. Closing it. Or leaving it closed. It is what the heart feels, not the head, not the law, not history. Simply the heart.

After a long beat, Agnieszka, looking from one to the other, then finally at Beniamin:

--The heart weeps its tears. It is so with all of us. It weeps for my son Kuba who I painfully miss when I wake, when I sleep. It weeps too for his great grandmother, my Hannah, my Hania. Perhaps in a different way to you. Or perhaps not. Perhaps, my dear friends, not.

*

Agnieszka and Beniamin asked for some time to consider all that Tom and Jenny had told them. They asked for some time to themselves.

Two days later Agnieszka telephoned and asked Jenny to come to the house alone. Jenny again sat in the leather chair. Agnieszka brought coffee, then sat opposite. Beniamin had gone to teach at his university.

--Tom probably told you about our Kuba, about the work he did. How he died.

--Yes.

--Kuba was interested in photography. He knew Tom's work long before Tom came here. He was very eager to meet him, although he was not a student at the college.

--I know.

--He had been taking photographs for some time before Tom took him under his wing, you might say. Kuba was particularly obsessed with the broken violin that is in the display case there, that has meant much to us. You know its story?

Jenny nods.

--For us it was…part of the story of my dear Pawel Weisz. And a curiosity but perhaps not much more. But for Kuba—

Agnieszka stops, takes a deep breath. The pain is evident.

--For Kuba it meant something much more. It was a symbol of who he was, of what he was. Maybe not just him, not just my family, my story. He talked about it with Tom perhaps even more than us. And he photographed it, quietly, without show, over and over and over, from every angle. These are a couple of those photographs.

Agnieszka pushes some photographs on the table towards Jenny, who stares at them silently.

--Music was everything to Pawel Weisz. It was within him, as it was within his mother. As it was part of her story, her loss. That music is what Kuba heard I think. Perhaps also what Robert, who Pawel loved as a boy, also loved. And why Robert wanted him to have this broken violin, this symbol of broken lives. Broken, but not lost. This last picture…

Here Agnieszka turns over a photograph of Kuba and Tom together, the photograph of a window reflection with them together that had so moved Tom and that he had put in the photographic exhibition in Jerusalem before he left.

--This picture moved Tom deeply. It is Kuba, and Tom, separate yet together. We have always felt that their journey, their search, while not the same, nevertheless needed one another. A search of one who is two; two who are one. Many questions. Answers so hard to find.

Jenny picks up the photograph, stares at it for the longest moment. In it, she sees not only the lost boy Kuba, she sees Tom as well, perhaps as she had not seen him, not fully, not wholly.

--I asked you when you first came here a couple of days ago, why? You said perhaps it was something you needed to do. What is your need, Jenny?

Jenny sits quietly in the chair. She looks over at the perspex case behind Agnieszka. She looks away. She looks within.

--I was in the north. Of Poland. Not far from the Ukrainian border. Working with a team, digging, keeping historical record. Memory alive. History alive.

Meaning…alive. Sites of so much—pain. The camps. The lies told…My work, my training was finding artefacts, defining buildings, finding…lives. Ghosts. I went there on the advice of a woman, a teacher, who loved me, who knew I was lost. Who found me. I loved her too, I…She understood my need. A few years earlier, my mother—took her life. I never really knew…never understood…

Jenny goes silent. Agnieszka watches her.

--Going to dig at the Site, it was to try to escape, to free myself, live again maybe. But the ghosts there consumed me. And then…the man I worked with, the head of the team: he knew. He knew more than I ever gave him credit for…My mentor friend back in England had told him about my love of sculpture, of art. It could have been my career, once. But it wasn't. So he suggested I use those talents, break away, create--something. I'd seen a wooden threshold where we had started digging again. Worn with the feet of thousands who had passed over it, shuffling into the…into what we knew was in fact once a large gas chamber made to look like a bath house. Shuffling to their deaths, their…

Jenny painfully looks for a moment at Agnieszka, then reaches down into her bag. She removes a photograph, folded. Unfolds it for the older woman, hands it over.

--It took months. During lockdown. The Project. It took--everything. Every detail is--as I saw it in my head. All my experience. My dreams; no, my nightmares. A lot of those. So I created. I took the image, made it real. I refused to use actual materials but I fabricated in such a way as for it to become real. A door that can never fully close and can never fully open. It was not meant to be a replica. Never meant to be that. Rather it was the 'thing'. And it wasn't simply to speak of what had happened once, there, of the deaths of thousands and thousands, and thousands. It was something that needed to speak to me, from me. It was a door through which I might walk to find my mother again. Just once more. To tell her that I loved her. To tell her that I had always loved her and always would and missed her and needed her and did not forget never forget never…Like for the men, the women, the children, so many who shuffled over a wooden floor threshold and did not return. Words. Of a story. An image that does not reveal, but rather speaks that story, sings that music, whispers with the sounds of loss and pain, and hope. There has to be hope. Has to be…Tom said this is what Kuba had said to him. About a violin. About Tom's work. And that is why I felt I needed to go to that place in the forest, that farm. That story that is your story but mine, too, everyone's maybe. Because I needed not to reveal, but to hear the words of what I might see. I needed to hear the music from a broken violin as well. That is why.

Agnieszka stares at the young woman for a long time, at the silent tears that gently, slowly, trace from her eyes, down her face. Neither woman, old, young, moves for the minutes that become more. Time passing slowly. Forever dripping slow.

Finally Agnieszka nods.

--I think you need to tell the authorities what you found up there. Convince them. If they will dig, you must dig. You need to know, and if Helena Kielar is buried there, she needs memory, from her people, from her world as from you. As from me. The only thing I would like to request is that, should the time come when you are ready to dig, I wish to be there. So that my story, my beautiful Grandmother Hania's story, may perhaps find its end as well. And finally rest.

Jenny nods. Sits quietly. Neither woman now speaks. In this way they sit, as the Jerusalem winter light fades, and dusk enters in shadows and in silence.

***

The thin layer of frozen snow crunches beneath her feet as she walks carefully up the path. A ghostly fog has set in; the air remains cold. The frost does not dissipate. Although relatively warm and dry for late January, she still feels the cold. Once more she has driven a rented car along the back lanes and parked it in the designated layby. She almost missed it when it somehow emerged through the grey dense air. She emerges, this time alone, blowing on her hands to keep them warm. And again, this month after they had all gathered, carefully walking along the path in order to make this final visit to the small excavation.

The quiet barely murmuring breeze chills. She shakes off the cold she feels. Shivering, although perhaps it is not the slight movement of air, the cold that causes her to do so. Perhaps it is the place. But she needs to return here. She knows it will be the last time.

There is to be another storm later in the week, or so the reports say. Nevertheless for January the season has been mild in Poland. As it was in December when the weather favoured the work they carried out. Or rather allowed the work to be done. That was a month ago.

So it is now Jenny. Only Jenny. Alone. Her feet slightly crunching over the thin layer of snow, nearly melted, disappeared. Everything disappears. The trees, the sky. The past. Slowly. Without protest. She makes her way into the clearing that was once a barn. Once that held little more than a message left for others to find. Initials on a collapsed beam. The barn has long since become earth. The message has long since rotted into slivers of insect housings and soil. The whispers however remain appearing over the crest of the slight hum of air that chills her now.

At the edge of the clearing a fallen tree, ghostly, fallen with time passing. Becoming eventually only part of a landscape, like all else. Becoming earth, like all else. The earth hides the dead as it will the stories of the living. The earth rarely reveals its secrets. Although sometimes secrets are revealed to eyes that can see despite life's best efforts. By eyes that search. And hearts that need to know.

Jenny wipes the thin layer of snow off the dead tree lying on its side and makes a seat. She wants a moment. She listens to the silence. Silences can be deafening. She takes out a cigarette. Lights it. Jenny has taken to smoking. She has not smoked since she was a teenager but lately has started every so often. Rarely, but every so often. She will stop when she is ready. She is not ready.

So she sits on the fallen tree, one trousered leg crossed over another, smokes a cigarette. In the misty landscape. Enveloping ghostly fog. She imagines pictures in the place where once was a barn, where once a young woman, exhausted, hid, then made a bed; souped, then became someone else's daughter, someone else's story. She pictures too only last December, stopping here with that woman's gentle granddaughter, Agnieszka, and the husband Beniamin, wrapped in heavy coats against mid-December chills, emerging from a path and stopping to look around at what remained. At the emptiness that remained.

That day there were clouds and sun. Cold, lifeless sun.

She had knelt then, she Jenny, knelt beside the remnants of foundations revealed by a small brick pillar, barely emerging from the ground like some sort of disappearing monument of sacrifice. She knelt on the cold, freezing earth, their eyes

255

watching her then, that cold silent month, watching with an indescribable sadness in their faces. A palpable pain of memory.

--These were the barn's support pillars, she told them. What's left of them. There is nothing else.

Agnieszka looked at the smallest echo of foundations that told a story, that told many stories, then looked back at Jenny. Shook her head, just slightly. Nothing else.

--It was very different, Beniamin had muttered.

Jenny had nodded in acknowledgement. It would have been. All life would have been different. Death as well.

Jenny then stood, continued leading them up the trail through the trees, slightly widened to continue through the forest up to where they would today excavate. The older couple, bound to one another, bound to this young woman herself searching, followed, all of them supplicants who slowly marched to the alter of a story, with a requiem's song dictating each laboured step.

That was December. Weeks ago. A cold but dry December.

When Tom was not there.

When Tom was already gone.

Even now, these weeks later, she still sees him sitting across from her in the café, quietly sipping his coffee, telling her that he had to leave, that he had accepted an assignment, that there was movement in the East that was troubling and that he felt he needed to go there. To see. To witness. He was going to the eastern borders, perhaps into Belarus, for how long he did not know. Perhaps on to Kyiv, to Crimea. Simply, it was time. They had asked him to go, and he felt in his gut that he needed to do so.

--The Nowy Wiśnicz Police Podkomisarz finally agreed, Jenny tells him trying not to sound as if she was pleading. She did not want to plead. Then she continues:

--The Priest helped convince him. I'll attend the excavation as will one of the Polish forensic archaeologists from Oświęcim. A pathologist from Krakow and some other medical types. When the weather clears. I need you there, Tom.

--I can't, Jenny. I'm sorry. You need to be there, but my work leads me elsewhere. It's simply time.

--And Agnieszka? Beniamin?

--I spoke to them. They know.

Jenny was quiet. She remembers being quiet. She remembers scrutinizing his face as he sipped his coffee, she sipping her coffee. The silence.

--Will I see you again?

--Yes. That's all I know. But yes.

--You brought me there. You did that. Why?

--Because—because you needed to go there, just as I did. And you need to return. You need to finish it.

--I wish I could stop you going. But I can't do that, can I? Still: it hurts.

--I know. I understand…This is what I said to Agnieszka and Beniamin: I said Kuba is within me. He showed me that seeking truth, that seeking what we are, who we are, is difficult. Painful. And I think he knew that it is perhaps something always just out of reach, just that one step further that you think you cannot make. And yet we have to keep trying. Keep moving. There is no one answer. And no final answer. Kuba knew that. He wanted me to understand. Needed me to. He was asking me to witness and to teach him to witness, because if we do not witness, we will never really know, never feel life. Never really know ourselves. Who we are. What we are.

Jenny nods. Hears. Hurts.

--They understood, and so do you. With them, you need to exhume the truth. Find what's there. Find the final notes of the song that Pawel Weisz composed about a woman named Hania. But witness too your own story. Hear the notes of that song as well. Let the music come to an end. It's just—time, Jenny.

That was at the beginning of December.

And then he was gone. She has not heard from him since.

Now it is late January. What is done, is done.

Jenny stamps out the remains of the cigarette into the thin layer of snow. She stands, starts up the track to the excavation area. The tracks of December, when others had come and gone—officials, the priest, the forensics people, the police, the visitants, all traces have disappeared. A couple branches lie on the ground, broken off by the cold days, branches of pine smelling of forest and winter and disappearance. Further above the small brook of water that she had cupped in her hands and washed over her face several months earlier has become a trickle she can easily step over.

She emerges through fog, still sitting on the ground, wrapping around her, to the excavation, or what is left of it. The ground shows disturbance still but the small pit of their digging was filled in after several days. In December.

After.

Two junior medical people had offered to remain. And promised to fill in what had been disturbed, once several days of examination were completed. What had been disturbed.

What had been revealed.

After.

After the surveys, the images, the walk overs, the drawn plans, the records. After the professional work that could not yet quell the broken heart.

And now.

And now Jenny stands silently, thoughtfully, staring at the small grove opening in the forest, yet slowly returning to itself. She stares down at the disturbed earth settling, until soon it will not exist. A yellow piece of boundary tape the police had placed around it a month before still flutters, stuck to an errant branch. But that is all. Soon nothing will exist to say they were here. To say what they found as she knew they would find. The ghosts moved elsewhere, finally silenced into forever.

She hears the slight breeze in the treetops. It calls to her. The heavy grey air swirls, then settles like the earth itself.

She remembers another Site and a battered, rusted empty tube of lipstick. And nearby that small pit, at the end of a path they called Heaven Street, a worn, smooth wooden threshold. She remembers the Project. She remembers the tears. She remembers her mother, hanging, swaying just slightly. She remembers this grave before her.

She hears too, sees too, even now, their own December whispers on the breeze: Beniamin, a man still struggling with private pain, standing near the edge of the excavation where only a few feet of earth they had carefully removed revealed the remains they were meant to find, so that they stopped digging for a moment. They stood. Became quiet. Each one looked at the others surrounding. And as they stood in silence Beniamin pulled out a small book of prayers and recited words of Hebrew. Words of the dead and remembrance. Kaddish. He said them quietly as others stood and bowed their heads with respect.

And Agnieszka, she grieving the grief of mother, of granddaughter, as descendant of a story, stared straight ahead, her face frozen. Jenny held her own gaze all the while on Agnieszka: Agnieszka who had become a mirror of her own Grandmother. And a mirror of Jenny herself.

She listened to the words of Kaddish that Jenny could not speak, could not recite, because they were not Jenny's own words but that nevertheless she had heard spoken and sung quietly often enough. Too often.

The priest with them as well, the local priest from the village, a young man still, who had eased their passage and encouraged the police and local medical authorities to investigate based on the evidence presented, he too lowered his eyes with respect before it was his turn to make the sign of the cross above the excavation.

W imieniu ojca i syna…In the name of Father and Son and…And. And. The words in Polish, in English; the same. Words for two who they now remembered. Those who had no names. Only earth-eaten bones and memories and the remains of a moment past, a time past. And a song chanting the words of Kaddish and the muttering Polish words of a Catholic verse. The final chapter of a story. Now their names would be returned. It was right that it was so.

Jenny, standing here now, weeks later, this cold January early afternoon with the fog surrounding her, dead fog, cold mist, she hears it again, sees it again.

And sees nothing at all but the still disturbed earth of the excavation settling into disappearance. Disappearing into memory and time and that which will be forgotten. Disappearing.

Tom was not there.

He is not here now.

Jenny, standing before the earth slowly settling after those hours, those weeks ago, closes her eyes. She sees them yesterday. Photos were taken. The police officers discussed a dormant crime scene. The forensics examiners took samples of the earth, dusted at skulls and bones, brushed away time. Jenny knew some time cannot be brushed away.

He who was Podkomisarz Rudetski, in charge of the operation for the local police, turned to them.

--This will take some time. Our people will be here for several hours before the remains are removed for examination by the pathologist at the laboratory. I understand this is difficult. If you wish to stay you are welcome to do so. You can sit in the vehicles below. Or you can return to Nowy Wiśnicz, wait in my office. I can ring you when we are prepared to remove the remains. I am of course at your service.

Despite the cold, Agnieszka shook her head.

--If it is acceptable, Podkomisarz, we would like to stay here. If we may.

Agnieszka looked at Beniamin, who nodded his head with agreement and support, just slightly. And so they remained, all of them, pushing the cold away. Waiting. The officials. The police pathologist. The priest. They all stood quietly. After some time Beniamin had found some fallen pine branches. He pulled them to the edge of the small clearing. He carried a blanket from a small bag and made a seat for Agnieszka. She sat, her back straight, her eyes looking straight ahead, looking inwards. Jenny watched her. Then did not watch her.

The painstaking work took a few hours. Podkomisarz Rudetski and a young police officer Rudetski referred to as Posterunkowy disappeared for a while, then reappeared with four thermoses of coffee and a bottle of Sliwowica, making sure both Jenny and Agnieszka drank. Even the Priest had a small sip, watching carefully. They also carried up a few black body bags that they put to one side.

Jenny had rarely but occasionally seen work like this in her own work. Not at the Sites; this was not allowed by Jewish Halacha law. But in her training, during her initial work, she had watched other forensic exhumations where it was allowed. She knew the care the forensic pathologists would take now, seeking definitions and understanding even as they brushed away the earth, took photographs, prepared to exhume those bones and fragments they would find.

Eventually they handed the heavy black body bags down to those with brushes and shovels, who carefully placed all the bones within. As they gently raised these from the excavation, the Priest quietly read from his bible. Once the remains were laid in two bags at the side of the grave, all those there silently gathered around. The

Priest quietly read a final prayer. He closed his bible. As he did, Agnieszka began to sing, quietly, alone, until the police officers and the forensics people and the colleague from work joined her, singing slowly, a hymn Jenny recognized having heard before at funerals, *Serdeczna Matko*. When they were finished they stood quietly for a moment, after which Podkomisarz Rudetski nodded and men, one on each side of the two bags, a group of four young officers, lifted the remains of so little weight and started to walk carefully down the trail towards the clearings, and ultimately to the vehicles.

The Podkomisarz and another government official turned to follow, leaving forensics people, suited in white, going over the site. Before they had gone, however, one of the forensics men called them back.

The man still standing in the small gravesite held something he had found at the base of the excavation: a small, tarnished neck chain with a tiny muddied cross attached. He handed this to the police officer, who stared at it. Jenny watched as he fingered it, then closed his palm around it. He looked up at the sky, now largely grey with winter clouds, a day that spoke of sadness and loss. He then looked at Agnieszka, at Jenny, nodding his head.

--Madame Unger here was insistent and as we now see correct in her observations and research work. We are grateful to her. She also pushed me to read the manuscript you have written about your Grandmother, Madame Janiec. The story moves me, greatly. When I was a younger man, I remember seeing you perform in a film about Janusz Korczak, a story that also moved me. As did your performance. This…this is something we will not need for examination. You have written about it as your Grandmother wrote to you. I have no doubt that the examinations will confirm all that she wrote, that you wrote… and that you in turn have gifted to us. Please…

He handed Agnieszka the chain and cross, smiled just slightly, then turned and followed his men and the pathologist down the path, joined by the Priest.

Jenny, Agnieszka and Beniamin remained for a few more minutes as the forensics people continued carefully sifting through the lower bits of the excavation. Agnieszka held the chain tightly in her hand. She stared at the grave, closed her eyes. Beniamin put his arm around her shoulders. After a quiet few minutes, together they turned and started back down the trail leading eventually to Jenny's car.

Jenny drove them back to their hotel in Krakow.

She drove up beside its door, turned off the motor.

Agnieszka, beside her, put her hand on Jenny's.

--Thank you.

Jenny nods, without words.

Agnieszka opened her small purse, took out the chain and cross. Held it in her fingers, staring at it.

--This was given to my Grandmother as she finally left Warsaw having escaped from the Ghetto, given by a woman she never knew. My Grandmother wrote that the woman, whose name was never spoken, had told her to 'go with God'. And so she did. My Grandmother wrote how, after the death of Helena Kielar, as my Grandmother buried her, my Grandmother so alone and very lost on that farm, she threw the chain and cross into the grave. I think she was always grateful to the woman in Warsaw. Yes, I think so. But I think she also wished that Helena Kielar, that her daughter Hannah whose name my Grandmother would be gifted, should also go with God. I think this was a final offering to them, their pain, their deaths. It is something I wish you to have, my Jenny. Tom, he will return, or he will not. But you also go with God. May it be so.

Agnieszka placed the chain and cross in Jenny's hand. She kissed Jenny gently on her cheek. Beniamin then accompanied her to the door of the hotel, and both of them, slightly hunched, tired from a long, difficult day, disappeared within.

But today, this day, this January day, Jenny stands alone. The day is cold but the weather dry. And this day Jenny makes her own way here through fog and silence. She needs to return here this once more. She needs to see the excavated grave one more time, alone. The disturbed earth, settling, disappearing. This place of rest and memory.

She stands before that small plot now, that disturbed earth finally allowed to return to the forest. Jenny stands here remembering what happened in December, remembering also what happened here almost eighty years prior. She remembers.

Jenny drops to her knees in the middle of the disturbed earth. She brushes away the light layer of snow becoming slush, the top soil. She reaches into the bag at her side and pulls out a small trowel. She had used it once on a site, on the Site. It had gently revealed to her a burnished, dented lipstick tube in the earth, much as here they had found the broken, somewhat charred bones of a life lost, of lives lost, to reclaim, to give closure. With that same trowel that had spoken the words of a different story, Jenny now digs a hole into the earth, perhaps a foot deep. She then places the trowel back into her bag. From her pocket she removes a small chain that has attached a small cross, now cleaned, polished, gold once again.

Jenny stares at it, holds it up to the light, holds it up towards the fog encrusted sky.

She smiles, quietly, to herself, then buries it in the hole that she has created, placing it gently at the bottom, covering it again with dirt and packing it down. Disturbed earth that will not remain disturbed for long but will settle, will return to the forest, that will disappear as the earth, as indeed all life is transitory from one beginning moment to one final moment but the earth, the earth remains.

It is where it belongs, Jenny thinks. In this resting place, in the hallowed ground, where a young woman Hania once gifted it to an old woman who had paid with her life to give Hania a new self, a new possibility. Who had helped Hania become Hannah, leading her onto a road of redemption and hope. This symbol, chain, cross, brought Hania here. It helped her to live, whatever she believed.

--And it brought me home as well, Jenny says quietly to herself, to no one but herself.

She stays on her knees, closing her eyes. She sees an image that speaks a story, an image of Hania become Hannah. She sees too Agnieszka even as that older grieving woman places her hand on Jenny's. And she sees her Mother, watching her, taking her to her breast. The three together. The three as one.

--It is okay now, she hears her Mother say. It is well. It is time, Jenny. You can be. We are of the earth, all of us, and we are free. It was not your fault, my daughter. Try to remember that. It was never your fault. I love you my child. As I always loved you.

Jenny bows her head, just slightly. Then she stands, looks around. The forest embraces. And just as she stands, strangely, the fog around her lifts. Disappears. A full sun burned winter orange just peeks through the treetops. She smiles. Closes her eyes. Feels the slightest heat, the slightest warmth touch her face, run its fingers along her cheek. It simply is.

Tom was right: she had needed to hear the final notes of Hania's requiem, and hear the final notes of her own song as well. Yes he was right. It was time.

She stares at the forest before her and behind. Yes, it does indeed embrace. And she holds that embrace tightly around her, and deeply within.

IV

"I did not want to go on," he said then. "But I saw that
I had to. I saw because you came to tell me that I had to go
on. I had to bear witness. I had to know. It had been a search.
And so a third movement, sacrifice. A movement that spoke
of so much sacrificed in the desire for understanding. The
need for that understanding. You had come to know when
truth came knocking at your door. As in time you would
come to find me. And knock as well. The journey for all
of us was not simply a journey of the past. It was of the
present. A journey that was, if I can say, a love story. A
story of lovers desperately reaching for one another. The
world can be so hard, so cruel. The pain so real. Such a
sacrifice made. But the sacrifice was a gift, my friends. A
gift to me. And to you. I was once wrong. So now I beg
forgiveness. Understanding. My music is my supplication."
                                    --A Requiem For Hania

1. Jenny

The Border
Late March, 2022

--Mówisz po polsku?

The young woman holding the infant in her lap shakes her head no.

--English? Do you speak English?

--Yes, I can speak a little.

Jenny smiles at her. Nods.

--Your baby is beautiful…You need to fill out this form. Here; this is in English. I can help you if you need.

--Yes, okay. Yes.

--Here…

Jenny hands the woman, wrapped in her heavy coat, a pen and shows her where she can sit in the tent.

--Let me help.

Jenny reaches out for the infant. The woman hesitates, then nods, hands the baby to Jenny so that she can finally drop her numerous plastic bags, then removes her coat and sits. Jenny stares down at the sleeping, silent face of a tiny girl. Smiles at her. Runs her fingers over the child's brow. The mother does not take her eyes off Jenny.

--She is beautiful. It has not been easy, Jenny says, part statement, part question.

--No.

--Where did you come from? Your home?

--Horodnya. Near Chernihiv.

--Your partner, husband?

The young woman looks at Jenny. Shakes her head slightly. Looks away. Jenny knows what it means. Jenny puts her hand on the woman's shoulder. Puts the infant in the woman's lap. Kneels in front of her.

--You are safe here. Safe…If you need help with the form, with the baby…look for me.

--Thank you, the young woman says almost in a whisper.

Jenny smiles. Places her hand gently on the woman's arm, then moves on to yet another young woman who sits with a form in front of her, two children playing with toys on the floor beside. Jenny kneels before the woman, who smiles.

It is not easy.

It is late March, 2022. Jenny has volunteered with an NGO group here at the border town. She spends long hours trying to help the thousands of Ukrainians arriving hourly to the Polish border crossing of Medyka, seeking to escape the Russian invasion of their country. She knows from figures that as many as a million refugees have crossed into Poland. Sometimes it feels to her as if they have all arrived here in Medyka at the same time.

The work exhausts her. The work is necessary.

When the full scale invasion began on 24 February and the Ukrainian refugees began to flow into Poland, Jenny felt she could no longer sit in the silence of her Krakow flat staring at her computer. She joined a group set up through her work colleagues in Oświęcim to drive to Przemyśl near the border, basing themselves there while daily driving the thirty minutes further to Medyka to assist. That was two weeks ago.

Jenny cannot allow herself to return to Krakow. Not yet.

So she remains, living for now in a backstreet apart-hotel in Przemyśl, assisting those refugees crossing at Medyka for sixteen hours a day. Returning to the hotel to work on her laptop for two or three hours, grabbing a few hours of sleep, starting again at dawn.

Yes the work exhausts her. Yes she feels it necessary. She cannot stop. Not yet.

*

Jenny walks into the cold outside. She needs the cold. She needs air. She walks down the alley formed between tents crowded with refugees towards the immigration and information centre where the refugees arriving on foot emerge. She silently stares at the long line of humanity, mostly women and children, still waiting to cross from Ukraine into Poland and thus the safety of the European Union. Some arrive in cars. Some in buses or from taxis that have dropped them off. Some walk. Some are carried. Men other than the very old are turned around; they are not allowed to leave their country. The line snakes back to the Ukrainian border immigration building, and beyond that. Hundreds becoming a few thousand. A kilometre of a line. Hours of wait. Hours to seek safety. They carry plastic bags, sometimes suitcases, often their dogs or cats. They carry their children. They carry anything and everything they can. Everything they have sometimes. Sometimes they have nothing.

They have left most things behind. For many they have left nothing because there is nothing to leave. Their houses, their dreams, their lives destroyed by an onslaught they had not wanted, had not sought.

Jenny stares at them waiting, constantly waiting; she shakes her head in slight despair. Once they cross they arrive into the chaos of NGOs, the UN, the Red Cross, military, government officials, volunteers, the many who have come to help. There is food, clothing, shelter. Warmth. Too much of some things. Not enough of others. They will need money. They will need possibility. They will need a place to go. Some have a place to go. Others do not. Do not know where to go. Where to start. Where to live again.

They need psychologists too, the adults and particularly the children. Jenny has seen the children hide beneath the blankets of camp cots, refusing to emerge, breaking into tears at the sound of a truck backfiring, or someone screaming, even the sound of a food tray banging down onto a table. They are safe, but it will be a long time before they are safe. Before they know they are safe.

Jenny's role is simply to assist. She helps them fill out the forms that will be used to direct those who have no family or housing to find countries offering asylum. She helps them settle for the few days they might be in the camp here at the border, finding a cot to rest on in the warehouse now filled with rows and rows of cots, most occupied, showing where the bathrooms are, where buses can be caught, where food is offered. Often she just sits and listens. Or watches. Or holds a hand.

She looks at the many, so many, and wonders how she can help change their lives from two dimensional fear into three dimensional hope. She has to find an answer for that.

She fears too for those who have not made it. And for some of those who have, particularly young women. She knows there are those in the shadows who watch. She knows there is great risk for some. Great danger. There is only so much they can do. Only so much she can do.

Jenny is needed; Jenny needs too for herself. She has for so very long but never recognized it. Here she understands that the algorithms she has for so many months mastered and depended upon cannot replace human touch. What is wanted here is touch: for those who have come so far, but too for those such as Jenny who in her own way has come a distance immeasurable.

She stands near the border arrivals building now, the entryway into the EU, the passage from war to uncertainty, asking those arriving if they need help, if someone is waiting for them. So many have no one waiting. She stares once more at the line of people stretching back along the pathway, prevented from moving right or left by the high fences topped with spikes on either side, a path down which they must make the long walk from one border to another. The line stretches back far further than the border itself; it stretches back to their home cities and villages and families, back to memory. Memory they retain; the rest is gone. Perhaps forever gone. They stand in the very cold weather. And the light snow. They wait mostly in silence.

There are those too who head in the other direction, those who brought an aging relative, or a pregnant daughter, grandchildren and children, but who refuse to remain. Who are determined to fight, somehow. Fighting ghosts. Fighting for belief. Those who return.

She knows too a lot are dying for that belief. It is not easy. No.

--Jenny?

She turns. Ewa, one of her colleagues. A PhD in forensic biology but for now simply trying to keep arrivals fed and warm. Basic biology. Life and death is always basic biology.

--Yes. Right there.

Ewa nods, turns away. Jenny takes another look at the line snaking from one world to another, one life to another, and turns away. Walks down the frozen mud alley between tents of NGOs and helpers giving out food and clothes and blankets.

She begins to turn into her own tent where she has been helping refugees fill out the necessary governmental forms when something catches her eye. Registers. Something. She stops, unsure. Unsure.

Turns back and looks between two of the tents and the hundreds of people milling about in the passageway. She thought she saw, but she did not see.

--Hey, you all right?

Ewa again.

--Yes…Yes. Just a minute. I'll be right there. In a minute.

She gently pushes through the throngs of confused people, the chaos around her, pushing between some tents.

Something.

Behind the tents, a road full of buses, vans and cars, offering those who wish rides towards Krakow, to other parts of Poland, or to Hungary, to Slovenia, to Germany. Friends and family searching for other friends and family. Jenny looks right and left. Down the road many buses along, she is not sure, the back of…of a figure she thought she saw from behind, the back of a man carrying a child in one arm, leaning on a walking stick or supporting crutch from the other, a young woman beside him. But it…no.

Jenny pushes her way through the crowd, trying to hurry. Towards the buses. Towards…

No.

Someone grabs her arm.

--Bus for Germany? Is bus for Germany?

--I'm sorry, I don't know. I'm sorry. If you ask…there, they might know. Yes? Yes?

Jenny points for the old woman who is seeking directions. The woman nods, grateful.

Jenny looks back again. And cannot find the figure whose back seemed so familiar. Holding a child in one arm, and limping with a walking stick or crutch beside a young woman.

She cannot find him. Who she thought. She cannot find Tom.

Because it was not him. It could not have been him. It was not…

Jenny turns away and returns to her colleagues. Too much to do. Simply, too much.

*

Two hours later she emerges from the tent into the alley again, still filled with throngs of people milling about. Looking for answers.

She needs a break. She needs a rest.

She needs too to know.

She wanders. Looks in various tents. Cuts between two tents to the road. Strolls along the buses and cars, looking in vehicle windows. Watches reunions, watches tears. Wanders. People talking to one another. People talking on phones. The fear with possibility, without possibility. A sim card away from some sort of hope. Please can I…? Please do you have space…? Please if we can stay with you for a few days. Help us. Help me.

Help.

It is then that she sees. And stops in her tracks. And steps back into the shadow of a tent's canopied entryway. And stops. And watches.

Down the alleyway thronged with humanity and uncertainty, she sees a figure whose back is to her, holding a camera. Lens angled on a refugee face. Photograph taken. That figure holding a camera. Another photograph. Another face. A camera. She sees this photographer squat in front of a child. Close up, and another photograph.

The photographer stands, leaning on a stick. Holds a camera beside. A familiar camera. Familiar. Now takes another photograph. And another.

His back only. But she… she thinks, she… She…

Another photograph. An old woman in tears. A young woman with a baby strapped to her chest. An old man exhausted. A group of women chatting, shaking their heads. Another sitting on the ground, head in her hands. Fear.

And the photographer.

And the photographer turns slowly, leaning on that stick. Turns and looks around. And away.

And yes.

Yes, it is him.

271

It is Tom. It is.

Jenny feels a pain in her chest. A knot. She stops breathing, just for a short moment. Time itself stops. Tom. Yes.

She wants to run. She wants to embrace. She wants to feel him in her arms. She wants his arms around her. She wants. But she does nothing. Stands, and watches. Nothing.

He disappears into a large tent.

Jenny, motionless. Frozen. Thinks hard. Makes herself breathe. Breathe. Breathe. She hears voices to the right, to the left, behind her, in front of her. She hears nothing. And slowly she moves one step, and another, and another. She makes herself move. Move. A step at a time. A forever step at a time.

She enters the tent where she saw him disappear. Rows and rows of tables where people can sit. Free food; a line in front of large vats of soup being doled out. Coffee and tea. Sandwiches. Rows of tables. Hushed voices. Some children running, trying to be normal.

Nothing is normal.

Blank stares and silences. Little chatter. Whispered stories. So many stories. So many whispers.

The story speaks. The photograph speaks. It does not reveal; it speaks of loss and journeys.

Someone weeps. Most just sit. Some sip at bowls of soup. Shaking of heads. More hushed voices. A radio plays quietly. Music. Another radio gives news. There is a constant flow of news; from expressions it is not good.

Rows and rows of tables of people waiting and shaking heads with worry and despair and need and bags of belongings and small children and older children and young and old and fatigue and uncertainty and...

And there. At a far table. Sitting alone. A camera resting on the table in front of him. A walking stick leaning against his chair. Staring at nothing but sipping from a styrofoam cup of coffee or tea or soup or warmth or nothing. Sitting. Nothing. Just sitting. Just...sitting.

Jenny slowly walks towards him. He does not see her. He does not look up. He sips from his drink. One hand feels the workings of his camera resting in front of him, as if it is the singular security of time and place and existence. Rubs along the top of the camera body simply to confirm he is at this place, this moment, his eyes, his ears, the camera. Nothing else to see unless seen through the lens of a camera. One he calls Annabel, Jenny remembers. As if it reminds him of who he is. As if it speaks—a story.

Jenny walks slowly to the back table. He does not look up. He does not see her.

She sits down in a chair directly opposite him.

He does not look up. He does not see her.

He sees only the camera in front of him. And the coffee in his hand, sipping, sip, hard metal camera body, sip, sip, sip. He does not look up.

He puts down the coffee in one hand, letting it rest on the table. Staring within himself. Rubbing the fingers of his other hand still over the camera resting silently too on the table. Looking down, deep in thought, deep in story, deep in exhaustion, deep away.

Jenny slowly reaches over and puts her hand on his, his hand with its fingers resting now on top of a camera called Annabel, this camera that has given him so much sight, too much sight over too many years, too much suffering, this camera that is an extension of him as is no human being. His Annabel Leika M4, eyes and heart and story. Memory. And he looks up. And he sees her. And he recognizes. And just the slightest reaction in his eyes, in the smallest nod of a head, in the quiet sigh and quieter smile. He turns his hand, just slightly, and with a single finger that has been running along the metal body of his Annabel he rubs the back of her hand. Touching to substantiate her reality. Her presence. Touching her as his own. He knows.

--Tom, she says, with pain, and relief, and need, and hurt. Tom, she says again.

She turns her hand over, grasps his searching finger, then the rest of his hand, grasps it in her own. She feels his beating pulse, his beating heart. She does not let go.

*

They sit in silence in the back of the taxi that takes them to her apartment-hotel in Przemyśl. She leads him up to her room. She helps him undress so that he can bathe. She unwinds the bandage wrapped around his left thigh where the wound had cut deep, blood red with pain and anger, scar tissue healing only slowly. She does not ask him. Not yet. There will be time.

She runs the bath so that it is hot. She tells him it will make him feel human. Let the heat enter. Let it burn.

He smiles gently. He says he does not want to talk, not just yet. He does not want to speak of anything just now. He needs the quiet. He lies back in the water to soak. Closes his eyes.

She tells him she will be gone for a short time, hurrying from the hotel to the small restaurant where for the last several days she has ordered food and brought her meals back to her room: safer there, time there, a bite at the room's small desk while staring at a computer for an hour longer before she falls into bed with mindless exhaustion.

She orders rosol soup, sausage and cheese, then hurries back. She finds him sound asleep in bed. He does not wake as she puts down the bag of food. He does not know she is there.

She stares at him for a long moment.

She sees his camera bag and clothes sitting on top of his small backpack. All he has. She opens the camera bag and removes his beloved Annabel. She turns it over and over in her hands. Then she focuses on his face, his eyes closed, his expression even in sleep troubled. And shoots. Click. To remember. Click. Memory. Click. Moment.

She returns the camera to the bag, removes her clothes and climbs into the bed beside him. She presses her warm body against his back. Her breasts against his back. Feminine to broken spirit. He does not wake. Her eyes close.

Exhaustion.

They both sleep without dreaming, without waking.

*

She rises at dawn, dresses and returns to the border. She leaves a note for him. *Please be here when I return this evening. Please stay with me for now. I need you.*

*

She thinks of him all during the day. She thinks only of him.

So much help is needed at the border. So many crossing this day, running away every day. So much chaos. She spends the hours helping to fill out forms. To find a bed. To find a bus here, a family member waiting there. She arranges medicines for those needing. Food to nourish. Tissues to wipe tears. There are always tears.

She does not wipe her own.

She embraces those in need of human compassion. She holds.

She needs to be held.

She returns to the hotel as soon as she can. Tom sleeps. Did he ever wake? The food she bought the night before remains uneaten despite the small microwave that is in the room. She watches him. Dream. Bad dream. He moans. Then falls silent.

Jenny removes her clothes and fills the bath. Hot as she can take it. The heat heals. She lies in the water for a long period, staring at the ceiling. Badly painted white ceiling. Stories remembered. Stories told. She prefers not to think of stories. Not now.

She emerges and climbs into the bed beside him.

He turns and his eyes open. He stares at her. Places his hand gently against her cheek. She closes her eyes.

They make love, slowly. She whispers his name and he holds her against him, tight against him. She weaves her legs within his. Two bodies one. Human touch.

He lies back. She leans over him, running her finger gently along the wound so red, so angry. Blood red. Blood. Pain. Running her finger over scar tissue. Wound. She stares at him. He closes his eyes.

She lies against him, resting her head on his naked shoulder.

She sleeps.

They both sleep.

*

--When I left Krakow I went to the Belarus border with Poland. That was the assignment. Refugees from Syria, Iraq, Pakistan, from Africa, all trying to cross into Poland. Political footballs. Belarus gangs and military pushing them into Poland to undermine the EU. Poland pushing them back to Belarus. Footballs. People freezing, dying. Hiding. Living in hovels. Even hiding in trees. Back and forth. No one cared. I saw a woman who had bled to death after giving birth to a still born. Lost people. Confused because of promises that weren't. A boy with a bloody deep gash in his arm where he fell crossing over barbed wire. What we have become.

It is in early hours. He wants to talk. He needs to talk.

--I was there for ten days, then managed to get into Belarus. Some opposition journalists helped me. They feared for what the country had become. They feared for themselves, their families. Hopeless. I photographed in secret. Military. Police. Thugs. The fear of those fighting against it all. I returned to Poland after a time, back to the border to take photographs of border police on that side. Their indifference. Their hate sometimes too.

He shakes his head, looks away, remembers. Looks back towards the vanishing point of a bedroom where memory does not vanish, where he vanishes only behind a camera searching through a viewfinder, hidden by a lens that replaces his point of view, and replaces it still.

--I thought to return to you. Return to Krakow. But I couldn't. Not then. Not yet. I waited. Listened. Waited longer. Somewhere I lost my phone. I could have got another if I'd tried. I don't know why I didn't try. I don't know why.

--I understand.

She kisses his hand. Holds it against her. He looks far away, images far away. Liturgy in monotone.

--We began to hear rumours of the Russian buildup on the Ukrainian-Belarus border. The Ukrainians did not believe they would invade, but many did not trust the buildup. Even the American government sent warnings. I'd seen it before. I'd seen lies before. Disbelief in the possible. You can never stop believing the possible. The possible becomes the likely. So I went into Ukraine. I took a room in Kyiv. Waited. Drank. I met up with some journalist friends. Brent Renaud. He used to work with the New York Times. Masha Lavrova who I had met briefly at a party somewhere, can't even remember now where it was. I remember being drunk. Damien Turner, a wire services hack. I joined up with him. An old friend. Old...I'd known him a long time. Even Bosnia, he...

Tom goes quiet. Jenny's head rests on his chest. He breathes. Inhale, exhale. Inhale, exhale. He remembers.

--Waiting. We waited. People like us, we wait, knowing what may be coming, almost willing it to come. So the adrenalin can flow. It's bullshit, what we do, what

276

we are…And then they crossed the border. Just like we knew they would. Almost like we willed…Damien and I went north; the Russian battle convoy heading south. We decided to base ourselves in Bucha. We would report. First on the scene. Witnesses. Journalists…Journalists, sure. In a town not far from Kyiv, right in the path of the invading army coming south. I suspect you've heard of Bucha.

--Yes.

Now she can guess. She lowers her eyes.

--They were fast. They appeared. We thought they'd simply say they had liberated. Would take control. But they began to kill. Civilians in cars. Women and children. Torturing, they…bodies in the streets. The gardens. Rapes. Summary executions. We saw…we…In the shadows Annabel clicks, and clicks, and clicks, and I am so afraid they can hear the clicking. Maybe it's age, maybe it's being tired. Or maybe it's the thought of Kuba keeping me going. Get the photograph. Whatever it takes. Take the risk. Keep going. Madness.

He looks at her, then looks away.

--Damien and I had been hiding in the cellar of some locals' house. We knew we couldn't stay. They helped us get to a village nearby. Irpin. We hid in an apartment block with a family. Two kids. Young. But the Russians, they came. The road to Kyiv. The Ukrainians slowed the Russians here. We thought it might stop. But it didn't. Then Russian fighters jets. Sukhoi SU-25s. Killers. A missile hit a building next to us. A gash in concrete, and a body hanging somehow from a kitchen railing three stories up. A refrigerator door hanging open where there were once walls and someone's home. Trophy shot for a camera and you lose your humanity. Hanging…

He remembers. He is there again. He has no choice to talk. The story.

--They were everywhere, killing everything that moved. Shooting. Looting. I've seen it all before. Maybe I needed to see it. To witness. I don't know. I don't know…The Ukrainians started to evacuate civilians. We'd heard that journalists were at particular risk. We met up with Brent Renaud and decided we all should leave, but we missed the rendezvous. Turns out his car ran into a checkpoint. They killed him there.

--Tom…

--No. I…no. I need to remember. To…see…The family we were with, we jumped into a car. They took Damien and me with them. They told me to hide the cameras. But I can't hide, I… We started out of town towards Kyiv. A back road. But we came around a corner and saw a checkpoint. The family with us, Andrii, the father…he backed away fast but they spotted us. He pulled the car into the shelter of some forest and we all ran. Damien and Andrii took one child. I carried the other. Nadia, the mother, running beside. We cut through the forest, heading to the Irpin river. Andrii knew, he knew, he… Somehow we separated. Then we saw soldiers again behind, near the road. I saw Damien. I waved. Go this way. This way. Hurry. Waving at them to run, to run, to…I stopped, pulled Nadia down, the child down. I needed to photograph. I needed to witness. Damien now running. Andrii holding his small son. I needed to wait for them, to bring them to us, to photograph the fear, to photograph the event. The war. Always the war. I…the camera…I… They were running and through the lens I saw the explosion of a mortar hit them. And then they weren't. They…Nothing. Empty sky. Dirt and dust. Nothing. I saw blood on the ground. I saw…Nadia screaming. She wouldn't stop screaming. We have to run I said. We have to run. For this child. Screaming. For this child. Five children playing football in a playground. But this child, this…

--Jesus.

--I put my hand over her mouth until she stopped. And she did, holding her other child. And we lay there, waiting for our turn. Turn to die. Turn to run. Silence. You hear the insects. You hear the wind. You hear fear. Finally I pulled her up, forced Nadia up and her child, the screams, stop, stop, and we ran, we ran, heading to the river we could see. Shooting nearby. Ran. The bridge had been blown to keep the Russians from crossing. There were people climbing over fallen vehicles in the water, a van hanging, just hanging. We saw someone point further down. Ropes and people trying to help. We ran to the bank, Nadia, the child… I pushed her down towards the water and as I did an explosion. I was thrown to the ground. My leg bleeding from shrapnel, blood flowing down my leg, my body, but not dead, maybe I should have died, I don't know, maybe… I don't know. She pulled me after. Gunshots. Screams. Dopomozhit′ meni. Dopomozhit′ meni…Help me.

He hesitates. He wills himself to remember. He needs to remember, now.

--A small boat appeared, a rowboat, I don't know. It pulled to us and we held on.

The child in my arms. My camera bag held high. The cameras kept dry because you have to send off the photographs, make them see, make them understand, tell the story. Witness. You have to witness. I'm swallowing water trying to hold her up the camera bag up the living up and they are shooting and trying to keep her breathing, breathe…breathe. Nadia holding on, screaming. They pulled us to the other bank. They pulled us out. Run. Bullets and explosions nearby but run and they helped us away, they, they…I'm sorry. Damien. I'm sorry. I hate it. I hate it. I hate it.

Jenny holds onto him tightly. He struggles to breathe. Then calms. His body, so tight, grows limp.

--I'm sorry, Tom.

--We went to Kyiv. So many refugees. So much fear that the Russians would enter. A hospital checked my leg. Pumped antibiotics into me. Cut out a piece of a mortar lying within. Flesh and blood. I could have stayed. Developed the photographs. I could have fallen back into who I am, into what I am. Sometimes I don't know what I…I don't know what I thought. But Nadia, she had no one there. She was empty, numb and I told her I would help. She has a sister in Slovakia. I said I'd get her through the border, to Poland. She and the child. She…Maybe if we'd stayed. They were trying to help us. Maybe we shouldn't have been there. Maybe Andrii wouldn't have…I don't know. I don't know. I…

He closes his eyes. Goes silent. She holds onto him. He lies motionless. Finally, he sleeps.

Jenny's eyes do not close. She does not sleep.

*

She leaves him for much of the day. She had hoped she might be able to spend only a few hours at the Medyka border crossing. But a young woman she is trying to help, pregnant, afraid, goes into labour. She begs Jenny to go with her to the hospital. She has no one else. No one away from her home. Her home there no longer.

An ambulance takes them both to a hospital in Przemyśl. Saint Padre Pio. While she sits with the girl Jenny looks up the saint's story on her phone. A saint of healing. Healing is needed, she thinks. For this girl. For the many coming over the border. For Tom. For her too.

She telephones the hotel, asks that a message be left for Tom. She hopes to be able to return later. She's at the hospital with a girl in labour. She'll bring food for him. Wait.

Always wait.

Meanwhile Jenny sits. She too waits. She holds the girl's hand. She wipes the girl's brow as she screams. She prays. Padre Pio keep her safe.

Safe. You're safe here. Safe.

At six minutes past eight that evening, the girl gives birth to a baby boy.

--What will you call him?

The young girl, confused by the English. Confused.

--Name?

--Ah. Svoboda.

--Svoboda.

--Yes. Is word freedom.

May he be free, Jenny thinks as she squeezes the girl's hand, the newborn child now sleeping on her breast. A nurse and Ukrainian volunteer arrive later. Jenny kisses the girl on the forehead and leaves her in their care.

She stops to pick up pizza on the way back. When she opens the door to the room she does not think he is there. But his bag remains. Then she hears movement from the bathroom, its door closed.

--Tom?

--Wait. I'll come out.

She sits on the bed. She looks at his few clothes scattered about. At the camera bag open on the desk beside her computer. At a mobile phone now lying beside. Written work notes. His. Hers as well. After a few minutes he emerges from the dark bathroom.

--I've got pizza. You need to eat.

He nods. She stands and as she does she looks into the open door of the bathroom. Strips and strips of developed film hang down. He sees her staring.

--I went out this morning. Bought a new phone. I'll give you the number. Polish. I found a photography shop. No chemicals but I made a deal with the assistant. He drove to Krakow. There's a shop I know there. He brought back chemicals and gear

I asked for. I need to develop all these rolls. There are a couple tanks in the bath. I'll move them.

--Leave them. It's okay. I've pizza.

They sit on the bed and eat slowly. She has also bought a bottle of wine and they drink from the plastic cups from the bathroom.

--There was a Ukrainian girl in labour. I took her to the hospital. I held her hand while she gave birth.

--The baby?

--A boy. He's okay. Some way to start life.

--Good you were there. She had someone.

--I don't know what will happen.

--People are resilient. The baby will give her cause. She's one of the lucky ones. A survivor.

--Is it always lucky, surviving?

He does not answer her question. He does not know the answer to her question. They sip their wine silently.

Later he moves his tanks to the bedroom, leaving enough space to run a bath, hot as he can stand it. He climbs in. Lies back. Jenny climbs in beside him. He holds her tightly against him. The hot water soothes. She stares at the strips of film hanging at the edges of the room.

--I'd always wanted a scene like this. A scene from a movie. One of those erotic love stories with a background of film hanging down from the ceiling.

He laughs, just a little. It is the first time she has seen him laugh since the border.

--The baths are always bigger in movies. The plots easier to understand.

--This will do.

They lie there quietly. She runs her fingers on the surface of the water. She watches it ripple. The ripples widen just a little, then disappear. Everything disappears.

--What will happen now, Tom?

--In the morning you'll return to the border. I'll stay here, begin to go through the negatives. See what they say. What story. See what I need to keep. There's a wire service offer. And a rep contact in New York. I'll send some off if any are good enough. If I think I need to share them.

--That's not what I mean.

His expression remains looking within, without. He stares at the film hanging near the walls. The images he cannot read from where he is. He thinks about the images he remembers shooting. He thinks about five children in Sarajevo and a little girl now gone after running from her home in Irpin. He thinks about his friend Damien, lost too.

--I don't know. I hate this war.

--But you may return.

--I may return. I don't know.

She lies beside him, staring at their distorted reflection in the water. She splashes some drops away from her. She turns on more hot water. More heat. She does not want it to turn cold. She is afraid of the inevitability of it turning cold.

--I had an email from Agnieszka Janiec when I was in Kyiv. She said you had been right. That's all she said. Jenny's voices spoke, she said, and we listened. You haven't told me what happened at the farm.

--No.

--Why?

Jenny thinks how to answer. She is not sure she can answer.

--Hallowed ground. The young woman Hania became Hannah. She survived. Others did not. People disappear in war. Perhaps it's not my story. Not mine to tell.

--People disappear in war.

--Sometimes they don't. The threshold of wood remains buried, awaiting its resurfacing. The shoeless feet shuffle across. Fingernail scratches on a door. Sometimes they don't disappear.

--We find ways to tell a story. As do you, Jenny. Let the story speak. It's not a moment that's captured. It's a life. Many lives. Not a moment transfixed but a heartbeat that does not stop beating.

--Do you believe that?

--I didn't. And then the boy.

--The boy Kuba?

--Boy man. Man boy. I think he heard too. Like you hear...

She holds him tighter.

--Tell me about the farm.

She hesitates. Sees the image. Feels the cold. Is there. Speaks in monotone.

--They found the remains of two females. Lying beside one another. The pathology noted that one of the remains was of a much older woman.

--Helena Kielar

--Half of her skull was fragmented, as if by a bullet wound to the head. Those remains also showed evidence of calcination consistent with fire. Hania—Hannah--only said in her notes and memoires that Helena Kielar had been killed by retreating German soldiers. But both the archive evidence for the area and statements from local farmers at the time said as the local German soldiers left in disarray with the Russian advance, there was looting. Some farms were burned, some people killed. The priest who eventually found Hania living wild on the property, assuming she was Hannah as she had the identification documents, assuming her mute, said that the farm had been largely destroyed by fire. Despite there being no remaining family for DNA confirmation, the examiner agreed these were the remains of Helena Kielar who Hania wrote was killed in early 1945 when the Germans withdrew.

--And the other?

Jenny sighs. And speaks still in monotone, officiously, trying to sublimate the pain she felt in December. The pain she still feels.

--Those remains were of a young woman who had never given birth. They showed evidence of upper cervical spine injury consistent with hanging. This was also the story Hania relayed in her notes, that the daughter Hannah whose identity Hania assumed had hanged herself some time prior. It was just as Hania, as Hannah, had largely explained in her story that she left for Agnieszka. That we read in the manuscript.

--You were right. What you saw. Heard there in the forest.

--Right? What is right? What war does, is…what it does to both of us. All of us. Witnessing is hell.

--And when you were there, with the others. With Agnieszka and Beniamin. What did you hear there? What do you think you heard?

Jenny considers the question.

--I heard loss. And loss is painful. Loss needs to rest. I heard a loss of humanity, and a need for humanity to one day, finally, one final day to be at peace. The past speaks a story. And the story is within each of us, if we listen quietly to what is inside. To what we are. Who we are.

--It's taken me a lifetime to learn that. It too is what I know.

--The two women had one another. And they will forever. Mother and daughter. Mother…They had one a—they had one another. All that was left to them. Nothing else.

Jenny feels tears. She takes a quiet breath.

--The remains have been buried in the church graveyard in Nowy Wiśnicz. The priest, the Podkomisarz who oversaw the exhumation, a local official of some sort and me. We alone who witnessed it. Who stood quietly in the cold. Who bowed heads at muttered a prayer. But we were enough. The priest told me Agnieszka and Beniamin wrote to him to say they wished to pay for a stone for the two women. He said it will hold their names and a short inscription: *what was once lost gave life, and hope. Memory remains.* Those are the words Agnieszka requested, he said.

Tom nods. And wipes away her tears.

He stares at the film negatives hanging.

The water grows cold.

*

Jenny again returns to the border early in the morning. Refugees continue streaming through. The word from Ukraine is very bad. Mariupol remains under siege and the Russians have advanced. Rumours of mass graves are on every refugee's lips. They talk too of the Zaporizhzhia nuclear power plant and how afraid they are now that Russian troops have taken control. They talk of family and friends killed in the war, in shelling, hiding in shelters, running. Sometimes they do not talk at all.

Words and rumours, exhaustion and fear for husbands and fathers and sons. There are moments Jenny does not know how to respond, how to comfort. There are moments when she simply wants to run away from it. From the present as she wanted to run from the past. She does not run.

She tries not to think of Tom. She tries not to think of the future. She tries not to think of an excavation in the forest where was once a farm. Or of an excavation at a Site where stones and a wooden threshold's whispers speak to her when she wakes, and when she sleeps. She tries to tell herself that the heavy door with bars locking entrance and exit remains closed forever. But she knows that the trying is in vain.

She helps to fill out forms. She dries tears. She shows where to get food, a coat, rest for a few days before moving on. She holds a hand. She tells herself it gives purpose to so much that is purposeless.

In the evening she returns to the apart-hotel room, entering with the fear that he will be gone. But he is not gone. Not yet.

Tom has picked up pierogi and bigos for two. They sit on the floor and eat. They do not say much. Neither wants to talk about the war but it is impossible not to talk about the war. She says a lot of people are dying. Young people. He nods and says yes a lot of people are dying. Sighs. They both care but they do not want to care. There is no choice but to care.

Later Jenny lies in the bath alone. She closes her eyes. She wishes she would see nothing with her eyes closed. But she cannot stop seeing whether her eyes open or shut. She sees a grey closed door. And she looks through a peephole covered with an unremovable wire grill into her mind's eye. She sees a city under siege, apartments and hospitals on fire. She sees a woman farmer on her knees, shot through the head while some men in grey uniforms laugh and curse and piss and spit. She opens her eyes and stares at an empty white ceiling but her glance is trapped by the single hanging lightbulb; from it she sees her Mother hanging and swaying and a young girl hanging and swaying and Jenny wants to see freedom and wants release but wonders if she can ever be released, ever herself be cut down, ever find peace in a world without. Her world.

She dries herself and puts on a long t-shirt.

Tom is hunched over the desk, Jenny's laptop on the floor. He stares through a slide viewer at image after image from his cut film strips. Image after image. Three dimensional memory without joy. Loss.

--I cleared the bathroom for you, he says.

--Thank you. What happened to the two developing tanks?

--Gave them to the assistant back in the photography shop. I'm done with them.

He can use them.

She nods. Watches him.

--Can I?

--Here. Sit, he tells her.

She sits at the desk, looks through the negative viewer. He shows her just a few of his images: a family in a cellar looking frightened. Cars with bullet holes. Apartment buildings with their sides blown away. A body lying in the street. A field with distant figures running. A field empty. A woman holding a child, looking vacant. A close up of a still hand lying on the ground without movement. A close up of the back of a head in grass. Then a school class of young children sitting in an underground metro station somewhere, huddled. An empty school playground. A fallen statue with a bullet hole in its metal skull. Destruction.

--It's what they are all running from.

--Yes.

--Will it end?

--One day. And then it will move somewhere else. It always moves somewhere else.

--Why do you do it?

He looks at her, seeks within for a response.

--Why do you?, he asks in return.

--I don't know.

--I think we are both looking for ourselves.

--Have you found yourself, Tom? In the photos?

He smiles just slightly, shakes his head just slightly.

--I always thought I was there not to be there. To disappear behind the camera. Within the camera.

--But?

--But...but my young friend Kuba said he could see me in all the photographs. He said he saw me even in the extreme closeups of things, of lifeless walls or fabrics or ruins or stone paths. Faces. He said I was there whatever I thought.

--He was right.

--He was right.

--I can see you in these. Not because of the stories you told me. But because you too are the story.

--As are you.

--...As am I, you're right, Jenny tells him.

She leans back and rests her head against Tom, standing just behind her.

--What will happen?

--We'll keep going.

She looks up at him. Smiles, sadly, and takes his hand.

--You're going to leave, aren't you, Tom. Where will you go?

He hesitates. Looks away. Looks back.

--I don't know. I really just don't know.

--It's okay, she says...Tom: it's okay.

Later she lies in bed against him, her head in the hollow of his shoulder.

--I think we both are at the border, she says. And we both have to cross over. In Agnieszka's manuscript, talking about Hania: she writes about Hania having to walk across Poland in the dead of winter, almost dying of sickness. She writes that a father and two sons helped her to survive when she didn't think she would survive. Do you remember?

--Yes.

--Agnieszka wrote that her grandmother Hania broke a rule, that she told one of the boys her name, although she never knew his. Because she wanted him to remember. He promised her he would.

--He did. Yes.

--That's memory, Jenny says. Will you remember too, Tom?

He is quiet for a moment. Then:

--I will remember.

--I know. I know you will.

Jenny closes her eyes. Weary. As she starts to drift to sleep, hearing Tom's regular breathing telling her that he too now sleeps, she has a final thought, and a final image. She thinks he will remember and that brings her comfort. And she sees herself sitting on the edge of a rectangular shallow excavation site staring at a perfectly formed shining golden tube of lipstick, shining in sunlight, from which she looks up and sees a woman smiling at her.

--Svoboda, the young woman seems to whisper to Jenny. We call it Svoboda.

Jenny disappears into sleep.

*

It is five in the morning when she wakes with a start. Dream or nightmare, now she cannot remember. Her eyes stare at the ceiling in the hotel room, staring through darkness. She lies there on her back wearing only her t-shirt, lying there simply staring upwards, the outside streetlamp casting minimal shadows over the ceiling. She chooses not to move. Not yet.

She finally turns her head to look at the empty space beside her. She pushes her hand along that side of the bed. His warmth is there, but he is not. She knows he is gone. Perhaps it was the click of the room door closing that woke her. Perhaps it was its lack. Jenny is hardly surprised. She expected him to go. She expects he will not return.

She tiredly climbs out of the bed in the apart-hotel room, in the town that is not hers, this time that is not hers. She pulls a blanket from the bed and wraps it around her mostly naked frame. She walks over to the window, pulls aside the thin worn curtain. She looks down towards the street below. A light snow had fallen leaving a slight trace. It is only now beginning to turn to rain quietly weeping, washing away to nothing. She hopes perhaps she will see him walking away, but there is no one on the street, still hiding from dawn. Only shadows from lamps. A few dead white bulbs that illuminate a doorway, a shop front, the street beyond. A few footstep shadows in the layer of white. Perhaps they are his footsteps. She cannot know but she wishes to think so. There are however no people. No life. Dead silence.

We live in dead times, she thinks. We live for the dead.

She sits down at the desk in the hotel room. Her laptop has been placed back on top. On its keyboard he has left a note. *I am catching an early train towards Warsaw. There is a bureau there. After I don't know. I think I need to return there. It is what I need to say, words in a photograph. Perhaps no choice. You have my Polish number if you wish. And I shall try to find you again. One day, may it be soon. Love T*

She has his number but she will not call, as much as she wishes she could. Maybe in a few days. Or a week. Or not at all. He needs to see himself in photographs, and show himself to the world. He is no different than she is.

Jenny puts the note aside. She sits in the darkness, asking questions of herself. But she cannot hear the questions and even if she could, she would not have the answers. She begins to think she does not need the answers.

She turns on her computer. Still on the screen from two days prior one of the artefact images they had sent to her. She stares at the image: two dimensions only, she stares at it in the darkness and silence of this night. Soon she will leave to return to the border, to the camp, to offer a welcome to so many who have lost everything, who still shiver with fear. She will tell them they are safe. She knows they are not safe. No one is really safe. Not really safe.

But for now she stares at the image. A pair of eyeglasses found recently. Digging. Scratching the surface. She stares at the image. Wire frame bent, its shape distorted. The glass on the left side long since gone. On the right, shattered but still intact, the glass remains.

Jenny considers the man who wore them a long time ago. He used them for seeing. She thinks about her own connection to seeing. There was a time she thinks when she saw little. Knew little. When light entering her thoughts was dulled innocence, indifference maybe. Now she thinks she can see more clearly. She can hear more clearly. She can see herself reflected. And reflected in the fragments of glass on one side of a pair of glasses.

She thinks too of Tom. He also has had to see, to witness, sight through the lens of a camera. His sight has perhaps been clearer. Sharper. The sharpness too of fragments, cutting.

He too needs to see, as does she. The past. The present. The pain. The search for hope. Tom seeks to see not just through the lens of a camera but ultimately with his own eyes. Just as she herself does. Bearing witness, both of them, to pain. Funny how the necessity of seeing the past, hearing it and feeling it and yes touching it, necessitates pain more often than joy. Joy is perhaps transitory; the pain of the past, spoken in stories, in images that speak the story, lasts forever.

Jenny turns off the computer. Closes the screen over the keyboard. Only then does she notice, hanging from the small table light on the desk that had been largely hidden by the screen, a simple chain with a simple charm attached: a somewhat misshapen tiny violin.

She had not seen it before. It must have been in his camera case, but it clearly has not been forgotten. Jenny knows it is a gift, left with intent. His way of saying he will remember. She knows it is memory. So much memory. Jenny pulls the thin chain off the light frame from where it had been hanging, releases the catch and places the chain around her neck. To remember, not Tom alone, to remember the words. So many words. She hears them now. And she hears the quiet song from a violin.

It speaks. She sits and listens.

V

"And they begin to hear the story. And the story will be retold. The truth told, retold, diverts, becomes lost, becomes found, following an inevitable path, an inevitable journey. They will listen....

Thus they each separately, and together, finally hear the music. And their journey can begin. But only just the beginning. Only the first step.

Thus listen. Witness. Hear."

--A Requiem For Hania

1. Agnieszka and Beniamin

Havat HaGitot
February, 2024

Beniamin parks the car at the lower campsite of the Havat HaGitot trail. The sun is already low in the sky but they know the walk to the spot she has chosen will only take fifteen minutes or so up the path. Beniamin takes the large backpack, large enough to hold the box. Agnieszka has a smaller backpack with the bottle of wine they have chosen, two small glasses and a corkscrew. They had debated whether to bring snacks, but have decided against it. The wine will do.

The trail is lined with blue green spruce trees stretching as far as they can see. They walk the remainder of the way up the mountain to the viewing spot that both Agnieszka and Jakub had always loved, and had wanted to return to. Knowing now too it might well be the final time they will come here together.

When they reach the spot, Agnieszka sits on the large rock that she has always called her throne, the cool rock waiting for her here still as it has on previous visits. The sun has set ever lower, casting a golden spring glow on the valley of trees that falls away below. Up here they are alone with their thoughts and their memories; it is as Agnieszka had wanted it to be. Beniamin takes the box from the backpack, sets it on the ground, then tells Agnieszka to wait while he returns to the car where he has left several bags of olive wood. She had insisted upon olive wood and he had not objected. He tells her to open the bottle of wine, a fine burgundy, to let it breathe for the half hour or so it will take.

She sits quietly as he disappears, grateful that he has offered to return to the car by himself, allowing her the bit of space to fill with her own thoughts, with memories that she carries within. A familiar, gentle song sings in her mind. She lets the notes play in her head. The piece is the final movement from her beloved Pawel Weisz's 'Requiem For Hania'; from this music she has always drawn comfort.

Even as the notes hold her tightly in her mind's eye, cradling her as they always have, she thinks too of what all now lies before them. The past two years have been so incredibly difficult, with Kuba's loss and the investigation and hearing they had refused to attend, knowing it was little more than a government and military whitewash.

But then the events of last October, and the eruption of violence and hate that followed. Huge grief gave way to anger and despair that Agnieszka could have never imagined. If she has learned anything from her Grandmother Hannah, her Grandmother Hania, it is that grief and hate should always remain separate. Events of the past had once made Agnieszka hate, until she found that such consumed her. So it is now in this country as it consumes itself. So much death and pain, and Aga no longer recognizes it as her home. She needs redemption and absolution and freedom. Mostly, she tells herself, she needs freedom.

When the offer was made to Beniamin, it seemed a godsend. She has never been to Berkeley, California, but she knows in her heart she will find some sort of solace there. Some sort of peace. Peace is what she desires more than anything. So they sold their house in Ein Karem and rented a house in Berkeley through an agent. Beniamin visited it twice and said each time he thought she would be happy there. She is sure she will. They have spent the last few weeks selling things they do not want, and packing. Family and friends say they understand, that they will be well to leave Israel now. She tells herself it is indeed a country she no longer understands, and she can see that Beniamin has no regrets. But they both know politics and violence are not the real reason they have to go.

They have to go away in order to live again. Yes, with sadness. With a huge hole of loss within each of them that will never be filled. But still they have to leave, while there is time. They have to find a way to live again.

Clearing Kuba's room has been the hardest thing they needed to do. Twice she walked out in tears. She could see too that Beniamin was shaken. But they pushed themselves, and propped up one another. They removed things in silence. Words were not needed. Between them there was enough love residing in the silence. And the thought of him.

They still have goodbyes to make and some packing to do. Then they will fly to

Warsaw to see some friends and family there, before continuing on first to New York, then to Berkeley. A publisher contact in New York has offered to publish Agnieszka's manuscript, and she feels it might be time. So she has agreed to work with an editor there, as well as to visit a few friends who have made it their home. She wants too to leave stones at Pawel and Arthur's grave. She has not been there in some years, but the sadness of visiting it is always mitigated by knowing they are together in whatever might be their final place, listening to wonderful music, smiling at one another, bickering with warmth, perhaps embracing. It is the image she carries with her. It gives her solace.

Beniamin now returns, the backpack filled with small and large pieces of olive wood, a plastic bag filled with more carried at his side. He huffs a bit from the walk up.

--Not as light as I thought.

--You're getting old.

--We're both getting old, Aga.

--Yes. You're lucky though that I'm here to look after you.

--Agreed. Agreed, my love.

Beniamin pulls out the logs he has carried up in the backpack and bag. He wanders around collecting some twigs and evergreen needles. He uses this kindling to create the base of a fire, then lights it with the small cube of fire starter he has brought in his pocket. The flame catches the smaller wood. He puts more on top, then slowly begins to add bits of olive wood to the burning spruce. Before long a small bonfire is burning.

He sits; Agnieszka pours him a glass of wine, as well as another for herself. They sit drinking, staring at the small fire. The smell of olive wood, the beautiful locale, the flames all offer solace. Warmth in many ways.

--So, Beniamin says after a time, are you really certain about this?

Agnieszka does not answer immediately. She stares at the fire, sips from her glass. She sighs, smiles gently at him.

--Yes, Beniamin. I am sure. I think...I think it is right. For Pawel. For Arthur and the young boy Robert who took his life. And most of all for Kuba. I think, somehow, this is what we should do.

Beniamin looks at her and nods

--I think Aga you are right. As difficult as it is, but…yes.

He opens the box, lying on the ground between them, and removes the cracked, rather broken violin that they had placed within. He holds it in his arms and stares at it, turns it over one way, then another, then another. He smiles gently. Looks at his wife, watching him.

--I think…perhaps I understand. He was looking not at one memory, but at many: the grain of the wood here, the crack, the colour, the textures. That's what Kuba was looking to understand.

--Yes. The stories. All of them.

Beniamin nods. And he hands the broken disfigured instrument to Agnieszka. She takes it gently. Runs her fingers over it. Closes her eyes. Sighs. Then opens them and looks at Beniamin. He nods again.

And gently, with great love, with both pain and a gentle sadness, Agnieszka places the broken violin onto the small bonfire, its embers glowing red against the shadows of the early notes of evening. After a moment, the violin catches a flame. It smoulders at first, then begins to burn, the fire beginning to embrace it as one of its own.

Agnieszka sits on the rock that is her throne, and Beniamin sits beside her. They sip from their glasses of wine, watching the violin slowly consumed by gentle flames. Beniamin puts his arm around this woman who he so loves. He sees that she is gently crying. He thinks the tears should fall, so does not attempt to dry them. He raises his small glass.

--I hope the smoke reaches our Kuba in heaven. I hope he is sitting with Hania, and Pawel, and all his forebearers. May they hear the music of their lives, their warmth and humanity in the notes of this offering.

Agnieszka smiles sadly. She takes Beniamin's hand in hers.

--We don't need the broken violin, my Beniamin. We have each other still. Together we remember and speak of our Kuba. That is enough.

--Yes. Yes, it is. We will always hold him within, we will remember him and such memory shall be a blessing of peace. May it be so.

--May it be so…May it be.

They watch the flames reach higher into the sky, into the heart of their son so deeply missed this as every moment, as indeed into their own.

They quietly sip and the dusk settles towards darkness.

And they remember.

2. Jenny

Near Portree, Skye
August, 2024

Sometimes she wonders why she bothers. She spends two quiet hours cleaning the small cottage, scrubbing the floors, wiping surfaces, putting her belongings, few as they are, in their specific place, only to find the sand and dirt and sea salt return as soon as she has wiped every corner of the four small rooms. Uninvited but unrelenting. Jenny smiles gently, thinking of excavations from the past, sifting through dirt finding evidence of living, evidence of dying. She smiles because living here in the cottage is a bit like the constant sifting through excavations. Perhaps that is why she has come to feel so comfortable.

Jenny has lived in the cottage for almost a year now. She had seen a notice about it after returning to Manchester, and decided this was the place she wanted to be. She had no hesitation in renting it, and now considers that she will take up the owner's offer to purchase. It suits her, being here outside the small town of Portree, close enough to have neighbours, a bit of a social life, but far enough away to find the peace she seeks. She needs the peace. And the silence but for the waves of the sea just over the field. Yes, it suits.

Jenny puts the dirty rags in the laundry, picks up her bundle of joy, terror that he is, and strolls outside to feel the warmth of the summer sun against her face. The cat follows her out. The cat always follows her out. The cat and Jacob, her two constant companions. The two true joys of her life. It is simple now. She knows it will not always be so.

Jacob is almost twenty months a part of her life. And she a part of his. Jenny had never considered motherhood, had never thought it would be something she would desire. But in fact it fills her both with joy and terror, mostly the former. Her son does not represent some sort of absolute fulfillment, but it seems to her that he adds

297

dimension, and possibility, and in his little way a bit of hope just when she thought hope might have disappeared from her life.

She looks down at his sleepy expression, his head resting against her, his weight on her hip. He is still small. And he is warm. She smiles as she looks back up at the blue sky and bright summer's day, relishing the sun's light, its heat. She puts her hand gently against the side of her son's head, pressing his warmth against the jumper at her breast. Jacob is a quiet child, but his own smile warms hearts. It certainly warms hers.

For no reason in particular she thinks about Agnieszka. She remembers the question Agnieszka once asked her: what is your need? Looking down at the simple sleepy smile of this small child, Jenny finally has the answer to that question. There will be other needs, other wants. But in that smile Jenny has found something simple. Trust perhaps. Simple love perhaps. An infant's need. Her own. Jenny wonders if it was always there, but hidden. Or if from pain it emerged even as the child emerged from her womb, a part of her yet a voice of his own. Perhaps only time will tell, but for the moment Jenny feels lucky, and quietly happy.

--I will try harder, Mother, Jenny whispers to the air. And I think I understand now. In this little one a bit of peace, eh Mother? Just a soupçon of peace for both of us. I know. That I do.

She smiles quietly. She must take up the invitation to visit Agnieszka and Beniamin in Berkeley one day soon, she thinks. They were touched by the name she chose to give her son and clearly delighted with the photos she sent. She feels a bond with them like with few others. Perhaps she will visit one day soon. They would like that. So would she.

Holding Jacob on her hip, Jenny kneels down to look at the row of leeks she has planted. And the rows of onions and cabbage. All seem to be surviving. Thriving even. She runs her fingers on some of the green stalks. Life, she thinks. Simple life.

--Good, eh little one?

The child looks at her with his large brown eyes, but offers no answer.

Jenny stands again, staring down the field towards the sea beyond. She loves it here. Yes she thinks she will buy the cottage. At times it may be too much for her, this commitment to place, but for now it suits. Even if there will be reasons to travel in the future—work, relief from grey days—it will always be a home to come back to. Her home. And she can build a small studio at the side for her art projects. Her many projects. She thinks too that Sofia will like it when she comes to visit with her own little Svoboda. Jenny is pleased Sofia found a home, a refuge in Glasgow, not all that far away. She and Sofia became friends after she had sat with Sofia in the Przemyśl hospital, holding her hand during the birth of her own little boy. During such dark times that friendship had become a small bit of light in darkness. Light for them both. Yes, Sofia and her son will like it here, and the two boys will grow close. Brothers too of a time and place. They will both need memories, memories that Sofia and Jenny will give them. Such memories as we are made, she thinks.

With her son resting at her hip, Jenny walks to the side of the house to see how her sunflowers fare. She had planted them thinking they would never grow in such a place, but was surprised to find not only did they grow, they flourished. A metaphor for her own life now perhaps. She stares at the six foot stalks and the large orange and yellow flowers hanging down. Beautiful, she thinks. Sunshine.

--Sunshine, she says to Jacob. They are sunshine and beautiful. Pretty flowers.

And then she speaks quietly to the wind.

--Yes, pretty flowers.

Jenny turns back towards the house, when something catches her eye. Or rather someone. A good distance away, walking slowly down her long road, she sees a figure heading in her direction. Perhaps a tourist, she thinks. They occasionally take the side road, hiking through the landscape of sea and rock. It cannot be the postman for he rarely drives his red van down this way. She watches the figure grow ever closer.

Something in his gait. Something cautious but with purpose.

Jenny watches without knowing particularly why she does so.

--A visitor, she says to Jakub. Will we have tea and scones?

And she laughs at the thought. Just a tourist, lost perhaps or not. Jenny turns to go back into the cottage. Except that she stops herself. Except that she does not turn away. She hesitates, looking back over her shoulder. Something. Something…

The figure getting closer. He getting closer. The slightest limp she notices. Slightest hesitation.

And he… but no…but he… Jenny lifts the quiet child from her hip to her chest, holds him tightly against her. Takes a step forward. And another step. But no, it…he…and another step.

And Jenny begins to walk towards him. Walking faster now. Faster into a run. She feels something inside, her heart suddenly racing. No.

And he walks more quickly towards her, despite his slight limp.

And she runs, holding the child, the baby against her. No. But no, but…

He stops, watching her. She runs and she sees him lift a camera in his hand as he shoots a photograph, aiming his lens towards her, towards the child. His camera. His story. Her story. Him.

She runs as he lowers the camera and smiles, just slightly. Nods just slightly.

She runs as he stands tall, tired, but warmth in his face, his expression, even his eyes that she can see now.

She runs to him.

And a promise kept. A promise finally kept after so long. He embraces her, the boy. And she feels his warmth, and his strength, and his being, and his love. And he is there. He is there after so long. His arms around her, the child. A promise kept. A promise kept.

I remember, she thinks. I remember I remember I remember…I remember.

And Jenny stands there, at the side of the cottage, staring at the road winding away, at a figure who is not there, at the emptiness that holds both her longing and her loss. Despite feeling such loss even still, despite trying to hold onto the need and the desire and the hope, she pushes away any despair. She pushes it away from her, and from the child on her hip, looking up at her calmly, with a wisdom she sees evidenced and waiting.

She will no longer despair. She is at ease and no, no longer will despair. She smiles to herself, and shrugs. There is grief, yes, but there is also a need and desire to move forward.

Jenny walks back into the cottage. She finds a rusk for Jakub to suck on because she thinks he deserves a treat. Still holding him on her hip, she walks over to the chest of drawers against the wall, with the framed photograph sitting on top.

--Look, Jenny says to her son. That's Tom. See? There? Sleeping? That's him.

That is him.

She had framed the photograph when she received it in the post from New York, forwarded from one country to another, one city to another. Tom's agent there had sent it to her at Tom's request. It is the photograph that Jenny herself took of Tom asleep in an apart-hotel room in Przemyśl, where once they lay together, where they had been lovers, and had made promises, and had had hopes and dreams. It now seems so long ago, so distant. But still she holds it close. The memory of the hotel room. The feel of his touch on her. The warmth. The photograph has always made her smile: Tom at peace. She at peace.

The agent had sent her two photographs, but the second she will only show to Jacob when he is older, along with the explanation the agent had sent to her in his letter. It is the final photograph Tom shot, a photograph of two thin, wounded soldiers still smiling, giving thumbs up despite the carnage and destruction. It was taken in Azovstal plant in Mariupol the day before the thermobaric bomb hit the plant and Tom disappeared forever. When the time comes, Jenny will show Jacob the photograph, and the agent's note saying that Tom had been caught in the explosion. And Jenny will explain to Jacob, when the time comes, and it will, that although Tom is not seen in the photograph, he is there. Just as Tom is there in all his photographs, there as he is in the photograph Jenny shot of him sleeping soundly in an apart-hotel room in Przemyśl. Perhaps not immediately evident. Not immediately seen. But she will explain that if you know how to look, he is always there, because he is part of all you can see, the photograph that does not simply capture a particular moment at a particular time, but that speaks a story.

And a story is spoken.

--That is him too, Jenny says to Jacob. That is Tom. That is him.

Jenny now puts the tired child into his bed and watches as his eyes close. She smiles gently, runs her hand along his little head.

--Sleep, little one. Sleep.

She turns and walks back to the cottage door, still ajar. She stares out towards the sea in the distance, and at the road that runs past. Tom had of course walked towards her, even though he had not been there. But she had seen him because of course even when he is not there in the landscape, he is within her, always keeping his promise, returning, embracing her. He remains part of the story. It is so.

Standing quietly, Jenny listens to the wind. She feels the warmth of the sun still on her face. She feels the whispers of ghosts talking to her as they do so often. Strangely she remembers the image of a young woman she once saw at a site, at the Site, a young woman with bright red lips glistening in sunshine. One of many ghosts who remain at Jenny's side and who whisper gentleness into her ear. I carry you with me, Jenny thinks. And you carry me with you. And hold me in your hands. Yes, she thinks. Yes.

Then strangely, uncertainly, Jenny thinks she hears something else in the gentle breeze that envelops her. She listens until her breath stops, so that she hears the wind talk. Like a photograph the wind too speaks a story. Now she closes her eyes and hears the quiet sounds of a violin. Broken perhaps, but the music gives heart. The quiet violin of a requiem's final notes. It plays for her.

Jenny smiles. A requiem for those past, those passing, but one that gives hope. Music of possibility. The harmonies travel across the earth, across generations, across time. The song sings, yes, of loss, of five children playing football on a weed covered playground and a young man marching through winter snows towards his fate. It sings of Kuba who stands in front of a little girl, protecting her from an onslaught no one wants, and a poor young tanner in a rag-worn coat who holds the dreams of a tavern girl in his heart. Its notes are written by the many who cross a border and do not know when they will ever see their homes again, and written by a young woman who survived to fill in a silent grave, speaking words of mourning for one who gave the young woman back her life and another who gave her a name. And finally its haunting melody from this broken but still beautiful wooden instrument that Jenny hears on the wind, ashes and dust floating towards the sun, sings of Tom, so that on the wind, in the notes and the melody and the song, she can still feel his arms around her, the warmth of his body with hers, the gift called life that he gives to her.

She can feel it still, that life. She can feel him still, this life. It is hers, and she embraces.

In all these stories of time and place, the requiem sings of hope. Of what is lost, and what is found.

Because in that sound, in those last few notes of music that Jenny even now hears over the waves of the sea just beyond, beckoning, a voice of life itself calling her forward and forever, she hears memory. And she finally understands that memory is not simply that which happened before, it is ever present within her, memory lived and living. She carries it within herself. She will share this warmth with her child. One day with her son, Jacob, also Jakub, also Kuba. And also Tom.

Memory, she hears on the wind, in the song, is life itself. And she embraces.

Jenny smiles quietly, as she hears the low murmurs of the child dreaming within her heart. A gentle dreaming that comforts.

It is enough.

She quietly lowers her gaze. And closes the door behind her.

Acknowledgements

This book could not have been written without the financial support of Ireland's An Roinn Turasóireachta, Cultúir, Ealaíon, Gaeltachta, Spóirt agus Meán. I am grateful. Milliún go raibh maith agat.

*

Fragments *was a difficult book to write, with a long gestation period and a long writing period. There are many who deeply influenced the writing of this book, some cognizant, others unaware. I wish to acknowledge and offer thanks to two in particular:*

I first encountered historian Dr. Natalia Romik's work and lectures for her historical art installation 'Hideouts' at the Zachęta National Art Gallery in Warsaw. Without Dr. Romik's work that straddles art and forensic archaeology, this book would not have been written. Her explorations and discussions about the secret places where Jews were able to hide during the Holocaust period proved a stimulus and background to the stories I sought to tell. I cannot thank her enough.

I have not had the chance to meet Professor Caroline Sturdy Colls, although she was kind enough in correspondence to point me in certain directions at Auschwitz-Birkenau, most helpfully. Her work particularly in 'Holocaust Archaeologies: Approaches and Future Directions' as well as her video presentation in 'Unearthing Treblinka', her documentary 'Treblinka: Hitler's Killing Machine' for the Smithsonian Institute, her 2024 Holocaust Memorial Lecture and so much of her work have proved invaluable in ways I can barely document. I can only apologize for scratching the surface of her incredible scientific exploration and revelation, for getting various archaeological techniques and instruments incorrectly presented here in this fiction; I ask her forgiveness for inaccuracies suggested in trying to tell a personal story.

Neither Dr. Romik nor Professor Sturdy Colls are personal models for Jenny in this story, but without their work I could neither have created the stories per se, nor explored the characterization that came to define a young woman in crisis personally and professionally, and how such work might mirror and come to define personality. I also admit to their work being too complex at times for a simple mind, and I offer my apologies for suggested similarities in research that I portrayed incorrectly.

Mostly, I wish to offer a heartfelt thank you to both.

*

Background and stories of the Pale of Settlement:

The Shchuchin Yizkor book proved invaluable: stories and background from Dr. Abraham Alpert, Sare-Gitel Boyarsky (Boyer), Tzipora Boyarksy (Wiel), Etel and Chaya Kravitz (Albert) I particularly acknowledge, as well as the words of Judith Liepah Slobin. The discussion paper 'Micro-Perspectives on 19th-century Russian Living Standards 1' by Tracy Dennison (Caltech) & Steven Nafziger (Williams College) November 2007 also assisted in research.

Poland:

Thanks to Klaudia Kiercz-Długołęcka and her work concerning three dimensional matzevot; Karolina Dryzner for directions and the source of many stories; the Auschwitz Museum; Julia Ain-Krupa who was so very helpful in the

Krakow research. Her novel 'The Upright Heart' is a fine read. Thank you too to Christian Maly-Motta in an article for WP Magazine, providing helpful information and recollections about Kobierzyn and the Babinski Institute where his great grandfather was a patient, as well as helpful information about the true life of Waleria Białońska rather than my imagined fiction.

Bosnia:

Photographer Fabrice Dekoninck's work on Bosnia in his book collection 'Between Fears and Hope' demonstrates his fine photographer's eye. His exhibition in Srebrenica also gave much food for thought in my research; thank you, Fabrice. Also thanks and recognition for filmmaker Elma Tataragić. To the team at 'Meet Bosnia' in Sarajevo who helped with both Sarajevo and Srebrenica travels, thank you. Journalist and Professor Janine di Giovanni's reporting on Bosnia was as always a great assistance in past and present.

Ukraine:

I am forever grateful to PEN Ukraine, the writers, poets, journalists, philosophers who stimulated and kept me safe and informed whilst traveling between Lviv, Ivano Frankivsk, Kyiv and Chernihiv as well as the wonderful towns large and small in the north. In particular I want to thank Tetyana Teren, Maksym Sytnikov, Anna Vovchenko who guided me through Bucha, Irpin and Borodyanka; to Sofia Andrukovych, a most brilliant writer, whose novel 'Amadoka' is a wonder and a true source of inspiration; to Sofia Cheliak who stood beside me at the gravesite of Victoria Amelina and quietly teared as I said kaddish at a loss so great; to the Centre for Urban History of East Central Europe in Lviv, its director Sofia Dyak whose contribution at Warsaw's Zachęta National Art Gallery with Natalia Romik touched a heart and thoughts, as well as both Maryana Mazurak and Taras Nazaruk, thank you for the direction, the discussion and the engagement with a stranger from afar. To the many people I met on my travels in Ukraine who only treated me with kindness and respect, I am deeply grateful beyond what words can say.

Israel:

Particular thanks to the Berman family, especially to sisters Rena, Ilana and Ora: for connections that touched a heart and a story that was told.

US:

My thanks to Sandie Lustig and in particular Mark Barnett who provided information about the Zask family, with helpful background about Louis Dinner and Ida Feldman, information that planted seeds for the development of story and place. To Rick Kornfeld, Julie Malek, Brad Kornfeld, Lisa Kornfeld and Kristi Dinner for the platform and for helping disseminate one story and support that led to another; and to Scott Levin of the ADL who asked probing questions, helping me to ask such of myself.

Ireland:

Thanks to Dr. Shauna Gilligan for suggesting the germ of an idea; to Oliver Sears and Holocaust Awareness Ireland for stories remembered.

UK:

To the Hurndall family, particularly Sophie and especially Jocelyn (Josie), who I remembered from so long ago and for whom I maintain my highest respect.

And finally as always to Annie, without whom this story, so many stories, would never find voice.

www.ingramcontent.com/pod-product-compliance
Ingram Content Group UK Ltd.
Pitfield, Milton Keynes, MK11 3LW, UK
UKHW041256110325
4948UKWH00004B/5/J